Praise for **MIDN**

"I tore through this one wit
I guarantee you will too!"

"*Midnight Rambler* is an extraordinary thriller."
—*The Kingston Observer*

"A superb thriller . . . action-packed."
—*Lansing State Journal*

"A story sure to put [Swain] in the ranks of superb Florida thriller writers like James W. Hall and Randy Wayne White." —*Rocky Mountain News*

"Compelling . . . suspense-laden . . . Swain doesn't miss a beat." —*South Florida Sun-Sentinel*

"*Midnight Rambler* is an immensely satisfying tale by a writer at the top of his game."
—*The Providence Journal*

"An exciting book." —*Florida Today*

"Well-defined characters and intricately woven subplots . . . make this a page-turner." —*Publishers Weekly*

"Swain is nothing short of marvelous. This is a book destined for this year's 'best of' lists."
—Bookreporter

Praise for James Swain

"Swain is one terrific writer."—*The Wall Street Journal*

"James Swain is the real thing, a writer of pure, athletic prose, capable of bringing alive characters as original and three-dimensional as our best novelists."
—JAMES W. HALL

ALSO BY JAMES SWAIN

Grift Sense
Funny Money
Sucker Bet
Loaded Dice
Mr. Lucky
Deadman's Poker
Deadman's Bluff

A Novel of Suspense

JAMES SWAIN

BALLANTINE BOOKS • NEW YORK

Midnight Rambler is a work of fiction. Names, characters, places, and incidents are the products of the author's imagination or are used fictitiously. Any resemblance to actual events, locales, or persons, living or dead, is entirely coincidental.

2008 Ballantine Books Mass Market Edition

Published in the United States by Ballantine Books, an imprint of The Random House Publishing Group, a division of Random House, Inc., New York.

BALLANTINE and colophon are registered trademarks of Random House, Inc.

Originally published in hardcover in the United States by Ballantine Books, an imprint of The Random House Publishing Group, a division of Random House, Inc., in 2007.

This book contains an excerpt from the forthcoming book *Night Stalker* by James Swain. This excerpt has been set for this edition only and may not reflect the final content of the forthcoming edition.

ISBN 978-0-345-47547-3

Cover design: Marc Cohen
Cover photograph: © David Perry/Getty Images

Printed in the United States of America

www.ballantinebooks.com

OPM 9 8 7 6 5 4 3

FOR ANDY VITA

Do justly . . . love mercy, and . . .
walk humbly with thy god.

—Micah 6:8

PART ONE

MERCY

CHAPTER ONE

My cell phone awoke me from a deep sleep.

I didn't get a lot of calls. Especially in the middle of the night. Opening my eyes, I stared into the darkness of my rented room. Hanging on the ceiling above my head were the smiling faces of my wife and daughter. They were like after-images of my former life, and they filled me with sadness. Lifting my arm, I tried to touch them, only to watch them melt away.

My phone continued to ring. Grabbing it off the night table, I stared at its face. Caller ID showed a 305 area code, which was Miami/Dade County. The only people I knew in Dade were cops. I decided to answer.

"Carpenter here."

"Jack, this is Tommy Gonzalez. Sorry to wake you up."

"What time is it?"

"Six in the morning. I'm in a jam, Jack. I wouldn't have called you otherwise."

Tommy ran the Missing Persons Division of the Miami/Dade Police Department and had gotten his training under me during a stint he did in Broward. Although he was only a few years my junior, I still considered him a kid.

"I'm listening," I said.

"We lost a newborn at Mercy Hospital this morning," Tommy said.

A knifelike pain stabbed my gut. "Abduction?"

"That's what it looks like. I need help. Are you available?"

"I'm giving testimony at a homicide trial tomorrow. I'm supposed to be spending the day preparing for it."

"Is this about the Midnight Rambler?" Tommy asked.

Another pain jabbed my gut, this one much deeper. The Midnight Rambler was my last case as a detective, and it had ruined both my career and my personal life. Each day I awoke wondering if I'd ever escape its dark shadow.

"No, this is another murder case," I said. "I can come down and help you, but I can't stay all day."

"That's fantastic," Tommy said. "What's your going rate these days?"

I was wide awake now, and I propped my back against the wall, which was cool against my bare flesh. My rent was due next week, and I was flat broke.

"Four hundred and fifty bucks," I said.

"How'd you come up with that figure?"

"Need. Now tell me what happened."

"Baby was born yesterday, name's Isabella Marie Vasquez. Parents are a couple of well-known architects, built those fancy downtown skyscrapers that look like giant kid's toys. Isabella got fed at four a.m. and was gone from her crib when a nurse checked fifteen minutes later. None of the other newborns in the maternity ward were touched. I sent my best investigator, and she combed the ward and interviewed the nursing staff, doctors, and cleaning people. No one saw anything, heard anything, or knows anything."

"Think it's an inside job?"

"I don't know what to think," Tommy said, sounding exasperated. "Mercy is one of the best hospitals in south Florida. I go there every year with a group from NCMEC, and we lecture the staff and administrators on how to lessen the likelihood of an abduction. When it comes to protecting babies, they know their stuff."

"So they've hardened the target."

"Absolutely."

NCMEC, the National Center for Missing and Exploited Children, had done more to prevent child abductions than any other grassroots organization in the country. They lectured school and hospital staffs on how to make children safe, or what they called hardening the target. I didn't like the sound of what Tommy had described, and climbed out of bed. My dog, sleeping beside me, got up as well.

"I'm leaving right now," I said. "Depending on traffic, I should be there within the hour."

"Park in the back and come through the emergency door," Tommy said.

CHAPTER TWO

Dressing is easy when you own only three pairs of pants and four shirts. Hanging up with Tommy, I put on the clothes that looked the cleanest, threw my dog into my car, and headed south to Miami.

The day my wife walked out on me, I went to the Broward County Humane Society to find a new companion. Forty dogs had been sitting on doggy death row, ranging from cuddly miniature dachshunds to snarling pit bulls. The orderly had suggested that I walk past their cages and see which one tugged at my heartstrings. Buster, a chocolate short-haired Australian shepherd, had done just that.

The dog had problems. He was not socially inclined and would curl his lip the moment you turned your back on him. My vet called him a potential fear-biter and suggested he be put to sleep. I had balked at the idea. The fact that Buster hated the world and adored me made him aces in my book.

Traffic was light on I-95, and I did seventy in the left lane. Flipping on my radio, I found a local shock jock named Neil Bash. Bash had vilified me on his show during the Midnight Rambler trial, and I got so many threatening phone calls that I had to change my number. Today he was attacking blacks and gays. It turned my stomach, so I turned him off.

I-95 ended just south of the city of Miami, the last exit a half mile from Mercy Hospital. I parked in the back as Tommy had suggested. It was a cool morning, and I left the windows down and filled up a plastic bowl with water for Buster. When I walked into the emergency room, Tommy was waiting for me.

Tommy was a tall, lanky Hispanic with a mop of jet-black hair, expressive brown eyes, and more energy than a litter of puppies. He pumped my hand and thanked me for coming, then led me to the maternity ward.

"Who's your chief investigator on the case?" I asked.

"Detective Tracy Margolin," Tommy replied.

"Any good?"

"She's one of my best."

We stopped at the maternity ward viewing area to stare through the glass at the bundles of joy on the other side. Babies rarely disappeared these days. It was one of the few arenas where the cops had actually won. I pressed my face to the glass and stared at the empty crib that Isabella Vasquez had occupied less than a few hours ago.

A thirtyish woman wearing a moss-green pantsuit made greener by the hospital walls appeared by Tommy's side. Tommy introduced her as Detective Margolin, and as we shook hands I studied her face. It was as round as a coin, her honey-blond hair swept back, the skin ringing her eyes puffy. Most cops become immune to the work they do, but it doesn't work that way when kids disappear.

Margolin went over her investigation, telling us the last person to see the child, the approximate time of the abduction, and how she'd broadcast the details on police communications channels in Dade, Broward, and Palm Beach counties while also notifying the FBI and the Florida Department of Law Enforcement.

"What's the parents' marital status?" I asked.

"They're happily married," Margolin said.

"This the first marriage for both of them?"

"Yes."

"Any other children?"

"This is their first."

"How are they taking this?"

"They're devastated."

"What about the nursing staff and doctors? How do they look?"

"Their alibis are airtight," Margolin said.

"How about the cleaning staff and maintenance people?"

"The same. I'm convinced it was an outsider."

"So you have a theory of how the abduction took place?"

"More or less."

"Show me," I said.

We followed Margolin back to the emergency room. Sometimes an investigator's first reaction was more important than the facts, and Margolin explained how she believed the abductor had entered the emergency room doors during a busy period at around four a.m. and slipped down to the maternity ward. Going outside, she pointed at a concrete bench where she believed the abductor had waited. The ground was littered with cigarette butts.

Back inside, Margolin showed us the zig-zagging path the abductor would have taken to reach the maternity ward, while speculating that he might have worn a white doctor's coat to avoid detection. When we reached the maternity ward, she stopped talking and stared at the newborns, then resumed.

"Somehow, he gained entrance to the ward, even though the door is locked at all times. My guess is, he waited for one of the nurses to come out after feeding, then grabbed the door before it closed. He rushed in, snatched the Vasquez baby, and ran."

I processed everything Margolin had said. Her assumptions rang true, but I wasn't buying this final scenario. Waiting for a nurse to leave was a risk, and I felt certain the abductor had used a different method to gain access to the ward.

Across the hall from the ward was a door with a brass nameplate. Crossing the hall, I read the name. Mercedes Fernandez.

"Who is this?" I asked.

"The head nurse for the night shift," Margolin said.

"Did you speak with her?"

"I tried."

"No luck?"

"She's out sick."

An alarm went off inside my head. The walk to the maternity ward was filled with turns, and I couldn't see someone unfamiliar with Mercy's layout not getting lost. The abductor had a map. And if he had a map, he probably also had a key.

I pointed at the night nurse's door. "Can we go in there?"

"You think she's involved?" Tommy asked.

"Could be," I said.

Tommy got a key from the hospital supervisor and unlocked the door. The room was a windowless square. I sat at Mercedes Fernandez's messy desk and booted up her computer. The screen came to life, and I entered her Web browser and checked e-mails. There were plenty, all work-related. Then I checked the sent e-mails. The Sent box was empty. Behind me Margolin was sifting through the garbage pail.

"Tell me what you think of this," I said.

Margolin peered over my shoulder at the screen. "Looks like Fernandez erased all the e-mails she sent before leaving work yesterday."

"That look strange to you?"

"Yes."

"Let's see if she erased her deleted bin."

I dragged the cursor over the deleted bin and double-clicked on it. It was filled with messages that were deleted but not permanently erased. I scrolled through them. Halfway down, I saw one that lifted me out of my chair.

Jorge, I've got what you're looking for. FBB. Call me.

I glanced at Margolin, who was blowing air down my neck as if we were on a hot date. "Have you seen a picture of the Vasquez baby?"

"No," she said.

I asked Tommy and got the same answer.

"Where're her parents?" I asked.

"The mother's in a room upstairs. She was sedated after hearing the news," Tommy said. "The last time I checked, the father was in the visitors' room pulling his hair out."

"I need to talk to him."

Mercy's visitors' room was painted in warm earth tones, the round coffee table overflowing with glossy parenting magazines, the TV tuned to *Dr. Phil.* Isabella's father sat anxiously in the corner, the only male in the room.

"Mr. Vasquez, we need to talk with you in private," Tommy said.

Vasquez rose stiffly from his chair and followed us into the hallway. He was bearded and heavyset, his clothes as rumpled as an unmade bed. Judging by the diamond-studded platinum Rolex on his wrist, he was also loaded.

Tommy walked down the hallway so we could talk in private. When we stopped, Vasquez recognized me and exploded.

"I know who you are," he said. "You're that sick cop from Broward that beat the shit out of that suspect. You're John Carpenter."

"It's Jack," I said.

"Well, Jack, I saw your smiling face on television the other day. You must be real proud of yourself, taking the law into your own hands like that. It's sick guys like you that give the police a bad name." Vasquez turned to Tommy. "Please don't tell me you've got him working on my daughter's case."

"Jack is one of the best in the business at finding missing kids," Tommy said.

"I won't stand for this," Vasquez said. "This man is a menace."

"It's my call," Tommy said.

"Don't talk back to me, goddamn it. This is my daughter's life we're talking about. I don't want *him* involved."

It was normal for family members of missing kids to take out their anger on the very people who were trying to help them. It was part of coping.

"Jack has a lead," Tommy said.

Vasquez blushed and looked at me.

"You do?" he squeaked.

"Yes. Does your daughter have blond hair and blue eyes?" I asked.

"Why is that important?"

"Just answer the question."

"Yes, she does," Vasquez said.

I looked at Tommy. "The e-mail said FBB. Female, blond, blue-eyed. Whoever Jorge is, he was shopping for a baby, and Mercedes Fernandez helped him find one."

"We need to talk to her," Tommy said.

There was a loud clacking of heels as Margolin came sprinting down the hallway. She was running so hard that she slid when she stopped, and nearly barreled into us.

"Got him," she blurted out.

"Who?" Tommy asked.

"Jorge Castillo. I found his name in Mercedes Fernandez's computer, along with his phone number and address. I called it in to headquarters, and they ran a background check. He's an ex-con who's already done time in the federal pen for kidnapping. The department is sending a cruiser to his house right now."

"Where does he live?" Tommy asked.

"On Tigertail in Coconut Grove. It's only a couple of miles from here."

Tommy looked at me. "You up for paying him a visit?"

There was a fire in Tommy's eyes that I knew all too well, for that same fire had burned in me every single day I'd been a cop.

"You bet," I said.

CHAPTER THREE

The city of Coconut Grove was a funky jungle of overgrown foliage, gourmet restaurants, and late-night bars. It was a far cry from the rest of Miami, which had been scraped clean by development, and I cracked the passenger window to let Buster sniff the many strange and wonderful odors.

I followed Tommy down Tigertail Avenue. The street was a mix of eclectic office buildings and Bahamian-style homes nestled behind protective stone walls. Tommy drove past Jorge Castillo's address and parked farther down the street. I parked in front of Tommy's car and lowered my windows, not wanting Buster to die of heatstroke while I was gone.

Tommy, Margolin, and I met on the cracked sidewalk outside of Castillo's house. There was no sign of the Miami police, which was irritating but not unusual. The city's crime rate was high, and cops were always busy answering calls.

Tommy came up with a plan. While he and Margolin knocked on the front door, I would watch the back of the house to make sure Castillo didn't escape with the baby. As we started to separate, a black BMW 745 came down the street and parked in front of our cars. It was Vasquez, and Tommy let out an exasperated breath.

"This guy is going to fuck this up."

"Let me handle him," I suggested.

"You sure?"

"Positive."

I walked down the sidewalk to the BMW. I should probably have let Tommy deal with Vasquez, but I was afraid Vasquez would start arguing and cause a scene. Not being a cop had its advantages, and I confronted Vasquez as he got out.

"Get back in your car," I said.

"You don't have the right to tell me what to do," he said indignantly.

I wagged my finger in his face. "This is my case, whether you like it or not. Either you get in the car, or I'll throw you in the trunk. It's your call."

Vasquez looked at me with murderous intensity. Sweat was marching down his face, the loss of his baby driving him insane. I softened my voice.

"Let us handle this. Please, Mr. Vasquez."

His face suddenly cracked.

"I want my baby," he said, tearing up.

"I know you do. So do I. We all do. Just do as I say. It's for the best."

He nodded his head woodenly and climbed back into his car. I returned to where Tommy and Margolin were standing. They'd drawn their weapons and were ready to make the rescue.

"You carrying any heat?" Tommy asked.

"It's back at my office," I said.

"Sure you want to do this? This guy has done time, Jack. He might be armed."

My adrenaline was pumping, and I felt better than I had in a long time.

"I'm not backing out," I said.

"Okay. See you in a few."

Tommy and Margolin hopped the front wall and walked up the path. At the same time I walked through the next-door neighbor's property and opened a gate into Castillo's backyard. His house was a Spanish-style single-story, the barrel-tiled roof turned black from age. The grass hadn't been mowed in a while and was knee high.

I cautiously approached the back door. It was ajar, and I pushed it open farther and stuck my head in. Three voices were talking in Spanish at the front of the house. Margolin, Tommy, and a man with a booming voice, whom I assumed was Jorge Castillo. My wife was Mexican, and I knew enough Spanish to understand what was being said. Castillo had invited Margolin and Tommy inside to have a look around. It could mean only one thing. He'd spotted us on the sidewalk and ditched the Vasquez baby.

I did a quick search of the backyard. Lying in the grass were the remains of a window-unit air conditioner and some rusted junk, but no place to hide an infant. Going to the gate, I put my fingers to my lips and let out a harsh whistle. Within moments Buster was out of the car and on the other side of the gate.

"Find the baby, boy. Find the baby."

I opened the gate, but my dog did not come onto Castillo's property. Instead, he stayed in the neighbor's yard and threw his front paws onto a large plastic garbage pail that I'd walked by moments ago.

"Good boy."

I made him get down and gently tugged off the lid. The

sports section of *El Nuevo Herald* lay on top of some bags of garbage. I gently pulled the newspaper away, and there she was, Isabella Vasquez, wrapped in a blue beach towel, her eyes firmly shut. She did not appear to be breathing, and an invisible fist tightened inside my chest.

I ran my fingertip down the side of her angelic face, then said something meant only for God's ears. Her eyelids parted, and she looked up at me in wonder.

"Hey, kiddo."

I lifted her from the pail and held her protectively against my chest. When my daughter was born, I stayed home for two weeks and let my wife recover while I took care of her. It was one of the greatest experiences of my life.

This was a close second.

I entered Castillo's backyard cooing to Isabella. I am one of those people who never grows tired of looking at babies. As I neared the house a large Hispanic male whom I assumed was Castillo marched through the back door. He was wearing a sleeveless black muscle shirt and carrying an old-fashioned Colt Peacemaker by his side. The gun was as big as anything Clint Eastwood ever carried in the movies, and I retreated backwards into the yard.

Castillo followed me, then fired a single round into the house. Through a window I could see Tommy and Margolin standing in the kitchen. They both hit the floor.

Castillo faced me. He pointed at the baby as if I was supposed to understand.

"No," I said firmly.

He aimed the Peacemaker's smoking barrel at my head.

"No," I repeated.

Our eyes locked. It was the first good look I'd gotten of

him. Fleshy jowls, skin savaged by acne, a flattened nose. A face only a mother could love. Or not.

"Give me the baby," he demanded in broken English.

"How much did they pay you for her?" I asked.

Castillo aimed at my left ear. I didn't want to lose it, or go deaf, but I wasn't giving this soulless bastard this child. Not now, not ever.

"Ten grand? Fifteen?" I asked.

Castillo lined up his shot. "Last chance."

"Sorry."

There was a swishing sound in the grass. It sounded like a giant snake, and Castillo looked fearfully around him. Then he let out a startled scream.

I ducked as the gun discharged. Castillo continued to scream, and he did a complete revolution. Buster had bitten Castillo in the ass and was hanging off him like a Christmas ornament. Fear-biters don't bark before they bite. My vet said that was what made Buster so dangerous and why he should be destroyed. Personally, I see it as an asset.

Two of Miami's finest appeared in the backyard with their weapons drawn. They cornered Castillo and disarmed him. I kept my distance, content to hold Isabella against my chest and let the scene play itself out. One of the cops said, "Is that your dog?"

"Sure is," I said.

"Make him let the guy go, or I'll have to shoot him."

Buster's hackles were up, and he looked twice as big as his sixty pounds. I slapped his nose, and he released Castillo and pinned himself to my side.

Margolin and Tommy came out of the house, covered in dirt. While Tommy explained the situation to the cops,

Margolin came over to me. She could not stop admiring the baby.

"She's beautiful. Look at those golden locks of hair."

"Want to do the honors?" I asked.

She almost said yes, then shook her head.

"You do it."

"You were first responder," I reminded her.

"You cracked the case. You deserve it."

"That's very nice of you," I said.

Margolin put her hand on my cheek and looked deeply into my eyes. She was the kind of woman I find attractive, and her smile ignited emotions buried deep within me. As she walked away, my eyes followed her longer than they probably should have.

Babies are perfect; ask any parent. I walked up the street to Vasquez's BMW, admiring Isabella. I had saved a lot of kids, and it never got old.

Exhaust was coming out of the BMW's tailpipe, and the windows were shut tight. I still wore my wedding ring, and I used it to tap on the driver's window. Vasquez was deep in prayer and lifted his head.

"You can come out now," I said.

Vasquez got out of the car saying, "Oh, my God, oh, my God," with tears streaming down his face. I handed him his daughter, and he nearly dropped her. I realized he'd never held his child before, and showed him how to do it.

"Keep her head up," I said.

"Like this?" he asked, cradling her head with his hand.

"That's it. Don't worry. She won't break."

Holding Isabella against his chest, he pulled out his cell

phone to call his wife. I started to walk away, and he stopped me.

"I'm sorry for what I said at the hospital," he said.

"Don't worry about it," I said.

"I was wrong."

"Heat of the moment."

He took out a business card and shoved it into my hand. "That's my card. My cell phone number's on the bottom. Call me if you ever need anything."

"That's not necessary, Mr. Vasquez."

"I mean it. Anytime, day or night, call me. I won't ever forget this."

I pocketed the card. When I was a cop, a lot of people I helped find loved ones made me similar offers, and I always turned them down. But times had changed. My life was a train wreck, and I needed all the friends I could get.

"Thank you, Mr. Vasquez," I said.

I followed Tommy and Margolin to police headquarters in downtown Miami to get my money. Tommy paid me out of petty cash and did not make me sign a receipt. Then he and Margolin offered to buy me brunch.

I was tempted to say yes. I was hungry, and I wanted to celebrate with them. It was not every day that things went this well. But there was the matter of the homicide trial that I was expected to appear at tomorrow. I was the prosecution's key witness, and I needed to spend time going over my testimony. I'd been told by the prosecutor that I would be grilled by the defense and would need to be ready.

I asked them for a rain check. Tommy said okay, while Margolin just smiled with her eyes. She was a nice lady, and if I hadn't been clinging to the falsehood that my wife and I would someday reunite, I would have asked her on a date.

Outside, in the visitors' parking lot, I found a uniformed cop standing beside my car. It was the same cop who had threatened to shoot my dog if he wouldn't let Castillo go.

"Something wrong?" I asked.

"That's some dog you've got," the cop said.

I didn't know if he meant this as a compliment, and grunted under my breath.

"You thinking of breeding him?" the cop asked.

"Actually, I was going to neuter him."

"Get puppies first," he said.

"You want one?"

"Yeah. I'll give you a hundred bucks for one of the males."

"He's a purebred Australian shepherd," I said.

"Two hundred," he countered.

I was desperate enough for cash to take the guy's name and number. As I climbed into my car, Buster stuck his head into my lap.

"You just might get laid," I told him.

CHAPTER FOUR

State your name," the bailiff declared.

"Jack Harold Carpenter," I replied.

"Place your left hand on the Bible, your right hand in the air. Do you solemnly swear to tell the truth, the whole truth, and nothing but the truth, so help you God?"

My fingertips rested lightly on the Bible's cracked leather cover. I hadn't given testimony at a trial in six months, and I felt out of place standing in a courtroom. My navy Ralph Lauren suit was too large for my thinned-down, six-foot frame, and the skinny necktie I'd purchased at a thrift shop that morning didn't adequately hide the monstrous coffee stain on my white cotton shirt. Although my life had changed drastically since my departure from the police force, its purpose had not, and I straightened my shoulders.

"I do," I replied.

"Please be seated," the bailiff said.

I took the hard wooden chair in the witness stand and felt the previous witness's warmth. Wilson Battles, the silver-haired judge presiding over the case, acknowledged me with a nod. I'd testified in his courtroom before, and I nodded back.

Then I looked at the jury of eight women and four men.

Their faces were hard, filled with skepticism and doubt. I was not a popular person. Back when I was a detective, I put a murder suspect named Simon Skell into the hospital for an extended stay. The case was still discussed in the newspapers and on TV. One editorial had called me a stain on the conscience of the community.

But that wasn't why I was here. Before my fall from grace, I had been a damn good cop and had pulled plenty of monsters off the streets. One of those monsters was sitting in this courtroom. By the time my testimony was over, I wanted there to be no doubt in this jury's minds as to who that monster was, and what he'd done.

Lars Johannsen sat at the defense table flanked by two high-priced defense attorneys. Lars was a big Swede with a face shaped like a milk bottle and a shock of blond hair. He stared coldly at me. His petite wife sat behind him in the spectator gallery, tearfully shredding a Kleenex.

The prosecutor stepped forward to begin her questioning. Her name was Veronica Cabrero, and she wore heavy makeup and an emerald-green dress that clung to her body like Saran wrap. Around the courthouse she was called the Cuban firecracker, and she had been fined for contempt by several judges for outbursts in their courtrooms. I would do just about anything for her.

"Mr. Carpenter, you were formerly chief investigator of the Broward County Missing Persons unit, correct?" she began.

"Yes," I answered into the microphone perched by my chair.

"How long did you hold this position?"

"Sixteen years."

"Would you say you're an expert at locating missing people?"

I'd heard it said that an expert was someone who lived a hundred miles away. The truth was, I enjoyed finding missing people and had never wanted to do anything else. When people went missing, there was always the hope of finding them alive. And even the tiniest ray of hope looked bright compared to the blackness of most police work.

"Yes," I said.

"The afternoon of Abby Fox's disappearance, you were the first policeman to arrive at Lars Johannsen's house," she went on. "As chief investigator, did you normally handle cases like this?"

"No."

"Who did?"

"Usually one of my people."

"Why did you take this case?"

All good testimony is rehearsed, and mine was no exception. Facing the jury, I explained how years earlier I'd found Abby Fox working the streets of Fort Lauderdale as a teenage prostitute. She'd been tossed out of her house by her parents and was what people in law enforcement call a "thrownaway." I'd gotten her into a shelter and, over time, helped her get her life together. Since then, we'd talked on a regular basis, and I knew that she'd gone to work as a nanny for a big Swede who'd been giving her funny looks. When the call came in that she was missing, I took it.

"Please describe what you found when you arrived at Lars Johannsen's house," Cabrero said.

Lars had met me at the front door. He'd explained how Abby had left five hours earlier to buy groceries and had not returned. I immediately got the color and model of

Abby's car from him and issued a tri-county alert for the vehicle.

An hour later, Abby's car was found parked near a wooded area a few miles from Lars's home. I decided to conduct a search using several sheriff's deputies, plus some neighbors who'd volunteered to help. I also let Lars tag along.

The search was conducted by the book. Everyone lined up six feet apart in the woods, took one giant step, stopped and visually inspected the ground, then repeated the process. After a few hours, everyone had started to slow down.

Then something odd happened. Lars sped up and started plowing through the woods. As a result, the rest of the search party also sped up. It felt like a ploy, and I instructed the deputies to remain with the group while I stayed behind to search the area.

It did not take me long to find Abby's shallow grave. She'd been buried in a shaded area behind a stand of thick cypress trees. I cleared away the earth with my hands until her head was uncovered. She was an attractive girl, and the ring of purple bruises around her neck made me choke up.

There was also a white handkerchief covering her eyes. The placement of the handkerchief told me a lot. It said that the killer had known Abby and had feared her gaze, even in death.

I caught up to the search party, found Lars, and took him to my car. I told him that I'd located Abby's body and watched his reaction. When he refused to meet my gaze, I took the handkerchief out of my pocket and showed it to him. It was in a plastic evidence bag, which I dangled in front of his nose.

"Whose fingerprints do you think we'll find on this?" I asked.

Lars looked away. The truth was, his fingerprints on the handkerchief wouldn't have proved a thing. It could have been Abby's handkerchief, which he might have touched at some time. Only Lars hadn't known this, so he broke down and confessed. A voice-activated tape recorder in the glove compartment had recorded everything.

"Is that when you arrested him?" Cabrero asked.

"Yes," I said.

I leaned back in my chair and took a deep breath. I had avoided looking at the jury while speaking, but I looked at them now. Their icy resolve had melted away. I'd swayed them.

"Did Lars Johannsen tell you why he killed Abby?" Cabrero asked.

"No," I said.

"Do you have any theories why he did it?"

One of Lars's defense attorneys sprang to his feet.

"Objection!" he said.

"Sustained," Judge Battles said. "Ms. Cabrero, this courtroom is no place for theories, despite the witness's obvious credentials."

"I'm sorry, Your Honor," Cabrero said. "I have no further questions."

"Your witness," Battles told the defense.

I *did* have a theory as to why Lars Johannsen strangled Abby Fox, and it went like this: Lars matched the description of a guy who'd been picking up prostitutes in Fort Lauderdale and brutalizing them. It had gotten so bad that Vice had set up a sting operation in an attempt to catch him.

My theory was that Lars knew about the sting and had decided to lie low. But over time, his cravings became too strong, so he hired Abby to watch his daughter. In Abby he saw a perfect victim. She was young and attractive and had no family. By having her in his employ, he could abuse her whenever he wished—what cops call one-stop shopping.

Only Lars's plan had a flaw. Abby had gone through intensive counseling, and along with no longer being a prostitute, she was also no longer a victim. She was her own person, and when she rebuffed Lars's advances, he flew into a rage, strangled her, and buried her body in the woods.

I didn't have a shred of proof to support this theory, just sixteen years of dealing with scum like Lars to know I'm right. Lars had hurt many women before Abby and, if let back into society, was going to hurt many more.

The shorter of Lars's defense attorneys approached the witness stand. I disliked defense attorneys who work in pairs. They reminded me of tag teams in wrestling matches, with neither member strong enough to go solo.

This one was named Bernie Howe. Howe had a clogged-sinus voice and a hair transplant that looked like rows of miniature cornstalks. Clutched in his hand were several sheets of paper, the top of which I was able to read upside down. It was a certificate of death, commonly called a COD, from Starke State Prison.

"Mr. Carpenter," Howe began, "isn't it true that when Lars Johannsen confessed in your car, you in fact were physically assaulting him, and inflicting such pain that he was forced to say that he'd killed Abby Fox?"

"No," I replied.

"Isn't it true that you put your hands around the defendant's neck, choked him for over a minute, and threatened to kill him if he didn't confess?"

"No."

"Mr. Carpenter, isn't it true that without your taped confession, there is no other solid evidence linking my client to this crime?"

"Yes."

"Mr. Carpenter, two weeks after my client was arrested, you were thrown off the police force, correct?"

Cabrero jumped to her feet and started to object. With a stare, I killed the words coming out of her mouth. The defense had only one tactic, and that was to turn the case against Lars Johannsen to one against me. I was ready for it. Cabrero sat back down, and I answered the question.

"I wasn't thrown off the force," I replied.

"But you were asked to step down," Howe said.

"I resigned."

"So you did remove yourself from the force."

"That is correct."

"Before you resigned, didn't the police conduct a hearing where you were accused of assaulting a suspected serial killer named Simon Skell, also known as the Midnight Rambler, who spent two weeks in the hospital as a result of a beating you inflicted upon him?"

"Yes."

"Isn't it true that you fractured Simon Skell's nose, jaw, and arm; knocked out several of his front teeth; threw him through a window; and fractured three of his ribs during that beating?"

"He attacked me during his arrest."

"Please answer the question."

The injuries that I'd inflicted upon Simon Skell had been in the newspapers enough times that I imagined every person in the courtroom could recite them from memory.

"Yes," I said.

"Mr. Carpenter, isn't it true that while you ran the Missing Persons unit of the Broward County Police Department, you conducted a personal vendetta against people committing violent crimes of a sexual nature?"

"No, I did not."

Howe flipped over the sheets of paper in his hand and shoved them beneath my nose. "Do you recognize these, Mr. Carpenter?"

I looked down and studied the pages.

"No," I said.

"You're saying you don't know what they are?"

"No, I didn't bring my glasses."

The jury rewarded me with a few thin smiles. Scowling, Howe displayed the sheets to them. "These are certificates of death issued by the warden at Florida State Prison in Starke for three sexual predators who Jack Carpenter sent there. These certificates were found thumbtacked to Jack Carpenter's office door the day he left the police force."

Howe faced me. "You put them on your door, didn't you, Mr. Carpenter?"

"That's correct," I said.

"Would you care to explain why?"

"If a bad guy died in the joint, I usually let the other detectives know. We liked to keep up on that sort of thing."

Howe bore a hole into me with his eyes. "Isn't it true, Mr. Carpenter, that you sent information to the warden at Starke that was so damaging to these men's reputations that it eventually led to them being murdered by other inmates?"

"I'm sorry, but which men are you talking about?" I asked.

Howe read off the three men's names from the CODs. Finished, he glanced up at me with a smug look on his face.

"Recognize them, Mr. Carpenter?"

"They sound familiar, but I'm not sure," I said.

Howe looked to the judge's box. "Your Honor, the witness is being evasive."

"Mr. Carpenter, you are required to answer the question," Battles said in a scolding voice. "Do you recognize the three names Mr. Howe just read, or don't you?"

Howe was accusing me of ethical misconduct. It was a hard charge to make stick, and it would have been easy for me to deny that I'd set those three men up. But I had something else in mind.

"Your Honor, I honestly don't remember if I did or not," I said. "Perhaps the defense would be so kind as to jog my memory."

Battles was a thirty-year veteran of the legal system and had seen his share of artful dodges in the courtroom. He studied me before replying.

"How would you propose Mr. Howe do that?" Battles asked.

"Have the defense read aloud the crimes these three men committed. I'm sure that once I hear what they did, I'll remember them and can tell Mr. Howe if I sent information to the warden at Starke that was inappropriate."

A disapproving howl came out of Howe's throat. The last thing he wanted was to have his client associated with the heinous crimes committed by the three men whose names were on those CODs.

Battles silenced Howe with a wave of the hand. Then he

removed his glasses and massaged the bridge of his nose. There were many people in the Broward legal system who did not approve of the things I did as a cop. But there were also many who did. I had always wondered which side of the fence Battles stood on.

"That sounds like a fine idea," Battles said. "Mr. Howe, read the crimes."

CHAPTER FIVE

I descended the courthouse steps, tugging off my tie. Howe had spent another twenty minutes soiling me before finally quitting. I am a big guy with a reputation for being tough, but it doesn't mean I don't feel pain. The tie landed in a trash bin, which I kicked for good measure.

Crossing the parking lot, I tried to put the trial out of my mind. I could not change the past or predict the future, so I'd learned to accept the present for what it is. My daughter taught me this trick, and so far, it seemed to be working.

My car was parked in the back of the lot. I drove a dinosaur called an Acura Legend. The salesman had said it would be a classic one day, but he'd never mentioned that the line was being discontinued. I left it unlocked with the windows open, and no one had tried to steal it.

Buster was asleep on the passenger seat and didn't stir until I opened my door. Remembering my manners, I let him out. He hiked his leg on a Porsche with a vanity plate that read ISUE, then circled my car while sniffing the ground. Something was bothering him, and I came around the passenger side to have a look.

Then I cursed.

Someone had keyed the passenger door and left a message.

SICK COP

I ran my fingers across the words. They were too deep to buff out. The door would have to be repainted. Only I didn't have the money. I looked disdainfully at Buster.

"Some watchdog you are," I said.

I lived in nearby Dania, a sleepy beach town known for its musty consignment shops and antique stores that sold the world's best junk. Most days, time stood still here, which suited me just fine. As I drove down Dania Beach Boulevard toward home, the ocean's dank, funky smell filled my car.

Pulling into the Sunset Bar and Grille on the northern tip of Dania Beach, I parked in the building's shade. The Sunset was a rough-hewn two-story structure, with half sitting on the beach and the other half resting on wood stilts over the ocean. I lived in a rented studio directly above the bar. My room was small, but the ocean view made it feel big. My rent was four hundred and fifty bucks a month, plus sitting on a stool next to the cash register on busy nights with a mean look on my face. So far, no one had robbed the place, and the owner seemed happy with the arrangement.

My cell phone rang, and I glanced at the Caller ID. It was Jessie, checking up on me. My daughter did this every day. I knew I should be grateful, but all it did was remind me of how far I'd fallen.

"Hey, honey, how's it going?" I answered.

"Great," Jessie said. "How are you? How's Buster?"

"I'm okay. Buster is Buster."

"How was the trial? Did you make out okay?"

"I survived."

"I hope they strap that son of a bitch into Sparky and fry his brains out."

Sparky was the infamous malfunctioning electric chair at Starke prison. A few days after Ted Bundy got juiced, the favorite joke among cops was to call each other and say, "Did you hear the news? Ted Bundy just stopped smoking."

"I hate to be the bearer of bad news," I said, "but the state has switched to lethal injection."

"That sucks," Jessie said. "Do you have any tips for me? The game is tomorrow night, and I need to get the team ready. We've got practice in an hour."

I grabbed a legal pad covered with scribble off the backseat. I hadn't done much with my daughter until she started playing basketball. Then I attended every high school game she played, and traveled with her to state finals. When she went to Florida State University on a basketball scholarship, I started calling a local bookie I knew. Women's hoops are big in Florida and, as a result, had a betting line. My bookie would get the skinny on the teams Florida State was playing and pass it on to me.

"Here you go," I said. "Mayweather, their leading scorer, is in a slump. She picks up her shooting in the second half, so double-team her late in the game. Cooper, one of their forwards, missed December with a mystery illness, and is only good for twenty minutes. Run her around and she'll fold. Fisher, Cooper's sub, can't shoot but is a good passer. The team has a tendency to rush their shots when they get behind. That's it."

"That's brilliant," my daughter said. "Coach wants to take you out to dinner the next time you visit."

"Tell her she's on."

"I will. Have you talked to Mom? I did. She asked about you the other day, wanted to know how you were making out."

"I'm doing fine. Tell her that, okay?"

"Why don't you tell her?"

I stared through the windshield at the Sunset. Talking about my wife made me want to get drunk. I had screwed up our marriage and couldn't bear discussing it.

"Mom wants to know how you're doing financially," my daughter went on. "How *are* you making out, Dad?"

My financial situation was a disaster, courtesy of Simon Skell's sister, who had brought a civil suit against me for the beating I'd inflicted upon her brother. The cost of hiring a lawyer to defend me had wiped me out.

"I'm living like a king," I said.

"But where's the money coming from? You're not robbing banks, are you?"

"I'm doing jobs for people."

"You mean detective jobs that you don't want to talk about."

Most of the work I did these days was helping understaffed police forces around the state find missing kids. It was my specialty, and the departments paid me under the table for my services, not wanting my name to appear on any internal documents.

"That's right," I said.

"Oh crap, look at the time," my daughter said. "I've got to run. Love you, Daddy."

"I love you, too."

* * *

A cold beer was calling me as I walked into the Sunset's horseshoe-shaped bar. Sitting at the bar were the same seven sunburned rummies who had been there since I started renting my room. I called them the Seven Dwarfs, since it was rare to see any of them standing upright. Sonny, the multitattooed, multipierced, shaven-headed bartender, sauntered over.

"Nice suit," Sonny said. "You getting married or laid out?"

"I was in court," I said.

"All those traffic tickets finally catch up with you?"

"What do you want?" I asked.

"Peace, love, and understanding. Barring that, a good blow job."

Sonny was an ex-con and loved to get under my skin. Because of his record, he legally shouldn't have been tending bar, just as I shouldn't have been doing private jobs for the police. Knowing each other's secret had formed a special bond between us.

"What do you want?" I repeated.

"A woman has been calling for you," Sonny said. "She sounded hysterical, said she needed to talk to you. Sounds like a booty call."

"What's her name?"

He started to wipe the bar with a dirty rag. "I put it in the till."

"You going to get it for me?"

"What's it worth to you?"

Sonny was going to end up back in prison if someone didn't straighten him out. I dropped my voice. "A punch in the face—that's what it's worth."

"You'd hit me in front of all these customers?"

"If I ask them, they'll probably hold you down."

The loopy grin left Sonny's face. He got a slip of paper from the till and slapped it on the bar. I read the name printed on it and felt myself shudder. Julie Lopez. Six months earlier, I had helped Julie come to grips with a loss that no one should have to bear. I hadn't seen her since, knowing that my presence would only open deep wounds.

I walked outside and punched her number into my cell phone. Julie answered immediately, her voice riddled with grief.

"It's Jack Carpenter," I said. "What's wrong?"

"The police found Carmella," she wailed.

"Where?"

"In my backyard!"

My head started to spin, and I leaned against the building and tried to compose myself. What Julie was saying couldn't be true. Carmella Lopez was murdered by Simon Skell, who made her disappear just the way he made seven other young women disappear. Of all the places he might have put Carmella's body, Julie's backyard couldn't be one of them.

"What are the police saying?"

"They think Ernesto did it."

"Is Ernesto there with you?"

"The police arrested him and took him away."

"Did you call a lawyer?"

"I ain't got no money. You've got to help me. I don't know what to do."

My head would not stop spinning. The police were wrong. I told myself that if I went to Julie's house I would get to the truth of the matter.

"I'm coming right now," I said.

"Hurry," she begged me.

Dania Beach was separated from the mainland by a short steel bridge. I raced across it and soon was on 595, driving toward the western reaches of the county. The sky was a murderous black, and large drops of rain pelted my windshield. I was heading into a storm, but I didn't slow down.

CHAPTER SIX

I parked at the end of Julie Lopez's driveway, my wipers furiously beating back the rain. The neighborhood had always been marginal but had slipped further since my last visit, with cars parked on lawns and black security bars on most windows.

Two police cruisers were parked in front of me. The cops were not going to be happy to see me, but it was a free country. I told Buster to lie down, and he shot me a disapproving look. Aussies are bred for herding, and my dog would have liked nothing better than to spend every waking moment by my side.

I got out and within seconds was soaked to the bone. I trudged up the driveway to the wooden privacy fence that enclosed Julie's backyard. When I stepped through the gate, my feet went ankle-deep in water. If lightning hit nearby, I would be history, yet I continued to slosh ahead. Four uniformed cops and a plainclothes detective were huddled in the backyard. They were looking at something, and I wanted to see what it was.

Carmella Lopez had been my last case as a cop. She and her sister were both prostitutes. Carmella turned tricks in a massage parlor, Julie through a live-in pimp named Ernesto. When Carmella went missing one day, Julie called and asked me to find her. I took the case and during my investigation stumbled across Simon Skell, whom I linked to Carmella's disappearance as well as to seven other missing women in the sex business. There wasn't much hard evidence, just a lot of circumstantial threads that pointed to a rampaging sociopath. The district attorney bought my theories and took Skell to trial. The judge threw out everything but Carmella's case, so the DA tried that. We won, and Skell was sent to Starke.

Yellow police tape lay on the grass. Ignoring it, I sneaked up behind two uniforms and peeked through the gap between their broad shoulders. They were standing beside a coffin-shaped hole. A decomposed woman's body rested at the bottom of the hole. Dressed in a red bikini, she clutched an object between two hands propped on her stomach.

Something in my chest dropped. Even though the woman's face was gone, I knew who it was. Carmella.

Lightning crashed nearby, rocking the ground. None of us flinched. We'd all stood in this shit before. I started backing up. This was the last place on earth I should've been. Suddenly a voice roared my name.

"*Carpenter!*"

Plainclothes detective Bobby Russo broke from the group and rushed toward me. The head of Broward Homicide, his meaty Irish face resembled a four-alarm blaze. Around his neck hung a necktie painted to look like a dead fish. It was Russo who'd coined the phrase "My day starts when your day ends."

Russo threw me to the ground and started kicking me. He was out of shape, and the kicks lacked sting. He shouted my name as if he'd already looked into the future and seen what a nightmare I'd created for him and the other detectives who'd helped put Skell away. It was hard to believe that I'd ushered at his wedding and that we were once friends.

The uniforms pulled Russo back. I got in a sitting position and assessed the damage. Nothing felt broken, and I stood up and faced him.

"What the hell are you doing here?" Russo shouted.

"She called me," I answered.

"Who?"

"Julie Lopez. She called me. What happened?"

"That's none of your business."

"Come on, Bobby. It was my case."

Russo cocked his fist as if he was going to take my head off. Instead of throwing the punch, he spoke to one of the uniforms.

"Arrest him."

"On what charge?" I asked incredulously.

Russo pointed at the police tape lying on the ground. "Trespassing on a crime scene."

"This is bullshit," I said.

"Welcome to my world," Russo said.

The uniform patted me down and handcuffed me. Together we walked down the driveway. He pulled my wallet from my hip pocket, then got into a cruiser and called in my driver's license on his radio. He knew I wasn't wanted for anything, just as Russo knew. They just wanted to harass me. Another crash of lightning shook the ground.

"I'm going to get killed out here," I yelled.

The uniform's face appeared in the driver's window. His eyes were lifeless, his face the same. I cursed, and saw him flash a smile.

* * *

The rain continued to drench me. I had planned to go swimming later, and I told myself that standing in a downpour accomplished the same thing. This was another of my daughter's maxims. I'm supposed to look on the bright side of things.

The uniform took his sweet time, and I let my eyes roam. A cable company repair truck sat on the street with two workers inside. Trenching equipment was in the truck, and I imagined the workers running a line across the backyard and happening upon Carmella's grave.

"Jack, is that you?" Julie Lopez stood inside the open garage, her face ravaged from crying. Shaped like an hourglass, she wore ragged cutoffs and a Miami Heat athletic shirt.

"Hey, Julie," I said.

"It's Carmella's body, isn't it?" she asked.

I nodded, and Julie stifled a sob. She had clung to the hope that her sister Carmella would turn up alive one day, even though Skell had been put away for her murder. A false hope, but sometimes those are the ones that keep us going.

"They took Ernesto away," Julie said. "What am I going to do, Jack? Will you tell me what I'm going to do?"

During the trial, Simon Skell's defense attorney had tried to paint Ernesto as Carmella's real killer. Ernesto was no angel, but I'd never pegged him for a killer, and neither had any of the homicide detectives who'd worked the case.

"I don't know," I told her.

"Please come inside and talk to me," she said.

"I can't."

"You don't want to talk to me?"

I showed her my cuffed wrists.

"I'm under arrest."

"What did *you* do?"

I took a deep breath. My brain was on overdrive trying to come up with a way to tie the body in Julie's backyard to Simon Skell. Only I couldn't make the connection. My case against Skell had just gone up in flames.

"I fucked up," I replied.

Julie shut the garage door in my face. My shoulders sagged. As a cop I had never left a stone unturned. When I was hunting for Carmella, I had the sheriff's office search Julie's property. The backyard was searched several times, including after Simon Skell was arrested. There had been no body.

The uniform climbed out of the cruiser and shoved my wallet into my hip pocket. The look on his face said I checked out. I showed him my handcuffs.

"Let me go, will you?"

"I need to get permission from Russo," the uniform said.

"Come on. I'm going to get struck by lightning."

"It's Russo's call," he said.

"That's horseshit and you know it."

"Sorry," he said.

A CSI van appeared on the street and parked behind the cable truck. A two-man forensic crew got out, griping about the weather. The uniform escorted them past me and into the backyard.

I'd reached my boiling point. I opened the driver's door of my car, and Buster stuck his head out and licked my fingers.

"Get the keys," I told him.

Buster's previous owners had done a helluva job training him. He pulled the keys out of the ignition with his teeth and dropped them on my palm. I carried a cigar punch on the ring, which was the same size as a handcuff key. I quickly freed myself.

If there's one thing that's gotten me in trouble, it's my temper. I walked down to the street and located Russo's car, a black Suburban. I tossed the cuffs onto the hood, causing a sizeable dent. Russo would go ballistic when he saw it.

Climbing into my car, I hugged my dog and drove away.

CHAPTER SEVEN

I didn't go far.

My head was filled with contradictions that needed sorting out. At a convenience store near Julie's house I purchased a sixteen-ounce coffee and a package of Slim Jims for Buster. The cashier stared at my wet clothes but said nothing.

I drank the coffee in my car while listening to the rain. Back when I was a kid, I was afraid of lightning storms. Sometimes my older sister, Donna, would invite me to her room, and we'd sit on her bed and listen to record albums. One album in particular still stands out: *Everything You Know Is Wrong*, by a comedy troupe called The Firesign Theatre. I blew steam off my drink thinking of that album.

Everything I knew was wrong.

I was not a new age cop. Forensics were great for solving tough cases, but they never stopped anyone from committing a crime. It took instincts to stop crimes. My instincts led me to Simon Skell, and I arrested him before he could kill any more young women. The fact that a piece of evidence had turned up that said I was wrong about how Carmella Lopez's body was disposed of didn't mean Skell wasn't guilty. He *was* guilty; I just couldn't prove it anymore.

My thoughts shifted to Bobby Russo. Russo was going to do everything in his power to divert blame from himself and his department over what had happened. Which meant *I'd* get the blame, whether I deserved it or not. My reputation had taken a pounding during Skell's trial, and I sensed another beating coming on.

Now the rain was coming down sideways. Jessie was always telling me to look on the bright side of things. Well, the bright side was that my wife and daughter no longer lived in Fort Lauderdale, and they wouldn't have to endure the shit storm I was about to go through.

I got on 595 and headed east. A part of me wanted to drink cold beer at the Sunset until I passed out, but my conscience wouldn't allow it. There were other people to think about. Namely Melinda Peters.

Melinda had been the prosecution's key witness at Skell's trial. I'd discovered her name in an old file in the National Runaway Switchboard's computer database that linked her to Skell. She'd been a reluctant witness, and it had taken every trick I knew to get her to testify. On the witness stand, Melinda had told in chilling detail how Skell picked her up when she was a sixteen-year-old runaway, drugged her, and kept her locked inside a dog crate in his house with a spiked collar on. He tortured her when the mood struck him and played rock 'n' roll music to drown out her cries for help. Skell was partial to the Rolling Stones, and he played one song repeatedly, "Midnight Rambler," a tune about a sicko breaking into women's homes and brutally murdering them. Out of desperation, Melinda talked Skell into having sex with her, and when he let her out of her cage, she jumped through a window. Instead of calling the police, she ran to a homeless shelter and went into hiding. She told another runaway at the shelter her story, and that girl told a phone counselor at the National Runaway Switchboard, who wrote up the incident and filed it in the computer. During my investigation I stumbled across the file and tracked Melinda down.

That was our history. Melinda had helped me, and it was my responsibility to tell her about the body in Julie Lopez's backyard. I didn't want her hearing about it on the TV and freaking out. I owed her the decency of a face-to-face.

The hard part was going to be finding her. Melinda was a stripper and bounced between clubs. I didn't have her address, and the phone number she'd given me was an answering service. Then I had an idea.

Since resigning, I'd stayed friendly with a handful of cops. One was a redneck named Claude Cheever. Although Cheever and I were on opposite sides of the spectrum on every issue you could name, he had come forward at my hearing and testified that every move I'd made during the Skell investigation was by the book. None of my friends had stuck up for me like that. Not a single one.

Cheever was also a sex hound and on a first-name basis with every stripper in town. Pulling up his cell number, I called him.

"Cheever here," he answered.

Blaring disco music in the background made me guess he was at a club.

"Carpenter here," I said. "Can you talk?"

"As good as the next guy," Cheever said. "How you been?"

"I'm hanging in there. You?"

"Loving life. What's up?"

"I'm looking for Melinda Peters. Any idea where she's working these days?"

"About three feet from my drooling face." His voice changed. "Ooh, baby, you are so damn beautiful. Come over here and make me smile."

"You talking to her right now?" I asked.

"No, this is another hottie," he said.

"Is Melinda really there?"

"Of course she's here. She just went on break."

"Which dollar store are you at?"

"The Body Shot on State Road 80," Cheever said. "I'll hold you a seat."

If there was one business that flourished in Broward County, it was strip clubs. There were so many that several glossy magazines were published each month to highlight the girls who danced in them. The clubs near the ocean attracted tourists and were high priced, while those out west were dives catering to locals. The Body Shot was out west, the parking lot filled with cars in worse shape than mine.

The club smelled of cheap beer and failed deodorant. Up on the oval stage, three women in G-strings danced to Santana's "Everybody's Everything" beneath a pulsating strobe light. As I crossed the room the strobe's clockwise rotation made me feel as if I were circling a giant drain.

Cheever was at the bar. With Claude, "cop" was never the first word that came to mind. In his mid-forties, he had a droopy mustache, a hard-looking belly, and a short choppy haircut that was the worst I'd seen on a grown man. He pumped my hand.

"You look good," I shouted over the music.

"Liar," he said.

I caught the bartender's eye and ordered two beers. Moments later, she slapped down two bottles and said, "Sixteen bucks" as if expecting a fight. I paid up, and we clinked bottles.

"Didn't anyone ever tell you not to shower with your clothes on?" Cheever asked.

I was still soaking wet. These clothes were my last link to my old life, and I didn't know if I should feel sad or elated. Taking a swig of beer, I decided on elation.

"Did you tell Melinda I was coming?" I asked.

"No. Was I supposed to?"

I threw a five at the bartender and asked her to find Melinda. The bartender disappeared, and Cheever nudged me in the ribs with his elbow.

"This little old lady in Fort Lauderdale goes to the supermarket to buy groceries," he said. "When she comes out, she finds two guys stealing her car. She whips out a handgun and screams, 'Out of the car, mother-fuckers. I have a gun, and I know how to use it.'

"The guys run like hell. The old lady loads her groceries and gets behind the wheel. Then she sees a football and a twelve-pack of beer on the front seat. She gets out of the car and sees her own car, same model and color, parked four spots away.

"She loads her groceries into her own car and drives to the police station to report her mistake. The sergeant on duty bursts out laughing when he hears her story, and points to the other end of the counter, where two guys are reporting a carjacking by a mad old woman. So what's the moral of the story?"

I shook my head and killed my beer.

"If you're having a senior moment, make it special."

Cheever snorted with laughter. I felt a tap on my shoulder and turned. Melinda stood behind me, her long blond hair resting seductively on her shoulder, her gorgeous bikini-clad body visible through black fishnet. In high heels, she was nearly as tall as me. She offered me her hand like a princess.

"Hello, darling," she said.

We retreated to the VIP lounge and sat on a couch with a large tear in the fabric. The lounge had a partial wall separating it from the rest of the club that afforded us some privacy. Melinda cuddled up next to me and rested her hand on my stomach.

"Hey, handsome."

"Hey," I replied.

"Did you miss me?"

"Sure."

"Marry me."

I swallowed hard, wishing I hadn't drunk a beer. I won't lie and say that Melinda didn't arouse me. I'd have to be stone-cold dead for that not to happen. But this come-on was just a game she played whenever we got together.

"I'm taken," I said.

She withdrew her hand and created distance between us on the couch. It was only a few feet, just enough for her to feel safe.

"Haven't seen you in a while."

"I've been busy," I said.

"Catching bad guys?"

"Sometimes."

"What happened to your clothes?"

"I got caught in the storm."

She pulled a pack of Kools out of a pocket in her fishnet, banged one out, and stuck it between her lips. I fumbled pulling a book of matches out of the pack's cellophane and lighting her cigarette. She blew a monster cloud over our heads.

"So what do you want, Jack, a lap dance?"

"I've got some bad news."

Her eyebrows went up. "What's that?"

"A body was found buried in a backyard this afternoon. The police think it belongs to Carmella Lopez, the girl Simon Skell went down for. The police arrested a pimp they think put it there."

It took Melinda a moment to process what I'd said. Panic distorted her face.

"What's going to happen to Skell?" she asked. "They're not going to let him out of prison, are they?"

"They might."

"But you said he killed Carmella and all those other girls."

"That's right."

"Then how can they let him out?"

"The evidence doesn't support the police's case anymore."

"Don't talk to me like that," she snapped.

"Like what?"

"Like a fucking automated answering machine. I hate that."

"I'm sorry."

Melinda put her hand on my leg and sank her dragon-lady nails into my skin. I'd forgotten who I was talking to. This was the girl who stopped being a victim long enough to put her abuser behind bars. There weren't many like her, and I'd just told her that it was all for nothing.

"*How* can they let him out, Jack?" she spat at me. "Didn't the judge hear what I said on the witness stand? How Skell tortured me? How he wouldn't feed me or give me water? How he made me piss into a Dixie cup? How he told me about the girls he'd tortured, and how I was going to join their little club? How he made me bark like a dog while he played that fucking song? Didn't the judge hear any of that, Jack?"

I fell mute. The sad truth is, it was not Melinda's trial. It was Carmella's trial, and although Melinda's testimony had helped send Skell to prison, it was not the crime he had been tried for. Which was a nice way of saying that Skell would never be punished for the crimes he'd committed against Melinda. Only I couldn't tell her that.

"It's not a done deal," I said instead.

"Meaning what?"

"Meaning that it's not certain Skell will be released from prison. His lawyer will have to go in front of a judge and present the evidence."

Her nails sunk deeper into my flesh.

"They're going to let him out, aren't they, Jack?" she said. "That's why you came here. They're going to let him out, and you wanted me to know so I could put extra locks on my apartment and buy a gun for when he comes tippy-toeing to my bedroom door."

I lowered my head. She'd hit the nail on the head. It was exactly why I'd come.

"I'm sorry, Melinda," I said.

She slapped my face. It stung, and I reflexively grabbed her arm before she could do it again. She let out a blood-curdling scream.

A huge bouncer stepped into the lounge. He yanked me

off the couch and hustled me through the club. I looked for Cheever at the bar, but he was gone.

As we went through the club's front door I expected the bouncer to stop, but he instead gave me a mighty shove. I flew forward with my arms flapping like a bird and hit the pavement hard.

"Stay out of here," the bouncer yelled.

I lay on the pavement and watched the rain come down in sheets. The knees of my pants were shredded, my jacket torn. I tried to find the bright side, only there was no bright side. I walked stiff-legged to my car.

As I got in, Buster cowered fearfully against the passenger door. Then the rancid smell hit me. My dog had puked Slim Jims on the floor.

"It's okay, boy," I told him. "It's okay."

The words seemed to reassure him, and Buster slithered into my lap. He stayed there all the way back to the Sunset.

CHAPTER EIGHT

The storm skirted south of Dania, and I reached the Sunset in blinding sunshine. I washed the floor mat in the ocean and placed it on the hood to dry. A few hours of daylight were left, and I went inside to change.

In my room I tugged on my Speedo bathing trunks. I'd lost twenty pounds in the past six months and acquired a flat stomach and deep tan. Although my hair has thinned, my friends said I looked younger than my forty years. Maybe I had found the fountain of youth. It was called hitting the skids.

I rolled my wet clothes into a ball and headed downstairs. At the bar, one of the Seven Dwarfs, Whitey, was doing a magic trick with a book of burning matches. The comic effect was great, only he was enough of a menace to burn the place down. I extinguished the matches in a glass of water, and he howled in protest.

I tried to catch Sonny's eye. He wouldn't meet my gaze, and I guessed he was still ticked off about the punch-in-the-face crack. I said, "Heads up," and tossed my clothes over the bar like a basketball. Sonny caught them with a puzzled look on his face.

"Throw those out for me, will you?" I said.

"Your suit?" Sonny asked.

"Yeah. I'm shedding my old skin. And while you're at it, give everybody a round of drinks, including yourself."

The Dwarfs gleefully pounded the bar. Sonny tossed the clothes into the trash with a grin on his face. All was forgiven.

"You want the drinks on the big tab, or the little tab?" Sonny asked.

"The little tab. I'm trying to balance them out."

"Little tab it is."

I lowered my voice. "I need a favor. You might get some calls from people looking for me. Reporters, police, that sort of thing. Tell them I haven't been around, okay?"

"You in trouble?" Sonny asked.

Normally, I would have lied to him, but with my ever-dwindling pool of resources, I needed all the friends I could get. I nodded. Reaching into a cooler, Sonny removed a sixteen-ounce can of Budweiser, my signature drink, and stuck it into the ice chest.

"Have a nice swim," he said.

The day my wife walked out on me, I took a drive. I didn't know how I was going to cope with her being gone, and eventually I found myself parked on the northern tip of Dania Beach. Then, I'd done what any heartbroken male would do. I got naked and went for a swim. I don't know why I did this; it just seemed the right thing to do at the time. And when I stepped out of the water an hour later, I knew I was going to be all right.

I started swimming competitively when I was ten and was good enough to get my name engraved on a plaque at the Swimming Hall of Fame in Fort Lauderdale. My specialty was the backstroke. What started out as a sport had become my daily therapy. I made it a point to swim every day, rain or shine. When I didn't, I got grouchy as hell.

The ocean was the temperature of bathwater, and I waded in with minnows darting between my legs. A hundred feet from shore I began my laps. I started with the crawl, then reverted to the backstroke. There was no lifeguard at this end of the beach, or other swimmers to call if I should need help. If I cramped and drowned, no one would know. I'd sink like a stone and get swept out to sea. Death scared me as much as the next guy, but the idea of drowning never had.

Perhaps it was because I was not truly alone. Lurking just beneath the water's surface were scores of stingrays, tiger sharks, and jellyfish. I supposed I should be wary of these creatures, but I wasn't. Not once had I been stung, nibbled on, or had my space invaded. Someday I might get my arm chewed off, but until then, I was willing to take my chances.

I swam for an hour, then headed back to shore. I heard a siren coming over the bridge. Dania was God's waiting room, and I assumed it was an ambulance. But then the siren multiplied: two, three, four. Police cruisers, all in a line.

I hit the shore running. Sonny met me halfway, looking panicked.

"I blew it," he said.

"What happened?"

"I went to piss, and the phone rang. Whitey grabbed it. Some cop asked if you were here. Whitey told them you'd gone swimming."

My feet took the stairs to my room three at a time. Banging open the door, I called for my faithful companion.

Buster jumped off the bed and followed me downstairs. Sonny stood in the bar's entryway.

"Hold my calls," I said.

Beneath the Sunset was a shady space where the sand and the wood meet that was impossible to see from the beach. I hid there with my dog and peered out through a decorative latticework nailed to the side of the building. Four wailing police cruisers pulled into the lot, and a gang in blue piled out. Russo was with them and looked mad as hell. I guessed he'd already taken his Suburban to the shop.

The cops entered the Sunset, flat feet pounding hard boards.

"Where the hell is Carpenter?" Russo roared.

"Swimming!" Whitey replied.

I listened to Russo walk out of the bar and climb the narrow stairwell. At the top he addressed the uniforms searching my room.

"It's clean," a cop said loudly.

"You couldn't have searched it that quickly," Russo said.

"There's nothing in it," the cop said.

"Search it again," Russo said. "Tear the place upside down, rip the mattress in half, I don't fucking care. That file has to be here."

I leaned back in the sand and shut my eyes. I'd forgotten all about the file.

The day I'd left my job with the sheriff's department, I'd taken Simon Skell's case file with me, intent on poring over clues until I could unravel the mystery of how he'd made his victims vanish without a trace. I hadn't thought the file would be missed. So many things have vanished from the Broward County Sheriff Department's building, like bales of marijuana and thousands of rounds of ammunition, that one stinking file should have gone unnoticed. Stupid me.

Russo padded down the stairs and reentered the bar.

"That Acura parked in the lot. That's Carpenter's, isn't it?" he asked.

"That's his car," Sonny said.

"You got a key?"

"No, but he leaves it unlocked."

"I'm going to search it. I don't want any of you to move, understand?"

"No sir," the Seven Dwarfs replied in a drunken chorus.

"That goes for you, too," Russo said.

"I'm not going anywhere," Sonny said.

Russo left the building and shuffled through the sand to the lot. He was twenty feet from where I was hiding, and I could hear him muttering under his breath. He was going to have a stroke someday, I'd make book on it.

Russo searched my car and returned to the Sunset, muttering even louder than before. One of the boys in blue met him at the door.

"Carpenter's room is clean," the uniform said.

"Fuck, shit, piss," Russo said, kicking the door. "Get the men out here. I want you to look up and down this stinking beach until you find him. We're not leaving here without that file, understand?"

"Yes, sir."

An incoming wave broke over me, and I spit out a mouthful of salt water. Russo needed the Skell file to make his case to the district attorney, who was breathing down Russo's throat about the body in Julie Lopez's backyard. Only I wasn't going to give Russo the file. It was my last tie to the case, and I wasn't ready to let go.

The cops hit the beach and spread out. Because the tide was up, the team assigned to search the north end walked around the Sunset instead of coming down to the shoreline. It was the first break I'd caught all day.

Russo stayed behind and searched my car again, giving special attention to the cavity where the spare tire sat. Another wave broke over me. I realized that if I stayed here much longer, I was going to drown.

I slipped into the Sunset with my dog. As Buster raced upstairs I entered the bar. Sonny and the Dwarfs were watching old fight films on ESPN. I put my finger to my lips and shushed them, then took the lone stool at the bar.

My body temperature was dropping and I could not stop shivering. Sonny loaned me a spare T-shirt, one of the Dwarfs floppy fisherman's hat, and I was in business. Taking my beer out of the ice chest, Sonny filled a frosted mug.

"You really think this is going to work?" he asked.

"It beats drowning," I replied. "How about another round for my mates?"

"Big tab or little tab?"

"Little tab."

The Dwarfs' collective memory span was about five seconds, and they applauded my generosity. Through the window I saw Russo lift his head from the trunk of my car. His radar told him something wasn't right, and he made a beeline for the building.

I did what any self-respecting drunk would do and buried my face in my suds. Russo barged into the room with flushed cheeks.

"What's with all the racket?" he demanded.

Sonny pointed at the TV. "Ali just knocked out Foreman."

"That's old news," Russo said.

"Not to these guys."

Russo glared at him. If he'd bothered to count heads when he'd come in the first time, he'd notice we'd multiplied. But he didn't, his mind wrapped up in other things. Like how he was going to tell the DA there was no file.

Muttering to himself, Russo went back outside. I continued to buy rounds while the cops conducted their snipe hunt. As the sun set, they returned to their cruisers and drove away. Russo was the last to leave, the interior light of his car illuminating a solitary man wrestling with his situation.

Soon everything was back to normal. Sonny served me a bowl of house chili with some crackers. I ate quickly, then caught myself yawning and decided it was time for bed. As I rose from my stool, the Dwarfs broke into a rousing rendition of "For He's a Jolly Good Fellow." It was a fine way to end a lousy day. Returning the clothes I'd borrowed, I bid them all good night.

CHAPTER NINE

Morning came hard and bright.

Lying in bed, I watched a seagull float outside my window while trying to make sense of what had happened last night. The cops had torn apart my room searching for the Skell file, but they'd managed to put everything back in its place. That wasn't normal behavior, and I supposed the special treatment came from having been one of them. Or maybe Russo told them to. I decided the latter was probably what happened, meaning Bobby didn't hate me as much as I thought he did.

An immovable object lay beside me: Buster was positioned so snugly against my body that I could not get out of bed. I grabbed a hind leg and pulled.

"Rise and shine."

We were both creatures of habit. Buster drank out of the toilet before I used it, then waited by the door. I washed up, threw on shorts and a long-sleeved running shirt, and took my dog outside for a run.

Breakfast awaited us at the bar upon our return. A bowl of table scraps for my dog, a cup of coffee and a copy of the *Fort Lauderdale Sun-Sentinel* for me. It was part of my rent, and I thanked Sonny, who sat on a stool behind the bar, half asleep.

Normally, I read the sports section first, but today it was the headlines. On the front page was a ghoulish overhead photo of the corpse in Julie Lopez's backyard. It was a good clear shot taken overhead from a helicopter. In journalism there were big murders and little murders, and this was being sold as a big murder. Something was clutched between the skeleton's hands. I asked Sonny his opinion, and he opened his eyes and studied the paper.

"Looks like a gold crucifix," Sonny said.

I had another look.

"I think you're right."

"This was your last case, wasn't it?"

I sipped my coffee and nodded. I was thinking about Julie Lopez's pimp, Ernesto, who according to the paper was being held without bail. Ernesto was deeply religious, and I wondered if this was his way of giving Carmella a proper burial. I didn't want to believe it, but facts were facts. Ernesto must have killed Carmella, then waited until Skell was in prison before plopping her in the ground. I had sent away the right man for the wrong crime. It made my head hurt.

"A guy was checking out your car when I pulled in this morning," Sonny said a few minutes later.

"Checking it out how?" I asked.

"Looking it over, reading the license plate."

"What did he look like?"

"He was in plain clothes, late forties, short hair."

"Think he was a cop?"

"I made him for a private dick."

"How can you tell the difference?"

"Cops don't get up that early."

The Legend was the only thing of value I owned, and I was sick of people messing with it. Going outside, I inspected my car, including the undercarriage. The black transmitter stuck to the gas tank was hard to miss. I went back inside.

"I need your help," I said.

"Name it," Sonny replied.

"This private dick put a transmitter on my car. I want you to take my car out for a spin. I'll follow you and see if I can nail this guy."

"I got DUIed last month and had my license suspended," Sonny said. "Why don't you ask Whitey?"

"Is he around?"

"Sure. Hey, Whitey, get up."

There was stirring from the other side of the room. Whitey's snow-white head appeared an inch at a time over the bar as he pulled himself off the floor. He was wearing yesterday's clothes, his face a mosaic of broken blood vessels and gin blossoms. He brushed himself off while grinning lopsidedly.

"Wass up, captain?" Whitey asked.

"You got a car?" I asked.

"Last time I checked."

"Your driver's license any good?"

Whitey jerked out his wallet, spilled his credit cards onto the bar, and extracted his driver's license. He scrutinized it, then nodded enthusiastically.

"Here's what I want you to do," I said.

Five minutes later we put my plan into action. Whitey drove south on A1A in my car while I followed in his filthy Corolla. Whitey was impaired and probably shouldn't have been driving, but that was true for a lot of folks in south Florida.

As I drove I watched the side streets. If my hunch was correct, the private dick hired by Simon Skell's sister would soon appear and start following Whitey. Most dicks were failed cops, which explained the harsh treatment I'd been getting.

Two blocks later, I was proved right. A black Toyota 4Runner with tinted windows pulled out and started tailing the Legend. At the next intersection, Whitey pulled into a 7-Eleven and hustled inside, the ten bucks I'd given him burning a hole in his pocket. The 4Runner also pulled into the lot, and the driver followed Whitey in. He was my size, with gunmetal hair and a dark suit that made him stand out like a sore thumb. The look on his face spelled trouble, and I parked on the street and hurried inside.

I found the guy in the rear of the store. He had cornered Whitey in the potato chip aisle and had his back to me. I shot my hands through his armpits and put him in a full nelson.

"Hey!" he yelled in alarm.

"Hey yourself," I replied. "I'm sick of your crap."

"Let me go."

"Not until you answer a couple of questions."

His muscles tensed. He felt powerful, and I sensed a fight coming on.

"Are you Jack Carpenter?" he asked.

"Whatever gave you that idea?" I replied.

"I need to talk to you."

"Call my secretary and set up an appointment."

"Come on. Stop acting like a fool," he said. "I just want to talk."

"Isn't that what we're doing?"

"Are you going to let me go?"

"Not until you apologize to me and my friend."

"I have nothing to apologize for," he said.

The guy was both stubborn and strong. There are some people in this world you can't reason with, and I decided he was one of them. Releasing my grip, I shoved him forward. To my surprise, Whitey stuck his leg out. The guy fell headfirst into the potato chips and took down the entire aisle.

Whitey ran out of the store laughing like a delinquent kid. I followed him, apologizing to the manager as I passed the register.

"Stay out of here!" the manager shouted.

Whitey and I exchanged keys in the parking lot. I pulled out of the lot just as the guy staggered out. His jacket was ripped at the shoulder, and there was defeat in his eyes. Honking my horn, I waved and drove away.

I went to the Sunset and picked up my dog. I hadn't felt this pumped in a long time. I decided to go to my office and get some work done.

I took the bridge back to civilization and headed toward town. Halfway there, I turned down a dusty two-lane road flanked by palmetto trees and a junk-filled boatyard. My destination was a local hideaway called Tugboat Louie's that had everything a person could want: bar, grille, dockside dining, and a marina with dry dock storage.

The bar was a ramshackle affair with bleached shingles and hurricane shutters. Inside, I found the owner behind the bar checking inventory. His name was Kumar, and he wore a white Egyptian cotton shirt and an oversized black bow tie. He was a small Indian man with a big personality, and he shook my hand.

"Jack, how are you? You are looking well. Is everything

good? What can I get you? Coffee, tea? How about something to eat? Scrambled eggs, perhaps?"

"I'm fine," I said.

"How about your dog?"

"He's fine, too. How are you?"

"Wonderful, fantastic. Business is good. I have no complaints."

"You're a lucky man," I said.

Belly-dancing music filled the air. It was the ring tone to Kumar's cell phone, and he removed it from his belt and took the call. Behind the bar was a stairwell with a chain strung across it and a sign marked PRIVATE. Stepping behind the bar, I unclipped the chain and headed upstairs.

The second floor had two offices: Kumar's and my own, which I occupied rent free. I'd worked here for six months in total anonymity, with no one except Kumar and a handful of employees knowing about it.

My relationship with Kumar was based upon a single act, which he seemed obsessed with repaying. On a summer weekend two years earlier, I had come in with my wife and daughter for dinner. Outside a bikini contest was taking place, its sponsor a local rum distributor. Rum and beautiful girls are what made south Florida great, and they were flowing in abundance, with a gang of drunks ogling ten scantily clad ladies standing on a makeshift stage. A local DJ was hosting, and in a moment of true stupidity, he'd invited the drunks to dance with the ladies, then played Steppenwolf's "Born to Be Wild."

The drunks had rushed the stage and started groping the ladies. Sensing a disaster, I went behind the DJ's equipment and pulled the plug on the main electrical outlet, then marched onto the stage holding my detective's badge over my head. I led the ladies into the bar and stood by while they got dressed. Within minutes everything was back to normal.

Ever since, when I wasn't doing odd jobs, I was here in my office. Along with a great view of the intercoastal waterway, my office contained a desk and chair, a dartboard with Michael Jackson's picture, an ancient PC and printer, and the Skell case file. I got behind my desk and went to work.

The Skell file sat on the floor, separated into eight piles. Each pile represented one of the victims and contained a police report, dozens of interviews with friends and neighbors, and a personal history. On the wall above the files I'd taped the victims' photographs. Their names were Chantel, Maggie, Carmen, Jen, Krista, Brie, Lola, and Carmella. I'd known them all as teenagers living on the streets. They were all either thrownaways or runaways. I'd seen them grow up and helped them out whenever I could. I'd never stopped caring for them, even in death.

Behind my desk hung a map of Broward County with colored pins showing where each victim was last seen. The victims were not defined by a common geography but lived in rural areas, in the city, and in residential neighborhoods. What tied them together was the completeness of their disappearances. One day they were here; the next they were simply gone. No witnesses, no trace, nothing.

I studied this evidence whenever I could. It was my obsession, and for good reason. Because I'd beaten Skell up, I'd cast him in a sympathetic light with the media. As a result, his trial had been scrutinized, and it was apparent that the state's case was weak. Every legal expert I'd talked to had said that Skell would either get a new trial or have his case thrown out on appeal. And all because of me.

I was reading my e-mails when my cell phone rang. Caller ID said Bobby Russo. I let it go into voice mail, then picked up his message.

"Jack, you stupid son of a bitch," Bobby Russo's voice rang out. "I'm about to issue a warrant for your arrest."

I'd fallen pretty hard in the past six months, but getting thrown in the county lockup would be a new low. I called Russo back.

"Tell me you're kidding," I said.

"No joke," Russo said.

"What's the warrant for?"

"Assault and battery on an FBI agent."

I nearly dropped the phone on my desk.

"That guy you roughed up in the convenience store this morning is an FBI agent," Russo said. "He paid me a visit yesterday. He's got an interest in the Skell case and wants to talk to you. Being a nice guy, I told him where you lived."

I shut my eyes and listened to my beating heart.

"I thought he was this private dick who's been harassing me."

"You thought wrong," Russo said.

"Is he pressing charges?"

"No, he doesn't want to press charges," Russo said.

"Then how can you arrest me?"

"Easy. The manager of the convenience store wants to press charges and was kind enough to provide me with a surveillance tape of what you did."

"Shit," I said.

"Shit is right," Russo said. "You're busted, Jack. Unless you'd like to do a little horse trade."

Russo was the master of getting what he wanted. Without missing a beat, I said, "You want the Skell file in return for dropping charges."

"That's exactly what I want, plus three hundred bucks to pay the deductible for getting my car fixed," Russo said. "You've got until three o'clock this afternoon to get the file and the money to my office. Otherwise, you're getting three hots and a cot."

Before I could bargain with him, I was listening to a dial tone.

CHAPTER TEN

Ex-cops don't do well in jail. Other prisoners harass them, and usually so do the guards. Then there was this little thing called my ego. It had taken a pounding recently, and I wasn't sure it could deal with this.

I had no choice but to cave to Russo's demands. Facing the victims, I started to take their photographs down. I felt that I'd failed them, and I was unable to look in their eyes.

I also took down the map above my desk. It wasn't part of the file, but I might as well include it and let Russo and the other homicide detectives working the case see what they could come up with.

I put everything in the cardboard box it had originally come in. As I hoisted it off my desk, my cell phone rang. I wasn't usually this popular, and I put the box down and pulled the phone from my pocket. It was Jessie, the light of my life.

"Hey, honey," I answered.

"Dad, I'm sitting here in my dorm room, watching you on TV," my daughter said. "I can't believe what they're saying about you."

"Who's they, honey?"

"That crummy lawyer representing Simon Skell. He's

on Court TV showing pictures of you and saying you're a psychopathic cop who framed his client."

"Are they good pictures?"

"Dad, this isn't funny. I read about this dirty trick in my criminology class. He's courting public opinion to pressure the judge. He's making you look *horrible.*"

I trudged downstairs with the phone pressed to my ear. I asked the bartender to find Court TV on the TV hanging over the bar, and he picked up the remote and obliged me. Skell's attorney, the infamous Leonard Snook, appeared on-screen.

Snook was in his early sixties, with a silver goatee, tailored clothes, and a movie-star tan. He practiced out of Miami and had built his reputation on representing lowlifes and scumbags. He'd gone over to the dark side long ago, and he floated in his chair like grease simmering in a frying pan.

Beside him was a big-haired, big-bosomed woman named Lorna Sue Mutter. Lorna Sue had materialized in the spectator gallery during Skell's trial and had been seen slipping notes to him. Two months after Skell went to prison, they got married. I know a psychiatrist who believes that if you did a TV show starring nothing but convicted murderers, millions of women would watch. Lorna Sue would be president of their club.

Two photographs of Skell appeared on the screen. Before I beat him up, and after. Skell was trim and athletic, with surfer-white hair, a paintbrush-blond beard, and eyes too small for his face. For reasons no one knew, both of his hands had missing fingers; half the pinky was gone on his left, half the index finger on his right. He had been semi-normal-looking until I got my hands on him.

"Oh, man, did you kick his ass," my daughter said.

I'd forgotten Jessie was there.

"Shouldn't you be in class?" I asked.

"Dad, this is important. That bastard Snook is slandering you."

"Let him," I said.

"Is his client going to get out? Will they let Skell go?"

More pictures appeared on the screen, showing the studio in Skell's house and several framed photographs of Florida landscapes. Skell claimed to be a professional photographer, but no evidence existed of him ever being paid for a job.

"Answer me, Daddy."

I was "Daddy" when Jessie wanted something. I didn't give in.

"Go to class. Please."

"But—"

"Everything's going to be okay, trust me."

"Are you sure?"

"Positive."

"I love you, Daddy."

"I love you, too."

I folded my phone while staring at the TV. The show's host let Snook present his case, and Snook put all his cards on the table. His client didn't put Carmella Lopez's skeleton in her sister's backyard; someone else did. Therefore, his client didn't murder Carmella Lopez, and he should be released from prison. Lorna Sue Mutter said nothing, content to nod like a bobblehead doll whenever Snook made a salient point.

The segment ended, and I found myself agreeing with my daughter. Snook was trying his case in the court of public opinion. If he could get a couple of newspaper editors and TV commentators to support him, he'd run to a judge.

I went upstairs to my office. Buster was on the other side of the door, panting frantically. Leaving him behind usually resulted in a piece of furniture being destroyed. He'd spared me this time, and I scratched behind his ears.

The Skell file sat on my desk. Beside it was a handful of mail. Most of what I got these days were flyers and solicitations for credit cards. A mailing on top of the stack caught my eye.

Kinko's.

That gave me an idea, and I spent thirty minutes counting each page in the Skell file. All totaled, there were eight hundred and ninety-five pages of evidence.

I called the number on the Kinko's flyer. The guy who answered was polite and helpful. I asked for a ballpark quote on copying everything.

"That it?" he asked.

I started to say yes, then realized I'd need copies of the victims' photographs as well.

"Do you copy photographs?"

"Of course."

I added the photographs to the quote.

"How quickly do you need this?" the guy asked.

"Zoom," I said.

The guy put me on hold, and returned to the line a minute later.

"That's going to cost you four hundred and twenty-two dollars, plus sales tax."

It was money I didn't have. I thanked him and killed the connection.

I made a list of the names of people I could hit up for a loan. I started calling them and got the usual excuses. After each call was finished, I drew a line through the person's name. Finally, only one name was left.

Sonny.

Taking out my wallet, I removed the money I'd been paid by Tommy Gonzalez for rescuing Isabella Vasquez. I'd earmarked the money to pay my rent. I decided to use it for the copies and called the Sunset to tell Sonny. He answered on the tenth ring.

"You working?" I asked.

"Not so you'd notice," Sonny said.

"Listen, I'm going to be late on the rent this month."

The news was greeted by a stony silence.

"You still there?" I asked.

"How late?" Sonny said.

"I don't know—a week at best. Can you cover for me?"

In the background, I could hear a women's exercise show on the TV. Sonny and the Dwarfs got their kicks watching women's exercise shows—the more strenuous the better. I was convinced they were suffering from some strange psychosexual disorder; not that any of them cared.

"I guess," Sonny finally said. "Look, Jack, you're good for it, aren't you?"

"Of course I'm good for it," I said. "See you in a few hours."

"I'm not going anywhere," Sonny replied.

The line at the Kinko's in Coral Springs was out the door. The concept of waiting to give people money didn't appeal to me, so I drove back to Dania. There was a copy shop across from the jai alai fronton. The owner was rude, the help unfriendly, and the place was generally empty. I decided to give him a shot at my business.

The owner agreed to match Kinko's quote and said the job would take at least twenty minutes. I handed him the box containing the file and walked out. Claire's Sub Shop was across the street, and I decided to grab lunch. As I entered the restaurant an athletic-looking woman with a radioactive tan greeted me.

"Hey, mister, can't you read the sign? No dogs."

I bellied up to the counter. "I don't see very well."

"You see well enough to cross the street."

Lifting my arms, I knocked over several condiment dispensers sitting on the counter.

"Oh, great, a smart-ass," she said. "What do you want?"

"Two chicken sandwiches on lightly toasted rye bread with lettuce, tomato, and mayo. On one of the sandwiches, hold the bread and the other stuff."

Her face turned mean. "You going to feed the dog in here?"

"Wouldn't dream of it."

"Ten minutes. The cook's kinda busy."

I took a table with a view of the street. Although there was plenty to look at, I focused on the copy shop. The building was easily fifty years old, with spaghetti wires running from a transformer on a pole to a black box on the roof. The place was a firetrap, and I imagined it burning to the ground, and the Skell file destroyed.

The thought unsettled me. What would I do if that happened? Get a new job? Go back to Rose? Or would I move somewhere else and start over? It should have been easy to make an imaginary decision, only I couldn't. For the time being, that file was my life. I couldn't let go of it, and it wouldn't let go of me.

Claire slapped a plate down on the counter and rang a bell. As I paid up the abrasive voice of Neil Bash came over a radio in the kitchen. The shock jock was talking about me, and it wasn't pretty.

"Detective Carpenter tortured your husband after he arrested him," Bash said.

"He most certainly did," a woman's static-filled voice replied.

"In his cell?"

"Yes, in his cell."

"This man is a menace."

"He most certainly is."

I made the voice. It was Lorna Sue Mutter, calling in the interview. I gripped the counter edge.

"How did Detective Carpenter torture your husband?" Bash asked.

"With a lit cigarette," Lorna Sue said. "He burned my husband and tried to make him confess to a crime he didn't commit."

"The murder of Carmella Lopez," Bash said.

"My husband did not kill that woman or anyone else."

"Your husband is not the Midnight Rambler who the police have linked to the disappearances of eight young women?"

"No! My husband is a professional photographer and an artist. He's a warm, sensitive man."

"Getting back to the alleged torture," Bash said. "I followed your husband's trial. A doctor testified about the beating that Detective Carpenter inflicted upon your husband, but never mentioned any cigarette burns."

"That's because my husband didn't show them to the doctor," she said.

"Why not?"

"Because he was afraid of what Detective Carpenter would do to him."

"Which is what?"

"Kill him."

"Did you see the cigarette burns?"

There was a pause. Then a little pathetic sob. Lorna Sue was crying.

Bash repeated himself. "Did you?"

"Yes," she whispered.

"Where?"

"In prison when I went to visit him."

"I mean on his body."

Another pause, this one a little longer.

"On his genitals," Lorna Sue said.

Bash said something that sounded like Jesus. It was the only part of the conversation that didn't feel scripted. I felt Buster against my leg and released the counter edge.

"Detective Carpenter burned your husband's genitals with a cigarette to make him confess to a crime that he didn't commit?" Bash asked.

"He most certainly did," Lorna Sue whispered.

"Folks, we need to hear from one of our sponsors. We'll be back in sixty."

I felt like I'd been kicked. Lorna Sue was lying through her teeth. But until someone disputed her claims, they'd stick. And I didn't see Bobby Russo or the district attorney jumping in to defend me.

Buster let out a whine. I slipped him a piece of chicken while thinking about the timing of Lorna Sue's appearance on Court TV and now Bash's show. She was trying to publicly assassinate me, and I wondered who was pushing her. Was it Leonard Snook, or was Skell manipulating her from behind bars?

"I saw that!" Claire said.

I snapped back to the present. Claire stood behind the counter, glaring at me. Her husband, a skinny guy with a mullet cut morphing into a ponytail, hovered behind her.

"Saw what?" I asked innocently.

"You fed your dog in my restaurant."

No clever retort came to mind. Guilty as charged.

"Sorry, I wasn't thinking," I said.

"Leave," Claire demanded.

"Excuse me?"

"And never come back."

"I didn't mean any harm."

"You heard me. We know who you are."

"You do?"

Her husband piped up. "Yeah, you're that stinking cop with the sadistic temper. Everyone knows what you did, buddy."

I blew out my cheeks. *Busted.*

"Get out, or we'll call the police," Claire threatened.

I've never been thrown out of a place before. It made me feel lower than a snake's belly. I grabbed my order off the counter and left with my dog.

CHAPTER ELEVEN

The next hour passed in a blur. I left the Skell file at the Sheriff's Department headquarters along with an IOU for three hundred bucks for Russo. Back at my office, I hung the copies of the victims' photographs and spread the copied files on the floor, just as they were before. Carmella's photo gave me pause, and I wondered if the body in her sister's backyard had been identified as hers. I supposed I'd find out like everyone else—from the TV.

Then I drove to the Sunset. I needed to jump into the ocean and wash away the scene at Claire's. Of all the rotten things that had happened to me recently, getting eighty-sixed from a crummy sandwich shop had been the most humiliating.

Parking in the Sunset's lot I remembered the transmitter attached to my gas tank. Whoever had put it there was probably still tailing me. I pulled the device free and walked down to the shoreline. Before I could throw it into the ocean, a black 4Runner pulled into the lot and parked beside my car. The FBI agent I'd roughed up earlier got out and came toward me.

The agent stopped when he was fifteen feet away. The first thing I noticed about him were his eyes. They were sad-looking and matched the gunmetal of his close-cropped hair. I pointed at Buster, who stood protectively by my side.

"He isn't friendly," I said.

"Neither's his owner," the FBI agent said.

He said this in a good-natured way. I told Buster to heel and showed the agent the transmitter.

"Looking for this?" I asked.

"What is it?"

"An electronic transmitter. Someone stuck it beneath my car."

"Not me," he said.

I heaved the transmitter into the ocean. Then I peeled off my clothes until I was standing in my underwear. My regard for the law had changed since my departure from the force, and I wasn't going to let this guy stop me from taking my swim.

"Jack, I need to talk to you," the FBI agent said.

"That's nice," I replied.

"Do you know who I am?"

"No, should I?"

He took out his wallet and showed me his credentials. Special Agent Ken Linderman, Quantico, Virginia. I'd heard of him. Linderman was the only living agent to receive the FBI Director's Award for Special Achievement for his accomplishments in hunting serial killers. Five years earlier, his daughter had vanished while jogging near the University of Miami, and it was no secret that he'd been hunting for her ever since.

"I'll be right back," I said, and dove into the water.

Ten minutes later my mood had lifted, and I swam back to shore. Linderman sat in the sand, making nice with my dog. Standing in front of him, I let myself drip dry.

"What brings you to sunny Florida?" I asked.

"I moved to Miami six weeks ago," he explained. "I'm running the Bureau's Child Abduction Rapid Deployment Teams throughout the state."

I'd worked with plenty of CARD teams. The FBI had established them to deal with the overwhelming number of child abductions throughout the country. Each team had four members: two field agents supported by two profilers from the Behavioral Sciences Unit in Quantico.

"Is there someplace we can talk in private?" Linderman asked.

"Do you want to interrogate me?"

"Actually, I was hoping we could share information about Simon Skell."

I felt myself stiffen. Linderman had dug up new evidence. That was why he'd tracked me down. I wanted to kick myself.

"How about my office?" I suggested.

"Your office it is," Linderman said.

He followed me to Tugboat Louie's. My office was dark, and I opened the blinds and flipped on the overhead lights. He instinctively went to the wall where the victims' photographs hung and studied them. I went to Kumar's office and got another chair. When I returned, he was sitting cross-legged on the floor, poring through the Skell file.

"Feel free to look around," I said.

He looked up, embarrassed.

"Sorry. I should have asked."

"That's okay," I said.

He spent several minutes with the file. Knowing he had lost a child made me see him in a different light. I listened to the music coming from downstairs, the Doobie Brothers' "China Grove" rocking the house. Finally he got up and took a chair.

"Sorry, but I have an insatiable curiosity for cases that perplex me," he said. "My wife says it borders on rudeness."

Rose had told me the same thing many times. Taking a quarter from my pocket, I balanced it on my fingertips.

"Call it," I said.

"Tails," he said.

The quarter did several lazy gyrations above our heads. I slapped it on the back of my hand.

"Tails it is. You want to go first, or should I?"

Linderman hesitated. The sadness in his eyes was still there. I've heard it said that when you lose a child, you die every day.

"You go first," he said. "I want to hear how you figured out Simon Skell was the Midnight Rambler."

I paused to gather my thoughts. I'd spoken to no one about the case since the trial, and I didn't want to sound resentful for how things had turned out. As Jessie was fond of saying, it was water under the bridge.

Linderman sat with his hands folded in his lap. Something about his demeanor told me I could confide in him. Reaching across my desk, I punched a button on the CD player, and the Rolling Stones' "Midnight Rambler" came out of the speaker. The song, a thinly veiled homage to a notorious serial killer called the Boston Strangler, described a man breaking into women's houses late at night and brutally murdering them. The song was filled with rage; it described furniture and plateglass windows being broken, and how the Midnight Rambler tracked and killed his victims with a knife or a gun. Written by Mick

Jagger and Keith Richards in Positano, Italy, in 1969, it was recorded that same year at Olympic Studios in London and Elektra Studios in Los Angeles. At the time, the Stones were being billed as the Beatles' evil antithesis, and at their producer's urging, they wrote and recorded many dark songs, including "Sympathy for the Devil," "Let it Bleed," and "Paint it Black." But nothing they recorded compared to the evil of "Midnight Rambler."

The song was six minutes and fifty-two seconds long and had four distinct tempo changes, each rapidly building upon the next. I could not hear it played without imagining a terrified woman running for her life.

"Two and a half years ago, I went to an apartment complex in Fort Lauderdale where a prostitute named Chantel Roberts lived," I began. "I'd known Chantel as a teenager when she was living on the streets, and I'd helped her out. We spoke about once a month. When the calls stopped, I decided to check up on her.

"Chantel's neighbors hadn't seen her in a while. I got the super to open her apartment, and there was no sign of foul play. Her car was also parked downstairs. I left the complex not sure what was going on. Driving away, I spotted graffiti on a schoolyard wall across the street and stopped to have a look. The graffiti was the opening lyrics to 'Midnight Rambler,' and included the words 'The one that shut the kitchen door.'

"The graffiti disturbed me, so I drove back to Chantel's apartment and got the super to open her place back up. In the kitchen was a swinging door, and I saw a man's shoe print to one side of where it had been kicked.

"I kept looking for Chantel but never found her. I knew she hadn't run away or just skipped town. I knew something was wrong."

"How did you know that?" Linderman asked.

"On her kitchen table was a brochure for Broward Community College, with pencil checks next to classes for cosmetology. I called the school and learned she'd enrolled."

"So she had dreams," Linderman said.

I thought of his lost daughter and nodded.

"Yes. Chantel had dreams. Over the next fourteen months, I stopped hearing from other young women I knew in the sex industry, with each vanishing every few months. I'd go to their apartments or houses and find lyrics from 'Midnight Rambler' painted on a wall outside. If the lyric referenced something being smashed or broken, I would find that inside the dwelling.

"For a while, the case went nowhere. Then one day, a prostitute named Julie Lopez called, and said her sister Carmella, who was also a prostitute, was missing. I decided to visit Carmella's apartment and do a search. Nothing appeared out of place. Then I went outside and looked around. The lyrics were painted on the parking garage wall. Carmella had disappeared the day before, so I knew her trail was warm.

"I went to Bobby Russo, who heads up the homicide division of the Broward County Police Department, and asked for help. Russo put half his team on the case. One of them tracked down Carmella's cell phone service and obtained a list of phone calls Carmella had made the day she went missing.

"There were over forty messages. Carmella did outcalls, so we knew most of them were johns. Russo's detectives got the names and addresses for every one. We split them up, with each person taking five names.

"Simon Skell was on my list. I went to his house in

Lauderdale Lakes and spoke with him. He was cordial and let me look around. I asked about Carmella, and he admitted hiring her for sex a few days before but said he hadn't seen her since. I asked him if he'd let a forensic team search his place, and he said yes.

"At that point, I didn't think Skell was our killer. He wasn't hiding anything and was actually quite friendly. His house was filled with books, and I saw a certificate from Mensa, the genius organization, hanging in his study, which didn't fit the profile of any killer I've ever hunted.

"I started to leave, and he offered me a cold drink. I said sure and followed him into the kitchen. A CD player was on the kitchen table, and I realized that I'd seen stereos and boom boxes and CD players in every room of the house. Skell was also wearing an iPod, and I asked him what kind of music he listened to.

"Skell just stared at me. He has strange eyes that are too small for his face. I saw a darkness in them that hadn't been there before. I knew something was wrong, and I hit the Play button on the CD player on the table, and 'Midnight Rambler' came out of the speaker. That's when I knew it was him."

"Is that when he became violent?" Linderman asked.

I nodded solemnly.

"Did you provoke him?"

It's a question that I'd asked myself many times.

"No," I said firmly.

"Then why did he become violent?"

"I have a couple of theories," I said.

Linderman straightened in his chair. "Go ahead."

"Skell's reaction to being arrested reminded me of

many pedophiles I've arrested. They know their lives are about to become a living hell, so they get crazy."

"Do you think Skell is a pedophile?"

I nodded again.

"But he doesn't have a record for pedophilia," Linderman said.

"I think he's a closet pedophile," I said. "Look at the victims he picked. They'd all been robbed of their childhoods and were emotionally immature."

"Children in adult bodies," Linderman said.

"That's right. I think Skell knew the consequences of preying on kids were severe, so he targeted immature women as a substitute. He chose women in the sex industry because he knew there would be less concern if they went missing."

"Perfect victims," Linderman said.

"Exactly. My other theory concerns Melinda Peters, the prosecution's key witness at Skell's trial. Skell kept her locked in a dog crate and played 'Midnight Rambler' on his stereo while standing in the next room. Melinda told me she thought he was masturbating. One day, Skell acted stressed out, and Melinda sensed he couldn't get an erection. She offered to have sex with him, and he let her out of the cage. That's when she bolted.

"I think Melinda's escaping sent Skell over the edge, and he went from being a closet pedophile to being a killer. He started picking up women who'd say they'd have sex with him, and murdered them."

"So his fantasy changed from torturing women to killing them, with Melinda Peters fueling his rages."

"That's correct."

"I read in the newspaper that Skell's house was examined from top to bottom by a team of forensic experts and was absolutely clean," Linderman said.

"Correct again."

"So if you hadn't started his CD player, Skell would still be on the loose."

"Yes."

There was a brief silence as Linderman digested everything I'd said. Talking about the investigation had made me feel better, and I leaned back in my chair.

"Your turn," I said.

CHAPTER TWELVE

Linderman went to the blinds and darkened the room. I like to work in the light, and he was obviously someone who gravitated toward the dark. When he sat down, I saw weariness in his face and offered to get coffee from the bar.

"That would be great," he said.

While waiting for my order, I called Jessie and got voice mail. I wished her luck in her basketball game tonight and told her about a dream I had where she was hitting three-pointers from all over the court. The bartender delivered a steaming pot and two mugs on a tray, and I went upstairs and served my guest.

Caffeine takes ten seconds to hit your bloodstream. Linderman's face sparked to life, and I topped off his cup without being asked. He nodded his appreciation and began.

"I happen to share one of your theories, which is that sexual killers like Skell start out as sexual predators and over time evolve into killers," Linderman said. "This evolution is one of the reasons they're so difficult to apprehend. They often become experts at deception, learning to hide their impulses from society for many years."

"So my assumption that Skell was a pedophile is probably true," I said.

He placed his empty cup on the tray. "Oh, it's definitely true. I started looking at Skell the moment I came to Florida. He's lived all over the state. While living in Tampa he was suspected of being a pedophile. The police saw him in his car near several schools. He was also caught frequenting teenage girl chat rooms on the Internet. It wasn't enough to enable us to arrest him, but he was definitely on everyone's radar."

"Why did you start looking at him?" I asked out of curiosity.

"He lived in Miami five years ago," Linderman said.

The same time Linderman's daughter lived there, I thought.

"Part of my job is to analyze killers like Skell to find recognizable behavioral patterns," Linderman said. "These patterns usually explain motivation, which is essential to prosecution and conviction. Recently, I began examining the transcripts of Skell's trial. I believe I may have uncovered something."

I grew rigid in my chair.

"Something I missed?"

"Yes. I'm sure it did not seem significant at the time, but that's because you're not trained in criminal psychology. But it was significant to me."

"What did you find?"

"Melinda Peters testified that 'Midnight Rambler' was constantly played during her imprisonment in Skell's home. The song she heard was a different version of the song you just played for me. Skell played the live version for Melinda Peters, taken off an album called *Get Your Ya Yas Out*."

I knew this, having listened to the live version as well. The lyrics were the same as the album cut, and I hadn't given the detail any weight.

"So?"

"The live version has a unique lineage," Linderman said. "It was recorded during the Stones' 1969 tour of the United States and is part of the soundtrack of a documentary called *Gimme Shelter.* The film chronicles a free concert given at Altamont Speedway in California. The concert was a disaster, with eight hundred and fifty people injured, three killed, and a black man murdered by a gang of Hells Angels hired as security in plain view of the band.

"The resulting publicity nearly destroyed the Stones' careers. If you watch the film carefully, the band appears to *want* something violent to happen during their set. When it does, the Stones are playing 'Sympathy for the Devil,' and they *continue* to play."

"Goading the violence on?"

"It certainly looks that way on the film. Vincent Canby, the film critic for the *New York Times,* was so outraged that he called the movie an opportunistic snuff flick."

"And you think this is what fuels Simon Skell's rages."

"No. They fuel his rituals," Linderman said.

"What's the difference?"

"Psychosexual disorders are defined as paraphilias, which are recurrent, intense, and sexually arousing fantasies that involve humiliation or suffering. The partners in these fantasies are often minors or nonconsenting partners."

"I'm with you so far," I said.

"The presence of paraphilias in sex crimes generally means highly repetitive and predictable behavior patterns focused on specific sexual acts. The repetitive nature of the paraphilia is the ritual. To become aroused, Skell must engage in the act."

"And Skell's paraphilia is to listen to the live version of 'Midnight Rambler' while torturing his victims," I said.

"All evidence points to that," Linderman said. "*Gimme Shelter* was released in 1970, when Skell was seven years old. That's the age when paraphilias usually develop. My guess is, he saw the film and was sexually stimulated by the song's violence toward women and the film's violence. Over time, the two became linked."

"And a deviant was born."

"Precisely. But that's the problem with this case. Based upon everything we know about sexual killers, Skell should have been caught long ago, and with far more evidence than what was presented at his trial."

I swallowed the rising lump in my throat. The faces of the victims were staring at us, and I could almost feel their shame.

"Did I screw up the investigation?" I asked.

"Far from it," Linderman said. "If not for you, Skell would still be murdering young women."

"Then what are you saying?"

"What I'm saying, Jack, is that it's amazing you *did* catch him. Most people who engage in sexual rituals cannot change their habits, even when they suspect law-enforcement scrutiny. As a result, they make need-driven mistakes and are their own worst enemies. But this isn't true with Skell. He chose his victims with utmost care and made them disappear in a way that so far has defied detection."

"Why is Skell different?"

Linderman paused to give me a probing stare.

"That's a good question. You believe that Skell is a pedophile who evolved into a serial killer. I think he's evolved even further. He's used his superior intellect to become organized and ruthlessly efficient. A killing machine, if you like. Only he can't do any killing from behind bars, so he's now orchestrating his own release from prison."

"You think he's behind this smear campaign against me?"

"Absolutely."

"What do Leonard Snook and Lorna Sue Mutter stand to gain, besides seeing themselves on TV?"

"A million-dollar movie deal."

"But that's illegal."

"Skell can't profit from his crimes, but his wife can, and she's signed a contract with a Hollywood studio," Linderman said. "According to the FBI's sources, she's cut Snook in on the deal. He's getting a 20 percent cut and is executive producer."

"Did you tell the police and the DA?"

"I briefed Bobby Russo and the district attorney yesterday," Linderman said. "They both felt that unless more evidence was found linking Skell to his victims, he'll be released from Starke."

Linderman was describing my worst nightmare, and I slowly came out of my chair.

"What can I do?"

"Keep digging for evidence," Linderman said. "You should also be thinking about what you're going to do if Skell is released."

His words were slow to register.

"Do?" I asked.

"If Skell walks, he'll come after you. You're the person he's most afraid of, as evidenced by the campaign he's waging against you. In order for him to continue to survive and practice his rituals, he'll have to take you out of the picture."

My office grew deathly still. The silence was so complete that I felt as if I were underwater.

"What about Melinda Peters?" I asked. "Will Skell go after her, too?"

"That would be a logical assumption. Melinda is the object of Skell's murderous fantasies *and* is responsible for him going to jail. More than likely, she will be his first target."

"What do you suggest she do?"

"Run."

That was easy for Linderman to say. Melinda had left home as a teenager, and like so many runaways, she had no place to run *to*.

Linderman looked at his watch. Then he stood up.

"I'm sorry, but I need to go."

"Of course," I said.

Linderman took out his business card and placed it on my desk. He thanked me for the coffee and urged me to stay in touch. Then he walked out the door.

CHAPTER THIRTEEN

Bob Dylan said, "You don't need a weatherman to know which way the wind blows."

I sat at my desk and stared into space. Although Linderman had left an hour ago, his presence hung like an odorless cloud. I thought about the timing of his appearance and the fact that our meeting had ended with a warning about my safety. It could mean only one thing: he knew something I didn't.

But *what*? Before paying me a visit, Linderman had met with Bobby Russo and the DA and shared the same information that he gave me. I had worked with the FBI enough times to know that this sharing didn't come without a price. Linderman got something in return, and I spent the next twenty minutes trying to determine what it was.

Buster crawled out from beneath my desk and stuck his head in my crotch, a cue that he wanted his ears scratched. I obliged him, and when I was done, he wagged his butt, then went to the door and whined. It was the same routine every day. Nap, scratch, pee. If only my own life were so simple.

I put my elbows on my desk and rested my head in my hands. I'd never been good for sitting in one place for very long pondering life's impossibilities. I was better on my feet and moving around. But this situation deserved serious thought, and I played back Linderman's warning.

If Skell walks, he'll come after you.

It wasn't the kind of thing someone in law enforcement would say to a brother-in-arms. Skell was in prison for first-degree murder, and for him to be set free, certain legal steps had to be followed, like his attorney petitioning the court, the judge finding the space on his docket to listen, and then the judge taking the new evidence and weighing it against the evidence presented at trial. The wheels of the legal system moved notoriously slow, and it might be weeks or even months before Skell was released, if the judge decided to swing that way.

So why did Linderman warn me? What disaster was on the horizon that warranted his seeking me out and telling me that Skell might be knocking on my door?

Five minutes later, it hit me.

It wasn't *if* Skell would be released from jail, it was *when*. Russo must have told Linderman that the body in Julie Lopez's backyard had been positively identified as Carmella's and that he was going to take the unusual step of asking the judge to release Skell so his department could save face. Learning this, Linderman had sought me out, hoping I might have uncovered additional evidence to keep Skell behind bars. And when he discovered I had none, he warned me.

I got on 595 and became a prisoner of late-afternoon traffic. Buster sat at stiff attention in the passenger seat, tuned in to my apprehension. Only one thought was running through my mind, and that was to provide safe haven for Melinda. I got her into this, and it was my responsibility to make sure nothing happened to her. My own safety was not important to me. I'd already had one confrontation with Skell and come out on the winning end. Until we tangoed again, I was alpha dog.

But Melinda was a different story. Despite her tough exterior, she was no fighter. She'd be easy prey for Skell once he was released from prison. I needed to track her down, and I called Cheever on my cell.

"Claude, it's Jack," I said. "You looking at naked women?"

"Yes, Mr. President," Cheever replied.

"Which club?"

"Church of the Sacred Body Shot."

"Is Melinda Peters working there now?"

"Yes, if you call making guys horny working."

"I'm coming over. Wait for me, okay?"

"Sure," Cheever said. "This is two days in a row. Want me to get you a membership card?"

"No, but thanks for asking."

Hanging up, I retrieved Dennis Vasquez's business card from my wallet and called his cell phone. He answered, and I heard Beethoven's Fifth Symphony playing loudly in the background and the joyful sounds of a woman's laughter.

"Mr. Vasquez?" I said.

"Who's calling?" he asked suspiciously.

"This is Jack Carpenter."

"Jack, Jack! How are you?"

"Just great," I said.

"Your ears must be burning. My wife and I were just talking about you. Hold on for a second, will you?" Taking his mouth away from the receiver, Vasquez said, "Honey, Jack Carpenter's on the line."

The phone was passed to a woman with a breathless

voice and a slight Spanish accent. "Oh, Mr. Carpenter, it's so wonderful you called. We brought Isabella home this afternoon, and we were sitting here, thanking God that you appeared when you did."

"She's a beautiful child," I said. "I hope you and your husband make more of them."

She squealed with delight and invited me to dinner Saturday night. Their address was in Key Biscayne. I envisioned them living in an estate home on the water, and knew I wouldn't fit in with my ratty clothes and aging car, even for a few hours. I asked for a rain check and got one. Her husband came back on the line.

"I need a favor, Mr. Vasquez."

"Anything, Jack. Anything at all," he said.

"I know this is presumptuous of me to ask, but do you own a second home?"

"We have two. A weekend place in Key West, and a four-bedroom house in Aspen. Either one is at your disposal."

"Does your house in Aspen have security?"

"The best money can buy," he said. "Besides the security system, the house is inside a walled community with a guard at the front gate, and another guard that patrols the grounds at night. Since my wife and I don't plan to use it for a while, you can have it for as long as you like."

"It's not for me," I said.

"A friend?"

"She's a witness in a case. I need to get her out of the state, let her lie low for a while. You're sure this won't be any trouble?"

"Consider it done. Just give me the dates she'll be arriving, and I'll arrange everything. She'll be very safe there, Jack."

"Thank you, Mr. Vasquez. I really appreciate this."

"There's no need to thank me, Jack," he said. "No need at all."

The sky was a dying amber when I arrived at the Body Shot. Parking in a strip center across the street, I told Buster to mind the fort.

The club was packed, and I elbowed my way through a mob of working-class guys leering at naked women dancing on the elevated stage. Being unemployed had its drawbacks, one of which was that I could easily lose track of the days. It was Thursday, which in south Florida was the official beginning to the weekend.

Cheever hailed me from the bar. A cold beer awaited me when I reached him.

"Sorry I split last night, but I got an emergency call," he said, clinking his bottle against mine. "How did it go with Melinda?"

"She had me tossed," I shouted in his ear.

"And you came back for more?"

"I need to talk with her. They're going to let Simon Skell out of prison."

His bottle hit the bar. "Fucking what did you say?"

"You heard me. I found out from the FBI. I need to get Melinda someplace safe."

Cheever gave me a thoughtful look. Even in the club's crummy neon I could see he was way drunk. He grabbed my shoulder and squeezed it.

"That's my Jack."

"I'm going to the VIP lounge. When you see Melinda, ask her to join me. She'll listen to you."

"Sure, man. Anything to help."

"And make sure the bouncer doesn't come looking for me."

I started to leave. Cheever got a fresh beer from the bartender and forced it into my hands.

"You deserve it," he told me.

The VIP lounge was normally reserved for friction dances and, if you were not careful, a five-hundred-dollar bottle of pink champagne. I settled onto a couch as the perennial strip club favorite, "Shake Your Booty" by KC and the Sunshine Band, blasted over the speakers. KC was a Miami band, and you could not spend any serious time in a south Florida bar without hearing at least one of their songs.

The set ended and the house lights flickered. Three new dancers came out and peeled off their clothes. I sucked on my beer, thinking of Skell. One of his victims was a stripper, one worked in a massage parlor, and the rest were prostitutes employed by escort services. Yet, except for the phone call Skell had made to Carmella Lopez, no evidence existed of him ever being inside a strip club or massage parlor, or using an escort service. He did not know his victims either personally or professionally, even though they all fit the same profile. It was another piece of the puzzle with a question mark hanging over it.

I had a theory about this, which along with eight bucks would buy me another beer. It went like this. We all walk around in life with different odds. Some people have good odds; some have bad. Your odds are determined by your upbringing, your luck, and the strength of your desires. My guess was that everyone in this club had bad odds, myself included.

Skell's victims all had bad odds. They had chosen their professions out of necessity, and lived on the edge of despair. They'd been thrown away not only by their families but by society and were struggling not to fall into the abyss. Somehow, Skell knew this about his victims, which was why he chose them. Someday, I was going to find out how he knew.

Melinda entered the VIP lounge with a glazed look in her eyes. She was every hot-blooded male's dream: white toga, six-inch stiletto heels, her hair in a single braid resting on her shoulder. Sitting beside me, she pulled at a knot in her garment. It parted, revealing nothing but a G-string. Her reaction to danger was to snort coke, and I could tell she was higher than a kite.

"Oh, it's my knight in shining armor," she said.

Her breasts gently swayed as she spoke. She had never gotten implants, and her natural beauty set her apart from every other woman in the club.

"We need to talk," I said.

Her face turned dreamy.

"Do you love me?" she asked.

I hesitated. Taking my head in her hands, she kissed me on the lips.

"You *do* love me," she said.

I gazed into her eyes. It was hard to tell how far gone she was.

"I have a solution to the problem," I said.

"You want to run away with me?"

"Listen to me. I have a solution to the problem."

"What problem is that, Jack?"

"The one we talked about last night. Simon Skell."

"I don't want to talk about him."

"We *have* to talk about him."

Her face turned dark. Then tears rolled down her cheeks, and she started to crack. I sensed another presence in the lounge and looked up. The bouncer from last night was back. I offered no resistance as he lifted me off the couch.

"I told you to stay out of here," he said.

Melinda held her head in her hands. I spotted Cheever at the bar and waved. He came running and pulled the bouncer off me. The bouncer cocked his fist, and Cheever showed him his badge.

"Fucking shit," the bouncer said.

Cheever made him empty his pockets. The bouncer was carrying several fat joints and enough nose candy for the Mexican Army. Cheever read him his rights. I returned to the couch and pulled Melinda's toga together.

"I don't want to die," she sobbed. "I don't want to die."

"You're not going to die," I said.

"Yes, I am. Skell's going to kill me."

"No, you're not," I told her. "You're not going to die."

I fed Melinda pigs in a blanket at the local IHOP, and the life came back to her cheeks. She tried to talk, but I wouldn't let her. She was still messed up. Drugs mixed with fear produces something akin to insanity. She desperately needed to get straight.

"What's going to happen to Ray?" she asked after her third cup of coffee.

I assumed Ray was the bouncer and said, "He'll cop a plea, maybe do a couple of months, probably just house arrest or probation."

She twirled her coffee with the tip of her pinky. She'd cried away her makeup, and beneath the restaurant's harsh neon she looked like a kid. I assumed Ray's coke was the carrot that kept her coming back to the club and saw her shrug indifferently.

"So what's your solution?" she asked.

I told her about rescuing the Vasquez baby and how it had led to my getting the house in Aspen.

"Ever been to Aspen?" I asked.

"I've never been out of Florida," she said.

"I want you to go there and lie low for a while."

"Let me think about it, okay?"

Melinda didn't own a car and relied on the largesse of other dancers for rides. I drove her to a sprawling apartment complex near Weston and parked outside her unit. A giant palmetto bug smacked into the windshield, making us both jump.

"Oh, Jesus, I hate those things," Melinda said. "Make it go away."

I cleaned the bug's remains off the glass and got back in.

"Will you do it?" I asked.

She looked away. "Leave Florida? I don't know."

"You need to get out of here for a few weeks," I said. "I'll buy the airline ticket, send you money for food."

She placed her hand on my thigh. "Will that make me your kept woman?"

I got out, came around to her side, and opened her door. I was all business walking her up the path to her ground-floor unit. She caught my drift, but at the door she embraced me anyway.

"One day, Jack. One day."

"Will you do it?"

"You sound like a recorded message. I hate that."

"I'm sorry. Will you?"

Her key ring came out, and she unlocked her door.

"Let me sleep on it," and she was gone before I could reply.

During the drive home I remembered Jessie's basketball game. It was late and she was probably asleep in her dorm room, but I called her anyway. Her voice was groggy when she answered.

"I'm sorry I woke you," I said. "How was the game?"

"We won," my daughter said. "Your dream was right. I shot eight for twelve from the three-point line and hit 80 percent of my free throws."

"You're a star."

My daughter giggled. "Thanks for calling. How was your day?"

"Couldn't of been better."

"Good. Good night, Daddy. Love you."

"Love you, too."

I ended the call. Talking to Jessie gave purpose to my day, and I looked out my window at the shimmering lights from hundreds of houses visible from the interstate. It wasn't that long ago that I'd lived in one of those neighborhoods, with a wife and a child and a big backyard, where I'd hoped to put a swimming pool. Back then, my life had been filled with headaches and dreams, and I was always wishing for things I didn't own. It had never occurred to me how good things really were and that I should have been content with what I'd had. Now, I knew. And I wanted that life back, and all the problems that went with it. Somehow I didn't think that was too much to ask for.

PART TWO

GOD BLINKED

CHAPTER FOURTEEN

God blinked.

My five-year-old daughter stood before me, wearing a pink polka-dot bikini and clutching a plastic bucket. We were visiting friends on Hutchinson Island for the weekend, and Jessie wanted to go shell hunting on the beach with the older kids.

"Please, Daddy, I want to go," she pleaded.

The beer bottle in my hand was empty, and I was craving another. Outside the screened porch stood the other children, waiting expectantly. I did not like letting Jessie out of my sight. Seeing my hesitation, Jessie stomped her foot.

"Please, Daddy!"

I sensed a tantrum coming on and felt myself start to cave.

"Promise me you won't bother the turtles we saw last night," I said.

Jessie began to pout. Last night, under a full moon, our family had watched giant loggerhead turtles that had swum all the way from South Africa lay dozens of perfectly round white eggs in nests they'd dug on the beach. Jessie hadn't stopped talking about it.

"But I wanna see them," she said.

"I'll take you later," I said.

"You will?"

"Yes. Now promise me you'll stay away from them."

She stared at the floor. "Okay."

"Good. Now go have fun."

I watched her leave, then went to the kitchen for a fresh beer. On the way I was besieged with orders from my friends.

"Hey Jack, how about another cold one?"

"Jack, I could use more wine."

Jack, Jack, Jack.

We'd been partying all day long, and no one was feeling any pain. In the kitchen I fixed the drinks and put them on a tray, then returned to my friends. I served Rose, and she kissed me. Then I served my friends, and they tried to kiss me, too.

I returned to my chair. Something didn't feel right. Rising, I went to the screened window and stared at the sand dunes behind the house. The kids were having a blast and making plenty of noise. Finally I realized what was wrong. I didn't hear Jessie. Opening the screen door, I called her name.

No answer.

The dreadful void of silence was a sound worse than any cry or scream. Stepping outside, I went to where the older kids were playing in the dunes, half expecting to have my daughter jump up and yell "Boo!"

But she didn't.

"Where's Jessie?" I asked them. "Where is she?"

The older kids gave me blank stares. Then one pointed down the beach. I ran to the next dune and found Jessie's bucket. There were three sand dollars in it.

I couldn't believe this was happening. I was a cop. I should know better.

"Dad-dy!"

I ran to the sound of her voice. Twenty yards away, Jessie sat in the tall grass, crying and clutching herself. I gathered her into my arms.

"Make him go away," she sobbed. "Make him go away!"

"Who, honey? Make who go away?"

"The man in the grass!"

"What man?"

"The naked man! He said he wanted to play with me. Make him go away!"

I clutched my daughter against my chest. My heart was pounding out of control, and I could not stop blaming myself for what had happened. Rose appeared, looking shaken, and I handed my daughter to her.

"Don't let her out of your sight," I said.

Then I ran down the beach as fast as my legs would carry me and searched for the man who'd tried to molest my daughter.

CHAPTER FIFTEEN

A pounding on my door awakened me the next morning. Pulling the sheet over my bare torso, I grabbed Buster by the collar.

"We're all friends here," I said.

Sonny entered my rented room wearing black jeans, a Black Sabbath T-shirt with holes in the armpits, and a black crucifix—a dark messenger if there ever was one.

"Hey, Sleeping Beauty, you need to see this," he said.

I threw on yesterday's clothes and followed him downstairs. A steaming cup of coffee awaited me in the bar. I sipped my drink and watched Bobby Russo on the TV. Russo was holding a news conference at police headquarters and fielding questions from a handful of reporters. He was dressed up and had traded his trademark fish tie for a more respectable solid blue one.

"How did the police confirm that the body found in Julie Lopez's backyard was her sister Carmella's?" a reporter asked.

"Dental records," Russo said.

"How long was the body there?"

"There's no way for us to know. The rain washed away a great deal of evidence."

"Have the police confirmed she was murdered?"

"Yes."

"Do you know the cause of death?"

"Strangulation."

"Do you have a suspect?" another reporter asked.

"We do," Russo said. "Ernesto Sanchez."

"Can you tell us what evidence you have against him?"

"Mr. Sanchez was an acquaintance of Carmella Lopez and lives in the same house with her sister," Russo said. "We also found an item of Mr. Sanchez's clutched in the victim's hands."

"Can you tell us what the item was?"

"A gold crucifix."

"Has the suspect been charged?"

"The suspect has not been arraigned," Russo said.

"When will that happen?"

"I can't comment at this time."

The news conference ended. Russo was stalling Ernesto's arraignment to give his detectives more time to study the Skell file. It was a smart tactic, but he was only delaying the inevitable. I finished my coffee and told myself that I had done everything I could. I'd fought the good fight, and tomorrow would be another day. The words were hollow, but they were all I had left.

A perky female newscaster came on the screen. Imposed on a screen behind her was a photo of Simon Skell with a banner that read HOLLYWOOD CALLING?

"The Simon Skell case is attracting attention in Hollywood," she said cheerfully. "According to *Variety,* Paramount Studios is purchasing the rights to Skell's life story from Skell's wife, Lorna Sue Mutter. Possible stars being considered to play Skell are Brad Pitt, Tom Cruise, and Russell Crowe. No word on who might play Jack Carpenter, the

Broward County detective who Lorna Sue claims tortured and framed her husband."

I cursed like someone with Tourette's syndrome. On the TV, a blow-dried male newscaster appeared beside his perky colleague.

"How about Vince Vaughn?" the male newscaster suggested.

"You mean to play Jack Carpenter?" the female newscaster said.

"Absolutely. I saw him play a sociopathic killer in a movie called *Domestic Disturbance* with John Travolta," the male newscaster said. "He was terrific."

"I saw that movie, too. Good choice!"

I picked up the napkin dispenser on the bar. Sonny yelled "No!" but it was too late. The dispenser left my hand and shattered the TV screen. Glass rained down on the bar. Sonny said something about history, then got a broom and started cleaning up.

"What did you say?" I asked.

"You're history if you don't replace the TV."

"You're going to throw me out?"

"I will if you don't replace the TV."

"Can you lend me the money?"

He swept around my chair. "No."

"Come on, just for a couple of days," I said. "I'll pay you back. You know I'm good for it."

Going behind the bar, Sonny removed a black box from behind the register, pulled out a card, and showed it to me. It contained my two tabs. The little tab had caught up to the big tab, and I owed the bar nearly five hundred bucks.

"Replace the TV and pay your tabs and your rent, or you're history."

"You're serious."

"Damn straight."

He retrieved the napkin dispenser and replaced it on the bar, then resumed his sweeping. I felt as if I'd lost my last friend in the world.

I turned on my stool and looked out the window at the bright blue ocean. Should I just go take a swim and not come back? The thought had crossed my mind before, but never seriously. This time, it was serious.

The bar phone rang. Sonny answered it, then handed me the receiver.

"It's your girlfriend."

I figured it was Melinda accepting my offer from last night, but I was wrong. It was Julie Lopez.

"I know who put my sister's body in my backyard," Julie said.

I drove past Julie Lopez's house a couple of times, not wanting to run into any cops or reporters who might be hanging around. The place was quiet, but I still looked over my shoulder when I knocked on her front door.

Julie ushered me into the living room and bolted the door behind me. Her eyes were ringed from lack of sleep, her puffy face void of makeup. Her dirty short-sleeved shirt and faded cutoffs only hardened the picture.

There was no real furniture in the living room, just three folding metal chairs and a card table with a greasy bag from McDonald's in its center. The last time Julie saw her sister it was over breakfast at McDonald's, and I was surprised that she still ate their food. We sat on two of the chairs and faced each other.

"Who put your sister's body in your backyard?" I asked.

Julie looked around the room before answering me.

The look on her face was best described as paranoid. I looked around the room as well. There were no wall hangings, unless you considered mold art.

"Are you afraid of something?" I asked.

She nodded. She was a big woman, with large breasts and curvaceous hips, and was considered a hot number with the older Hispanic men who enjoyed her services. In a whisper she said, "It was the cable TV guys. They put Carmella in the backyard."

"The cable guys?" I repeated.

"Yeah."

"Is that why you called me over here?"

"Yeah, Jack."

I felt the strength leave my body. Opening the McDonald's bag, I removed a large order of french fries and helped myself. Julie threw me a wicked stare.

"That's my breakfast," she said angrily.

"You get any for me?"

Julie didn't understand the question. I was pissed off and not ashamed to show it. I had important things to do. Like replace the TV in the Sunset and figure out what I was going to do with the rest of my life. She grabbed the fries out of my hands with a catlike quickness and shoved several into her mouth.

"I can prove it," she said.

"All right, prove it."

"Last week the cable on the TV stopped working. Ernesto called the cable company, and two repairmen came out that afternoon. They said the wire in the backyard was old. They dug a trench and laid a new wire. But guess what?"

I had no idea where this was heading, and shook my head.

"The cable don't come back on. Ernesto looked at the

work they did. Then he climbed up on the pole. When he came back in the house, he called them dumb fucks. I ask him why, and he said the problem was on the pole. That was why we weren't getting HBO. The problem was on the pole."

"So?"

"Don't you get it?"

"No."

"What you acting so pissed off about, Jack?"

"I'm sorry, Julie, but you're wasting my time."

She threw the french fries and hit me in the head. I jumped out of my chair.

"I don't have time for this," I said angrily.

She wagged her finger in my face. "Listen to me. The cable guys didn't have to dig in the yard. The problem was on the pole."

"So?"

"The cable guys knocked the cable out on purpose. Then they dug a hole when me and Ernesto were sleeping, and put my sister's body in it. Get it?"

Hookers work at night, sleep during the day. Someone could have come into Julie's backyard and dug a grave while she and Ernesto were sleeping.

"What about the gold crucifix that was in your sister's hand?" I asked. "It was identified as Ernesto's."

Julie dragged me into the kitchen and pointed at a bookshelf beside the rattling fridge. Two gold crucifixes stood upright in a display meant to hold three. The middle crucifix was missing.

"One of the cable guys came inside to get a glass of water, and he stole one," Julie said.

I stared at the display. Two days earlier, when I'd stood in the driveway in handcuffs, there was a truck on the street with a trenching machine and two guys inside. Cable guys.

"Show me the pole," I said.

We went outside to the backyard. Carmella's grave was still open, and it gave me goose bumps. Julie pointed at the telephone pole in the corner of her property.

"That one," she said.

I borrowed a ladder from the garage, put it on the pole, and climbed up. The cable had been stapled to the pole, and halfway up I found where it had been cut. The cut was right above a staple, which minimized the chance that anyone might see it from the ground. I looked down at Julie, who had her arms crossed.

"See?" she said.

"Yeah, I see." My eyes drifted to the open grave. "Who called the police and told them about the skeleton?"

"The cable guys. They were trenching and said they found pieces of jewelry in the yard. They started digging and found Carmella's body."

"Or so they said."

"You finally believe me?"

I nodded.

"It's about fucking time."

I started to climb down, then froze. I could see over Julie's house to the street. A white van with two Hispanic guys was parked behind my Legend. The guy in the passenger seat got out and approached my car. He was husky and wore a red bandanna around his head. He got on his knees and began looking beneath my car. It took a moment before I realized what he was looking for.

The transmitter.

Buster was asleep on the backseat. Waking up, he began barking through the half-closed window. The Hispanic guy jumped to his feet and saw me perched on the ladder. He got into the van, and it pulled away with a squeal.

I scurried down the ladder. I wanted to tell Julie I was sorry, but there was no time. Instead, I told her to go inside and lock the doors.

"And call the police," I said.

As I started my car, I made a decision. If I were running from someone, where would I go? I decided on the interstate.

Within minutes I reached 595. Traffic was heavy heading into Fort Lauderdale, and I guessed this was the way the van had gone. Soon I was heading east doing ninety, the wind punishing my face through my open window.

A lone white van occupied the left lane. I pulled up alongside it and made eye contact with a thirtyish male talking on a cell phone. He winked flirtatiously, and I roared past him.

Hope is something I never give up on. Several exits later, I spotted another white van hurtling down the interstate like a stock car. I floored my accelerator and got behind its bumper. The license plate was from Broward and was caked with mud. Three digits were visible. I memorized them.

Getting in the right lane, I eased up to the van's passenger side. The Hispanic with the bandanna was leaning out the passenger window, smoking a cigarette. He was in his forties and had a pirate's scar running down the side of his face. Something told me he was a Mariel refugee, the most notorious group of criminals ever to invade south Florida. He tossed his cigarette, then saw me.

The Hispanic scrunched up his face as if trying to place

me. Then he spotted Buster, and panic set in. Ducking down, he grabbed something off the floor.

I knew I was in trouble, but I didn't think my car was powerful enough to pass him. I tried to slow down, only a delivery truck was riding my bumper. I was stuck.

The Hispanic leaned out his window. In his hand was a steel pipe, which he threw at me. The pipe hit my windshield lengthwise, and a thousand spiderwebs appeared in the glass. Unable to see, I banged out the broken glass with my fist.

My car was like a wind tunnel without a windshield. I tried to watch the road, but a popping sound that reminded me of firecrackers made me look at the van. The Hispanic was holding a shiny revolver and taking target practice at my car.

Buster yelped in fear as I swerved off the interstate.

CHAPTER SIXTEEN

I stood on the shoulder of 595 with Buster pressed to my side, the white van long gone.

My Legend sat twenty feet away. The windshield was a memory, and there were smoldering bullet holes in the passenger seat and both backseats. One bullet had missed my head by less than six inches. I should have been grateful that I was still breathing, but all I wanted to do was run those bastards down.

Cars roared past, but no one stopped. Their drivers stared through me as if I were invisible. Next to a deserted island, there was no lonelier place than the shoulder of a highway. I called 911, and an automated answering service put me on hold.

Buster barked at the cars. I had leashed him out of fear that he might step into traffic and add an exclamation point to my already miserable day. I went to the Legend and turned the radio to my favorite FM station. They were playing a song by the Fine Young Cannibals called "She Drives Me Crazy." Once upon a time they were my favorite band; then they suddenly disappeared. It seemed like a metaphor for my own sorry situation, and I leaned against my car and sang along.

I should have been dead. Three shots and you're usually

out. I got spared, except now I didn't have wheels. I was one step closer to becoming a homeless person. I imagined myself pushing a shopping cart filled with garbage through Dania, a beaten and forgotten man.

A female dispatcher came on the line. I gave her my name and explained what had happened. She asked if I was hurt. I knew that if I said yes, a cruiser would be here in a New York minute.

"I'm okay," I said.

"Hold tight," the dispatcher said. "I'll get a car out there soon."

I folded my phone. A tow truck was barreling down the interstate toward me. I'd been saved.

The tow truck parked, and an enterprising young guy hopped out. He gave my car a cursory inspection, then shoved a business card into my hand. It had his smiling picture on it and embossed lettering. LARRY LITTLEJOHN'S 24-HOUR TOWING. I TOW, YOU GO!

"What the heck happened?" Larry asked.

"I ran into some old friends. Can you tow me to Dania?"

"What's the address?"

"Sunset Bar and Grille. It's over on the beach."

He scratched his chin. "Yeah. I can do that."

"Second question. Do you take IOUs?"

As the tow truck drove away I tore up Larry's card. The radio was playing another song from a vanished band. This time, I didn't sing along.

Fifteen minutes later a cruiser appeared with Bobby Russo at the wheel. He parked on the shoulder in front of my car and got out. He was wearing his suit from the news conference and steel-framed aviator's glasses turned to mirrors by the blinding Florida sun. He halted six feet from where I stood.

"Keep that monster back," Russo said.

"He's a nice dog once you get to know him."

"I heard he took a piece out of a guy's ass in the Grove."

"You talk to Tommy Gonzalez?"

"Yeah," Russo said. "He said you were a star."

It was the nicest thing anyone had said to me in a while.

"How did you know where to find me?" I asked.

"The dispatcher recognized your name and gave me a call. Mind if I examine your car?"

"Be my guest."

While Russo fly-specked my car, I told him what happened at Julie Lopez's house and gave him the numbers I'd memorized off the van's license along with a description of the vehicle. Without a word, he went to the cruiser and climbed in. I felt invisible again and knelt beside his open window.

"Are you going to help me or not?" I asked.

"What do you want me to do, Jack?" Russo said, staring straight ahead. "Kill my day figuring out which white van in Broward belongs to the guys who potshotted you?"

"You could run a partial license check."

"Those are expensive."

"That never stopped you before."

"In case you hadn't heard, we have a budget freeze. I now need authorization to run partial license checks. If I tell my boss you're involved, he'll say no."

"Tell him it's connected to the Skell case," I said.

"You don't know that for a fact."

"Yes, I do. These guys bugged my car. They also put Carmella Lopez's body in her sister's backyard. For Christ's sake, Bobby, they're *involved.* You need to drag them in and put their feet to the fire. You don't want to see Skell released from prison, do you?"

"That's the judge's decision, not mine."

"I have evidence that Skell isn't acting alone," I said. "Don't you think the judge needs to know that?"

Russo shook his head, his mind made up. He wasn't doing it.

"What the hell's wrong with you?" I asked.

"What's wrong with me? I'll tell you what's wrong with me," Russo said. "I have a wife and two kids and a sick mother-in-law. I have responsibilities, in case you've forgotten what those were."

I had no answer for this, and hung my head in shame.

"Jesus, Jack, I didn't mean that. I'm sorry."

I lifted my gaze. "Help me. Please."

"Do you have the transmitter these guys were using to bug your car?"

The transmitter was lying on the bottom of the ocean outside the Sunset. I decided to lie to him.

"Yes."

"Bring the transmitter to my office, and I'll put in a request for a partial license run to be done on all vans in Broward with those three numbers. If my boss squawks, I'll show him the transmitter, and tell him it's regarding another case."

Russo was in my corner again, fighting the good fight. He started the cruiser, and I asked him for a lift back to Dania.

"Why don't you take your own car?" he suggested.

"Last time I checked, not having a windshield was against the law."

"I'll escort you home," Russo said.

* * *

I dropped my car at a body shop in Dania, and Russo drove us to the Sunset. He parked in the lot and left the engine idling. It was another beautiful day in paradise, and we sat in his car and watched waves crash against the shoreline.

"I've got a gang examining the Skell file," Russo said. "Half of homicide, two investigators from Florida Department of Law Enforcement, and one of those crackerjacks from the FBI. I'd bring in the Boy Scouts if I thought it would do any good."

"Nothing, huh?"

"Actually, there is something I think we can use."

I felt a spark of hope. "What did you find?"

"Melinda Peters."

"But she testified at the trial. The judge has already heard her."

"I read her testimony and compared it with the deposition she gave before trial," Russo said. "Her testimony at the trial was shorter. She left out some really sick things that Skell did to her when she was locked up in the dog crate in his house."

"She was traumatized by the experience, so the prosecutor toned it down," I explained. "It was the only way Melinda would agree to testify."

"Would she tell the whole story now?"

I shook my head. Victims of sexual crimes were slow to heal and sometimes never healed at all. I couldn't see Melinda reliving the experience.

"I want a judge to hear what happened to her," Russo said. "It's hard evidence that Skell is a sexual predator. Predators can be held in jail indefinitely in Florida if they're considered a threat."

"But Skell wasn't put in prison for being a sexual predator."

"It doesn't matter. If the judge determines that he is one, the state will hold him. It's called the William's Law, and we'll ask him to invoke it."

I shook my head again. I didn't see Melinda doing it.

"Melinda likes you, doesn't she?" Russo asked.

"What does that have to do with this?" I asked.

"You can talk to her," Russo said. "Take her out to dinner, beg her; hell, sleep with her if you have to, but get her to help us. She's our last chance."

Melinda's coming on to me was still fresh in my mind. She probably would agree to testify if I tricked her by lying about my feelings, but I wasn't going down that road.

"I'll try," I said.

I got out and retrieved Buster from the backseat. Russo backed out of the spot and pulled up alongside me. He leaned out his open window.

"I'll be by later this afternoon with the transmitter, and we can run those list of partial license plates," I said.

"You do that," Russo said. "Oh, by the way. I don't take IOUs. You still owe me three hundred bucks for the repairs on my Suburban."

Before I could tell him I didn't have the money, Russo drove away.

CHAPTER SEVENTEEN

The ocean had turned rough.

With my flippers propelling me through the choppy waves, I swam to the spot where I believed the transmitter had sunk, stopped to adjust my mask, and dove down.

Nearing the ocean floor, I stopped as a sand shark with a mouthful of frightening-looking teeth and small darting eyes swam past. Having spent my life swimming in Florida's waters, I'd encountered sharks many times and did not fear them. They were docile creatures, generally content to prey on smaller fish and roam with other sharks.

The sand shark left, and I resumed my search. The ocean floor was covered in a brownish silt. Hovering about it, I paddled my flippers and moved the silt around. Broken seashells and an assortment of bottles and rusted cans appeared before my eyes, but no transmitter. I paddled for a minute, then went up for air.

Breaking the surface, I spotted Sonny on the shoreline, holding a cordless phone in his hand while looking up and down the beach.

"Over here," I yelled.

Seeing me, Sonny started to wave.

"I've got a phone call for you."

"Who is it?"

"Kumar."

"What's he want?"

"He's got a job for you, helping some couple find their lost kid."

"Tell him I'm busy."

"For Christ's sake, Jack. Ralph is coming by tomorrow. What am I going to tell him?"

Ralph was the Sunset's long-distance owner and made a monthly appearance to make sure the place hadn't burned down. Normally, Sonny didn't care about Ralph's visits, and I guessed he was afraid Ralph might fire him over the busted TV. The idea that Sonny might lose his job because of something I'd done didn't sit right with me.

"Tell Kumar I'll take it," I yelled back.

"For real?"

"Yeah, for real."

Sonny relayed the message, then ended the call.

"Kumar said the couple is coming to his restaurant, and you can meet them in his office," Sonny yelled.

"Right now?"

"Yeah."

I couldn't deal with Russo and try to help Kumar's friends at the same time. I decided Kumar's friends could wait, and dove back down.

Nearing bottom, I encountered another shark. This one was six feet long, with a yellowish brown tint, dual dorsal fins, and small pointed teeth. I decided it was an adult lemon shark, which was extremely rare. Fisherman believed lemon sharks brought good luck, and I was half tempted to rub my hand across its back.

Swimming away from the lemon shark, I picked another spot and started paddling my flippers. The silt lifted to reveal more garbage littering the ocean floor. The stuff was a distraction and made my task of finding the transmitter that much harder.

I repeated my routine several more times, then found myself growing frustrated. At this rate, it would take hours or even days to find the transmitter. There was even a chance I might never find it at all.

Then I had an idea. No one had seen the transmitter but me. The fact that I didn't have it anymore didn't matter. I'd get another transmitter, scuff it up, and present it to Russo as the original. It was the kind of crap dirty cops pulled all the time. Being desperate, I was willing to give it a try.

A pair of lemon sharks popped out from behind a coral ledge and began circling me. Sharks become aggressive only when antagonized, and I decided to wait them out. By conserving my movements, I could stretch the oxygen left in my lungs.

Soon more lemon sharks appeared. They continued to circle me, and I felt as if I were watching an underwater ballet. Seeing so many in one place was unusual, and I wondered what they were doing here. Had the water's warm temperature attracted them, or was it the ocean's salinity? Perhaps the females were in season, emitting strong chemical signals to their male suitors. Or maybe they'd been investigating tasty sacks of garbage dumped from a pleasure boat, and I'd spoiled their fun.

After a minute my lungs were aching, and I had no choice but to kick my legs and head up. To my great relief, the lemon sharks did not touch me. Moments before breaking the surface, I looked down and saw that they'd dispersed.

* * *

I threw on fresh clothes and drove to Tugboat Louie's. Sticking Buster in my office, I walked down to Kumar's office and knocked on the door. He bid me enter, and I poked my head in. Kumar and the couple with the missing child were waiting for me.

"Jack, Jack, we've been expecting you," Kumar said.

Whenever I've annoyed people, they tend to say my name twice. I proffered a lame apology and entered. I was wearing frayed cargo pants and a Tommy Bahama shirt minus two buttons, and my hair was uncombed. The couple eyed me suspiciously.

Kumar introduced them. Amrita and Sanji Kahn. I put her age at forty, his over fifty. She was pretty, with nutmeg skin and clear amber eyes; he was overweight and brooding, with capped teeth that clashed with his jet-black turban. They both wore expensive country club clothes and matching platinum watches. Opening her purse, Amrita removed a snapshot and handed it to me. I knew it was of their missing daughter without having to look.

But I did look. Their daughter was sixteen going on twenty-five, with multiple rings in each ear, bee-stung lips, and a dazzling smile. She was as dark-skinned as her parents, but the sparkle in her eyes said all-American girl. I let the appropriate amount of time pass before handing the photograph back.

"Her name is Katrina," her mother said.

"She's a very attractive young lady. How long has she been missing?"

"Three days," her father said.

"Have either of you spoken to her?"

"I have," Amrita said.

"Recently?"

"Last night. Actually, we didn't talk. My daughter

posted a message for me on the National Runaway Hotline, and I responded and posted one for her."

"So she wasn't abducted," I said.

"Oh, no, this is nothing like that," her father said.

"Her life is not endangered in any way?"

Both parents shook their heads.

"Did either of you ask her to leave?"

"No," they said at the same time.

"Where is she staying? With friends?"

"She's staying at a hotel," her mother said.

That told me a lot. Hotels don't take cash, only credit cards, which meant Katrina was staying on her parent's nickel. They could have forced their daughter's hand by cancelling the card and getting her thrown out, but they seemed divided on how to be handling this. I glanced at Kumar. He was sitting behind his desk with his hands steepled in front of his face. I gave him a look that said we needed some privacy.

"If you'll excuse me, I must go downstairs and check up on some things," Kumar said.

The door clicked behind him. I pulled my chair closer to the parents. Waiting three days to take action was a serious mistake and could lead to more trouble. I didn't want to divide them by pointing fingers, so I tried a different tack.

"Did you consider calling the police?" I asked the father.

Sanji's eyes locked on to my face. "Yes."

"Why didn't you?"

"I asked him not to," his wife said.

"Why?"

"I assumed our daughter would return home."

Sanji sat with his hands on his slacks, exposing his fingers. They were long and the nails were manicured, but without gloss. I pegged him as a surgeon.

"And when she didn't, you decided to get outside help," I said.

"Yes," Sanji said. "At first we considered hiring a private detective, but the ones we interviewed were too sleazy. Then Kumar told us about you. He said you were a good man, despite what the newspapers write about you."

"Sanji! That was not necessary," his wife scolded him.

Her husband looked at me.

"I'm sorry if I have offended you."

I leaned back in my chair. I'd run into my share of Sanjis over the years. Like many wealthy people, he thought his problems could be solved by swiping a credit card through a machine, or hiring someone to fix them, instead of fixing the problems himself. I wondered how well Kumar knew them, and how badly I'd damage the relationship by what I was about to say.

I decided I didn't care and said it anyway.

"You both should consider yourselves lucky."

Amrita looked at me with surprise, Sanji with a deep frown.

"Are you trying to be sarcastic?" Sanji asked.

"Not at all."

"Then explain yourself."

"Your daughter isn't dead. She hasn't been sold into the sex trade, or been locked in some psycho's basement. She wasn't abducted by a neighbor or someone else that she knew, and my guess is, neither of you was physically or sexually abusing her. Those are the kinds of cases I often deal with. They don't have happy endings.

"Your situation is different. Your daughter ran away, which is unfortunate, but not the worst that could happen. My guess is, you both know what the problem is and refuse to fix it."

Sanji looked ready to explode. "I don't want to talk about this! Will you find our daughter, or won't you?"

"I can find your daughter, but what good will it do?" I asked. "If you don't fix the problem, she'll only run away again. Fix the problem."

Amrita nodded her head like a metronome. I sensed she'd tried to reason with her husband and hit a brick wall.

"This is about a boy, isn't it?" I asked.

"You are very perceptive," she said.

Sanji jumped out of his chair and headed for the door.

"Come back here," I said.

"Why should I listen to you?" he replied angrily.

"Because I'm trying to help you."

Sanji stopped dead. He didn't return to his chair, but he didn't leave, either. Taking out my wallet, I removed a snapshot of Jessie and showed it to his wife. My baby looked enough like me that you didn't have to ask whose she was. Amrita smiled faintly.

"A lovely girl," she said.

"Her name's Jessie," I said. "When she was sixteen, she announced she was dating a nineteen-year-old boy she'd met. When I heard Jessie describe this boy, I knew that the relationship was serious, and my wife and I had a problem on our hands."

Sanji came back to his chair and sat down.

"I was certain my daughter was sleeping with this boy," I went on. "It made me so mad, I considered having him arrested for statutory rape. I saw my daughter as a victim. I also knew that the law was on my side. Only my wife talked me out of it."

Amrita's hand found her husband's and clasped it.

"Please go on," she said.

"My wife talked to my daughter and realized that my daughter didn't see herself as a victim. This boy was her best friend and confidant. He gave my daughter a level of attention that my wife and I could not. He *indulged* her. To my daughter, it was only natural to have sex with him."

"But the boy was taking advantage of your daughter," Sanji said.

"Yes, he was," I replied. "But that wasn't the issue."

"It wasn't?"

"No. The issue was pulling my daughter back into the fold. It was about maintaining our authority over her. And it was about controlling the situation without traumatizing her in the process."

"Did you succeed?" Amrita asked hopefully.

"Yes, thanks to my wife."

She looked at her husband. He swallowed hard.

"Will you share your solution with us?" he asked me.

"I'd be happy to. My wife asked the boy over for dinner. He accepted, and we spent the evening peppering him with questions. Was he going to college? How did he plan to make a living when he got out? What religion was he? When could we meet his parents? We made him realize that if he wanted to see our daughter, he was going to be part of the family, and with that came responsibilities. We treated him like a grown-up."

Amrita's dark eyes were dancing.

"Did it work?"

"They broke up a few weeks later. I can't guarantee that will happen with your daughter, but it will at least give you the upper hand for a while."

They shared a meaningful look. I know of no greater

telepathy than the silent communion shared by husband and wife. I slapped my knees and rose from my chair.

"Good luck," I said.

We went downstairs to the parking lot. They drove a white Mercedes with a bag of tennis rackets in the back-seat. Sanji opened his wife's door, then came over to me. From his pocket he removed an envelope and stuffed it into my hand.

"Kumar said that you would prefer cash."

The envelope was thick, and I felt my heart race. Sanji was an arrogant jerk, but most fathers were when it came to dealing with their teenage daughters. I know I was.

I offered my hand. He shook it warmly, and I decided that I liked the guy.

"I hope this works out."

"Thank you," he said.

Back in my office, I fanned twenty crisp hundred-dollar bills across my desk and let out a happy whistle. It was enough to pay my rent and my tabs and buy the Sunset a brand-new TV. I thought back to my encounter with the lemon sharks and decided that my luck had changed.

CHAPTER EIGHTEEN

Kumar gave me a lift to Big Al's body shop on Sheridan Street. My Legend was parked in front with a shiny new windshield. I loaded Buster into the back, then visited the office.

Big Al sat at his cluttered desk eating a sandwich. He was into steroids and body art, and every inch of his body was either ripped or inked. He was a high school classmate of mine who in the '80s got busted for importing bales of marijuana, or what locals fondly call square barracudas. I guessed he still peddled on the side; the lure of easy money was hard to get out of your system. I paid for the windshield, then asked if he had a transmitter for sale. Opening a desk drawer, he tossed me one. It was scratched and dirty and exactly what the doctor ordered. I asked him how much.

"On the house," Big Al said.

"Thanks. And thanks for fixing my windshield so fast."

"What are friends for?"

"You still dive, don't you?"

Big Al said yes, and I recounted the incident with the lemon sharks. I hadn't stopped thinking about them, and he listened attentively.

"Lemon sharks are strange," Big Al said. "I once encountered a school during a dive. They were hovering around a spot and wouldn't leave. Turns out, there was a wreck on the ocean floor. A boat had caught on fire and sunk the day before."

"Were they scavenging it?"

"No, they were protecting it," Big Al said.

"From what?"

"Beats me, Jack. But that's what they were doing."

We went outside. Big Al was six-six and cast a long shadow across the dusty yard. Reaching my car, he put his hand on my shoulder.

"I was listening to the news earlier," he said. "This Skell thing is getting out of hand. You going to leave town?"

"I wasn't planning to," I said.

"With all this shit flying around, I would."

"Where would you go?"

"West coast."

"Of Florida?"

"California. Southern part, where the weather's decent. You can get lost there."

I realized he was giving me advice. Since it came from a guy who had spent many years rebuilding his own life, I gave it some weight. Big Al knew the uphill battle I was facing, and he was telling me that staying and salvaging my reputation was a lost cause. He might have been right, only I wasn't willing to go there just yet. We shook hands, and I left.

At Best Buy I purchased a new TV for the Sunset. For an extra thirty bucks the salesman promised to have it delivered by that afternoon.

Then I drove to the Broward County sheriff's headquarters and circled the parking lot. Cars were parked illegally and in the handicap spots. I couldn't remember the place ever being so jammed.

Finally a spot opened up. I parked and, with transmitter in hand, headed across the lot toward the shining four-story building that I had once called home. Along the way, I noted all the cars owned by cops. They were easy to spot. Cops always backed in.

A well-dressed crowd of about twenty was gathered by the building's front steps. A news conference was taking place, and I heard a woman's voice speak my name.

"Jack Carpenter is a *goddamn monster*," Lorna Sue Mutter hissed into the mikes. She was wearing her trademark black dress and too much makeup. Behind her stood Leonard Snook in a black pin-striped suit with wide lapels, nodding beatifically.

"Jack Carpenter should be sitting in a prison cell, not my husband!" she went on. "Do the police need any more evidence than they heard today? Do they need more proof?"

"Have you asked a judge to release your husband?" a reporter asked.

Leonard Snook answered. "We cannot do that until the Broward County sheriff's office formally charges Ernesto Ramos with the murder of Carmella Lopez."

"Why haven't the police done that?" the same reporter asked.

"The sheriff's office is purposely dragging its heels," Snook replied. "What they need to do is face the truth. Simon Skell did not kill Carmella Lopez, nor did he kill seven other young women in Broward County, whose bodies, I might add, have never been located. My client is not the Midnight Rambler."

I stood on my tiptoes for a better look. Snook was

pressed up next to Lorna Sue, and there was a real sexual tension between them. I wondered if anyone else was picking up on it. Lorna Sue nudged Snook out of the way.

"My husband was convicted because of the testimony of a woman named Melinda Peters," Lorna Sue continued. "Melinda Peters said my husband abducted and tortured her. What she *didn't* say was that she had a relationship with my husband *and* an affair with Jack Carpenter. When Jack Carpenter found out, he forced Melinda Peters to fabricate a story about my husband and have him thrown in jail."

My mouth had been washed out with soap plenty when I was a kid, but it never stopped me from swearing when the situation warranted it. In a loud voice I said, "That's a fucking lie, and you know it."

The reporters parted like the Red Sea, leaving a clear path between me and my two accusers. Pointing my finger at them, I said, "Why don't you tell them the truth, which is that you have a movie deal in the works. The only reason you're here campaigning for Simon Skell is because you stand to make a bundle if he gets out of jail."

A reporter shoved a mike in Snook's face. "Is that true? Do you have a deal with a Hollywood studio?"

"No comment," Snook replied.

"He's getting 20 percent and his name in the credits," I yelled.

Someone must have told Snook that cowardice was the better part of valor. He retreated backwards, hit the steps, and fell down with a groan. Lorna Sue ignored him and pointed a manicured finger at me.

"You railroaded my husband," she screamed.

"Your husband is a serial killer, and you're a crazy lunatic bitch for marrying him."

"*How dare you!*"

Lorna Sue charged me. I hadn't battled with a member of the opposite sex since fighting with my sister, and I tried not to laugh as her balled fists bounced harmlessly off my arms. Instead of breaking up the melee, the TV crews filmed us. I realized how bad this was going to look on the six o'clock news and decided to extricate myself.

I feinted to my right. Lorna Sue took the bait and lunged at air. I scooted around her and darted up the steps. It was all I could do not to kick Snook in the stomach.

Reaching the building's front doors, I wondered where the cops were. Normally, they were the first to arrive when a fight took place on the grounds.

Inside, I discovered a gang in the lobby, standing by the windows. Many of the faces were familiar. Russo was one of them.

Russo hustled me into an elevator and took me to the War Room on the top floor. It was actually a spacious conference room outfitted with sixteen phone lines and a wall of TV sets that carried all the major networks, and was where strategy was coordinated when there were emergencies like major hurricanes and wildfires. The room resembled my office at Tugboat Louie's, with pictures of Skell's victims taped to the wall and the case files spread on a large oval desk. Dead coffee cups lay everywhere, and when Russo slammed the door, they started to shake.

"You are a bad news buffet, you know that?" he shouted at me. "Every time I turn around, this case gets worse, and you're standing in the middle of it, pretending you don't have a fucking clue as to what's going on."

I wanted to apologize for my behavior outside, but I

didn't see it doing much good. Instead I handed him the transmitter.

"This is the transmitter I found on my car. The guy I saw at Julie Lopez's house put it there. The same guy who shot three holes into my car on 595."

Bobby gave the transmitter a cursory look and tossed it into the trash.

"What are you doing?" I asked.

"Park your ass in a chair and shut up," he replied.

"But that's evidence."

"Leave it there."

There was real menace in his voice. I sat in the nearest chair and watched him remove a cassette tape from his pocket and insert it into a player on the desk.

"When was the last time you spoke with Melinda Peters?" Russo asked.

"Last night."

"What was her mood like?"

"She was scared out of her mind that Skell would get out."

"So she didn't tell you that she was going public."

"I don't know what you're talking about, Bobby."

Russo started the player. Music came out of the machine that faded into Neil Bash's abrasive voice. It was a tape of his talk show.

"I have a special guest on the line with me today," Bash said. "Her name is Melinda Peters, and along with being one of Fort Lauderdale's premier adult entertainers, she was a key witness in the murder trial of Simon Skell, aka the Midnight Rambler. How are you doing today, Melinda?"

There was a short pause.

"I'm okay," Melinda said.

"May I call you Melinda?"

"Sure."

"I appreciate your coming on the show. There's been a lot of buzz in the last few days about Simon Skell being railroaded by a Broward County detective named Jack Carpenter. So far, the sheriff's office hasn't responded. Since you were a witness at the trial, I was hoping you'd share your thoughts with our audience."

Another pause.

"It was all Jack's idea," Melinda said.

"What was Jack's idea?" Bash asked.

"My testifying."

"Well, that's his job. He's a detective and he gets people to testify. Nothing new there."

"He told me what to say," Melinda said.

My fist slammed the table, knocking several empty coffee cups to the floor.

"It gets worse," Russo said.

I leaned forward in my chair and stared at the tape player.

"Are you saying that Jack Carpenter *coached* you?" Bash asked.

"He made everything up," Melinda blurted out.

"*Everything?*"

"Yeah."

"But he is, or should I say was, a police officer. Why would he do that?"

Another pause. "Jack and I were going out together . . ."

"You mean you were having an affair," Bash jumped in.

"That's right. Then I met Simon Skell while I was dancing at a club, and he asked me out. He was nice, so I started seeing him on the side."

"So you were dating Simon Skell *and* Jack Carpenter."

"Yeah."

"What happened?"

"Jack found out and didn't like it."

"Now, wait a minute, Melinda," Bash said. "If I remember correctly, you testified at trial that Simon Skell abducted you and kept you locked in a dog cage in his house and tortured you while playing Rolling Stones songs, specifically 'Midnight Rambler.' Are you telling us now this wasn't true?"

"It didn't happen," Melinda said.

I closed my eyes and imagined I was still submerged in thirty feet of water and the lemon sharks were swarming around me, only this time they were tearing me apart, one limb at a time. The water clouded with blood, and I silently screamed.

"So everything you said was a lie, Melinda," Bash said.

Another pause.

"That's right," she replied.

"And you helped send an innocent man to jail," Bash said.

"Uh-huh," she said.

I opened my eyes. Now it all made sense. Big Al's questions about me leaving town, the crazy scene outside.

"Are you still there, Melinda?" Bash asked.

"Yeah," she said.

"Tell me why you did it."

Again, she didn't answer.

"Did you love him? I'm talking about Jack Carpenter."

"No," she said.

"But you had an affair with him."

"I found out he was cheating on me."

"He was seeing another woman?"

"Yes. Her name is Joy Chambers."

"Is she a dancer?"

"She's a prostitute," Melinda said.

"If you don't love Jack Carpenter, then why did you do it?"

Another pause.

"He threatened me. Said he'd make my life living hell if I didn't play along. He had all these cases of missing girls that he couldn't solve, and he saw Simon as the perfect suspect, if I'd just play ball."

"So you went along with him."

"That's right."

"Can I ask you one more question, Melinda?"

"Okay."

"Do you feel ashamed by what you did?"

There was a short silence, followed by a dial tone. Bash took a commercial break, and Russo turned off the cassette player while looking at me as if I were some piece of trash in a holding cell. I wanted to defend myself but didn't know where to start. I thought back to last night's conversation with Melinda. What had I said to cause her to turn on me this way?

Russo cleared his throat. He had lifted his arm and was pointing at the door. I pulled three hundred dollars out of my wallet and tossed it on the table.

"Fix your car," I said.

I left the War Room as fast as my legs would carry me.

CHAPTER NINETEEN

I decided to get drunk. Whatever was left of my reputation had gone up in flames, and Big Al's suggestion that I move out of the state suddenly seemed a good idea.

But before I got drunk, I wanted to look Melinda in the eye and ask her why she'd done this to me. It seemed cruel that she'd accuse me of sleeping with her when I'd spent so much energy fighting off her advances. It was also an accusation that I'd never live down. When a woman says you slept with her, there's no denying it.

I pointed the Legend toward her apartment complex. Buster had picked up on my sorry state and tried to crawl into my lap. He wanted to comfort me, but I wasn't in the mood and made him stay on the passenger seat.

I parked a few units down from her place. At her door I knocked loudly. When she didn't answer, I pounded. Then I started to kick.

"Open up. It's Jack Carpenter."

Sticking my face to the front window, I peered inside. Through a slit in the drapes I saw a floor plan like a cheap motel room. Everything looked in its place. A black kitty jumped at the glass, scratching at my face.

I knocked on her neighbors' doors. Melinda spent her days watching soap operas and reading romance novels.

That doesn't sound like much of a life, but it was a far cry from living on the street and not knowing where her next meal was coming from. An elderly neighbor wearing fuzzy bedroom slippers and a muumuu agreed to talk to me.

"I saw Melinda this morning," the neighbor said, her face shrouded by a cigarette's fog. "Lent her some Sweet'N Low. You a cop?"

"A friend."

"Boyfriend?"

"No, just a friend."

"You look like a cop," the neighbor said. "Act like one, too."

"I used to be. How was Melinda's demeanor?"

"Her what?"

"Her attitude. How was she acting? Was she happy or sad? That sort of thing."

The neighbor thought about it. "Pissed off was how I'd describe her."

"About what?"

"Her cable TV was on the blink."

An alarm went off inside my head.

"When did this happen?"

"This morning, I guess. Melinda got one of those plasma flat-screen TVs, and liked to watch the Discovery channel where they show those beautiful sunrises from all around the world. I've gone over to her place a couple of times and watched them with her. Ever seen the show?"

I nearly told her to drag her sorry ass out of bed some morning and come over to Dania and watch the real thing. Instead I shook my head.

"Did the cable repairman come?" I asked.

"I saw the van parked out front, so I guess they were here."

"Was it white?"

"Come to mention it, yeah."

"What time was this?"

"Couple hours ago."

"So they came right away."

She cackled. "Came like they were responding to a five-alarm fire. You ever see that girl in a bathing suit? That's all she wears in her apartment. Make your eyes pop out of your head. Even mine."

"She's a beauty," I said. "Can I go into your backyard, have a look around?"

"You don't think something's happened to Melinda, do you?" the neighbor asked.

"That's what I'm here to find out."

She hesitated. A teacup-sized poodle darted out, sniffed my sandals, and started dry-humping my leg. Any other time, I would have drop-kicked the dog into the next county. Instead, I scooped it up and scratched its head.

"You got a dog?" she asked.

I pointed at Buster sitting regally in the Legend. She nodded approvingly.

"Anyone who owns a dog is okay in my book. My name is Gladys."

"I'm Jack," I said.

"Nice to meet you, Jack. Come on in."

Gladys's backyard was the size of a postage stamp and surrounded by a sturdy picket fence. Hopping on the fence, I jumped onto the phone pole in the corner of the yard and started to climb. Running up the side of the pole was a black cable identical to the one I saw in Julie Lopez's backyard. Fifteen feet up, I stopped. The cable was cut right above the metal staple, same as Julie's pole. I climbed down.

"Find anything?" Gladys asked.

"The line's been cut."

"You think someone cut Melinda's cable on purpose?"

"Could be."

I hopped over the fence into Melinda's backyard and looked around. Through a glass slider I was able to peer into Melinda's kitchen. Everything looked normal except for a chair sitting upended on the floor. Taking out my cell phone, I called my police buddy Claude Cheever.

"I'm at Melinda Peters's place," I said. "Something's happened."

"I'll be right over," Cheever said.

Cheever pulled into the parking lot driving a filthy Pontiac Firebird. Besides the grime and dirt caked to the vehicle, an assortment of dead palmetto bugs, moths, and lovebugs was prominently displayed on the bumper and headlights. Claude's success as a cop did not come from his superior intellect or astonishing investigative technique. His gift was the ability to look like a lowlife. The fact that this came naturally simply made him that much more effective at what he did. I led him around to the back of Melinda's place.

"I heard what Melinda said on the radio," Claude said, his face pressed to the slider.

"Bad news sure travels fast."

"Did you fuck her?"

"No."

"Not even once?"

"No, not even once."

"Think someone forced her to do that interview?"

Claude was looking at me in the slider's reflection, and I nodded.

"I once called into Neil Bash's show when he was talking about gun control," Cheever said. "The show's broadcast live, you know."

It took me a moment to get his drift. If Melinda had been forced to call Bash's show, her abductors were taking a risk, since she could have blurted out the truth. Yet, it wasn't something that I saw Melinda doing on her own.

"Someone made Melinda say those lies," I said.

"That's good enough for me," Cheever said.

Cheever found the complex's superintendent and got him to unlock Melinda's front door. Cheever told the super to hang around, then went inside. I followed him and walked down a narrow hallway to the kitchen.

Everything looked normal except the upturned chair. I covered my hand with a paper towel and righted it, then studied the scratches running along one side. The marks were fresh, and I envisioned Melinda's kidnappers dragging her across the floor while she was still in it. I slid the chair back into its spot at the table.

Kitty was happy to see me, and I filled a bowl with crunchies and put it on the floor. Then I checked the countertops and table. Nothing looked out of place. Picking up a pencil, I used the eraser to press a button on the answering machine and check for messages. There were none.

Beside the phone was a notepad filled with cartoonlike drawings. I peeled the pages back with the tip of the pencil and saw pictures of cats, horses, and other domestic animals. The drawing on the last page caught my eye. It contained a pair of stick figures standing in front of a two-story house with lollipop trees and smoke billowing from its chimney. The figures were holding hands and sporting big smiles. They were a man and a woman, and the man wore a badge.

I gave the room another sweep. Beneath the table lay a book bag, which I pulled out and opened. It contained a GED prep book and a laminated badge for Broward Community College with Melinda's picture on it. She looked different from the woman I knew; her hair was pulled back in a ponytail, her face without makeup.

"Hey, Jack, come here," Cheever called out.

Closing the bag, I walked down the hallway and entered the bedroom. Cheever sat on a water bed with a collection of Winnie the Pooh teddy bears at its head. A suitcase lay on the floor, stuffed with winter clothes. Cheever was going through the suitcase and glanced suspiciously at me.

"Looks like Melinda was planning to take a trip," he said.

"She was going to Aspen," I said.

"She tell you that?"

"I arranged for her to stay at a house there. She was afraid of Skell coming after her once he got released."

"Were you going with her?"

"No, I wasn't going with her."

"You sure you're not fucking her, Jack?"

"Positive, Claude."

He patted the bed for me to sit down. The expression on his face was no longer that of a friend. He was wearing his cop face, and it was cold and unflinchingly hard.

As I sat the water bed shifted beneath me. It was an unsettling feeling, as were the words that next came out of Cheever's mouth.

"My guess is, you are fucking her, Jack, and don't have the courage to admit it. The two of you were going to leave town, only Melinda got cold feet, and she went on Neal Bash's show and spilled her guts. Then she split, and now you can't find her. So you called me, hoping I'd run her down. Well, I'm not going to do that. In fact, I'm not going to do another fucking thing until you come clean with me."

I was down for the count. I needed Cheever in my corner or I was finished.

"I'm not doing her, Claude," I said. "But she is my friend, just like plenty of other women I've helped who were living on the street."

"Ever fuck one of them?"

"Not a one."

"How about Joy Chambers? Melinda said you were seeing her on the side."

"For the love of Christ."

"Answer me."

"I never fucked Joy Chambers."

"You're a better man than me," he said.

I wasn't going to argue with Cheever there. Married with two kids, he had engaged in more cheap affairs than anyone I knew. It was astonishing that he was grilling me about adultery, but he was wearing the badge.

"You've got to help me find Melinda," I said. "Her testimony is the only thing that will keep Skell in prison. With her gone, the state has no case."

Cheever pulled at his walrus mustache.

"What do you think happened to her?" he asked.

"She was abducted by a pair of cable repairmen. They cut the cable outside her house, and she called for it to be repaired. They came this morning and took her. These same cable guys cut the cable outside Julie Lopez's house, and when they were called in for a repair, they dug a grave in the backyard and put Carmella Lopez's body in it. I saw these guys this morning and chased them on 595. They pumped three bullets into my car and tried to kill me."

"Where did you first see these guys?"

"On the street outside of Julie Lopez's house."

"She's a hooker, isn't she?"

"That's right."

"Were you fucking her, too?"

My eyes fell to the floor. Cops get a lot of free tail thrown at them, and many take advantage of it. But my conscience never let me. I rose from the water bed, and Cheever sank. It was as if we'd been riding a seesaw, and I'd decided to get off.

"I'll take that as a yes," Cheever said.

There was nothing left to say. We left the apartment. The super was waiting outside, and locked the door after we came out. Gladys stood at her front door, biting her nails.

"Is Melinda okay?" she asked.

"Melinda Peters isn't here," Cheever said.

"Oh, no," she said.

We went to my car. Cheever peered through the glass at the bullet holes in the upholstery, and I could almost hear the gears shifting in his head. I wanted to grab him by the shoulders and beg him to reconsider, but I was afraid he'd take it the wrong way. There was no trust left between us.

"How close were they when they shot your car?" he asked.

"Five or six feet. They were in another car."

"That's awfully close."

"Meaning what?"

"Meaning they might have been trying to warn you to stay away from Julie Lopez's house. Her boyfriend is also her pimp, right?"

"That's right," I said.

"Think he has friends?"

"I'm sure he does."

"Maybe he asked his buddies to watch Julie's house and make sure she didn't bang anyone on the side while he was cooling his heels in jail. And when they saw you, they decided to send you a little message."

"That's not what happened."

"I'm just looking at the evidence, Jack."

"Do you think I'm lying?"

"You're telling me one story, and the evidence is telling me another."

Lying to a cop was a crime, and Cheever had every right to arrest me. I decided to test him and got behind the wheel of my car. As I started the ignition he knelt down, and I lowered my window. His eyes locked on to my face.

"I need to ask you something, Jack."

"Fire away," I said.

"When you resigned from the force, whose side did you go on?"

The question stunned me.

"What is that supposed to mean?" I asked.

"You don't act like a cop anymore, and if your lifestyle is any indication, you're not a crook," Cheever said. "You're living in some gray area, making up the rules as you go along. I can't make heads or tails of it, and neither can anyone else on the force."

I wanted to yell at him at the top of my lungs. Eight women were dead and another one was missing, but no one seemed concerned about anything except my fucking behavior.

"I'm on *my* side, Claude," I said, throwing the car into reverse. "It's the only one that makes sense anymore."

CHAPTER TWENTY

I left the apartment complex with my head spinning.

I needed to prove Melinda was lying. That wasn't going to be easy, considering that it was her word against mine. But if I could punch holes in her story, people might stop believing her and start listening to me.

Joy Chambers was one way to do that. Joy was a local prostitute who'd dated several cops. I wasn't one of them, but I had done her a favor and helped her locate a child she'd put up for adoption years before. I knew a lot about Joy, including where she lived, and her real name, Joyce Perkowski. If I asked her to contact the newspapers and say we weren't sleeping together, I felt certain she'd do it.

I called Joy's number, and she didn't pick up. She lived in Tamarac, and fifteen minutes later I pulled into her driveway. Her gray clapboard house was eclipsed by the tangle of brush covering the front lawn and a veil of vines creeping down from the roof. It was an eyesore, which was how she liked it.

I banged on the front door, then tried the buzzer. It wasn't working, and I went around to the back. The kitchen door was open, and I tapped on the glass.

"Joy? Are you home? It's Jack Carpenter. I need to talk to you."

There was no answer. I entered the kitchen with my dog. It was spotlessly clean. Joy kept the interior of the house immaculate. She did not bring her johns here, or any of her suitors. Just a few trusted friends.

I went down a hallway to the front of the house. The living room had brand-new nice furniture and looked like a department store showroom. In the corner was a TV with lines of static running across the screen. A remote lay on the glass coffee table. I picked it up and pressed the Cable button. Nothing happened.

Buster let out a yip. I followed the sound to the master bedroom on the side of the house. Joy lay on the bed, stripped naked, her head twisted at an unnatural angle. Her face was ashen, her mouth wide open as if it were frozen. Buster stood beside the bed, licking the fingers of her outstretched hand.

I made my dog lie down, then studied her corpse. The position of her body indicated she'd been dragged into the room, tossed on the bed, and had her clothes torn off. Her attacker had straddled her—the imprints from his knees were still on the sheets—and strangled her. The purple bruises ringing her neck said he'd used his hands. He'd left quickly, not bothering to cover her body or close her mouth. It had happened fast, which I supposed was a blessing.

I knelt down beside the bed. Joy had been a fighter, and I could not envision this happening without some struggle. I looked at her hands. The left was clenched into a fist; the right wide open. The knuckles of the left were bruised. Joy had punched her attacker as he'd killed her, and left her mark on him.

"We'll get him," I told her.

I rose from the floor. I wanted to cover her but was afraid of contaminating the crime scene. I went into the kitchen to call 911. As I punched in the numbers an envelope on the kitchen table caught my eye. It was addressed to me.

I dropped the phone into the cradle, then picked up the envelope and tore it open. Inside was a handwritten letter. It was from Joy, dated two days earlier. She was breaking off the affair we'd never had. My hands began to tremble. Her killer had made her do this.

As I slipped the letter into my pocket a numbing realization swept over me. Joy had been killed in an effort to set me up. That setup included Melinda Peters telling Neil Bash that Joy and I were having an affair. As hard as it was for me to believe, Melinda was part of this.

I searched the house for anything else linking me to Joy. Finding nothing, I wetted a paper towel in the sink and wiped down everything I'd touched. This included the phone, but only after I dialed 911 and heard the call go through.

It was dark when I returned to the Sunset. The new TV was sitting over the bar, and the Dwarfs couldn't stop commenting about the sharpness of the picture. I bellied up to the bar and motioned to Sonny. He came over, and I handed him ten hundred-dollar bills to cover my double tabs and my rent. The sight of the money made his jaw drop.

"You don't have to pay me all at once," he said.

I was tempted to take some of it back.

"Keep it," I said.

Sonny slid a cold can of Budweiser toward me. "A reporter called for you earlier, said she wanted to talk about Melinda Peters. I've got her number in the till."

I groaned, and everyone in the bar looked at me.

"Shitty day," I said.

I killed the beer, then started to leave.

"Remember what the prophet said, Jack," Whitey called out.

I stopped in the doorway. "What's that?"

"In the land of the blind, a one-eyed man will be king."

"Hear, hear," several of the Dwarfs said.

Climbing the stairs to my room, I wondered if Whitey was right. Perhaps I was a one-eyed man, seeing only those things I chose to see.

Joy's murder was going to haunt me. Russo would want to question me about her murder. If he didn't like my answers, he'd arrest me as a suspect. Since I couldn't post bail, I'd go to jail for a few weeks, or even longer.

Melinda's lies were also going to haunt me. Not only was Skell going to walk, but the Midnight Rambler case would be reopened. This time, the scrutiny wouldn't be focused on Skell. It would be on me, and how I'd handled the investigation.

I entered my room and switched on the light. I was in a world of trouble. So much so that I found myself counting the people I could ask for help: Kumar, Sonny, my wife, and my daughter. Not a big group, but better than nothing.

My cell phone rang. I dug it out of my pocket. Caller ID said it was Jessie. I sat on the bed and kicked off my shoes. Then I answered it.

"How's the world's best basketball player?" I answered.

My daughter was sobbing. It made my mind return to that horrible day on Hutchinson Island.

"How *could* you?" she wailed.

"How could I what?" I asked.

"I was in my dorm watching CNN, and they showed your photo and a photograph of some stripper. They said you were screwing her and had fabricated evidence and all sorts of horrible things. *How could you do this to me and Mommy?*"

"It's all lies," I said emphatically.

"*Then why are they showing it on TV?*"

"It must be a slow news night."

Jessie didn't see the humor and screamed at me. I tried to explain, but she refused to listen. Finally I hit my tolerance point and jumped in.

"Lower your voice, or I'm hanging up this phone," I said.

My daughter grew quiet, and I continued. "Whatever you might think of me at this moment in time, I'm still your father, remember?"

"Yes," she said softly.

"Good. Now, let me ask you a question. When have I ever lied to you?"

My words were met by a short silence.

"Never," she replied.

"That's right. Never, ever have I lied to you."

"Not that I know about," she chimed in.

"Never, ever," I said. "What you heard on the TV was a pack of lies."

"But that stripper said you had an affair with her, and another woman as well."

I could hear my teeth clench. I didn't give a rat's ass if

the rest of the world thought I was slime, but with Jessie it mattered.

"None of it is true," I said.

"You need to talk to Mom," my daughter said. "She heard it on the news in Tampa. She's awfully upset."

"I'll call her right now."

"Promise?"

"Yes, I promise. I love you."

"I love you, too, Daddy."

I ended the call. Then I spent a minute gathering the courage to call Rose.

I'd always blamed myself for our breakup. My wife was from Mexico and deeply religious. In her faith, the spirits of the dead hung around long after the body was gone. Many times she'd told me that Skell's victims were clinging to me and that she couldn't compete with them. Like a fool, I didn't argue, so she left me.

I punched her number into my cell phone.

"Hey, Rose," I said when she answered.

"Who is this?" she asked suspiciously.

"It's me. Jack."

"What do you want?"

"To apologize."

"It's too late for that."

"No, listen. Everything you heard on TV is a bunch of crap."

"I don't believe you."

"You have to believe me."

"No, I don't."

I put my hand over my eyes. "Rose, please, listen to me."

"I'm filing for a divorce."

"What? No. Please don't do that."

"Tomorrow. First thing in the morning. I already have

a lawyer. I'll send you the papers. Now I have to go to bed."

My heart felt ready to break. I could not let her go.

"You can't give up on me," I said.

"Give me one good reason why."

"Because I need you, and because I love you."

I heard my wife's sharp intake of breath.

"Go to hell, Jack Carpenter," she said.

I had no answer for that, and heard her hang up.

CHAPTER TWENTY-ONE

At four a.m. my alarm clock went off. I dragged myself out of bed and rousted Buster. My dog rolled over, expecting to get his tummy scratched. Instead, I tugged on his hind leg.

"Road trip," I said.

Five minutes later we pulled out of the Sunset's parking lot. Tampa was three hundred miles away, and my goal was to reach my wife's place before she left for work, and beg her for another chance. We'd been married for twenty years, and I wasn't going to let it end with a phone call.

Driving through the streets of Dania, I found myself wondering if I'd ever return to south Florida. I'd never run away from a fight before, but this fight was destroying me. I needed to regroup and come up with another strategy. Then I would come back.

But before I did any of those things, I needed to see Rose.

A1A took me to 595, which led to the Florida Turnpike. My car was old enough to have a tape deck, and I popped in a collection that I fondly called the soundtrack of my youth. It included songs by the Doors, the Allman Brothers Band, the Eagles, Crosby Stills Nash & Young, the Grateful Dead, and Led Zeppelin performing at New York's Madison Square Garden.

I reached the Vero Beach exit in two hours thirty minutes and got off. The sky was clear and there was a chill in the air. I took Highway 60 through Yeehaw Junction, a redneck burg of truck stops and squawking chickens strutting on the highway. Forty-five minutes later I stopped at a McDonald's in Bartow and ordered breakfast. As I pulled up to the take-out window, a teenage girl opened the slider.

"Two sausage biscuits and an OJ?" she asked.

"Not me," I said.

She stared at her computer screen. "One egg biscuit and a small coffee?"

"Wrong again."

"You'd better repeat your order. My computer's messed up."

There were no cars behind me in the take-out line, and I wondered how her computer could be placing orders for customers who didn't exist.

"Large coffee and hash browns," I said.

I was back on 60 sipping my drink when my cell phone rang. Central Florida used to be one giant dead zone, but modern technology changed that. Caller ID said Unknown.

"Carpenter here," I answered.

"Jack, this is Veronica Cabrero."

"How's my favorite prosecutor?"

"I'm afraid I've got some bad news."

Bartow was famous for its speed traps, and my foot eased up on the gas pedal.

"What's wrong? Don't tell me your case against Lars Johannsen went south."

"Lars was found dead in his cell this morning," she said.

"What happened?"

"He slit his wrists. The police think his wife slipped him a razor in court yesterday."

I nearly said "Good riddance" but bit my tongue instead. Veronica was a devout Catholic who did not believe in capital punishment, and I could tell this turn of events had upset her.

"Any idea why he did it?" I asked.

"Lars knew he was going down."

"How so?"

"I followed up on your hunch," Cabrero said. "You told me Lars matched the profile of a predator who'd been beating up hookers in western Broward. I ran an advertisement in one of those strip club magazines with Lars's picture and asked any women who'd been brutalized by him to come forward. One finally did, and she agreed to testify."

"So Lars knew you had him by the short hairs."

"Yes. Now, I need to ask you a question. The police are considering charging Lars's wife as an accessory. What do you think?"

I braked at a stoplight and considered Veronica's question. If there was anything I'd learned as a cop, it was that there was no understanding the tangled relationships between men and women. Perhaps Lars's wife was an accomplice and into the same twisted things as her husband. But more likely she loved the guy and, when the truth became known, afforded him a graceful exit.

"I think you should leave her alone," I said.

"Seriously?"

"Yes. She'll have to live with this for the rest of her life. That's punishment enough."

There was a short, thoughtful silence.

"Thanks, Jack. I really appreciate this."

"Anytime, Veronica," I said.

I crept into Tampa with the rush-hour traffic. Tampa had the feel of a small southern city, the downtown streets paved with brick and uneven. The people were a lot friendlier, and it was rare to hear anyone honk their horn. The beaches weren't as pretty, but a lot more of them were unspoiled. And the sunsets beat any in the state.

At eight-thirty I pulled into Rose's apartment complex in Hyde Park. I had her address written down on a piece of paper and found her building without trouble. Her blue Nova was parked in front, and I parked two down.

I left Buster in the car with the windows rolled down. Rose's unit was on the second floor, and I took the stairs, feeling apprehensive. It had been a while since my wife and I had seen each other, much less had a real conversation.

A copy of the *Tampa Tribune* was stuffed into her mailbox. I pulled it out, then knocked. Rose answered in her white nurse's uniform.

"Surprise," I said.

The resounding slap my wife delivered across my face had every ounce of venom in her body.

"You stinking bastard!"

She raised her arm to strike me again. I grabbed it in midair.

"I didn't sleep with Melinda Peters. Or Joy Chambers."

"Let go of my arm," Rose declared.

"You have to believe me."

"Let go."

I obeyed, and she slammed the door in my face.

"Don't you want your newspaper?" I asked.

"No," she shouted through the door.

"It has my picture on the front page."

"Lucky you."

"Yours, too."

The door opened, and my wife snatched the newspaper out of my hands. I got down on one knee and looked up into her face.

"I swear to you, Rose. I didn't sleep with them. You have to believe me."

Rose stared at me impassively. She looked no different from the day we met. Small-boned and perfectly proportioned, with toffee-colored skin and big round eyes. She was waiting tables in Fort Lauderdale while going to nursing school, and I was six weeks on the force. In my face she'd seen my daddy's Seminole genes, and mistakenly thought I was part Mexican. We'd started dating, and ten months later Jessie was born.

"A woman would not say those things unless they were true," she said.

"This woman did," I said. "They're not true."

"You'd better not be lying to me, Jack Carpenter."

"I didn't drive all this way to lie to you."

Rose scrutinized the newspaper to make sure her picture wasn't on the front page, then went inside. This time, she didn't slam the door in my face, and I followed her.

Rose's apartment was a one-bedroom with furnishings purchased from secondhand stores. My wife made enough money to spruce the place up, but instead she sent a monthly allowance to Jessie that I wasn't supposed to know about.

"You want a cup of coffee?" she asked.

"That would be great," I said.

I cleared off the coffee table in the living room while she brewed a pot. Sitting on the table were five hand-carved wooden boxes, which Rose had owned since I'd known her. Each box had a drawing of a skeleton and contained a belonging from one of her dead relatives. A button from her grandfather, a lock of hair from her grandmother, and other keepsakes from her aunts and uncles. The boxes were part of Dia de los Muertos, or Day of the Dead, a religious holiday celebrated in Mexico each year. In my wife's faith, not to remember the dead was considered a disgrace.

I handled the boxes gently as I placed them on the floor. Rose entered the room holding two steaming cups, and sat down beside me.

"Why did you come so early?" she asked.

"I wanted to catch you before you went to see the lawyer," I said.

We drank in silence. My eyes drifted around the apartment. Hanging from the wall was the family photograph that also sat on the night table beside my bed. It was a painful reminder of our past.

"You've lost weight," she said.

"Almost twenty pounds," I said.

"You look like you did when we met. Lean and tan and . . ."

"And what?"

She wouldn't let the word come out of her mouth.

"You look the same, too," I said.

"No, I don't," she said.

"You look beautiful."

"Why did you really come, Jack?"

"Because I love you and don't want to lose you."

Her cup hit the saucer hard. "Then why haven't you come for me? Why stay in south Florida and let people destroy your reputation? I love you, too."

"I know you do."

"Then why haven't you come for me?"

I moved closer on the couch and put my hand over hers. "Because I can't leave until I figure out how Simon Skell killed those women. If I do that, he stays in prison. If I don't, he goes free. I must resolve this. Then I'll come back to you."

Her face melted, and I watched her fight back tears.

"Is that a promise?" she asked.

"Yes, it's a promise."

She took my left hand and stared at the gold band encircling my third finger. Looked at it a long time, her eyes blinking with thought.

"Take it off," she said.

"You mean my wedding ring?"

She nodded, and I tugged my wedding ring off my finger. I didn't know what Rose was up to, and I watched her lift my left hand and stare. The place where the ring rested was milky white, the rest of my finger dark brown.

"You never took it off," she said.

Then I got it.

"Not once," I said.

"Never went out on a Friday night and played the field?"

"No, honey."

"No strippers on the side, or trysts with female cops? There were a couple who had their eye on you."

"Nope."

"You knew I was waiting, didn't you?"

"I hoped you were," I said, smiling.

She rose from the couch and motioned to me. I stood up, and she unbuttoned my shirt and ran her fingertips across my hairless stomach. Her nose twitched, sniffing my skin, and before I knew it, her head was resting on my chest and I was holding her.

"I love you so much," she whispered.

After a minute she called in late to work. Then, clasping my hand, she led me to her bedroom. She undressed me, then I undressed her. It was our little ritual and never failed to get us both aroused. We tossed the sheet on the floor and got into bed.

"I want to be on top," she said.

"You sure?"

"Yes. Lie down."

I was too tall for her bed, and my feet stuck out at the end. I wiggled my toes and pointed at them. She laughed and slapped me on the thigh.

"Move over, big boy."

I slid across the bed until I was lying crosswise. Then Rose mounted me. At first our lovemaking was awkward, and I felt like a teenager doing it in the backseat of my car. Rather than be annoyed, my wife smiled at me. If she'd needed any more convincing that I wasn't fooling around, she just got it.

It only took us a minute to get our rhythm back, and then we were flying through the clouds. Rose knew what made me happy, and as I climaxed I was reminded of all the times in our relationship that she'd pulled through for me.

When we were done, she snuggled up beside me and put her head on my chest. Then she drifted off to sleep. Her energy was flowing through my overheated skin, and for a little while I felt whole again.

CHAPTER TWENTY-TWO

At eleven we walked down to our cars and kissed each other good-bye. Rose was back in uniform and had her hair tied in a bun. Seeing Buster, she let out a happy squeal.

"You got a dog."

She stuck her hand through the open window and scratched the back of Buster's head. To my utter surprise, Buster wagged his tail and acted like a normal dog.

"I like this dog. You should breed him," she said.

"You're the second person who's told me that," I said.

"Then why don't you?"

"He's got a mean streak a mile long."

"Maybe it's the people you hang out with."

Rose got in her Nova and lowered her window. When I was a cop, we'd never said good-bye. It was always "See you later." I said that now and saw a tinge of doubt in her beautiful brown eyes. So I added a postscript.

"I promise."

"When will that be?" she asked.

"Once I get this mess cleaned up."

"Another six months?"

I shook my head. "They'll run me out of town before then. A couple of weeks."

"Don't make a promise you can't keep, Jack."

"I mean it."

"I know you mean it," she said. "But that doesn't mean you will. You have to figure out what Skell did with those girls. If you don't, you won't be able to live with yourself, and neither will I."

There was a finality to her voice that made arguing useless.

"I'll come the moment the case is solved," I said.

"Is that a promise?"

"Yes, it's a promise."

We kissed again, and then I watched my wife drive away.

I decided to get lunch and cruised the neighborhood. Hyde Park was an eclectic mix of old homes, funky watering holes, and ethnic restaurants. Rose liked it here, and I tried to imagine myself fitting in. A sign boasting the best sub sandwiches in town caught my eye, and I pulled in.

Soon Buster and I were sharing a steak hoagie in my car. My vet said that people food was bad for animals, so I asked him why we ate it. He didn't have a good answer, so I continued to share my meals with my dog.

On the other side of the street, two workers were replacing a billboard. They were fifty feet in the air and were using putty knives to strip away an ad for a popular lite beer. It looked like dangerous work, and I wondered why they did it.

As the lite beer ad came down, the old ad beneath it was exposed. That ad was for a morning radio program and showed a bad-boy DJ sitting on a throne with a pitchfork, his ears pointed to make him look like the

Devil. Printed beneath his picture were the words *Weekday Mornings, 6–10. Prepare to get Bashed!*

I handed the last piece of my sandwich to my dog. The poster was for Neil Bash. Although I'd heard him on the radio many times, I'd never seen his face. He was big and homely, with a flat nose and jug ears. As more of his face became exposed I saw how someone had defaced his likeness with red spray paint. It said:

THIS MAN'S A FUCKING PIG!

The words bothered me. Whoever had written them had taken a real risk climbing up there. I wanted to know why. I got out of my car and called up to the two workers.

"Hey! You up there."

One of the workers stopped, and found me with his eyes. His skin was the color of a pencil eraser, his hair jet black.

"What you want?" he called down.

"That guy in the sign. What did he do?"

"Dunno," the worker said.

"Ask your partner, would you?"

The worker asked his partner. The partner shook his head. I guessed they were both illegals and scared I was from Immigration. The first worker turned back to me.

"We're busy," the first worker said.

"Does your friend know?" I asked.

He hesitated.

"I just want to ask him a couple of questions."

"Come back later," the first worker said.

I knew what was going to happen if I came back later. They would both be gone.

The billboard had a ladder attached to it. I crossed the

street and started to climb up. A stiff breeze was blowing, and I stopped midway and held on for dear life. One of my greatest fears was getting killed doing something stupid, like crossing the street without looking. Yet, for some reason, I continued to do stupid things. Finally the wind died, and I resumed my climb.

Reaching the top, I grabbed a handrail and looked around. I could see downtown's shimmering skyscrapers and rows of gritty warehouses in the Port of Tampa. Seeing me, the workers stopped what they were doing. I pointed at the devilish face on the poster.

"Tell me what he did."

The second worker stepped forward. He was also Hispanic and looked scared out of his wits. I handed him and his partner some money, and they both relaxed.

"He did something bad," the second worker said.

"What was that?" I asked.

The man scratched his chin.

"I think it was with a girl," he said.

"A young girl?" I asked.

"Yeah. He did something bad on his radio show to a young girl. They ran him out of town."

"How long ago was this?"

"Two, maybe three years ago."

"Thank you very much," I said.

He smiled. I'd made his day, and he'd made mine. Neil Bash was living in Tampa at the same time as Simon Skell, and he was doing something with underage girls that got him in trouble.

I'd found a link.

I climbed down and got into my car. My cell phone was stuck to a piece of Velcro on the dash, and I retrieved Ken

Linderman's business card from my wallet and punched in his cell number. Getting voice mail, I told Linderman that I urgently needed to speak with him. Five minutes later, he called me back.

"I'm in Tampa, running down a lead on the Skell case," I said. "Do you have an agent I could team up with for a few hours?"

"Of course," Linderman said.

The drive to the FBI building on Gray Street was a short one. Although Tampa wasn't a big city, the FBI's presence was, and I waited on line at a security checkpoint for several minutes, then had a German Shepherd bomb-sniff my car before I was allowed to drive onto the manicured grounds.

The three-story FBI building sat on seven pristine acres overlooking glistening Tampa Bay. It resembled the headquarters of a Fortune 500 company, and I found a shady spot beneath a mature oak tree and parked. Buster was not having fun, and he curled up into a ball and went to sleep without being told.

I walked through the building's front doors, feeling out of place in my beach-bum clothes. Having worked with the FBI many times, I knew that behind these walls were several hundred dedicated agents who did everything from finding missing children to stopping domestic terrorism.

At the reception desk I presented my driver's license to the uniformed male guard on duty. The guard kept my license and told me to have a seat. A minute later he called me back to his desk and returned my license.

"Go over to those glass doors," the guard said. "Special Agent Saunders will be out shortly."

I thanked him and stood by the shimmering glass doors. Thirty seconds later Saunders marched out. He wore a starched white shirt and dark blue necktie, was about thirty-five, and had a football player's broad shoulders and imposing physique. His palm swallowed mine as we shook hands.

"Ken Linderman called and said you had a lead in the Midnight Rambler case," Saunders said when we were in his office, a tidy second-floor room with two chairs, a metal desk, and a spectacular view of the bay. "I was assigned to Skell when he lived here. I'll do whatever I can to help you."

"What do you know about Neil Bash?" I asked.

"The shock jock?"

"Yes. What can you tell me about him?"

Saunders was animated and didn't appear to enjoy sitting down. I recognized the trait and followed him to the window. We both stared out at the bay's choppy water.

"Bash was a twisted guy," Saunders said. "He seemed to get his kicks out of making his listeners uncomfortable. One time he had a hog castrated on his show. The station got fined two hundred grand by the FCC."

"Was he arrested?" I asked.

"Believe it or not, he didn't break any laws. The hog was to be castrated anyway. Bash just played it on the air."

A team of rowers with a coxswain passed by the building. When they were gone, Saunders said, "Okay, so how are Bash and Skell connected?"

"They lived in Tampa at the same time, and now Bash is promoting Skell on his radio show in Fort Lauderdale while attacking me."

Saunders's eyebrows went up. "Sounds like you're onto something."

"I hope so," I said. "I heard Bash got run out of Tampa

a while back. Something to do with an underage girl. Is he a pedophile?"

"He never showed up on our radar."

"Do you remember what the deal with the girl was?"

Saunders crossed his arms and gave it some thought.

"No, but I know someone who probably does," he said.

Saunders picked up the phone on his desk and called a feature writer at the *Tampa Tribune* named Gary Haber. They exchanged pleasantries, and Saunders put the call on speakerphone and introduced us. Haber had a watered-down New York accent and sounded like a decent sort, and I asked him about Neil Bash being run out of town.

"That was about three years ago," Haber said. "If I remember correctly, one of the newscasters over at Fox broke the story."

"What happened?" Saunders asked.

"A sixteen-year-old cheerleader at Plant High School accused her history teacher of having an affair with her," Haber said. "Somehow, Bash got the girl to call his show, then tricked her into saying that she'd initiated the relationship and that the teacher wasn't to blame."

"How did Bash do that?" I asked.

There was a pause as Haber dredged his memory.

"It had something to do with the equipment Bash had in his studio," the reporter finally said. "I don't remember how, but he used a piece of equipment to get the girl to say things that she really didn't mean to say."

"You're saying he manipulated her answers," I said.

"That's right," Haber replied.

"Wouldn't the girl have known what Bash was doing?"

"Somehow she didn't know. From what I remember, Bash did something that was really clever."

"Was this a live show?" I asked.

"Yeah, it was live," Haber said.

I thought back to Melinda's call-in performance to Bash's show the day before. Her answers had sounded strained, and there had been pregnant pauses between them. I wondered if this played into what Haber had just described.

"Who was the reporter over at Fox?" Saunders asked.

"Kathy Fountain," Haber said.

Saunders glanced at me. "I know Kathy. Want to take a ride over to the station and have a chat with her?"

"Absolutely," I said.

"We need to run," Saunders told Haber. "Thanks for your help."

"Anytime," Haber said.

CHAPTER TWENTY-THREE

I followed Saunders to the Fox News station on bustling Kennedy Boulevard. The building was sleek and ultra-modern, with large tinted windows that faced the street and a hundred-foot-tall white tower with the station's number, 13, printed on its side. My impression of Tampa as a sleepy burg was changing, one piece of architecture at a time.

I parked in the shaded Visitors parking area. Buster was still put out, and he refused to make eye contact with me.

Saunders and I went through a revolving door into the building's main reception area. The receptionist was a white-haired guard with an engaging smile. A small sign on his desk said Director of First Impressions. Saunders asked to see Kathy Fountain while displaying his badge and laminated ID. The guard pointed at the flat-screen TV hanging over our heads.

"She's in the studio doing her show. I'll tell her assistant you're here. Please have a seat."

We sat on a leather couch and watched Kathy Fountain interview two guests in her studio. An attractive woman in her early forties, she was blond and fair skinned, and had the sympathetic manner of someone who'd raised kids.

At one o'clock her show ended. Sixty seconds later she was standing in front of us, out of breath.

"Hello, Scott," Fountain said. "Is something wrong?"

"We need your help with an investigation," Saunders said.

"Certainly," she said.

"This is Jack Carpenter," Saunders said. "He's working with me."

A flicker of recognition registered in Fountain's face, and I was glad that I was with Saunders, and not by myself.

"I'd like to talk to you about Neil Bash," I said.

Fountain rolled her eyes. "Neil was one sick, sick man."

"So I hear."

"Has he done something wrong? It wouldn't surprise me."

"Yes," I said. "Is there someplace we can talk in private?"

"My office. Follow me."

Fountain took us to her office on the other side of the large mazelike building. The shades were drawn, and the air-conditioning was turned down low. A family photo sat on her desk, confirming my earlier suspicions. Saunders and I remained standing, as did she.

"Gary Haber at the *Tampa Tribune* told us you broke the story that sent Bash packing," I said. "Can you tell me what Bash did that got him in so much trouble?"

Fountain crossed her arms in front of her chest, and her pleasant demeanor vanished. "A local high school girl had an affair with her history teacher. One day the affair became public, and the history teacher was arrested. Somehow, Bash got the girl to call his show. Although the show was broadcast live, there was a fifteen-second time delay on the broadcast, which let Bash bleep out crank calls and obscenities. Bash used that delay to manipulate the girl's answers. He asked questions like 'You asked your history teacher to sleep with you, didn't you?' The girl said no, and Bash said, 'So you didn't ask him to sleep with you?' The girl said yes, and Bash would bleep out the first answer and substitute the second. It made listeners think the girl had said yes to the first question, when she really hadn't."

"Wouldn't the girl know she was being manipulated?" Saunders asked.

"That was the clever part," Fountain said. "Bash made her turn off her radio to prevent feedback. She didn't hear the interview until after it was broadcast."

"How did you figure out what Bash was doing?" I asked.

"To tell you the truth, I didn't," Fountain said. "There's a magician in town who's been on my show a few times. He heard the interview and called me. He said Bash was using a trick invented by a mind reader named the Amazing Dunninger. Dunninger did a radio program, where he used the trick to 'read the minds' of listeners who called in."

"Did you expose Bash on your show?" I asked.

"You bet I did," Fountain said, nodding vigorously.

"What happened?"

"At first he denied it and threatened to take us to court," she said. "Then the girl went to the newspapers and said she'd been tricked. Bash recanted and said some of her answers were edited. That's when the excrement hit the air-conditioning."

Saunders and I both smiled.

"What happened to the history teacher?" I asked.

"There was a trial, and he was found guilty and sent to jail," Fountain said. "If I remember correctly, Bash showed up at the courthouse to support him. Right after that, Bash's show was cancelled, and he left Tampa."

"Did your station cover the trial?"

"Of course. It was big news."

"Is there any available footage that I could see?"

Fountain offered to check and left us standing in her office. Saunders had a spark in his eyes and was nodding, a sign that he agreed Bash needed to be investigated. In criminal investigations there was no such thing as coincidence or happenstance. Saunders and I both knew that Bash was connected to Simon Skell. The trick would be proving it.

Fountain reappeared a few minutes later, wearing a smile.

"You gentlemen are in luck," she said. "Follow me."

The station was like a small factory, with shows about cooking, the weather, and raising children being recorded in different sound studios. Fountain led us to the back of the building to the station's video library and introduced us to a lanky young guy with curly dark hair named Kevin Ford. Fountain told Kevin what we were looking for, and Kevin searched his computer's database for footage of the history teacher's trial.

"This might take a while," Kevin said.

Kevin's desk was loaded with work, and I offered to buy him lunch.

"You're on," he said.

Fountain and Saunders also took me up on my offer, and I left the station and drove to a deli a few blocks from where Rose worked. I hadn't stopped thinking about her, and I was thrilled to see her picking up a lunch order when I walked in. Edging up behind her, I lowered my voice.

"Excuse me, miss. Aren't you Jennifer Lopez?"

"Get lost," she said without turning around.

"You sound just like my wife."

She stiffened, then turned around. I kissed her on the lips.

"Hey, Rose," an aproned woman working the register said.

My wife would not take her eyes off me.

"Yes, Cynthia," she said.

"That your husband?"

"Yes, it is."

"About fricking time he showed up."

I ordered four Cuban sandwiches to go. While my order was being prepared we took a table, and I told Rose everything that had happened since we'd parted. My wife believed that God talked to us through signs. If we chose to believe in Him, those signs would become apparent to us. To her, my seeing the defaced billboard with Neil Bash's picture was a sign, and she nodded approvingly when I was done.

"Everything happens for a reason," she said.

"You really believe that, don't you?" I said.

"Yes, Jack, I do."

My food came, and I paid up. I kissed her again at the front door. There was a coldness that hadn't been there before. I thought I understood. Rose wasn't going to invest any more emotion in me until I committed myself to her and to our marriage.

I told myself I could live with that.

* * *

The sandwiches were met with smiles at the station. Kevin had found a week's worth of footage from the history teacher's trial, and Fountain, Saunders, and I ate in Fountain's office while watching a plasma monitor mounted to the wall.

"Because the girl was a minor, the judge didn't allow TV cameras inside the courtroom," Fountain explained as the first clip ran. "As a result, we used a courthouse artist to capture renditions of the different witnesses who testified during the trial."

I ate my sandwich while trying to hide my disappointment. My reason for wanting to watch the trial was to see if Simon Skell had attended and sat in the spectator gallery. Without a camera inside the courtroom, there was no way for me to know.

Instead, I decided to focus on the film taken outside the courtroom each day after the trial, when both the prosecuting attorney and the defense attorney made statements to the media. If I was lucky, Skell's face might show up here.

On the fourth clip I got a hit. This was the day Bash came and the cameras caught him leaving the courthouse. Bash wore a flowing black garment that made him look downright evil. When a reporter asked him a question, he shoved his palm into the camera and said, "No comment, asshole!"

As Bash came down the steps I spotted a man walking beside him.

"Can I see this clip again?" I asked.

Fountain rewound the tape and started it over. I had her freeze the picture as Bash appeared at the top of the steps, then play it in slow motion. As Bash descended, another man also came down, walking to his right. We leaned in to stare.

"Any idea who that is?" Saunders asked.

"He looks familiar, but I'm not sure," I said.

"Think it might be Skell?"

"It could be."

We watched the clip again. The second man's face never became visible to the camera. I felt as if I were watching a Hitchcock film, and the master was taunting me.

"You had contact with Skell, didn't you?" Saunders asked.

"That's one way to put it," I said.

"Judging by the guy's size, do you think that might be him?"

I hesitated. Body parts were hard to distinguish, and I couldn't really be certain. The guy looked about six foot and one-eighty, which matched Skell's proportions. He also had a bounce to his step, and Skell was athletic. But there was no way of knowing for sure. Fountain rewound the tape, and we watched it again.

"I just don't know," I said.

The air had been let out of the room. We finished eating in silence. A tapping on the door lifted our heads. Kevin stood in the doorway, looking pleased with himself.

"Guess what I just found," he said, holding a Beta tape in his hand.

Kevin came into Fountain's office and handed her the tape with a flourish.

"I decided to search the video archives to see what we had on Bash," Kevin said. "Guess what turned up? The clip when he castrated the hog."

Fountain let out a sickening groan.

"Oh, please, Kevin, I just ate lunch," she said.

"The station filmed it," Kevin said, "but it was so gross it never aired."

I looked across the desk at Fountain. "Do you mind if we watch it?"

"Of course not," she said. "Do you mind if I leave the room?"

"Not at all."

Fountain left her office. When she was gone, Kevin inserted the tape into the deck attached to the TV and hit Play.

"You want it with or without audio?" he asked.

"With," Saunders said.

The screen flickered to life. Dressed in black, Bash stood in a grassy field clutching a cordless mike. Beside him stood a gap-toothed farmer wearing dirty coveralls. Behind the farmer was a large squealing hog tied to a stake in the ground.

Bash and the farmer bantered back and forth like a couple of frat house buddies. Then the farmer drew a curved knife from a sheath in his belt, and knelt down beside the hog. The castration took place with the farmer's back to the camera. There was nothing to see, but the sounds were gruesome.

"Enough of that," Saunders said.

Kevin muted the clip with the remote. Soon the segment ended, and the camera pulled back. I could see Bash standing beneath the shade of an enormous oak tree off to the side. With him were four men, their faces masked by shadows.

"Freeze it," I said.

Kevin froze the clip. I stared at the four faces, as did Saunders.

"Any of them look familiar?" Saunders asked.

I stared hard. Then I shook my head. The resolution on the clip was poor, and the faces were indistinguishable.

"I need this blown up and lightened," I said.

"Your wish is my command," Kevin said, popping the cassette out.

We followed him down a long hallway to an editing room, which was windowless and quite chilly. A black male technician was on duty, and Kevin explained what we needed. The tech inserted the tape into a deck, then had us go into the next room, a brightly lit soundstage with a giant video monitor hanging on the wall.

"I'd like to watch football on that baby," Saunders said.

The frame we'd just been watching appeared on the monitor. Now, Bash and the four men looked larger than life.

"Would you look at that," Saunders said.

Standing next to Bash was the history professor who'd molested his student. The teacher wore a baseball cap pulled down low, but it didn't hide enough of his face. It was definitely him.

"Do you recognize any of the others?" Saunders asked.

I stared at the other three men. They were smiling and looked like a bunch of guys having a barbecue in someone's backyard.

"Can you make the faces lighter?" I asked the tech.

"Sure," the tech said from the other room.

The faces turned a few shades lighter. The guy to Bash's left wore shades and a leather bombardier jacket and was trying to look cool. He bore more than a passing resemblance to Skell, and I looked at his hands. Fingers were missing on both.

"That's Skell," I said.

"Jesus, are you sure?" Saunders said.

"I'd bet my life on it."

"What about the other two?"

The third man's face was partially turned. Hispanic, broad-shouldered, with an ugly facial scar. It was the guy who'd pumped three bullets into my car on 595.

"This guy tried to kill me the other day," I said, pointing.

Saunders shouldered up beside me.

"What about the fourth one? Do you know who he is?"

The fourth man in the photograph was ten years older than the rest. He had meticulously styled blond hair and a beach-ball stomach. A thick gold necklace hung around his neck, and his watch looked like a Rolex.

"Never seen him before," I said.

Saunders looked at Kevin.

"How hard would it be for us to get prints of this?" he asked.

Kevin walked into the next room and spoke with the tech. A minute later Saunders and I were holding color prints done off a laser printer. As I stared at Bash and Skell and the other members of the gang, my hands started to tremble. Finally, after six months of scratching my head, I was beginning to understand what I was dealing with.

"I need to talk to Ken Linderman," I said.

CHAPTER TWENTY-FOUR

I have a theory I want to share with you," I told Linderman.

We'd driven back to the FBI building on Gray Street and were sitting in Saunders's office, talking on a squawk box.

"I'm listening," Linderman said through the box's speaker.

"I think Skell is part of a gang of sexual predators," I said. "Skell, a shock jock named Neil Bash, a high school history teacher, and two other men lived in Tampa three years ago, and if my hunch is correct, they preyed on underage girls. When the history teacher got busted and went to jail, the remaining members moved on to greener pastures."

"You mean Fort Lauderdale," Linderman said.

"That's right," I said. "They came to my town and started abducting young women and having their way with them. They picked women who had no families and wouldn't be missed. They also chose women who were emotionally immature, so they could pretend they were underage and indulge in their fantasies."

"Like role-playing," Linderman said.

"Exactly," I said. "Pedophiles do it all the time. But

Skell's group was different. Instead of letting the women go when they were done with them, they killed them. My guess is, they realized this was the best way to cover their tracks."

"Let me see if I get this right," Linderman said. "You think that Skell and his team *became* killers in order to hide what they really were."

"That's right," I said. "They never stopped being pedophiles. They just found a way to satisfy their sexual cravings with less fear of retribution."

Saunders was sitting directly across from me, hands on knees, listening intently to our conversation. He shot me a funny look.

"You think these guys kill their victims because it was *less* dangerous than what they were doing before?" Saunders asked.

"That's right," I said.

"Don't you think that's a bit of a stretch?"

Before I could answer him, Linderman jumped in.

"Not really," he said. "The justice and penal systems are less harsh on murderers than on sexual predators of children. This is especially true for first-time murderers. In terms of self-preservation, Skell and his friends made a wise choice."

Saunders leaned back in his chair and shook his head.

"Jesus," he said under his breath.

"I also think that the team divides up the duties," I went on. "Bash is the front man. He's a minor celebrity and gets them invited places. Maybe that's where they scout for victims. Bash also protects the other members if they get caught, the way he did with the history teacher, and the way he's doing now by attacking me."

"Damage control," Linderman said.

"Exactly. The Hispanic is the abductor. He works for a cable company. He goes to the victim's house and cuts the cable on a pole. Then he gets a call to fix the outage, goes back to the house, and snatches the victim. There's never been a sign of a struggle at any of the victims' houses, so my guess is he's chloroforming them. I also think he's disposing of the bodies."

"Why?" Saunders asked.

"He has the truck, and works with a partner. It's just a hunch."

"What about Skell?" Linderman asked. "What's his role?"

"He pulls the strings and directs the action," I replied.

"The mastermind?"

"Yes. He's got a genius IQ, so it would make sense that he's calling the shots and orchestrating the show."

The laser print of the gang sat on Saunders's desk. Saunders picked it up and pointed at the blond guy with the perfectly round stomach.

"What about the fourth guy? What's his role?"

"This is just a guess," I said.

"I like your guesses," Linderman said.

"The part no one's figured out is how Skell selects his victims," I said. "How does Skell know *which* women to abduct? My guess is, the fourth guy is behind it."

"Any ideas how?" Linderman asked.

"Maybe he owns a restaurant and is secretly bugging the ladies' room," I suggested. "I knew a restaurant owner in Fort Lauderdale who did that, and told his buddies what their girlfriends were saying about them behind their backs."

"What a sleaze," Saunders said.

"So the mystery man in our photograph is the information gatherer," Linderman said.

"That's right," I said.

"So we have a front man, an information gatherer, an abductor and disposer, and a mastermind," Linderman said. "This all sounds good, Jack, but can you prove any of it?"

"Not yet," I said.

"Then, I'm afraid I have some bad news for you. The Broward County police charged Ernesto Ramos with Carmella Lopez's murder earlier today. Skell's attorney is standing right now in front of a judge, asking for Skell to be released from prison."

Something hard dropped in the pit of my stomach.

"Are the Broward police going along with it?" I asked.

"I'm afraid so," Linderman said.

"So, we're too late," I said.

"There is no timetable on justice," Linderman replied.

I folded my hands in my lap and did not respond.

"Jack, the FBI is behind you on this," Linderman said.

I glanced at Saunders, who nodded in agreement.

"Behind me how?" I asked.

"If Skell is released, he'll be watched twenty-four hours a day, seven days a week, as well as have his phones wiretapped," Linderman said. "So will Neil Bash. We'll also take the laser print of the gang and compare the unknown men against photographs of known sexual predators. Assuming we make a match, we'll watch those two men as well. Skell may have won this battle, but he won't win the war."

It all sounded good, but I wanted to ask Linderman how long he planned to tail Skell and his gang. A few months, a year? At some point the FBI would lose interest and move on to other cases. It was the single greatest weakness of any law enforcement operation. And once they did, a group of monsters would go back to work.

I looked at the wall in Saunders's office. It was bare except for a ticking clock. I found myself blinking. The photographs of Skell's victims that hung in my office had appeared. Chantel, Maggie, Carmen, Jen, Krista, Brie, Lola, and Carmella. Tears ran down their faces, and I wondered if I was seeing them from exhaustion, or maybe I was losing my mind.

Reaching across the desk, Saunders squeezed my biceps.

"Jack, you okay?" he asked.

"What's wrong?" Linderman asked through the box.

"Jack's looking a little pale," Saunders said.

"Give him something to drink."

Saunders rose from his chair.

"I'm okay," I said.

"You sure, Jack?" Saunders asked.

I nodded while continuing to stare at the wall. The photographs faded away, leaving only the ticking clock. It was a perfect metaphor for what was about to happen. With the passage of time, the victims would be all but forgotten.

I thanked the special agents for their time and left the office.

I got into my car feeling angry at the world. Buster looked relieved to see me, and I scratched his head.

I decided to drive back to Dania and resume digging for evidence. It wasn't much of a plan, but I didn't see myself having any other choices. Rose was right. I wouldn't be able to live with myself until I knew what Skell had done with the victims.

As I backed out, my cell phone began beeping, indicating I had a message. I pulled my phone off the dash to see who'd called. Caller ID showed a number with a Fort Lauderdale area code. It wasn't one I knew.

I retrieved the message and listened. At first there was nothing. Then I heard a woman's voice. It was far away, as if coming from the bottom of a deep well.

"Jack."

I hit my brakes hard. It was Melinda.

"Jack, are you there?"

Her voice was strained. I couldn't tell if it was drugs or fear.

"Jack, you gotta help me. Oh, God, where are you?"

I pulled back in to my spot and threw the car into park.

"I'm sorry what I said on the radio. They made me say those terrible things. I know it hurt you, and I'm sorry."

She started to cry. She sounded messed up, and I decided it was drugs.

"I'll call you back as soon as I can. Please keep your phone nearby. And whatever you do, don't call me back. They don't know about the phone."

It was classic Melinda. First she led me on, then she pushed me away.

"Good-bye, Jack. Oh, wait."

In the background I heard a door open and the faint sound of music.

"Oh my God—here they come!"

The message ended. The music had sounded hauntingly familiar. I replayed the message and listened hard. It was the live version of "Midnight Rambler."

PART THREE
HIDDEN MICKEYS

CHAPTER TWENTY-FIVE

I wrestled with what to do with Melinda's message. It exonerated me, only I wasn't sure anyone else would interpret it that way. She sounded too messed up. If I called Russo or Cheever and played it for them, they might accuse me of doping her up and forcing her to talk. I decided to hold on to it and hope she called back.

As I drove away from the FBI building my cell phone rang. It made my heart race, and I answered without bothering to look at the Caller ID.

"Carpenter here."

"Jack, this is Sally McDermitt. I hope I'm not catching you at a bad time."

Sally was a former investigator with the Broward County Police Department who had worked in my department. I tried to hide the disappointment in my voice.

"Not at all. What's up?"

"I'm in a bind and need some advice," she said. "A little girl disappeared inside the Magic Kingdom this morning, and we can't find her."

Sally had left the force to take a great-paying job running internal security for the Walt Disney World theme parks in Orlando. The last time we'd spoken, she'd had over a thousand people working for her, was driving a

BMW convertible, and lived in a gated community whose other residents included a bunch of well-known professional golfers.

"How old?" I asked.

"Just turned three, a little red-haired cutie named Shannon Dockery. She's a roamer, so her parents didn't immediately notice she was missing."

"Where was she last seen?"

"Right outside the 'It's a Small World' exhibit."

I had worked with Disney on child abductions before. This exhibit was a favorite among toddlers and their parents.

"A pro," I said.

"That's what we think," Sally replied. "The park's exits have been closed. We're only letting people out through the main parking area. That way we can get a good look at everyone who leaves."

"You think the abductor is still inside the park?"

"I sure do. We looked at the videos at all the entrances right after this happened. No kids fitting Shannon's physical description have left the park today."

Sally had caught a live one. It was rare, and I'd compare it to catching a giant marlin on a fifty-pound reel. She didn't want him to break the line and get away, and for her sake, neither did I. I could drive home by way of Orlando, and I decided to offer my services.

"Want me to help you catch him?"

"But you're four hours away," she said.

"Actually I'm in Tampa, working on another case. I can give you a couple hours of my time, if you think it will do any good."

"Oh yes, please come. You were always the champ when it came to finding little kids."

I could hear the desperation in Sally's voice.

"I'm leaving right now," I said.

"See you in an hour," Sally said.

"You've never seen me drive," I told her.

An elevated section of I-275 ran over the city of Tampa, and I found an entrance ramp without trouble and headed east. Within minutes I was merging onto I-4, which dissected central Florida and led directly to the forty thousand acres owned by the Walt Disney World Corporation. I pushed the Legend up to eighty and kept it there.

Children had disappeared at Disney since the theme park opened over thirty years before, and many of those abductions had become case studies for people who made their living looking for missing kids. Ninety-nine percent of the time, the abductor was a parent who'd lost custody in a bitter divorce battle and decided to take the child back and go judge shopping. But every once in a while, a stranger stole a child.

The folks who ran Disney did everything imaginable to stop this from happening, and employed a small army of well-trained security people to keep the place safe. Public areas were outfitted with the latest in high-tech surveillance monitoring equipment, including a special magnetic bar code in every ticket that allowed Disney to monitor the flow of people around various attractions. But in the end, they couldn't protect every child who passed through the turnstiles, and the unthinkable happened.

Disney was not really in Orlando, despite what the television and magazine advertisements said. It was located in the tourist town of Kissimmee, ten miles due south. Forty minutes later I took the exit and followed the signs for the MGM Theme Park, one of five theme parks that Disney owned in Orlando. Buster's window was at half-mast and his ears were standing straight up.

I drove down the twisting road to MGM, then hung a right at the EMPLOYEES ONLY sign and spotted Sally standing in the parking lot. She wore chinos and a blue sports shirt with the Disney logo embroidered on the breast. Her hair was a natural gold, her eyes the color of the ocean. Like me, she was a native Floridian, and she lived for the outdoors. I once joined her for a run after work, and she nearly killed me. As I got out I offered her my hand, but she hugged me instead.

"It's good to see you, Jack," she said.

"It's good to see you, too," I said.

"I'm scared about this one."

"I know. That's why I came."

Sally led me into a four-story glass-and-concrete building with no markings. It was painted an earthy green and blended into the lush landscaping that towered around it. The security for Disney's theme parks happened here, though few people knew it. At Disney, buildings were either part of the experience or invisible.

A basement hallway echoed our footsteps, and we entered a small carpeted room with a one-way mirror covering one wall. On the other side of the mirror sat a young couple crying their eyes out. The girl was pleasantly plain and covered with freckles, while the boy had a pinched face and an old-fashioned crew cut. Both were small of stature and dressed in simple country clothes.

"Meet Peggy Sue and Tram Dockery," Sally said. "We kept them apart and interrogated them. Their stories are consistent."

My breath fogged the mirror. "That his real name?"

"Yes. Hails from Douglas, Georgia, which is about two hundred and fifty miles from here as the crow flies. He manages a barbecue restaurant that his father owns. First thing he told me was he'd done a stint in prison for selling weed, and had been on the straight and narrow ever since."

"Believe him?"

"He offered up the information. Yes, I believed him."

"His wife looks young," I said.

"Her driver's license says she's nineteen."

"How old is their little girl?"

"Nearly three."

"So he got her pregnant when she was sixteen."

Sally didn't respond. She'd already looked at the facts and decided the Dockerys hadn't orchestrated their daughter's disappearance and sold her for money to buy crack, or to pay off a loan shark, or put a down payment on a new car, or any of the other insane reasons that couples give when they get caught selling their children.

I continued to stare through the glass. Something about Tram's behavior didn't feel right, and after a few moments I realized what it was. Parents who lose kids do nothing but worry, and worrying is a manufactured fear. Tram's fear wasn't manufactured. It was real, and it told me that he knew something the rest of us didn't.

"Can I talk to him without the wife?" I asked.

"Be my guest," Sally said.

The couple were separated. I entered the room and introduced myself as park security without giving my name. Tram jumped out of his chair and pumped my hand. He was small and wiry, maybe one-forty soaking wet, with dozens of tiny black moles visible beneath his crew cut.

The words *Jimbo's Homestyle BBQ* were stitched in flaming red over the pocket of his denim shirt. He didn't look old enough to shave.

I told him to sit down and gave him my best no-nonsense look.

"I need to ask you a couple of questions, Mr. Dockery."

"It's Tram," he said.

"Mine's Jack. Let me get right to the point. We think the person who nabbed your daughter is a pro. More than likely, he'll try to leave the park when it closes and tens of thousands of people are going home. That gives us time to figure out a strategy."

"Great," he said.

"That's the good news," I said. "The bad new is, it won't be easy figuring out which child is yours. Your daughter's appearance will be drastically altered, and she may not look like a little girl anymore."

"I'll do whatever you want," Tram said.

"Good. Now, I want you to level with me. Did you sell your daughter to someone in the park and not tell your wife about it?"

Tram leaped out of his chair, and I reflexively jumped back. He threw his arms into the air while tears streamed down his face. "No! I'd never do that! You think I'm some kind of criminal—I can see it in your eyes! I'd never sell my daughter, not even to the richest man in the entire world."

"Sit down," I said.

"Do you believe me?"

I pointed at his chair.

"Do you?"

"Sit," I ordered him.

Finally he sat.

"No, I don't believe you," I said flatly.

"But I'm telling the truth," he wailed.

"Something's bothering you, son, and I want to know what it is."

Tram held his head with both his hands and looked down like there wasn't enough floor to stare at.

"Tell me," I said.

"This was my last chance, and I blew it," Tram said.

"What's that supposed to mean?"

"I've been straight for six months. No weed, no beer, going to church every Sunday, working eight-to-six in my daddy's restaurant. Peggy Sue told me if I didn't clean up my act, she'd divorce me and get sole custody of my daughter. And I've been doing good, until today."

"Do you blame yourself for what happened?"

He nodded, still looking down. "I was watching her."

"Tell me what happened. From the beginning."

"We came out of the 'It's a Small World' exhibit. Peggy Sue got on line to buy snacks, and me and Shannon went looking for hidden Mickeys."

"Hidden what?"

"Hidden Mickeys."

"Is that a game?"

"There's hundreds of hidden images of Mickey Mouse in the park," he explained. "They're in tables and on buildings and sometimes you see them in shadows at certain times of the day. We're staying at a Disney hotel, and they've got a promotion if you find a certain number of them. Shannon was looking at a hidden Mickey carved in a shrub, and I went to help Peggy Sue with the snacks. When I came back, my baby was gone."

"How long did you leave your daughter?"

"Half a minute."

"Do you consider Shannon's disappearance your fault?"

Tram choked up. "Yeah."

"So you screwed up."

"I've been doing that my whole life."

"Answer the question."

"Yeah, I screwed up."

"But you didn't sell her to someone."

Tram shook his head, and tears flowed down his cheeks. I didn't know whether to believe him or not. But I *wanted* to believe him, and sometimes that's the best emotion to run with. I placed my hand firmly on his shoulder, and he looked up at me hopefully.

"Okay," I said.

Tram and Peggy Sue were reunited, and Sally drove them to the front entrance of the Magic Kingdom in a golf cart. I followed in a separate cart, watching Tram from a distance. The kid was still bothering me, and I wondered if he was high on something when his daughter disappeared. That would explain his hyped-up behavior.

We reached the entrance, parked, and got out. There were ten turnstiles. A pair of Disney security guards stood at each turnstile, holding a picture of Shannon Dockery while watching people pass through. Characters in Mickey Mouse costumes also stood by the turnstiles. Sally must have heard about Shannon's fascination with hidden Mickeys and decided this would be a good way to draw the child out.

I stood with Tram and his wife and Sally on a patch of grass beside the entrance. Sally asked Peggy Sue what kind of shoes her daughter was wearing. She explained that while the abductors had probably changed Shannon's clothes, they wouldn't know what size shoes she wore and would have to leave those on her feet.

"Pink Reeboks," Peggy Sue said.

"You sure she wasn't wearing her flip-flops?" Tram asked.

"She wanted to wear her flip-flops, but I wouldn't let her," Peggy Sue said. "My daughter's wearing pink Reeboks."

Sally went to each pair of guards and instructed them to be on the lookout for a child wearing pink Reeboks. Ten minutes passed, and hundreds of families walked by. Everything was being done by the book, but there was a problem. Too many small children were walking past to let the guards get a good look at each one. I pulled Sally aside.

"This is only going to get worse as the park starts to clear out," I said.

"What should I do?" Sally asked.

"Slow the lines down."

"I can't do that."

"Why not?"

"Half the people inside the Magic Kingdom are infants," Sally explained. "These kids have to eat, go to the bathroom, take a nap. If the lines start backing up, they'll start screaming, and we'll have a full-blown catastrophe on our hands."

Sally was starting to sound desperate. She'd done everything she could, yet knew it wasn't good enough. I stared at the families pouring through the turnstiles. Fort Lauderdale also had theme parks, and I had lost a four-year-old girl on my watch two years earlier that I would forever lose sleep over. Her disappearance was a total mystery until a maintenance man told his bosses about some odd things he'd discovered in the trash.

"Can you get me into the park?" I asked.

"Sure. What do you have in mind?"

"I want to search the area where Shannon was abducted."

"I'll get one of the guards to drive you," Sally said.

I pointed at Tram standing nearby, holding his wife's hand.

"I want him to come with me," I said.

CHAPTER TWENTY-SIX

A Disney security guard drove us inside the Magic Kingdom in a golf cart. I sat behind Tram and watched him jerk his head at every infant we passed. He was crazy with worry and called out his daughter's name several times.

The guard parked near the "It's a Small World" exhibit, and we hopped out. This had been my daughter's favorite ride when she was little. If prompted, Jessie would sing the entire song from memory, although it had been years since I'd asked. I hummed the chorus and saw Tram stiffen.

"You trying to be funny?" he asked.

"No, just trying to stay calm. Mind my asking you a question?"

Tram didn't answer me.

"What are you on?" I asked.

Tram swallowed his Adam's apple.

"I ain't on nothing."

"Stick to telling the truth. You're better at it."

"I am telling the truth," he said defensively.

I was close enough to him to smell his breath. It was mint flavored with a hint of something acidic: The smell was one I'd encountered countless times before. He'd been drinking, and I grabbed him by the shoulders and shook him.

"Stop lying to me, you stupid little son of a bitch," I said. "You've been hitting the sauce, haven't you?"

His defiant attitude melted away. "I had a couple of beers for breakfast, that's all."

"Then what was the bullshit line about you quitting?"

"I slipped."

"How many is a couple?"

"A six-pack."

"Does your wife know that?"

Tram shook his head.

"So you were drunk when your daughter got snatched."

Tram's face twisted with agony. With many missing children cases, there was often another crime behind the abduction. Sometimes the crime was excusable, like a parent bowing to a child's demand to go inside a store alone. Other times, the crime was so damning that it could never be excused. In this case, Tram Dockery was not a fit parent and didn't deserve the second chance the world had given him.

"God damn you, son," I said.

I made Tram take me to the last place he'd seen Shannon. The guard tagged along and stood dutifully to one side. He was an older black man with wispy hair and watery eyes. His expression said he'd seen many like Tram before.

"Shannon was right here the last time I saw her," Tram said.

We were standing by an enormous bush carved to look like Mickey Mouse. Tram pointed at a concession stand thirty feet away.

"Peggy Sue was over there carrying two cardboard trays, and I went to help her," he said. "When I came back, my baby was gone."

I did a three-sixty revolution and looked for places where a person could have taken Shannon without being spotted. I was suspicious about the fact that Shannon wasn't heard during her abduction, until the doors to the "It's a Small World" exhibit opened. Then, five hundred noisy kids and their parents poured out, and I realized that Shannon could have been screaming her head off and not been heard.

"What's your name?" I asked the guard.

"Vernon," the guard replied. "People call me Vern."

"Vern, where's the closest restroom?"

"There are several," he said.

"Do they all have family restrooms?"

"No, only the restroom around the corner has that."

"Show me," I said.

Vern led us to a small redbrick building right off the main drag. It had three doors—His, Hers, and Family—and was a perfect place to bring a child to. I banged on the door for Family. Getting no answer, I went inside.

Like everything at Disney, the bathroom's interior was spotlessly clean. In the corner sat a metal trash can, and I dragged it outside onto the grass. Pulling off the top, I rummaged through the smelly diapers and other garbage stuffed inside.

"What you doing?" Tram asked.

"Looking for your daughter's clothes."

"You think they changed her, huh?"

"Yes, I do."

Tram started to help. His face was milk white, and he was sucking down air. If I hadn't known better, I would have thought he was having an epiphany and going through a life-altering experience. But more than likely, it was all the beer he'd drunk burning through his system. I held up a child's ripped T-shirt.

"This look familiar?"

Tram squinted at the piece of clothing and shook his head.

"No, that ain't hers."

We kept searching. Vern was a step ahead of us and pulled trash containers out of the two other lavatories, dumping their contents onto the grass as well. By the time we were done, garbage was strewn everywhere. Vern made a call on his walkie-talkie and told someone to send people to clean up our mess.

"There's another place we should check," Vern said.

"Lead the way," I told him.

We followed Vern a hundred feet down a path. He stopped at a trash container designed to look like a Chinese pagoda. Yanking open a metal door, Vern removed an enormous garbage bag and dumped the contents onto the walkway. We started to sift through the pile.

Mostly it contained wrappers with half-eaten food or juice containers. Near the bottom, Tram found a plastic bag with its mouth tied in rabbit ears. Tearing the bag open, he let out a shout. Stuffed inside were a child's pink shorts and matching pink shirt.

"Those are my baby's clothes," he said tearfully.

"You're sure?" I asked.

"Yes, sir."

I examined the clothes and found several long red hairs stuck in the fabric of the shirt. Shannon's abductor had given her a haircut.

"Let me see the bag," I said.

Tram handed me the bag. I turned it upside down, and a metal can fell out. It made a funny sound as it rolled down the pavement.

Tram ran after the can and snatched it off the ground. He tossed it to me, and I grabbed it out of the air and stared at the label. Blue spray paint.

"They must have changed her hair color," Tram said.

I continued to stare at the label. Blue hair would have made Shannon stand out like a sore thumb. There was another reason for the spray paint, something as devious as the people behind the abduction, only I didn't have a clue what it was.

I found myself thinking of the little girl who'd disappeared at the theme park in Fort Lauderdale. Her abductors had changed her appearance so that even her parents, who'd been standing by the turnstiles as the crowds left, couldn't identify her. Her clothes and a can of blue spray paint were later found in the trash, yet I was never able to make a connection between them.

I have a maxim that has served me well. I always assume that the criminals I'm chasing are as smart as I am, or smarter. It may not always be true, but it keeps me on my toes. Driving toward the Magic Kingdom's main entrance in the golf cart, I suddenly realized what the can of blue spray paint was for.

CHAPTER TWENTY-SEVEN

I jumped out of the cart as it reached the turnstiles. Catching Sally's eye, I held the can of blue spray paint triumphantly over my head. She hurried over to me.

"Please tell me you have some good news," she said.

"Shannon's abductors have cut her hair, changed her clothes, and also changed the color of her shoes," I said. "My guess is, they made her look like a little boy."

Sally took the can of paint out of my hand.

"Is this the new color of her shoes?"

"Yes. Get me some paper."

Sally went to her golf cart and removed all the paper from a clipboard on the dash. She handed the paper to me, and I sprayed all the sheets with blue paint and waved them in the air to dry. Then Sally and I approached each pair of guards watching a turnstile and handed them one of the sheets.

"Look at the shoes of each child leaving the park," I instructed them. "If you see this color, grab the kid and yell for us."

Sally repeated the instructions, making sure the guards understood. Then we went to where Tram and Peggy Sue stood on the side in the grass. Tram had brought Shannon's clothes out of the park, and Peggy Sue was clutching them against her chest. I gently touched her arm.

"Peggy Sue," I said.

"What do you want?" she whispered.

"You need to pull yourself together. If there's any person your daughter will run to, it's going to be you."

Peggy Sue swiped at her eyes. "What if she's gone? What if they already took her out of the park? What then?"

I wanted to tell Peggy Sue not to think those dark thoughts, but I bit my tongue instead. There was no greater sin in my line of work than making false promises.

"We're going to find her," Tram said, sounding strong.

I stood by the turnstiles with Sally and watched families leave the park. Each child passed briefly before my eyes, then was gone forever. More than once I thought I'd spotted Shannon, only to realize I was wrong. Finally Sally spoke up.

"Why are you so jumpy?" she asked.

"Times like this I can't stand still," I said.

"Why don't you go back inside and see if you can spot her?" she suggested.

It sounded like a good idea. An elderly couple wearing mouse ears walked past. They were smiling and holding hands like newlyweds. I approached the man and offered to buy the mouse ears from him. The man refused my money and handed the ears to me.

"Have fun," the man said.

Sally got me back inside the park. Thousands of people were waiting to leave, and I was reminded how incredibly loud small children could be, especially when they were unhappy.

I walked to the rear of the lines, feeling the hot macadam baking through my sandals. Reaching the lines' end, I turned around and started walking back, looking at little kids' shoes without being too obvious. Several irate fathers accused me of trying to cut in.

"I've lost my family," I said.

The ruse worked, and let me keep moving forward. It was a slow process, and after ten minutes, I called Sally on my cell to see how things were going.

"No sign of her yet," she said.

"Keep the faith," I said.

I slipped the phone into my pocket. I'd reached the middle of the lines and was standing in a sea of unhappy little kids. I reminded myself that Shannon's abductors were playing the roles of parents, and when they reached the turnstiles, they'd be giving star performances. Coming up from behind was the best way to go.

Lowering my head, I continued my search.

Most cops I knew believed in God. I'd always found this strange, considering the amount of human suffering and tragedy that cops were subjected to. Perhaps a religious belief was the best way to cope with these experiences. Or to explain when amazing things happened.

Right now, I was a believer.

I'd spotted Shannon Dockery. She was part of a family of five and was standing a hundred yards from the turnstiles with her thumb stuck in her mouth.

I quickly noted her abductors. The woman pretending to be Shannon's mom was a thirtyish brunette with permed hair and fake fingernails painted in custom-car colors, and the man pretending to be her dad was a bearded truck-driver type who spit out a steady banter of corny jokes. They looked just as ordinary as anyone else.

Then there were Shannon's fake brothers. The oldest boy was tall and string-bean thin and maybe ten years old, while the younger boy was short and round and didn't know how to tie his sneakers. Shannon stood between the boys, holding hands and doing the buddy system, the way kids in the park were supposed to.

The deception Mom and Dad had used to disguise Shannon's identity was extraordinary. Many families that visited Disney wore color-coordinated or themed clothing. They did it for fun and because it made it easier for parents to watch the kids. Shannon's fake mom and dad were also wearing themed clothing. "Support Our Troops!" was splashed across their T-shirts along with pictures of the burning World Trade Center towers, and each of the children wore patriotic colors: the oldest in red, the middle in white, Shannon in blue. Had I not found the can of spray paint in the park, the disguises would have flown right by me.

I called Sally on my cell phone.

"Any luck?" she asked.

"Got her," I said quietly.

Sally screamed into my ear. "You found her?"

"Yes."

"Oh, Jack, I love you!"

"They're about to come out, second turnstile from your right. It's a family of five, with three little kids dressed in red, white, and blue. Shannon is in blue. I'm going to come out right behind them."

"A family? How old are the other kids?"

"They're young."

"Hold me back if I hurt the parents, Jack."

Using children to commit crimes sickened even the most jaded law enforcement officers, and I understood Sally's feelings, for they were my own as well.

"I'll call you once they come out," I said.

Soon Shannon's false family reached the turnstiles. I watched Dad shoot a furtive glance at Mom. Together, they put their hands on their children's backs and pushed them ahead. They were going to exit as a group, making it harder for the guards to get a clear look at Shannon. It was another clever tactic to avoid detection, and my gut told me that they'd done this before. I called Sally back.

"Here we go," I said.

Private security forces were not bound to the same rules as the police. They did not have to identify themselves to suspected criminals, nor act with the same restraint that the law required of cops. As the family exited the turnstiles I threw my arms in the air and jumped up and down. Moments later, Disney security hit the family hard.

Three burly guards surrounded Dad, who immediately began pushing and shoving. In a flurry of flailing arms and legs, the guards wrestled him face-first to the ground. Dad was as slippery as an eel, and while two of the guards held his arms, the third sat on his back and pinned him down.

At the same time, a pair of female guards pinched Mom and led her away from the turnstiles. Mom did not go quietly. First she yelled at the top of her lungs. Then she tried to break free, forcing one of the guards to twist her arm behind her back. When Mom continued to resist, they cuffed her.

Individual security guards confronted the two boys,

who seemed baffled by what was happening. The guards hustled them off as well.

Coming up from behind, I scooped young Shannon into my arms. She was light as a feather, and her eyes looked mildly sedated.

"Hi, Shannon," I said.

"Hi," she said.

"How you doing?"

"I'm good! We're going to get ice cream."

"What kind?"

"Chocolate swirl."

"Is that your favorite?"

"Yes!"

Sally had pulled Shannon's parents away from the turnstiles to avoid a free-for-all.

Holding their daughter in my arms, I walked over to them. Seeing a look of disbelief in Tram's and Peggy Sue's faces, I realized they didn't recognize their own daughter.

But they did recognize me, and I flashed my best smile. Slowly their worried looks disappeared. Peggy Sue knelt down and spread her arms wide.

"Shannon, baby, come to me!"

I put Shannon down and let the little girl run into her mother's arms. Peggy Sue hugged her child while mouthing a silent prayer. Then she looked at me. In her face I saw a promise. She was never letting this child out of her sight again.

Tram came up to me. He wanted to say something, but the words had escaped him. Instead, he gave me a bear hug, the top of his head barely reaching my chin.

"You like barbecue?" he asked.

"Love it," I said.

"Good, because I'm sending you barbecue for the rest of my life."

I said good-bye to the Dockerys and went looking for Sally. With the crisis averted, families were being allowed to exit the park normally, and I became engulfed in the loud boisterous crowd. I found Sally standing by the golf carts talking on her cell phone.

"You know, you look cute with those mouse ears on," she said.

"I need to talk to you," I said.

"Go ahead. The Orange County Sheriff's Department has me on hold."

"Hang up on them."

Sally shot me a concerned look. "Why should I do that, Jack?"

"Because I want to talk with these two slimeballs without the police or lawyers in the room," I said.

Her face turned ice cold. "Jack, I'm in charge here, remember?"

"Didn't I just drop everything I was doing, run over here from Tampa, and save your ass?"

"Jack, what's come over you?"

"Didn't I?"

"Yes, you did."

"I just want to question them without some goddamn lawyers in the room or some cops reading them their rights."

"You going to beat them up?"

She had struck a nerve, and I nearly told her to go to hell.

"They've done this before," I said instead. "Look at the preparation they went through, dressing the boys in red and white clothing so they could make Shannon fit in by dressing her in blue. I'm convinced this couple used the same trick to snatch a little girl out of a park in Fort Lauderdale. Let me talk with them, Sally."

Sally chewed on a fingernail and considered my request.

"You sure about this, Jack?"

I had no proof of what I'd just said, just what my gut told me.

"Yes," I said emphatically.

She closed the phone and slipped it into her pocket. "I'll give you one hour with them, but you have to promise me you won't lay a finger on either one."

"I won't touch them."

"Is that a promise?"

I again suppressed the urge to curse her. I'd pushed her buttons plenty of times when she'd worked for me, and now she was pushing mine.

"Yes, it's a promise."

"Okay, they're yours."

We got into a golf cart, and Sally drove down a winding concrete path that led to the security building. Halfway there, we came upon another golf cart that contained three security guards and Dad. Dad was handcuffed and riding shotgun, with two guards sitting behind him while the third guard drove. The cart wasn't moving too fast, and Sally beeped her electric horn.

"Everything okay?" she called out.

The driver slowed even more and turned to look at us.

"Just a little problem with the brakes," he said.

"Need some help?"

"No, we'll be fine."

"Nice job back there," Sally said.

"Thank you, Ms. McDermitt," the driver replied.

As the cart pulled away, Dad jerked his head around and looked our way. His face was flushed, and he was sweating as if he were going to the electric chair. Our eyes locked, and I sensed he was trying to place me. For the hell of it, I removed the mouse ears. Cold hard fear spread across his face.

"Jesus," Sally said. "He knows you."

"Yes, I believe he does," I said.

CHAPTER TWENTY-EIGHT

In my next life, I want to be a dog. Not just any dog, but my dog. Pulling into the security parking area, I checked on Buster and found him lying on the backseat of the Legend cutting zzzs, his hind legs running in place as he chased an imaginary car.

Sally took me to the basement interrogation room. On the other side of the one-way mirror I saw Mom sitting in a plastic chair. She was talking out loud, threatening to sue the park for false arrest, her true character on full display.

Still handcuffed, Dad was dragged into the room and made to sit in another chair. His shirt and pants were covered in dirt, and his face was dripping with sweat. The guards left and shut the door behind them.

A standard procedure in interrogating suspects was to put them together and listen to them talk. Most of the time, nothing of value was gained. But every once in a while, a pearl of information slipped out of someone's mouth.

We watched Mom and Dad for several minutes but didn't learn much. There was a knock on the door. A guard entered our viewing room and handed Sally the couple's driver's licenses. Sally read them both, then passed them to me.

Their names were Cecil Cooper and Bonnie Sizemore. Cecil lived in Jacksonville on the east coast, while Bonnie resided in Lakeland, a sleepy town about thirty minutes away. Sally addressed the guard.

"Either one of them say anything during the drive over?"

"The woman cussed up a storm," the guard said. "The guy demanded that we let him call some hotshot lawyer in Miami."

My head snapped. "You sure it was Miami?"

"Positive," the guard said.

"Did he give you the lawyer's name?"

"Yes, sir. I've got it written down in the other room."

"Was it Leonard Snook?"

The guard acted startled. "Why yeah, I think it was."

"Would you mind checking?"

The guard went to find the lawyer's name, and returned holding a slip of paper in his hand. "Leonard Snook it is," he said.

I thanked him, and the guard left. Sally practically jumped out of her chair.

"Jack, how did you know that?"

My blood boiled. At the mirror I stared into the next room. Bonnie was slumped dejectedly in her chair, gazing at the floor. Her mascara had run from crying, giving her hideous raccoon eyes. In a stage whisper, Cecil was trying to coach her. I'd always been good at making snap decisions, and I made one right now. Cecil was the ringleader, Bonnie the pawn.

"Earth to Jack," Sally said.

"You sound just like my daughter."

"What in God's name is going on? How did you know his lawyer's name?"

I took a deep breath and continued looking through the glass. "Leonard Snook represents Simon Skell, the Midnight Rambler."

"*What?*"

"Our friends in the next room are part of an organized group that's making people disappear. Think back to when you were a cop. How many WATs did we deal with each year?"

WATs, a police acronym for Without a Trace, stood for people who vanished without any significant clues being left behind.

"About four or five," Sally said.

"Ever think the cases might be connected?"

"It crossed my mind, sure."

"But because there weren't any solid leads, the police couldn't act on those suspicions, could we?"

"That's right."

I jabbed my finger at Bonnie and Cecil. "Well, now you can. I'll bet you everything I own that they've been snatching kids here, and from other theme parks in Florida as well. I'll also bet you that these abductions are linked to the eight women the Midnight Rambler made disappear."

"Jack, look at me," Sally said.

I turned from the glass. Putting her hands on my shoulders, Sally gave me a no-nonsense stare. Her grip was as strong as any man's.

"Where's your proof?"

"The victims are proof."

"How so?"

"The part of the Midnight Rambler case that's so baffling is how did Skell identify his victims? How did he know *which* women were easy prey and wouldn't be missed when they disappeared?"

"Soft targets," Sally said.

"Exactly. Well, we have the same thing here. How did Bonnie and Cecil know that Shannon Dockery was a soft target?"

"Maybe they got lucky."

"Luck is the residue of design. Tram Dockery had a six-pack of beer for breakfast. He admitted it to me earlier. He's also very young and not very smart. He was the *perfect* parent to snatch a kid from. Bonnie and Cecil knew that, and they followed the Dockerys around the Magic Kingdom. When the opportunity presented itself, they grabbed Shannon and disguised her to look like one of their own. Remember the little girl that disappeared at the theme park in Fort Lauderdale a few years ago? The parents were just like the Dockerys."

Sally dropped her hands and thought about it.

"You're right, they were," she said.

Again I pointed into the next room. Bonnie had sunk farther into her chair, and was sadly shaking her head.

"Separate them, and let me have a crack at her," I said.

"What exactly are you going to do?"

"I'm going to put the fear of God into her and make her talk."

"Promise me you won't use any rough stuff."

"I already did."

"Promise again."

My face grew hot, and so did my emotions.

"What do you think I am, some kind of crazy vigilante?"

"No, just a man on a mission," she said, looking me straight in the eye.

I held her gaze. "All right. No rough stuff. That's a promise."

"Thank you."

"Do you have something I can record my interrogation with?"

"The room's already wired," Sally said.

Bonnie and Cecil were separated.

Before I went in to speak with Bonnie, I decided I needed to look like a Disney employee if my words were going to carry any weight. Sally tried to find a Disney shirt for me to wear, but nothing close to my size was available. I settled for a hastily constructed laminated badge with my name printed on it. To add to the picture, Sally gave me a copy of the internal newsletter that Disney's forty thousand employees received each week.

"Good luck," she said.

I entered the interrogation room with the newsletter tucked under my arm. Bonnie lifted her head but did not speak. I removed a pack of gum I'd bought from a hallway vending machine and offered her a stick. She refused with a shake of her head.

"Take one," I said. "It will make you feel better."

She changed her mind and took a stick.

"Who are you?" she demanded.

"Human resources. I came about your boys. They're yours, aren't they?"

She ripped the paper off the gum and shoved the stick into her mouth.

"I want to talk to a lawyer," she said, chewing vigorously.

"You mean Leonard Snook?"

"Whatever his name is, I want to talk to him."

"He's Cecil's lawyer. Is he your lawyer, too?"

"Damn straight," she said.

"Trust me, Bonnie, you *don't* want to talk to him," I said, pocketing the gum.

"Why the hell not?"

"Leonard Snook won't do those boys any good. Now, whose are they?"

She crossed her arms defiantly in front of her chest. "You're violating my civil rights. I'll sue this park and Michael Eisner and Walt Disney if you don't let me talk to my lawyer. Understand that, Mr. Human Resources?"

I casually leaned against the mirror, studying her. She had a perfectly even tan that I guessed had come from a tanning salon, and her eyes were too blue to be anything but contacts. The amazing artificial woman.

"Do you know anything about Leonard Snook?" I asked.

"What's there to know?" she snapped.

"Leonard Snook is a criminal defense attorney who represents serial murderers and career criminals. Call him, and you're all but admitting that you're guilty, and those two boys will get placed in a state foster home. You don't want that to happen, do you?"

"I want to speak with my lawyer."

"I'm here for the boys' sake," I said. "If you had an ounce of compassion for their well-being, you'd answer the question."

Bonnie's face started to crack. Then, just as quickly, her icy demeanor returned.

"Go away," she said.

* * *

I slammed the door behind me. The best way to deal with scum like Bonnie Sizemore was to scream at them while threatening bodily harm. It was the only way to penetrate the callous layer of skin that had wrapped itself around their hearts. But I had promised Sally I wouldn't resort to those tactics, and I was a man of my word.

I went down the hall to the room where Cecil was being held. Sally was working him over, and through the door I could hear Cecil telling her the same things Bonnie had told me. He wanted to speak to Leonard Snook, and he wanted to speak to him now.

I leaned against the wall and listened to Cecil's verbal barrage. He had his answers down pat and didn't sound intimidated by Sally's threats of a lifetime in jail. Eventually, Sally would have to turn him and Bonnie over to the Orange County Sheriff's Department or risk ruining the police's ability to prosecute.

I tore a corner off the Disney newsletter to stick my gum in. On the newsletter's cover was a photograph of a comic/impersonator named Brian Cox. Cox was headlining at Disney's Islands of Adventure nightclub, and the newsletter urged Disney employees to come out and see the show. It gave me an idea, and I knocked on the door. Sally opened the door with an exasperated look on her face.

"Any luck?" she asked.

"No, but I've got an idea," I said.

Sally came into the hall and shut the door. I showed her the article about Brian Cox.

"I once used an impersonator to crack a witness in Fort Lauderdale," I said. "Maybe I can get this guy to help me crack Bonnie. Think you can track him down?"

Sally read the article while studying Cox's photo. Cox had spiked hair, a lopsided grin, and bulging eyes.

"I don't know, Jack. He looks like a lunatic."

"The article says he does great impressions. It's worth a shot."

She handed me the newsletter. Her eyes looked tired.

"You don't give up, do you?" she said.

"Never," I said.

CHAPTER TWENTY-NINE

Sally made a couple of phone calls and located Brian Cox. He was staying at a hotel on International Drive. I called the hotel, and an operator put me through to his room. Cox answered and sounded dead-asleep. After some gentle persuasion he agreed to help.

Twenty minutes later, Cox pulled into the security area and got out of his rental car. He was unshaven, skinny to the point of being unhealthy, and clad in rumpled black clothes. His spiked hair was mashed to one side of his head. We shook hands.

"Thanks for coming so fast," I said.

"I'm a comic," he said. "What else have I got to do?"

I took him into the basement of the security building and introduced him to Sally, who'd remained outside the room Cecil Cooper was being kept in. Sally eyed Cox skeptically, then looked at me.

"Exactly what do you want to do?" she asked.

"I want Brian to listen to Cecil while you interrogate him," I said. "Hopefully, Brian will be able to mimic Cecil's voice, and we can trick Bonnie into confessing."

"How good are you?" Sally asked him.

Brian's face turned semiserious, and he launched into a series of famous voices, jumping from a mean Humphrey

Bogart to a boisterous John Wayne to a wimpy-voiced Mike Tyson without pausing to catch his breath.

"I'm impressed," Sally said. "Okay, let's give it a try."

Sally went into the room where Cecil was being kept, along with a guard who was watching him. She left the door ajar and began to question Cecil. Before she could finish her first sentence, Cecil exploded.

"I want to speak to my fucking attorney, and I want to speak to him right now," Cecil shouted. "You fucking people don't scare me. You think because you're rich you can push everyday folks around. Well, I ain't being pushed!"

Brian stood by the door, listening hard.

"Piece of cake," he said.

A few minutes later I entered the interrogation room where Bonnie Sizemore was sitting, and left the door open. I looked at Bonnie while sadly shaking my head.

"What do you want?" Bonnie asked.

"You had your chance, and you blew it," I said.

"What's that supposed to mean?"

"I told you to come clean, didn't I? Now you and your boys are screwed."

"Screwed how? What are you talking about?"

"Cecil sold you down the river."

The blood drained from her tanned face, leaving the skin a sickly caramel color. "Cecil wouldn't do that. You're lying, mister."

"I just heard him," I said. "Put a pair of mouse ears on him, and he'd look like a giant rat. Come here and listen if you don't believe me."

Bonnie joined me at the door. I glanced down the hallway at Sally, who stood inside the doorway to a vacant room where Brian was hiding. Cecil was gone, having been taken upstairs. I gave Sally the high sign.

"Listen," I told Bonnie.

"It was Bonnie's idea to grab the kid inside the park," Brian said in Cecil's rough voice. "I told her it was a big mistake, but she always wanted a little girl. She can be mighty demanding when she wants stuff. Fucking-A, sometimes I can't control her. So I just went along, you know what I'm saying? She grabbed the kid and cut her hair and spray-painted her sneakers blue. It was all her idea. I was just along for the ride."

"That's a fucking lie!" Bonnie screamed.

I shut the door and pointed at the chair. "Sit down."

"Cecil's lying. He talked me into it. You've got to believe me, mister."

"Are those boys your sons?" I asked.

Bonnie backed into the wall. Her hands had balled into fists and she was breathing hard, her conscience crashing down upon her like a suffocating wall of sand. I took out my pack of gum and put a stick into her hand. She unwrapped the stick and shoved it into her mouth. Her mouth worked the gum hard, and she calmed down. I repeated my question.

"Yeah, they're my kids," she said softly.

"They didn't know what was going on, did they?"

"No, sir."

"How about you?"

"Cecil told me it was a custody thing. He said the little girl's mother wanted her back and was paying Cecil five thousand dollars to snatch her inside the Magic Kingdom theme park. Cecil said the mother got screwed in a divorce, and that we'd be doing her a big favor."

"When did Cecil tell you this?"

"This morning. He called me from a motel in Kissimmee, asked me to drive over with my boys. I said sure."

"Did Cecil pay you, Bonnie?"

Shamed by the question, Bonnie looked up at the ceiling. "He was going to give me five hundred dollars. I ain't worked in a while and needed the money to buy clothes for my boys. I thought I was doing the mother a favor. I been divorced. I know what it's like to fight for your kids."

Bonnie started to cry. The tears were left to run their course, her hands pressed against the wall for support. I stepped back and cracked the door. Sally stood in the hallway with Brian. I gave her a thumbs-up. Sally and Brian exchanged jubilant high-fives, and I shut the door.

"Mister, will you answer a question for me?" Bonnie asked.

I already knew what the question was, and simply nodded.

"Am I going away? You know. To prison."

The answer was yes. Her attorney might convince a judge that Bonnie was lied to and manipulated by Cecil, and if the attorney was any good, he'd get the most serious charges against her dropped. But in the end, Bonnie would do hard time.

But I wasn't going to tell Bonnie that. I was not her friend, and was every bit as cunning and deceptive as she was. It was the only way justice could be served.

"It all depends on how cooperative you are," I said.

"I'll do whatever you want," she said.

CHAPTER THIRTY

Jack Carpenter, I can't believe you talked me into doing this," Sally scolded me a half hour later.

"Believe it," I replied, my eyes glued to the road.

"But this is wrong. We're breaking the law."

"What law is that?" I asked. "I just want to look inside Cecil Cooper's motel room before the police do. I won't touch anything or remove anything. I just want to see what the guy was up to. How is that breaking the law?"

"If the police find out, we're both screwed, and you know it."

"I thought Disney owned the police."

"That's not funny," Sally said.

We were driving down motel row in Kissimmee, staring at god-awful billboards and elevated signs. There were more motels, putt-putt golf courses, and cheap family restaurants on this nine-mile strip of highway than anyplace else on earth. We were looking for the motel whose name was printed on the plastic room key that Sally had found tucked inside Cecil's billfold. The motel was called Sleep & Save, its logo a cartoon of a man lying in bed, dreaming of dollar signs. Bonnie had told me that she'd seen computer equipment in the room when she'd met up with Cecil that morning, and I wanted to examine the equipment before the police did.

A mile later, Sally spotted the motel and jumped in her seat. "There it is. Sandwiched between the IHOP and the Big Boy."

I tapped my brakes while glancing in my mirror. A tourist driving a minivan was hugging my bumper, and I didn't want to get rear-ended. Seeing him slow down, I made my turn, parked in front of the Sleep & Save's main office, and killed the engine.

"Speaking of big boys, how's that guy you've been dating?" I asked.

"You mean Russ? Oh shit, I don't know."

Back when Sally lived in Fort Lauderdale, she had a slew of boyfriends, each one a bigger loser than the last. After she moved to Orlando, I started hearing about a subcontractor named Russ, and I'd been rooting for it to work out.

"What's wrong?" I asked.

She gave me a sly look out of the corner of her eye. Guys wouldn't admit this, but it was those little looks from women that turned them on more than anything else. Sally had always turned me on, and always would.

"Sure you want to hear?" she asked.

"Yes. Russ sounded like a good guy."

"He *is* a good guy. But I found out he's got a record and did time."

"What for?"

"Possession of narcotics."

"Sorry to hear that."

"Can I ask you a personal question, Jack?"

I didn't like talking about my personal life, for no other reason than it's such a mess. I nodded reluctantly.

"Do you believe that criminals can be reformed?" Sally asked. "Is it possible for people to truly change their behavior?"

I leaned back in my seat, the sound making a soft *whoosh*. Buster looked up from the back. He was acting great around Sally, and I was beginning to wonder if my wife's comment about his behavior being tied to my acquaintances in Fort Lauderdale was true.

"I'd have to say no to both questions," I answered.

Sally fell back in her seat as well.

"Well, that's a definitive answer."

"Criminals don't reform," I explained. "At least, not any I've encountered. They always walk around with larceny in their hearts. They might get scared into going straight, but they don't change. Now, let me ask you a question."

"Shoot."

"Is Russ really a criminal?"

"I told you, he's got a record and did time."

"But is he a criminal? Does he walk around every day with bad intentions and evil thoughts? That's a criminal. Or is Russ a decent guy who did something dumb and has paid his debt to society? If that's the case, you ought to give him a break."

"Aren't we being generous?" Sally said.

I turned and faced her. "I drove to Tampa this morning to apologize to my wife for fucking up our twenty-year marriage. She forgave me. It was one of the nicest things anyone's ever done for me."

"You're getting back together with Rose?"

I nodded, and Sally leaned across the seats and hugged me.

"Oh, Jack, I'm so happy for you."

* * *

Sleep & Save was part of a nationwide chain, if the sign by the front desk was to be believed. In reality, it was a world-class dump, with rooms going for $29.99 a night and a bank of vending machines that sold soft drinks and candy in the main office.

The manager was a smiling Pakistani with two rows of perfect white teeth. He stood behind the counter, tapping the keyboard to a computer. Sally and I had worked several cases together, and I knew her well enough to let her take the lead. Pressing her stomach to the counter, she batted her eyelashes.

"Hi," she said.

"Good afternoon," the manager said brightly.

"Can you help me?"

"I will certainly try."

"My brother is staying here, and we're supposed to be meeting him outside his room, only like a dummy I didn't write down the number when he gave it to me this morning. Can you help me?"

The manager stared at the Disney logo on Sally's shirt. Despite what Sally had said earlier, Disney ran Orlando and practically everything around it, and it wasn't uncommon for people to bend over backwards to help Disney employees. The manager flipped open the registration log lying on the desk.

"What is your brother's name?"

"Cecil Cooper."

The manager ran his finger down the page. "Here it is. C. Cooper. Room 42. Your brother is staying on the second floor."

"Oh, thank you so much. You're so sweet!"

Outside, we took a set of stairs to the second floor. The

motel was beside the highway, and the endless drone of passing cars was giving me a headache. We found Room 42 at the end of the building, a DO NOT DISTURB sign hanging from the knob. Sally extracted Cecil's room key from her purse, then grabbed my wrist with her other hand.

"You've been working out, haven't you?" I said.

"Promise me you won't take anything, Jack."

"Didn't you believe me the first time?"

"No, I have trust issues with men."

"I won't take anything," I promised.

Cecil's room was about what you'd expect for $29.99 a night. Rickety furniture, threadbare carpet, smoky mirrored walls that desperately needed a shot of Windex, a slab for a bed. Sally shut the door behind us, and we were thrown into darkness. I heard her hand scrape the wall, then the lights came on.

Sally checked the bathroom while I looked around the bedroom. Except for an ashtray overflowing with cigarette butts and several dead soldiers in the trash, the room was clean. Next to the telephone was a notepad with deep indentations in the top page, indicating that someone had recently written on it. Holding the notepad beneath the light, I attempted to read the indentations, only they were too faint.

"Have a pencil?" I asked Sally.

"There's a mechanical one in my purse," she said.

Sally's purse was on the bed. I removed the mechanical pencil from a side pocket and extended the lead. Holding the lead sideways, I used it to shade the top page of the notepad. Before my eyes, the indentations turned into words.

P: Tram, Peggy Sue
K: Shannon (age 3)
C: Ford Pickup
L: BSX 4V6
P: Magic Kingdom
KID LOVES MICKEY

Cecil hadn't impressed me as a detail guy, yet the notepad indicated otherwise. Cecil knew exactly who he was tracking, right down to which theme park the Dockerys were planning to visit, and Shannon's fascination with Mickey Mouse. Sally came out of the bathroom, and I showed her the notepad. Her eyes grew wide.

"Wow. How did he get all that information?"

"That's what I need to find out."

"Think he was stalking them?"

"Could be."

"Did you check beneath the bed?"

"Not yet."

Kneeling, Sally stuck her hands beneath the bed and pulled out a cracked leather satchel. I knelt down beside her, and our heads nearly knocked. She opened the satchel and dumped its contents onto the bed. It contained a thin Dell notebook computer, a portable HP printer, and four grainy eight-by-ten photographs.

"Aren't you glad I talked you into this?" I asked.

"Yes," she said.

Sally spread the photographs on the bed. The first three showed Tram Dockery behind the wheel of his pickup truck with a six-pack of Old Milwaukee in his lap. There was a baby seat in back, and Shannon was strapped in. Tram had told me he'd gotten drunk that morning, but he'd never mentioned his daughter was with him. The fourth photograph showed the rear of the pickup, the license plate plainly visible.

"Cecil must have snapped these pictures," Sally said.

I stared at the six-pack in the photo. There were five unopened cans in the pack. Tram wasn't drunk when the photographs were taken.

"Tram would have seen him," I said.

"Maybe Cecil used a telescopic lens."

I took one of the photographs off the bed and held it up to the light. It was printed on cheap paper, and I shook my head.

"Cecil didn't take these photographs. He printed them off his computer."

We both studied the photographs some more.

"You think someone e-mailed the photos to him on his computer?" Sally asked.

I nodded.

"What about the information on the pad? Did someone send him that as well?"

I nodded again.

"So there's a third person involved?"

I thought back to the photograph of Simon Skell's gang I'd seen at the Fox TV station. Skell was the mastermind, Bash the front man, the Hispanic the abductor, and the blond-haired mystery man the information-gatherer. If this was indeed an organized gang of abductors working together, then the mystery man was doing more than just gathering information. He was also forming profiles of victims for his gang, and possibly other gangs as well.

"Yes," I said.

"Do you think he's driving around and randomly photographing people?"

I studied the pad with the notations. "That wouldn't explain how's he getting the rest of the information."

"I don't know, Jack. I'm just stabbing in the dark."

I picked up the other three photographs from the bed. "I need to show these to Tram Dockery. He'll know where they were taken."

Sally snatched the photographs out of my hand.

"No, you don't," she said.

"What do you mean?"

"You're not taking the photographs to show Tram."

"Then just give me one. That's all I'll need to jar his memory."

"God damn it, Jack, you promised me."

I looked into her eyes. I had crossed over the fragile line of our friendship.

"Give me one, and tell the police you found three photographs in the satchel," I said. "What harm will that do?"

"They're evidence."

"I need to show one of the photographs to Tram. Come on, Sally, don't you want me to crack this thing?"

"You promised me. Isn't your word worth anything, Jack?"

I blew out my cheeks. A little voice inside my head was telling me to snatch one of the photographs out of Sally's hand and run for the door. Even if Sally caught up to me, she wasn't strong enough to make me give it back.

Only another little voice—perhaps my conscience—was telling me not to think these dangerous thoughts. Sally was my friend and confidante, and I'd given her my word. Once upon a time, my word had actually meant something.

So what had happened? I guess I'd changed. Now I was

willing to make promises that I didn't intend to keep, and do things I've never done before. I'd been pulled to the dark side. Yet, I didn't know what else to do.

"Think about it," I heard myself say. "Shannon Dockery was the *perfect* victim for an abduction. Someone secretly gathered that information and sent it to Cecil on his computer. A profiler."

Sally held the photographs protectively against her chest.

"No," she added for emphasis.

I couldn't be in the same room with Sally anymore. I went to the door, jerked it open, and stepped outside. The sky had blackened with storm clouds, and a stiff wind was shooting garbage around the parking lot. The day my sister died, she looked out her hospital room window at a storm similar to this one and told me how beautiful it looked. I was not born with my sister's optimism, and now I saw only bleakness and despair in the murderous clouds.

Inside the room, I heard Sally call the Orange County Sheriff's Department on her cell and ask for a certain detective by name. She told the detective everything that had happened in the past two hours, including Cecil's room number at the Sleep & Save. Hanging up, she came outside and took my hand.

"You okay?" she asked.

"I'll live," I said.

"Are we still friends?"

"I sure hope so."

"You are so pitiful when you pout," she said.

"You think so?"

"Yes. Most men are."

"And I thought I was special."

Sally led me downstairs. At the motel's front desk, she sweet-talked the manager into making copies of the photographs on his copier. I hugged her fiercely when we were outside, holding the copies in my hand.

"Now go figure this thing out," she said.

CHAPTER THIRTY-ONE

I could not find Tram Dockery.

Tram had told me his family was staying at a Disney hotel. I called Disney's main number and got patched into his room. When no one answered, an operator came on the line. I asked her which of Disney's twenty hotels the Dockerys were staying in. She refused to divulge the information.

I decided to wait Tram out. I was banking on his returning to their room, even though there was the chance he'd left without checking out and driven home to Georgia. After a day like he'd had, I wouldn't have blamed him.

I sat in my car in the Sleep & Save's parking lot and watched the storm, which had grown to biblical proportions. Sally was upstairs dealing with the police and had said she'd grab a lift back to her office.

Crashes of lightning and gusts of howling wind shook the ground, and Buster began to whine. Making him stay in the car during a storm was torture, and I went inside the motel's main office.

"I need a room for a few hours," I said.

The manager raised his eyebrows in alarm.

"To wait out the storm," I explained.

The manager cut me a deal, and I paid him up front.

Outside, I let Buster out of the car, and we ran to the room dodging raindrops.

The room was a newer version of Cecil's, the fabrics and carpet more alive. I lay on the bed with Buster curled up beside me. It was comforting being in bed during a storm, and before I knew it, I was sound asleep.

A clap of thunder awoke me. The digital clock on the night table said nine o'clock. I grabbed my phone and called the Disney main number. There was still no answer in Tram's room. I weighed leaving a message but wasn't sure how to tell him about the photographs without scaring the hell out of him. I hung up in frustration.

I powered up the TV. It had nine channels, just like the good old days. I found CNN, the clipped format exactly what my brain needed. At the top of the broadcast was a story about Skell's impending release from Starke. Leonard Snook stood on the Broward County courthouse steps, looking resplendent in a blue suit and glowing yellow tie. He was talking while triumphantly waving several sheets of paper in his hand. If I hadn't known better, I would have thought he'd just sold his first car.

Dressed in black, Lorna Sue Mutter stood beside him. She was content to bask in Snook's oratory and looked at him in a way that only confirmed my earlier suspicions about them sleeping together. I raised the volume with the remote.

"Today, my client, Simon Skell, was exonerated of the charge of murder in the first degree," Snook said into the reporters' bouquet of microphones. "Justice has been served."

"Will your client be suing the police for false imprisonment?" a reporter asked.

"No comment," Snook said.

"How about Detective Jack Carpenter? Will your client sue him?"

"No, he will not," Snook said.

Of course he wasn't suing me. I didn't have any money.

"When will Simon Skell be released from prison?" another reporter asked.

"The orders for my client's release have been sent to the warden at Starke," Snook replied. "Hopefully, he will act swiftly."

"Will Skell be released today?"

Snook frowned. The warden at Starke was a hard-ass named Einbinder. Einbinder knew all about Skell, courtesy of yours truly. My guess was Einbinder would delay Skell's release and give the police extra time to find evidence against him.

"That's out of my hands," Snook said.

A reporter shoved a mike into Lorna Sue's face.

"Have you spoken to your husband recently?" he asked.

Lorna Sue beamed beatifically. "Why yes, I spoke with Simon earlier. He asked me to personally thank everyone who's been praying for him. He looks forward to being a free man very soon."

My sandal hit the screen. Luckily it stayed intact, and I saw something that I hadn't seen before. Standing behind Lorna Sue was a man wearing stylish tinted glasses and a diamond stud earring. His name was Chase Winters, and he was a Hollywood producer of some repute. I knew Chase because I had nearly sold him my life story when I was desperate for cash. I'd thought he was a straight shooter until he told me over lunch that he needed to take "artistic license" with the facts of the case. When I asked what that meant, Winters explained that he wanted to turn all of the Midnight Rambler's victims into strippers because it would help sell the movie overseas. Instead of punching his lights out, I walked away from the deal. Seeing him with Lorna Sue, I assumed he'd found someone more willing to bend the truth to his liking.

I killed the TV. Then I called Disney's main number and asked for Tram Dockery's room. To my relief, Tram picked up.

"This is Jack," I said.

"Hey, Jack," Tram said brightly. "How's it going?"

"Not so good. You and I need to talk."

The Dockerys were staying at Disney's Wilderness Lodge. The lodge was situated on several heavily wooded acres, the roads unmarked and poorly lit. I pulled in twenty minutes later and let Buster sniff trees before entering the main building.

Wilderness Lodge was Jessie's favorite hotel growing up, and our family had stayed there many times on vacation. Modeled after the Old Faithful Inn at Yellowstone National Park, the main building was the world's largest man-made log structure, with each massive log fitted in place without the use of glue or nails. A woman in cowboy attire greeted me at the front desk.

"Howdy," she said.

"House phones," I said.

She pointed to a stand by the elevators, then handed me a brochure.

"Have a nice evening," she said.

I called Tram's room and asked him to meet me in the lobby. He sounded worried and said he'd be right down.

I made myself comfortable on a sprawling leather couch and leafed through the brochure the receptionist had given me. It was called the Hidden Mickey Hunt and was a special promotion for guests staying at the Lodge. Eight hidden images of Mickey Mouse were carved into the balconies of different rooms, while another eight were hidden around the property in the landscaping. Every guest who found all sixteen won a special prize. I thought of Shannon Dockery and wondered how many she'd found so far.

"Hey," a voice said.

I rose from the couch. Tram had come out of an elevator and was walking toward me. He wore a clean plaid shirt and had a fresh part in his hair. I didn't believe in beating around the bush, so I showed him the photographs from Cecil's room. He gasped.

"Who took these?" Tram asked.

"That was what I was hoping you'd tell me," I said.

He studied the photographs, then shook his head.

"I don't know," he said.

"Did you notice any cars following you this morning?" I asked.

"Not that I remember."

"Before you left the lodge, did someone talk to you in the lobby, or maybe outside when you got to your truck? Someone suspicious?"

Tram's eyes were burning a hole in the photographs, and I sensed he was having a hard time remembering. Scaring the living daylights out of people worked wonders on their memory. I led him over to the crackling fireplace in the room's center and put my hand on his shoulder.

"I'd like nothing better than to throw these photographs in the fire, but that won't change things," I said.

"What do you mean?" he asked.

"The police have a copy. They're going to want to talk to you."

"Shiiit." He drew the word out as if he was sliding in it. "So my wife's going to find out I was drinking with my daughter in my pickup."

"Yup."

"Oh, man, I'm screwed."

Everyone hates the bearer of bad news, and Tram shot me a mean stare. I felt bad for him. There was no greater shame than letting your kid down.

"I've got an idea," I said.

His eyes turned hopeful.

"Tell your wife you only drank one of the beers," I suggested. "Then you realized you were making a mistake and tossed the rest out."

Tram gave it some thought.

"Yeah, that will work," he said.

"But you still need to be apologetic."

"And admit I was wrong."

"Yes."

He studied the photographs some more.

"Where did you find these?" he asked.

"In the motel room of the man who snatched Shannon," I said. "Someone sent them to him on his computer, along with a lot of information about you and your wife and daughter."

"How the heck could someone know all that?"

"That's what I want to find out. I want you to reconstruct what you did this morning, from the moment you took your daughter out in your pickup."

The fire's flames illuminated Tram's face as he tried to reconstruct his morning.

"I took Shannon to McDonald's, bought a six-pack of

beer, drove around for a while, then came back here and picked up Peggy Sue. No, wait. I bought the six-pack first, then went to McD's."

He lifted the photograph, counting the beers left in the six-pack.

"Heck. I know where this was taken," he said.

"You do?"

"Yessir. On the drive-through at McD's."

"Are you sure?"

"Uh-huh. You know the expression 'Your first beer is your best beer'? Well, my first beer this morning was sitting on line at McD's drive-through, waiting for my grub. I placed my order, popped a brewski, and got a buzz on."

Tram impressed me as a guy who would remember something like this, and I stared deeply into the fire. Julie and Carmella Lopez had gone to a McDonald's restaurant in Fort Lauderdale the morning that Carmella disappeared. I'd found another link.

"They must've been listening to me inside the restaurant," Tram went on. "I called my sister on my cell and told her what we were doing today."

"You think someone inside the restaurant was listening through the order box," I said.

"Yessir," Tram said. "I bet they photographed me through that thing, and listened to me as well. That must be how they knew all that stuff."

I continued to stare into the flames. There was something wrong with Tram's explanation. I'd seen the order stations inside McDonald's restaurants, and they were right by the kitchens. An employee couldn't spy on cars in the drive-through without other employees noticing. I was still missing a piece of my puzzle, but I suspected that a trip to the local McDonald's would answer my questions.

"Thanks. You've been really helpful," I said.

"No problem," Tram said.

I handed him the brochure. "Does your daughter know about this?"

"Heck, yeah. She found them all. Bet you didn't see the one in front of us."

I shook my head, and Tram pointed at the protective metal screen covering the fireplace. A hidden silhouette of Mickey Mouse was carved into it. Mickey was waving to us, and I found myself nodding. If I'd learned anything as a cop, it was that you had to search for the good and bad in this world. It was all out there, if you knew where to look.

CHAPTER THIRTY-TWO

Tram walked me to the lodge's entrance. I asked him the location of the McDonald's where he'd bought breakfast, and he said it was in Kissimmee. When he described the landmarks, I realized it was a stone's throw from Sleep & Save. I started to leave.

"I need to ask you something," Tram said.

I stopped in the doorway and waited for him to finish.

"I never got your last name," he said. "Folks back home in Douglas are gonna want to know who you are when I tell them this story."

The idea that this kid was going to be telling stories about me made me smile.

"It's Carpenter," I said.

"That works."

I hesitated, unsure of what he meant.

"Carpenters fix things," he said.

I smiled at him. I'd come to the conclusion that he wasn't a criminal, just a young guy prone to making dumb decisions, and I hoped that this experience had taught him a lesson. Then I went outside.

A wet kiss on my wrist turned my head to the sky. Another storm had rolled in, and I reached my car just as the downpour began. Buster sat on the passenger seat, looking ready to call it a day.

I found the weather on the radio. A storm front was parked in the Gulf, and heavy rain was predicted for several days. It was the price you paid for living in the tropics. I left Disney unable to see twenty feet in front of my car.

Pulling into the Kissimmee McDonald's twenty minutes later, I was shocked to see it closing for the night. I entered to find a black kid wearing a hairnet mopping the floors. He shot me an annoyed look, and I stood on the mat with water dripping off my hair.

"We're closed," the kid said.

"The sign says 'Open 24 hours.' "

"I have to mop up," he explained. "Don't want customers coming in and slipping on the wet floor. Then we'll get sued."

"When will you reopen?"

"Once the night manager gets here."

"When will that be?"

The kid smirked, leaving me to believe the night manager would show up whenever he pleased.

"I need your help," I said.

The kid rested his chin on the end of his mop and gazed at me reflectively. He looked seventeen but had the eyes of a much older man. His name tag said Jerome.

"What's this about?" Jerome asked.

"I need to ask you a couple of questions. I'm doing some work for Disney. It's concerning a little girl who was abducted in the Magic Kingdom theme park earlier today."

Jerome looked me up and down. He would have made

a helluva poker player, because I couldn't read what he was thinking.

"No offense, but are you *really* working for Disney?" he asked.

It took me a moment to catch his drift. Disney didn't allow long hair or scruffy clothes on anyone in their ranks, and I had both. I extracted a dog-eared Broward County Sheriff's Department business card from my wallet and shoved it into Jerome's hand. His facial expression didn't change, so I showed him my driver's license. He studied the names on each, then handed both back.

"Ask away," he said.

"I need to see the computer that takes orders from customers in your drive-through," I said.

"Sure. You mind taking off your sandals? I don't feel like mopping the floor again."

I kicked off my sandals. I could feel my heart pounding in my chest the way it did when I ran track. The finish line was in sight, my marathon almost over.

I followed Jerome around the counter to a workstation beside the take-out window. The station was small and contained a computer, a flat touch-screen, and a microphone used to talk to customers outside. Something was wrong with the picture, and I felt myself shudder.

"Where's the printer?" I asked.

"There isn't one," Jerome said.

"How do you print the customer's orders?"

"We don't," Jerome said matter-of-factly. "Everything's computerized and appears on the screen. Only thing that gets printed is the customer's receipt."

In a panic, I pulled the photos of Tram from my pocket. Jerome examined each one, his demeanor of someone sincerely trying to help. Which is why the next words out of his mouth crushed me.

"Sorry, but these photographs didn't come from here," he said.

"But they were taken of someone sitting in your drive-through," I said.

"Maybe so, but there's nothing to print them in the restaurant. Even if there was, none of the managers would allow it. Now, if you don't mind, I need to finish mopping the floor."

The game was over. I had run out of road.

I sat in the suffocating darkness of my car and listened to the rain. Out in the road, a pair of police cruisers and an ambulance were attending to a collision at an intersection, their flashing bubble lights turning the night a sad pink. People were hurt, with medics attending to the drivers of both vehicles. I would have gone out and helped if I'd thought it would do some good. But I'd have only been in the way, making a bad situation worse.

Buster rested his head in my lap and began to snore. I decided to get back on the Florida Turnpike and head north to Starke. I needed to be there when Skell was released. I wanted him to know that he hadn't won. Being there was the only way I knew to tell him this.

My cell phone rang. I wanted it to be Ken Linderman or Scott Saunders calling with some piece of good news. Grabbing the phone off the dash, I stared at its face. It was Melinda. I said hello so loudly that Buster was jostled from his slumber.

There was no reply.

"Melinda, are you there?"

In the background, Mick Jagger was singing the chorus

from the live version of "Midnight Rambler": "Don't you do that. Oh, don't do that!"

"Jack," Melinda whispered.

"I'm here," I said.

"Help me."

There was a cloudburst directly over my car. I pressed the cell phone to my face.

"Tell me where you are, and I'll come and help you."

"I'm hanging in the closet of some fucking Cuban guy's house. I pulled my cell phone out of my purse with my toes. You gotta help me."

"Is that why you didn't want me calling you back?"

"Yeah."

"Did this Cuban guy kidnap you from your apartment?"

"Yeah. There were two of them."

"What does the Cuban guy look like?"

"I don't fucking know."

"Think hard. Does he have a scar running down the side of his face?"

"Yeah."

"Do you know where the house is?"

"Somewhere in western Broward. You gotta find me, Jack."

"I'm trying to. Do whatever he tells you to do. Okay?"

"I'm sorry for what I said on the radio. He made me. I yelled out a couple of times, but somehow it got bleeped out."

"It's okay, Melinda. It's okay."

"You sure?"

"Of course I'm sure."

"This guy said he's going to kill me."

"He told you that?"

"Yeah. But he said he was going to wait."

"Did he say why?"

"He said he's waiting for Skell to come back. Skell wants to be there when I die."

I realized what this meant. Melinda would be kept alive by her captors until Skell was out of prison and back in Fort Lauderdale. I could still save her.

"Do you have any idea where you're being kept?"

"Some black guy's house."

"Do you know the address, or a street name?"

"No. Will you do something for me?"

"Sure, whatever you want."

"Feed Razz."

"Who's that?"

"My cat. I don't want him to die."

"I was in your apartment yesterday. I put a bowl of food out for him."

"Thanks."

The music grew louder, the song's four distinct tempo changes picking up speed, driving the melody into my brain like a runaway train. Melinda began to weep. I tried to find something positive to say but came up empty. Finally the song ended.

"Jack, are you still there?"

"Yes, Melinda."

"I need to tell you something."

"I'm listening."

"I love you."

I didn't know how to respond to these words, and shut my eyes.

"Jack."

"Yes, Melinda."

"Do you love me?"

Chances were, I would never see her again. She knew this, and so did I.

"Yes, Melinda."

"Say it. Please."

"I love you, Melinda."

"I knew it."

I heard five short beeps. Melinda shrieked.

"My battery's dying!"

I tried to tell her to stay strong, and found myself talking to a dead phone.

CHAPTER THIRTY-THREE

I buried my face in my hands. The image of Melinda hanging in a killer's closet was tearing me apart. I had gotten her into this mess, and it was my responsibility to get her out.

Only I didn't know how.

The clock on my dash said it was eleven. I decided to call Scott Saunders in Tampa to see if the FBI had matched the Hispanic abductor in Skell's gang against the faces of any known sexual predators. If the FBI could tell me the Hispanic's identity, I could track him down and rescue Melinda. It was a big if, but it was all I had left.

I called Saunders's cell number and got voice mail. I explained my dilemma and left my number. Then I folded my phone and waited for him to call back.

Several cars appeared in the parking lot. Three teenagers wearing McDonald's uniforms went into the restaurant. Then a low-slung Acura coupe squealed in, and a guy with spiked hair and a necktie hurried inside. The night crew had arrived.

I heard my stomach growl. I hadn't eaten dinner. Worse, I hadn't fed my dog. I glanced at Buster and saw his little tail wag.

I entered the drive-through and faced an illuminated

menu with too many choices. Lowering my window, I addressed the order box.

"Ready when you are."

"Welcome to McDonald's," a perky female voice said through the box's speaker. "Would you like to try our dinner combo?"

"What's that?"

"One Big Mac, one bacon–double cheeseburger, one regular fries, and a soft drink for four dollars and ninety-nine cents."

"I'll take two of them. Skip the sodas, and give me a large coffee instead."

"Would you like an ice cream sundae with that?"

"No thanks."

"They're really good."

She was too cheerful, and I made a face at the order box.

"That will be ten dollars and seventy cents," she said. "Will you be paying with cash or a credit card?"

"Cash."

"Please drive forward. Thank you for eating at McDonald's."

I drove around the building. I took the opportunity to look at the outside of the restaurant and see where someone with a camera might hide, and secretly photograph a person sitting in the drive-through.

I studied the grounds but didn't see a good spot. The restaurant sat on a small parcel of land beside the highway. There were no bushes, trees, or trash receptacles where a person might hide. I'd reached another dead end.

I drove up to the take-out window. The guy with the necktie pulled back the slider. His name tag identified him as the night manager.

"Good evening," the manager said. "Two dinner specials and one large coffee for ten dollars and seventy cents."

I handed him a twenty.

"Out of a twenty," the manager said.

I watched him punch the transaction into a computer. Behind him, a uniformed guy worked the counter while two other guys in the kitchen prepared my food. It was a well-run operation, with each employee working at breakneck speed to fill orders. But something didn't feel right. As the manager counted out my change I realized what it was.

"Where's the girl who took my order?" I asked.

"What girl?" the manager said.

"The friendly girl who took my order a minute ago. Where is she?"

"She works someplace else."

The manager's words were slow to sink in.

"She isn't here?" I asked.

"She's in another state, for all I know," the manager said.

The manager was staring at his computer screen, and I stuck my head out my window. A small canopy above the window protected me from the rain.

"How does that work?" I asked.

"We employ a centralized call center to take our orders," he explained. "It speeds up the process, and it's one less employee for me to hassle with."

The manager passed me a bag containing my food. There were no cars behind me, and I pretended to check the bag's contents.

"How does someone in another state send you the order?" I asked.

He pointed at the computer screen. It was the same

computer that Jerome had shown me earlier. "The girl at the call center takes your order, and she also takes an electronic snapshot of you. She e-mails both to my computer, which lets me match you to your order."

"How does she take a picture of me?"

"There's a hidden camera inside the order box."

"Do you have a picture of me on your computer right now?" I asked.

The manager nodded.

"What are you going to do with it?"

"Erase it. What else?"

"Can I see it?"

Before he could answer, I stuck my head out my window, and nearly crawled through the take-out window. On the manager's computer screen was a matrix with four black-and-white photographs. Three of them showed me and Buster taken a few moments before. In one, Buster was licking his privates. Another showed me making a face at the order box. The fourth was a rear shot of the Legend that captured my license plate. I pulled back, and the manager looked relieved.

"I've got one more question," I said.

The manager had run out of patience and didn't reply.

"How many McDonald's use this service? I own a restaurant myself. I'd like to try it out."

"Most of them," the manager said.

"In Orlando?"

"In the state."

Parked in front of the restaurant, I sipped my coffee while watching the rain distort my windshield. I'd given Buster both our meals, and he'd spread the food onto the passenger seat. Normally I cared when he made a mess, but right now I didn't care at all. I'd found the fourth man in Skell's group, the blond-haired guy I'd decided was the information gatherer and profiler.

I'd found him.

The blond-haired guy operated a call center for McDonald's restaurants in Florida. Every day, his operators spoke with thousands of people as they placed orders for food. Because these people didn't know they were being spied upon, they let their guards down, just as I had minutes earlier. They said and did things they'd never do if they thought someone was watching them.

But someone *was* watching them. The blond-haired guy. He sat in the privacy of his office in front of his computer, studying electronic snapshots while eavesdropping on conversations. He told his employees it was for quality control, and no one argued with him because he was the boss. But in reality, he was hunting for victims.

But not just any victims. Like any other predator, he stalked the weak and defenseless. And when he found a young woman that matched his profile, he sent her information and license plate to the other members of the gang, who tracked her down and abducted her.

I thought about Carmella Lopez. She and her sister had gone to a McDonald's the morning of her disappearance, and I wondered what Carmella had done in her car that was a tip-off. Perhaps she'd made a call on her cell and booked a "massage" with a client. Or maybe she'd told Julie something in confidence. Whatever it was, Carmella didn't mean for anyone else to hear. But someone had, and now she was dead.

I cleaned up Buster's mess and tossed it into the bag. Then I drove around the restaurant and entered the drive-through. There were no other cars, and I pulled up to the order box and lowered my window.

"Welcome to McDonald's," a girl with a squeaky voice said. "Would you like to try our dinner combo?"

"Just give me a large coffee," I said.

"Would you like an ice cream sundae with that?"

"No thanks. Can I ask you a question?"

The girl hesitated. "Is this personal?"

"No, it's business related," I said.

"Oh. Well, go ahead."

"I own a couple of fast-food restaurants in Tampa, and I want to hire a company like yours to process my orders."

"No kidding?" she said. "I grew up in Tampa. Which restaurants do you own?"

I had to think fast. I didn't want to name any fast-food restaurants her company might already be doing business with. Near my wife's apartment was a hamburger joint that I'd only seen in Tampa, and I said, "Checkers."

"Really? I love their spicy french fries. They're the best."

"Thanks. So, can I hire you?"

The girl giggled. "You'll have to ask the boss."

"Who's that?"

"Paul Coffen. He owns the company."

"Is that who you report to?"

"Uh-huh."

"Is your company big?"

"Well, there's eighty order takers and Paul."

I hesitated. I wanted to be absolutely certain I had the right person, and said, "You know, I think I met your boss at a fast-food convention. Is he in his early fifties, has blond hair, and likes expensive jewelry?"

"That's him," she said.

"Great. When's a good time to speak with him?"

"Paul usually works really late, but today he went home early."

My skin turned ice cold. It had never occurred to me that her boss might be at work, watching me at this very moment.

"What's your company name?"

"Trojan Communications."

"Where are you located?"

"Fort Lauderdale. Are you really going to hire us? Paul will give me a bonus. He loves it when we bring him new business."

I'll bet he does, I nearly said.

"What's your name?"

"Sherry Collins."

"I'll make sure I mention your name, Sherry."

Sherry gave me the company's phone number and street address, and I scribbled both down on a piece of paper. Trojan Communications was located in downtown Fort Lauderdale, a block away from ritzy Las Olas Boulevard. As rents went, it was one of the more pricey areas of town, which told me that Coffen's company did well. It was another piece of the puzzle that up until now I hadn't understood. Criminal operations were expensive to run, and I'd been wondering who was financing this one. Now I knew.

I thanked Sherry and pulled the Legend up to the take-out window. The night manager was there, and he shot me a suspicious look.

"Back so soon?" he asked.

I handed him my money.

"It's the coffee," I said.

CHAPTER THIRTY-FOUR

I left the McDonald's and drove east through the pouring rain until I reached the entrance for the Florida Turnpike. There was a tollbooth, and I stopped in the median in front of it and threw my car into park.

I sipped my coffee, my mind racing. For the first time since starting my investigation of the Midnight Rambler killings, I had the name and address of someone who'd been involved besides Simon Skell, and I was going to take advantage of it.

I decided to call Ken Linderman and tell him what I'd learned. He was the one law enforcement person I could trust with the information. Linderman had moved to Florida because he believed that Skell was responsible for his daughter's disappearance, and he had as much at stake in bringing Skell's gang to justice as I did. I pulled out his business card and called his cell number. He answered on the first ring.

"This is Jack Carpenter. You awake?" I asked.

"Wide awake," he said. "I was just reaching for the phone to call you."

From anyone else I would have taken this as bullshit, but not Linderman.

"The FBI has identified the Hispanic in the picture from

the National Center for Missing and Exploited Children database," Linderman went on. "He's a known sexual predator named Ajony Perez, also goes by Jonny Perez. He served three years at Krome Prison in Miami for kidnapping and raping a fourteen-year-old girl, got out, and promptly disappeared. Believe it or not, he's got a brother named Paco, who's also in the NCMEC database."

"Predator?"

"Yes. So your theory about Perez having a partner is correct."

"Any luck tracking them down?"

"We contacted the cable company in Fort Lauderdale they work for," Linderman said. "They're both subs working for another subcontractor. The Perez brothers have no known address or phone number."

"Did you contact the Broward police?"

"I just got off the phone with them," Linderman said. "I e-mailed them the brothers' photographs and profiles, and they're going to start hunting for them as well. I'm also going to call the Florida Department of Law Enforcement and alert them."

Linderman's news wasn't great, but I forced myself to look on the bright side. Having the Broward police, the FDLE, and the FBI hunting for the Perez brothers was about as much as I could ask for.

"I've got some news of my own," I said. "Jonny Perez is holding Melinda Peters prisoner in a house in western Broward. He plans to kill her once Skell is released from prison and joins them."

There was silence on the line. Linderman was processing what I'd told him, something I did all the time when dealing with difficult cases. He spoke first.

"How do you know this?"

"Melinda called me a little while ago."

"She called you?"

"That's right. She's hanging by her wrists in Jonny Perez's closet and got her cell phone out of her purse. The phone died while I was talking to her."

"What are you going to do?"

"Rescue her."

There was another short silence. Again, Linderman spoke first.

"How are you going to do that, Jack?"

"I located the blond-haired guy in the photo. The profiler. He owns a call center business in Fort Lauderdale that processes drive-through orders for McDonald's restaurants in the state. That's how he's finding the gang's victims. I'm going to pay him a visit and make him tell me where Melinda is."

"Make him *how*?" Linderman asked.

I didn't answer, which was all the answer Linderman needed.

"Jack, this is a dangerous road you're going down," Linderman said.

I wasn't going to argue with him there.

"Care to join me?" I asked.

I heard Linderman breathing heavily into the phone. The truth was, there was no other road to go down. If the FBI or the police arrested Paul Coffen, he would hire an attorney and clam up, and we'd never find out where Melinda was being held, which was the equivalent of signing her death warrant.

I heard Linderman rise from his chair. Then I heard movement. I imagined him pacing the floor with the phone pressed to his ear while wrestling with his conscience. I'd done the same thing plenty of times when I was a cop. All cops did.

"All right, Jack," he said. "I'll do it your way. What's your game plan?"

"I'm in Orlando, about to drive back to Fort Lauderdale," I said. "I'll call you when I arrive, and we'll meet up at this guy's office, and pay him a visit."

"Are you going to tell me this guy's name?"

"Not until tomorrow," I said.

There was another silence, punctuated by Linderman's heavy breathing.

"Are you're planning to use force to make this guy talk?"

"Do you have another suggestion?" I asked.

Linderman did not reply.

"I also have a request," I said.

"What's that?"

"I want you to send your best agents to Starke to cover Skell when he's released."

"That's already been taken care of," Linderman said. "Special Agent Saunders and his partner are at Starke right now. They'll be tailing Skell the moment he walks out the front gates."

I watched a car pass through the tollbooth in front of me. The FBI had a high opinion of itself. But when it came to deception, my opinion of Skell was much higher. Two FBI agents could not adequately cover him, no matter how well trained.

"That's not good enough," I said.

"Excuse me?" Linderman said.

"Having two agents watch Skell isn't good enough," I said, raising my voice. "This guy is a meticulous planner. He's been thinking about this day for six months, and he has a plan that's taken all these things into consideration."

"How can you be so certain?" Linderman asked.

I sipped my coffee. The answer to that question was simple.

"I just am," I said.

"I'll call Saunders and suggest he add another team," Linderman said.

"Four agents total?"

"That's right."

"Make it six," I said.

"Excuse me?"

"Make it six agents. Three teams of two agents, each team assigned to watch Skell for four hours at a time so they're always sharp. Otherwise, they're bound to slip up."

"This is outrageous, Jack. You can't be telling the FBI what to do."

"If you don't do it, I won't call you tomorrow when I reach Fort Lauderdale."

"Are you trying to blackmail me?"

"Call it whatever you want. That's the deal."

I heard Linderman bump into something and curse.

"You're being unreasonable," he said. "The Bureau is fully aware of the threat that Skell poses. Come to Fort Lauderdale and I'll help you find Melinda Peters. In the meantime, stop worrying about Skell."

There was a finality to his words that should have made me stop. But I didn't.

"I want six agents watching Skell, and I won't settle for anything less," I said. "That's the deal. Take it or leave it."

"What has gotten into you?" he said angrily.

"I'm hanging up the phone," I said.

Linderman let out an exasperated breath.

"All right, Jack. You win. Six agents. You have my word."

"I'll call you when I arrive," I said.

Before I could say good-bye, Linderman slammed down the phone. He sounded mad as hell, and I told myself he'd get over it. I entered the tollbooth and got my ticket, then started my drive to Fort Lauderdale in the lightning and pouring rain.

PART FOUR

DIA DE LOS MUERTOS

CHAPTER THIRTY-FIVE

The downpour turned to a light drizzle around the Vero Beach exit. The highway was humming with vehicles, the water flying up from their wheels in a dangerous but hypnotic ballet. I stayed in the right lane, my speedometer clocking a steady fifty. I wanted to go faster, but there was too much standing water on the road. Barring any delays, I would be home by five a.m.

I had driven this stretch of highway enough times to know its landmarks. One of the most significant was the service center eight miles south of Vero. Reaching it, I left the dead zone I'd been traveling in since Kissimmee, and my cell phone came to life.

A minute later my phone's message bell chimed. I dialed up voice mail and found two messages waiting for me.

The first message was from Rose. It had come in shortly after I hit the road. My wife was lying in bed, and called to say how much she loved me. I'd forgotten the powerful effect those three words had on me, and I listened to the message several times before erasing it.

The second message was from Jessie, and it came in right after my wife's. I could tell from the exuberance in my daughter's voice that she'd spoken to Rose and heard the news about our reconciliation. When Jessie was happy, she talked a mile a minute, and the voice mail cut her off in midsentence. I listened to her message a second time, then erased it as well.

As I neared the Stuart exit fifty minutes later I weighed calling my wife and daughter back. Both were early risers, and I couldn't think of anything I would have enjoyed more than hearing their cheerful voices to begin my day.

I decided against it. If I called them, my wife and daughter would hear the apprehension in my voice and know something was wrong. To be honest, I didn't want to hear it myself, for I just might realize how afraid I was of what lay ahead.

So I played Tom Petty & the Heartbreakers *Damn the Torpedoes* on my tape player. Normally, Petty's sardonic lyrics and hard-driving music cheered me up, and I would join the chorus while tapping my fingers on the wheel. But their magic was lost on me this time, and I stared at the rain-soaked highway and watched the miles clock by.

A few minutes after five I pulled into Tugboat Louie's. A beer delivery truck was parked by the front entrance, and I parked beside it. Kumar had once told me that he trusted his employees with everything but money and alcohol, which was a nice way of saying that he didn't trust them at all. I found him in the bar counting cases of beer.

"Good morning, Jack! How are you? Not used to seeing you up so early in the morning," Kumar said. "How about a fresh cup of coffee?"

"That would be great," I said.

"Can I interest you in something to eat?"

I shook my head. "I just came to pick something up."

"Well, you have a good day."

I went upstairs to my office. Taking out my keys, I unlocked the center drawer of my desk and opened it. The drawer contained my detective's badge, which the department had never asked me to return; a box of .380 copper-jacketed bullets; a pocket holster; and my favorite gun, a Colt 1908 Pocket Hammerless, the best concealment weapon in the world.

I took the gun out of the drawer and cleaned it. The Colt 1908 carried seven rounds and was magazine fed, with a European-style release at the back bottom corner of the grip. It sat easily in my right pants pocket without making a bulge. The gun had gone wherever I had for sixteen years. At times it had been the only thing standing between me and a killer. Not once had it let me down.

I fitted the Colt into the pocket holster, then slipped both into my right pants pocket. The holster had been handmade by an ex-LAPD detective named Robert Mika and was constructed of a moisture-resistant material that kept its interior bone-dry. As a result, the Colt never got stuck because of perspiration, allowing me to draw it in the blink of an eye.

I picked up the box of bullets. Buster was curled at my feet and had not moved a muscle. He'd never liked firearms and would have made a lousy hunting dog.

"Want to go outside?" I asked.

Buster didn't move. I got the hint and left without him.

I walked down the dock that ran alongside the bar. The sky was lightening, and a flock of seagulls circled lazily overhead. My destination was a hangarlike building where people paid to dry-dock their boats. The building was a hundred yards from the bar. The Colt felt good in my pocket, and I tried to remember why I'd stopped carrying it. Perhaps leaving the force had something to do with it.

Or maybe I was afraid I'd use it unwisely, and permanently mess up my life.

Behind the dry-dock building was a clearing where Kumar's employees came during breaks to smoke cigarettes and talk. In the center of the clearing was a rusted garbage can filled with trash. Rummaging through the trash, I found an empty milk carton, tore off its top, and tossed a few rocks into it.

Printed on the milk carton's side was a photograph of a missing boy. His name was Mitchell Thompson, and he had dimples and a wonderfully engaging smile. He had last been seen in Boise, Idaho, over two years before.

On the other side of the milk carton was a picture of his abductor. I looked at the abductor's name to see if they were related. The abductor wasn't identified. He was just another nameless face who had stolen a child.

I put the carton on a tree stump and positioned it so the abductor's photo faced me. Just looking at him made my blood boil. I took ten giant steps back.

For several minutes I practiced drawing the Colt from its holster. The clearing was filled with buzzing mosquitoes, and I was constantly having to swat them away. They were a necessary distraction—there was never a perfect time or place to use a gun. It was all about adjusting.

Then I loaded my weapon and practiced shooting the carton. People think shooting a handgun is easy, but in reality there's nothing easy about it. I held the Colt with both hands in front of me and my knees slightly bent. It was called the Weaver position, considered the most efficient way to shoot a handgun. I pulled the trigger until my weapon was empty.

My aim was lousy. I'd never been a great shot, and time

had only worsened my skills. For every bullet that hit the carton, two missed it completely.

I kept shooting until I was hitting the carton every other time.

Hearing a sharp rustling of leaves, I lowered my weapon so the barrel was aimed at the ground, then looked over my shoulder. Kumar entered the clearing.

"Jack, how can you breathe in here?" he asked.

The air was dense with gunpowder. I picked up the empty casings scattered on the ground and tossed them into the can. Only a handful of bullets remained in the box. I dropped them into my pocket and left the clearing with Kumar by my side. We walked down the dock toward the bar.

"What is wrong, Jack?" he asked.

"Nothing," I said.

"A man does not practice shooting a gun unless something is wrong," Kumar said. "Tell me what the problem is, and I will try to help you."

The sun had popped over the horizon, and the new day had begun. I considered bringing Kumar into my confidence, then decided against it. The things I knew would only depress him. And there was nothing he could do to make them better.

"Who said I was practicing?" I said.

"Please don't play games with me," Kumar said. "I went to my office to do some paperwork. I opened the window, and heard you firing your weapon. I counted over eighty shots. A man does not shoot a weapon that many times unless he's preparing for a gunfight. Are you planning to shoot someone?"

Kumar's words had a powerful effect on me, and I realized he'd hit the nail on the head. Paul Coffen, Neil Bash, and Jonny Perez were more than just murderers. They were my mortal enemies, and I would kill them if I had to, just as I suspected they'd kill me if the opportunity presented itself. And as any cop would tell you, the first rule of a gunfight was to bring a gun.

"Yes," I said.

"Is this person a criminal?"

I nodded.

"Are you scared?" Kumar asked.

"I'd be lying if I said I wasn't," I said.

We had reached the bar. I put my hand on the door, then turned to look into my friend's face. His eyes were open wide. In them, I saw my own fear. Fear was a gift if you listened to it, and I touched the warm gun resting in my pocket.

"I'll be okay," I said.

"What if you are shot? Or killed?" Kumar asked.

"Better not to think that way," I said.

"But what if you are?"

I hadn't weighed that option. Yet, it was an easy one to consider. I had nothing of value to pass on. If I died, all my earthly possessions would probably end up in a Dumpster. Except one.

"If something happens to me, I'd like you to take care of Buster," I said.

"You would?"

"Yes. He likes you."

Kumar acted as if he was going to cry. Instead, he threw his arms around me and held me tightly against his body.

"May almighty God watch over you," he whispered in my ear.

CHAPTER THIRTY-SIX

Las Olas Boulevard was Fort Lauderdale's answer to Rodeo Drive. The three-mile-long, tree-lined street was filled with pricey clothing boutiques and epicurean restaurants. A handful of watering holes were within my price range, but mostly it was stuff I only dreamed about.

Trojan Communications was located one block south of Las Olas in a dramatic two-story building made of chrome and tinted glass. The company's logo—a crooked T made from shiny aluminum—sat by the front entrance in the grass.

At eight-thirty, I pulled in front of the building and called Linderman. He was waiting for my call, and I gave him the address and told him that our suspect worked for the company. I didn't give him Paul Coffen's name, and he didn't ask for it. He agreed to meet me in thirty minutes and said he'd call if traffic was bad.

I then drove east to the beach and walked my dog. The tide was up and the waves were big and loud, and I drank up all the sights and smells, my conversation with Kumar still fresh in my mind.

At eight-fifty I drove back to Trojan Communications and entered the company parking lot. A cream-colored Mercedes 500 SL was parked in a space marked Reserved

P. Coffen, President & CEO. I parked beside the Mercedes and waited.

At eight fifty-five, Linderman arrived and parked beside me. Sitting beside him was a sandy-haired man with a purple scar on his cheek shaped like a question mark. He wore Ray-Bans and a dark suit, as did Linderman. The three of us got out of our cars. Linderman introduced the second man as Special Agent Richard Theis.

"The suspect is named Paul Coffen," I said. "He owns the company and appears to be here. I think we should enter the building separately, in case he happens to be watching the front door on a surveillance camera. I'll go first, then you and Theis follow."

Both men nodded. Theis said, "What's the deal once we're inside?"

"I spoke with one of Coffen's phone operators earlier," I said. "I'm going to use her name with the receptionist, and tell Coffen I'm interested in hiring his company to process calls from a group of Checkers restaurants I own in Tampa."

"What's our role?" Theis asked.

"You're my business partners."

"Works for me," Linderman said.

Theis simply nodded.

I checked my watch. Nine o'clock on the nose. Without another word, I crossed the lot and entered Trojan Communications. I walked with my head bowed, my eyes peeled to the ground. Thirty seconds later, Linderman and Theis followed me.

When I was a cop, I was good at putting myself in the shoes of criminals I dealt with. It allowed me to anticipate how they were going to react when I confronted them.

Most cops are good at this, but I was particularly good at it.

I entered the reception area assuming that Coffen had taken precautionary measures to avoid being arrested. Like bugging his reception area or having a surveillance camera trained on the door. I scanned the reception area and, not seeing any cameras, approached the receptionist, a purple-haired young woman in a miniskirt sitting at a Lucite desk.

"Can I help you?" she asked, snapping her gum.

I was still wearing yesterday's clothes and hadn't shaved. It wasn't my best side, but it would have to do.

"I'm here to see Paul Coffen," I said.

"Do you have an appointment?"

"No."

"Sorry, Mr. Coffen is busy."

"I spoke with an operator named Sherry Collins about hiring your company to handle orders for several fast-food restaurants that I own in Tampa," I said.

Her eyes touched briefly on Linderman and Theis, who flanked me.

"Are these gentlemen with you?"

"Yes, they're my business partners."

"Let me see if Mr. Coffen is available. Can I have your name?"

I nearly said my real name, then caught myself.

"Ken Linderman," I said.

Linderman laughed under his breath. The receptionist pressed a button on the intercom sitting beside the phone. It came alive with a man's voice.

"I'm busy, Heidi."

"I have three gentlemen who are interested in hiring our company to service their restaurants."

"Then I'm not busy," the voice said with good humor. "Would you mind asking them to wait? I'm on a conference call."

The receptionist looked up into our faces expectantly. "Would you gentlemen mind waiting until Mr. Coffen is free?"

"How long do you expect him to be?" I asked.

She asked Coffen how long he was going to be.

"I don't know," Coffen said. "Just ask them to have a seat. I'll be out when I'm done with this call."

No smart businessman made potential customers wait, and I sensed that Coffen was stalling. I looked around the reception area again, then at the desk. The receptionist acted embarrassed and crossed her legs. A tiny button on the intercom caught my eye. It was a miniature camera. Coffen was looking right at us.

"He's onto us," I said.

Behind the desk was a black door marked Private. I started to walk around the desk, and the receptionist rose from her chair.

"You can't go in there," she said.

Linderman pulled out his wallet and showed his badge. "FBI. Sit down and don't move," he said.

She dropped into her chair.

"Jesus," she said.

The black door was locked. Lifting my leg, I kicked three inches above the knob. Both hinges broke at the same time, and the door came crashing down.

I pulled the door out of the way and entered a windowless hallway that ran the length of the building. Through its walls I could hear female phone operators processing fast-food orders from around the state. Their voices seemed to be coming out of nowhere.

Theis and Linderman were right behind me. Theis went left and started checking doors. I headed in the opposite direction with Linderman breathing down my neck.

"Are you armed?" Linderman asked.

"Yes," I said. "How about you?"

"You're a funny guy, Jack."

The hallway's carpet muted our footsteps. I assumed that like most CEOs, Coffen occupied the corner office. At the hallway's end I found his name printed on a plaque nailed to a door. The door was locked and I took it down with my foot. We rushed in.

"FBI," Linderman announced.

The office was light and airy. One wall was nothing but windows; the other three were decorated with paintings of naked girls in provocative poses. Coffen sat at a cherry-and-walnut desk wearing a black designer T-shirt and an array of gold necklaces, his chubby fingers banging the keyboard to his computer. His face was crimson and reminded me of someone having a heart attack. As I came around the desk, I saw why.

His computer had frozen. Imprisoned on the screen was a photograph of Julie and Carmella Lopez sitting inside a car at a McDonald's drive-through. Coffen was trying to erase the image, only the computer wouldn't let him.

"Stop what you're doing," Linderman said.

"Whatever you say," Coffen said.

Coffen pulled open the desk's middle drawer and reached for the automatic pistol resting inside. I threw my hip against the drawer, closing it on his hand. The automatic went off, and a bullet ripped through the desk. Linderman collapsed on the floor.

I punched Coffen in the face. His eyes rolled back into his head, and he passed out.

I retrieved the smoking automatic and placed the barrel under Coffen's nose. The fumes instantly revived him.

"Touch the computer again and I'll kill you," I said.

He gripped the arms of his chair and shook away the cobwebs.

"Whatever you say," he mumbled.

I went around the desk and knelt down beside Linderman. The bullet had clipped him, and he lay on the floor clutching his side.

"I think I cracked a rib," Linderman said.

"You wearing a bulletproof vest?" I asked.

"Yes. We both are."

"Thanks for offering me one."

Linderman didn't know what to say. Rising, I told Coffen to stand up. He slowly came out of his chair. He was flexing his right hand, which was turning an ugly purple.

"Tell me where Melinda Peters is being held," I said.

"Never heard of her," Coffen said.

I glanced at the frozen picture of the Lopez sisters on his computer. Then I looked at Linderman lying on the floor. His presence was only complicating things, and I found myself wishing I'd never asked for his help.

The automatic felt awkward in my hand. I lay it on the desk and drew my Colt. I aimed the Colt at Coffen's belly.

"If you don't tell me where Melinda is, I'm going to kill you," I said.

Coffen's expression was defiant. Like all predators, he was used to dominating the people around him. Nothing was ever going to change that. Not a lifetime in prison, nor endless psychiatric counseling. It was simply who he was.

"Last chance," I said.

Blood was pouring out of his mouth, and Coffen raised his hand and wiped it away. Then he stared at the blood. He looked at me and began to tremble.

"All right," he said.

I looked at the blood as well. I knew that it was a pre-cursor of his new life, for in prison he would be beaten by fellow inmates who felt the need to remind themselves that he was a worse breed than they were. His career as a successful businessman was over, while his role as a pariah was about to begin.

Coffen knew this as well. It was in his face and his pos-ture. His life was about to become a living hell. Which is why I was shocked but not surprised when he bolted around his desk and jumped headfirst through the wall of windows.

CHAPTER THIRTY-SEVEN

I didn't shoot Coffen as he burst through the glass. If I killed him he wouldn't be able to tell me where Melinda was being held, and that was all I cared about right now.

Going to the window, I kicked out the broken glass with my shoe. Coffen was staggering across the parking lot with hideous gashes in his black T-shirt and pants. He wasn't moving very fast, and I didn't anticipate any trouble running him down.

I jumped through the broken window and landed in a standing position. The fall was short, but it made my right knee sing with pain. Coffen was fifty feet away, and I watched him pull a key ring from his pocket as he staggered toward his Mercedes.

Linderman appeared in the broken window above me.

"He's getting away! Take him out!"

I aimed at Coffen's legs and fired. A large hole appeared in the Mercedes's gas tank, and gasoline began pouring out. Four more shots produced the same results. I missed Coffen but kept hitting his expensive sports car.

Coffen got into his car and backed out of his space. Instead of driving toward the exit, he went in reverse and plowed through a thick hibiscus hedge. Reaching the street, he spun the wheel until he was facing Las Olas.

I fired my last two bullets at the gas tank. The Mercedes began to make loud popping noises, followed by a muffled explosion. Within seconds the vehicle became engulfed in bright orange flames.

"Way to go!" Linderman shouted.

I limped toward the burning vehicle while reloading. The flames were intense, and I cautiously approached the driver's door and found it wide open. Coffen had escaped.

My eyes found his bloody trail. It crossed the street and went straight down the sidewalk of Las Olas. Linderman came out of the building and staggered toward me.

"Where's Coffen?"

I pointed down the sidewalk. Something wet touched my wrist, and I looked down to see Buster pinned by my leg.

"Can't you go anywhere without that dog?" Linderman asked.

"No," I said.

We limped down the sidewalk in pursuit. It was early, and most of the stores along Las Olas were closed. Halfway down the block I spotted Coffen hanging on to a lamppost. In his damaged hand was a cell phone, into which he was frantically punching numbers. I knew what he was doing. He was calling Jonny Perez to tell him to kill Melinda.

"Drop the phone!" I shouted.

Coffen saw me and pushed himself off the post. The life was draining from his face, and his eyes were out of focus. Throwing himself across the sidewalk, he disappeared inside a hotel restaurant.

"Get him," I told my dog.

Buster took off running.

* * *

I was moving faster than Linderman and hurried ahead. The restaurant Coffen had gone into was part of the Riverview Hotel, a local landmark. I walked through the main dining area to find several patrons hiding beneath tables.

"Stay down," I said.

I passed through the restaurant into the hotel lobby on the other side of the building, an airy room decorated with elegant rattan furniture and ceiling fans. There, Coffen's bloody trail mysteriously stopped.

"Buster! Here boy!" I called out.

I heard my dog's familiar yip. The hotel's entrance was on a backstreet, and I pushed open a swinging door with my gun and went outside.

Coffen stood by the valet stand, trying to punch numbers into his phone while kicking at my dog. His broken fingers were making this especially hard for him. I leveled the Colt at his chest.

"Drop the phone," I said.

"You're not a cop. You can't tell me what to do," he said.

He kept pressing numbers into the phone. Even Buster nipping at his ankles didn't seem to faze him.

"I'm giving you one more chance," I said.

He raised the phone triumphantly to his face. His call had gone through.

"Go fuck yourself," he said.

I fired the Colt three times. Coffen spun away from the valet stand, clutching his chest. The phone slipped from his hand and clattered to the pavement. He tried to speak, but instead of words, blood spilled from his mouth. He crumpled to the pavement.

I retrieved his cell phone and held it to my ear. It had gone dead. I attempted to power it up and retrieve the number he'd just dialed. The phone did not respond.

"Shit," I said.

Linderman came out of the hotel and said something. When I didn't reply, he knelt down and checked Coffen for a pulse. It was strictly a formality, and he looked up at me.

"He's dead. Did his call go through?"

"No," I said.

In the distance I could hear wailing sirens. I couldn't imagine how I was going to explain this to the police. Linderman stood up.

"Give me the phone," he said.

I handed him the damaged phone.

"Let me deal with the police," he said.

"Deal with them how?"

"I'll tell them I shot Coffen. It will take the heat off you."

"You sure?"

"Yes. It will make everything easier."

I suddenly felt light-headed. I had never shot an unarmed man before. It was a strange feeling, and I pointed at the doors leading inside.

"I'll be in there if you need me," I said.

The hotel lobby was filled with frightened guests and wide-eyed staff. I sat on a creaky rattan couch with Buster glued to my side. A white-jacketed waiter served me a cup of coffee without being asked. I thanked him and sucked it down.

The coffee brought me back to life. The couch faced a flat-screen, high-definition TV, the lobby's only nod to modernization. CNN was on, broadcasting live from Starke Prison. I stared at the screen and nearly got sick.

Simon Skell had been released.

Starke was in a rural area, the facility surrounded by a

six-foot-high chain-link fence topped with razor wire. A stretch limousine came through the front gates, followed by several news crews covering the event. There was a light drizzle, and the caravan inched down a muddy road to a field where a helicopter sat.

The limo stopped, and four figures piled out. Leonard Snook, Lorna Sue Mutter, Chase Winters, and Skell. Skell was dressed in jeans, an Old Navy sweatshirt, and white tennis sneakers. Everyone else wore raincoats.

The group climbed into the waiting chopper, and the door closed. Skell's face appeared in the side window, and he tugged on his paintbrush beard.

The chopper went airborne and briefly hovered in the gray sky.

A second chopper appeared and followed Skell's chopper. I guessed this chopper contained Scott Saunders and the other FBI agents tailing Skell.

As the choppers faded from view an icy finger ran down my spine. The FBI wasn't going to stop Skell. Skell had been on the FBI's radar for *three years*, and they hadn't gotten close. They didn't understand what made him tick. His motivation was a crazy song, one I knew by heart. Only I could stop him.

I grabbed Buster and went outside. Coffen lay beneath a white sheet. Two uniformed cops stood behind him, making small talk. They paid no attention to me.

Linderman stood by the valet stand, talking on his cell phone. In his face I saw something that resembled hope. He folded his phone and approached me.

"Tell me you've got good news," I said.

He nodded enthusiastically.

"Theis just cracked Coffen's computer," he said.

CHAPTER THIRTY-EIGHT

We limped down the sidewalk back to Trojan Communications.

"What's wrong with your dog?" Linderman asked.

Buster walked with his nose glued to the ground. The shooting had done a number on his head, and I promised myself to later take him running on Dania Beach. It was his favorite thing to do and would bring him around.

"He'll be okay," I said. "What did Theis find on Coffen's computer?"

"Hundreds of photographs are stored on the hard drive," Linderman said. "The memory's overloaded, which is why it froze on him. There's also a database. Theis is hoping it will lead us to the other members of the gang."

And Melinda Peters, I hoped but would not say aloud, as if uttering her name might jinx our ability to rescue her. We reached the parking lot, and I put my dog into my car. Then we went inside.

Heidi the receptionist was still at her desk. Seeing Linderman, she slammed her fists on her desk and flew into a rage.

"My friend at the Riverview Hotel called and said you killed Mr. Coffen!"

Linderman put his palms on her desk as if he were doing a push-up.

"Calm down, or I'll arrest you," he said.

"Why did you have to kill him?" she said.

"Let's see. For starters, he shot me."

"Couldn't you have just wounded him?"

"Your boss had his chance."

"You bastard!"

I walked around Heidi's desk and down the hallway to Coffen's office. Despite what had happened, it was business as usual, and through the walls came voices of faceless operators taking orders from around the state. They reminded me of Skell's victims, and how their voices were yet to be heard.

I stopped at the hallway's end and stuck my head into Coffen's office. Special Agent Theis sat at Coffen's desk, working the computer. He motioned me inside.

I stood behind Theis's chair. My eyes fell on the computer screen.

"How did you get it unfrozen?"

"I tried the idiot approach," Theis said. "I turned off the power, then rebooted it. I needed a password to gain entry and found it on a business card in Coffen's briefcase. There's a ton of stuff on the hard drive, including a file that has pictures of you."

"Let me see it," I said.

Theis opened up a file called ENEMY. It contained a photograph of me taken from a newspaper article along with a short biography. There were also photographs and bios of Tommy Gonzalez, Sally McDermitt, and dozens of other Florida law enforcement agents who specialized in finding missing people.

"What about Coffen's database?" I asked.

"Who are you looking for?"

"Jonny Perez. Jonny's spelled without the h."

Theis searched the database for Jonny Perez. Finding nothing, I suggested he try Ajony Perez. The results were the same.

"Try Neil Bash and Simon Skell," I said.

Theis did and found nothing. On a hunch, he exited the database and checked Coffen's e-mail, first looking at his address book, then his sent e-mail folder and deleted bin. Everything he came across was business related and worthless to our search.

I shut my eyes and took a deep breath. Each road in my investigation had taken me to a dead end, and only an act of luck or God had let me progress. How the hell was I going to save Melinda if I couldn't locate Jonny Perez?

"Want to look at his photograph collection?" Theis asked.

"Sure," I said quietly.

Theis exited the database and clicked on the My Pictures icon. It opened to reveal dozens of different folders. The ones at the top were labeled by city—Orlando, Miami, Tampa—while the ones on the bottom had cryptic notations. One file caught my eye:

MIDRAMB

"Open this one," I said.

Theis opened MIDRAMB, and a page containing eight JPEG files filled the screen. Each JPEG had a date attached to it, spanning the past two and a half years.

I gripped the back of Theis's chair. I knew what the JPEGs contained without having to look at them. They were electronic snapshots of Skell's victims taken at McDonald's drive-throughs. I was one step closer to learning their fate.

I had dreamed of this moment. I was finally going to find out what had happened to Skell's victims. Yet, I was also filled with dread. Throughout the investigation, I'd continued to hope that I'd get a phone call from each of them, saying they were okay. It was what every person who lost someone told themselves.

Theis opened the first JPEG. The picture was of Chantel, an African American girl who got tossed out of her home at fourteen. She'd lived near the beach, where she did her hooking. The picture showed her in a car with a white-haired guy chomping on a cigar. Chantel's hand was in his lap, the guy all smiles. Coffen had caught her servicing a john.

"Know her?" Theis asked.

"She was Skell's first victim," I said.

The next JPEG was of Maggie. Maggie worked for a Fort Lauderdale escort service, a fair-haired Irish girl whose stepfather had married her mother in order to sleep with Maggie. She worked the local hotels and was on a first-name basis with the concierges. In the picture, Maggie was on her cell while applying lipstick. Her face was all business, and I imagined Coffen overheard her getting a call for a job.

"What about her?" Theis asked.

"She was number two."

"You knew all of the victims, didn't you?"

"Yes."

"Want something to drink?"

"No thanks."

"Want my chair?"

"I'm fine, really."

Theis opened the rest of the JPEGs and let me study them. Had I not stuck the victims' photographs on the walls of my office, I wouldn't have recognized them so quickly. But I did, and their faces evoked a sharp pang of delayed grief.

In each photograph I searched for what Coffen saw, or heard, that alerted him to the potential for victimization. Most of the time it was obvious. Either the victim was talking on her cell, or she was talking to a passenger in the car. Some snippet of conversation must have tipped Coffen off to the type of person he was dealing with.

But in three of the photographs—those of Carmen, Lola, and Brie—there was no telltale clue. The women were in their cars, staring absently into space. They were all victims of family abuse, their faces hauntingly sad. I studied their photographs but learned nothing. Perhaps I would never know what Coffen had seen. Or perhaps he'd seen the same thing I just had. Three young women with faces like refugees. Maybe that was all he needed.

The office had a small refrigerator. Theis removed two bottles of Perrier and handed me one. Brie's picture was still on the screen. I drank while staring at her.

I'd stayed in contact with Brie for over ten years. Every few months we'd meet for a pancake breakfast, and she'd show me her most recent bank statement. She was saving up so that on her thirtieth birthday she could quit hooking and open a nail salon. She already had the location picked out, and the name: New Beginnings.

I pitched my empty bottle into the trash and headed for the door.

CHAPTER THIRTY-NINE

I'm sorry this was a dead end," Theis said.

Pulling his wallet out, Theis placed a snapshot of a young woman in a cap and gown on the desk, then got back on the computer. I stopped in the doorway.

"Who's that?" I asked.

"Danielle Linderman," Theis said.

"Ken's daughter?"

"Uh-huh."

"You going to look for her on Coffen's database?"

Theis mumbled yes, his fingers tapping the keyboard. I came around the desk to get a better look at the photograph. Danielle Linderman bore a strong resemblance to her father, with a pretty, intelligent face and soft hazel eyes. The faces of scores of missing kids were stored in my memory, and I added hers to the group.

"Good luck," I said.

I found Linderman in the reception area. He'd gotten Coffen's cell phone to work and was scrolling through the address book while pressing a hanky to his face. Lowering the hanky, he displayed a nasty gash running the length of his chin.

"Did the receptionist do that?" I asked.

He nodded grimly.

"Did you arrest her?"

"You're goddamn right I did," he snapped. "So help me God, if I find out that little bitch knew what Coffen was doing, I'll ruin her."

I didn't reply. More than likely, the receptionist didn't know that her boss was a predator. Coffen ran a respectable business and had a public face. That was the person she knew. Hearing he'd been killed, she'd snapped.

"How did you make out?" Linderman asked.

"We found photographs of Skell's victims on Coffen's computer, but nothing that will lead us to Jonny Perez," I said. "Any luck with the phone?"

Linderman reapplied the hanky to his face. "So far, every number in the address book is a client's."

"Who was he trying to call?"

"Another cell. I'm having the number traced."

I had traced cell numbers before. It could take days to track them down.

I went outside to my car. Looking at the victims' photographs had reminded me how much I'd cared for those young women. It was hard to believe that I'd never speak with any of them again.

Opening the passenger door, I knelt down so I was eye level with my dog. Buster propped a paw on my shoulder and licked my face. I did everything I could not to cry.

I got behind the wheel and spent a few minutes massaging my leg. It was starting to feel better; the injury I'd suffered from my jump was just a sprain. I watched an ambulance carrying Coffen's body go past the building. In my wife's religion, the spirits of the dead never leave this earth. I imagined Coffen's ghost hovering over the ambulance, mocking us as we tried to unearth his dark secrets.

My cell phone rang. I took it off the dash and looked at Caller ID. It was Claude Cheever. I didn't want to talk to him and let the call go into voice mail.

My last encounter with Claude was still fresh in my mind. While Claude had been accusing me of sleeping with Melinda I'd heard another accusation as well, which was that he'd suspected it for a while. Which meant that all the honorable things he'd said about me in front of the police review board had been lies.

The phone rang several times over the next few minutes. Each time, Caller ID said it was Cheever. Finally I answered it.

"What do you want?" I said by way of greeting.

"Melinda was just on Neil Bash's show, talking about your affair," Cheever said.

"Is that what you called to tell me?"

"No, no, calm down, buddy. I'm on your side."

"You weren't the last time we got together."

"I found Jesus and saw the light," Cheever said. "You were right. Melinda was abducted from her apartment yesterday."

You were right. I hadn't heard those words in a long time.

"What brought you to that conclusion?" I asked.

"While Bash was interviewing Melinda, he asked her where she was calling from," Cheever said. "Melinda told Bash she was at home. I was driving near her apartment and decided to pay her a visit. I banged on the front door, looked through the back slider, and talked to the next-door neighbor. Melinda hasn't been home since yesterday. I didn't like it, so I called Bash's show."

"You called Bash? Jesus Christ, Claude. Bash is part of it."

"Don't worry. I've called Bash's show plenty of times. He knows me."

"Why do you call his show?"

"For kicks. I go by a pseudonym: Sex Hound. Anyway, Bash let me talk to Melinda. Now, I'm going to tell you something in confidence, and you can't repeat it."

"I'm listening," I said.

"I had a fling with Melinda," Cheever said. "Lasted about a month. Sex every day, sometimes twice a day. She was a goddess. We had a special language all our own."

I shook my head in disbelief. I couldn't imagine Melinda and Claude in bed together, even with the shades drawn and the lights turned out.

"When I talked with Melinda I used a few of our code words, and she realized it was me," Cheever continued. "She told me she was being hurt, the fucking bastards."

Claude paused to compose himself.

"Jack, I want you to help me rescue her."

"How do you plan to do that?" I asked.

"I'm going to pay Bash a visit and make him tell me where she's being held."

"What about the police? Or the FBI?" I asked.

"They'll only slow us down," Cheever said.

I knew exactly how Cheever felt. Had I visited Trojan Communications without the FBI breathing down my neck, I could have made Coffen cough up Jonny Perez's address. It wouldn't have been pretty, but I could have done it.

"Count me in," I said.

CHAPTER FORTY

Neil Bash's radio station was in a semirural community called Davie in the center of Broward County. I agreed to meet Cheever there in thirty minutes. As I backed my car out, Linderman emerged from Trojan Communications. I lowered my window.

"The police want to talk with you," Linderman said.

I glanced at the street. While I'd been talking with Cheever, a pair of police cruisers had pulled in the front of the building, and several sheriffs had gone inside.

"I thought you had the police covered," I said.

"They're picking apart my story," Linderman said. "Coffen is a big mover and shaker in town, and the police want to know why I shot him when he was unarmed."

"Have Theis show them the photos of the victims on his computer," I suggested.

"Theis did. The police are saying the photos don't mean squat. They're saying we can't even prove those women are dead. You need to straighten them out, Jack."

"Me?"

"Yes, you."

I threw the car into drive. I couldn't see myself explaining how I knew eight women were dead to a legal system that had let their killer walk free.

"Fuck 'em," I said.

I drove to Davie, listening to Bash's talk show on my radio. Bash was ripping me apart and making me the poster boy for everything wrong with the criminal justice system. He recited every injury I had inflicted upon Skell, without mentioning the crime for which Skell had been sent to prison. He was brainwashing his listeners, one moron at a time.

Every few minutes, Bash took a call-in. As the Davie exit appeared in my windshield a caller came on whose voice was instantly familiar.

"Hey, Neil, it's your old buddy Sex Hound," Cheever said brightly.

"Sex Hound," Bash said. "You always lighten up my day. What's up?"

"You going to bring her back on?"

"Who's that?"

"Melinda Peters."

"Ah, yes, the lovely Melinda Peters, star of your friendly neighborhood strip club. Melinda has promised that she'll be calling again. Believe it or not, she actually has *more* dirt on our favorite cop, Jack Carpenter."

"What kind of dirt?" Cheever asked.

"She's going to tell us what Carpenter was *really* up to," Bash said.

"You mean there's more to the story?" Cheever said.

"Lots more," Bash said. "But to tell any more would be cheating."

"I'll be waiting," Cheever said. "Oh, and Neil? Love your show."

"Thanks, Sex Hound. And now it's time for a word from one of our sponsors."

I took the exit and headed south. Davie was a blue-collar area, and I drove down a two-lane road with trailer parks hugging each side. Two miles later, I spotted a cluster of trailers with large antennas on their roofs. Above the trailers hung an elevated billboard with the station's call letters and Bash's round, devilish face.

I'd found him.

Trailer parks were as much a part of Florida as alligators and Mickey Mouse. They sat on land scraped clean of trees and were usually the first casualties of hurricanes and electrical storms. Low-income families flocked to them, as did the retired. They were their own worlds, and could be good or bad places to live. I'd known many cops who refused to answer a call from one on a Saturday night.

Bash's radio station was inside a trailer park called Tropical Estates. It was a cheapo operation, the main building a series of double-wides attached by flimsy covered walkways. Cheever's car was parked by the entrance. I parked beside him.

We got out and faced each other. I was still pissed and glared at him.

"I'm sorry, Jack," Cheever said.

"You should be," I said.

"Hear me out, will you?"

Bread crumbs peppered his mustache. I couldn't imagine him screwing Melinda.

"I'm listening," I said.

"I'm sorry I doubted your story, and sorry I called you a liar. I hope you'll forgive me. I won't hold it against you if you don't."

"That's it?" I said.

He nodded solemnly.

"Maybe someday," I said.

He pretended to understand. Reaching into the backseat of his car, he removed a white box tied with string.

"It's a pound of homemade chocolate fudge for Bash," he explained. "I bought it from a candy store in my neighborhood. Eat one piece, and you can't stop."

"You going to bribe your way in?"

"That was the idea."

"What if he refuses?"

"He won't. A while back, he had a porno queen named Kissy in his studio taking calls. I'd seen her movies and wanted to get a glimpse of her in the flesh. I used the fudge then, and it worked fine."

Cheever again reached into the back of his car. This time, he came out with a pair of black cowboy hats. He put one on, and handed me the other.

"Disguises?" I asked.

"Yeah. You got shades?"

"In my car."

"Get them, and your dog. You're going to be my blind cousin."

"Isn't that a little hokey?"

"Not with these bozos. Listen, I got some bad news. Joy Chambers was found murdered yesterday in her house. There was a piece of skin under one of her fingernails. The lab ran a DNA check. It was from some Cuban guy."

"His name's Jonny Perez," I said.

Cheever blinked. "How the heck did you know that?"

"Jonny Perez shot out my car on 595. He's part of Skell's gang."

"You're one step ahead of me, aren't you?"

"Try a mile," I said.

We entered the trailer that served as the radio station's reception area. It was a low-ceilinged arrangement with paneled walls and carpet that wasn't tacked down. A receptionist with fake eyelashes and eye-popping cleavage beamed at us.

"Hey, I remember you," she said. "You're Sex Hound."

Cheever doffed his hat. "It's Janet from another planet, right?"

"Good memory. Bring any candy?"

Cheever untied the box and showed her the fudge. She filched the biggest piece and stuck it sideways in her mouth.

"Who's he?" she asked, nearly choking.

"This is my cousin LeRoy," Cheever said. "He's blind."

"What a shame. He's cute."

"Maybe you can babysit for him sometime," Cheever said.

"I think I'd like that," she said.

I kept my face expressionless. Janet from another planet looked like the type who'd molest me if given half a chance.

"Can I go see Neil?" Cheever asked.

"Be my guest," she said.

We walked down a claustrophobic hallway and entered a second trailer, where the studio was located. It had soundproof walls and a small glassed-in space where Bash sat, jabbering into a mike. His goatee was gone, revealing sunken eyes and a triple chin. Seeing Cheever, he cut to a commercial and clicked off his mike.

"Sex Hound," he yelled through the glass. "You bring candy?"

Cheever held the box of goodies up to the glass. Bash pushed himself out of his chair and emerged from the studio. He was about five-six and tipped the scales near three hundred pounds. I had expected the Devil incarnate, but he was nothing more than a sad little man. Cheever gave him the fudge, and Bash started shoving pieces into his mouth. He paid no attention to me or my dog.

"How's the fudge?" Cheever asked.

"Delicious," Bash said through a mouthful.

Cheever punched Bash in the stomach. Bash spit up the candy and fell backwards onto the floor. Cheever shoved his detective's badge in Bash's face.

"You're under arrest, asshole," he said.

Some cops will tell you that ethics are situational and that there is a time and a place for just about anything. I kept my mouth shut as Cheever silenced Bash's screams with several well-placed kicks to the ribs.

Buster seemed perplexed by the whole scene. I made him sit in the corner and removed his leash. If anyone walked into the studio unannounced, I was hoping his presence would slow them down.

"You going to cooperate?" Cheever asked.

Lying on the floor, Bash groaned in the affirmative.

"Good," Cheever said. "Now get up."

Bash pulled himself off the floor. His lips were smeared with fudge, and he was gasping for breath. Cheever pushed him into the studio and threw him into his chair. ZZ Top's "Sharp Dressed Man" was playing over the room's speakers.

I followed them in, shut the door, and removed my disguise. Bash stared at me.

"You're Jack Carpenter," he said.

"That's right," I said. "I just came from seeing a friend of yours."

"Who's that?"

"Paul Coffen. He told us about the girls you and Skell

and Jonny Perez molested in Tampa, and how you came down here and set up shop. He's selling you down the river."

Bash squirmed in his chair. "Paul wouldn't do that."

"He showed us the surveillance photographs of Skell's victims he kept stored on his hard drive," I went on. "We've also connected him to a child abduction case at Disney World. He named you and Perez and Skell as his co-conspirators."

"What?" Bash said.

"There's enough evidence to have all of you put to death," I said. "Think about it, Neil. Fifteen years on death row, waiting on appeals, then one day they march you into the death chamber and it's lights out."

The song ended, and silence filled the studio. Bash reflexively pressed a button on the master console, and another song came on: George Thorogood's "Bad to the Bone."

Cheever was standing behind the chair and dropped his hand on Bash's shoulder. "Tell us where Jonny Perez is keeping Melinda, and we'll help you."

Bash looked up beseechingly into Cheever's face.

"Help me how?"

"We'll tell the district attorney that you pulled through for us," Cheever said. "We'll say that without your help, we couldn't have solved the case."

"You mean you'll cut me a deal?"

"That's right," Cheever said.

Swiveling in his chair, Bash looked at me.

"Is he telling the truth?"

"Yes," I said. "Help us find Melinda, and you won't go down."

"You mean I won't die?"

We both nodded.

Bash covered his face and began to weep. I believe that evil people all think about the day when they will be held accountable for the things they've done. It's called Judgment Day, and there's no escaping it. Bash was living that day.

"Jonny Perez lives with his brother Paco in a rented house a few miles west of here," Bash said. "He's keeping Melinda there. That's where he kept all the girls."

I leaned closer.

"What's the address?"

"It's written down in my trailer."

"Is your trailer here?"

"Yeah. It's part of my deal with the station."

I glanced up at Cheever to gauge his reaction. He nodded grimly.

"Take us there," I said.

CHAPTER FORTY-ONE

Before we left the studio, Bash slipped a tape of an old show into a player on the console. He hit the Play button, and his abrasive voice filled the trailer.

"Won't your listeners notice it's a repeat?" Cheever asked.

"Who cares?" the DJ said.

We left the studio through a back door and walked down a dusty road into the bowels of the trailer park. Each trailer in the park sat on a tiny sliver of land. Many were sinking into the ground, their roofs patched with asphalt shingles and plywood. On screened porches sat shapeless women fanning themselves while shirtless men sucked cans of beer. No one said hello.

Bash's footsteps were measured, his hands gripping his gut. Turning down a street called Majesty Lane, he went to the last trailer. It was newer, with bright aluminum siding and a giant satellite dish on the roof. He unlocked the front door, then faced us.

"I need to tell you guys something," Bash said.

We waited, the midday sun burning our faces.

"I was never *there* when the girls died," he said emphatically.

"Where were you?" I asked.

"I was *here*, in my trailer," Bash said.

"So what's your point?" Cheever asked.

"I never laid a finger on any of them, or did anything horrible to them, or made them suffer or cry," Bash said. "I just watched."

"Is that your thing?" Cheever asked.

"Yeah," Bash said. "I like to watch. My heart don't work so good anymore, so I never went down on them like Coffen and Jonny and Skell did. I didn't hurt them, either. I just stayed in my trailer and watched."

His words sounded like a confession. Only something was missing. Guilt. His eyes were empty and soulless, and I wondered what event in his life had caused him to participate in the deaths of so many innocent young women and not regret it.

"Did you watch them die?" I asked.

Bash stared down at his scuffed shoes.

"Most of them," he said quietly.

"Not all?"

"I missed a couple," he admitted.

"What happened?"

"Skell killed them when I was on the air doing my show."

"Which ones did you miss?" Cheever asked.

"I don't know," Bash said.

"What do you mean, you don't know?" Cheever said.

"I never knew the girls' names," he said.

Cheever threw a right hand into Bash's face. The DJ let out a muffled yell and tumbled backwards into the trailer. Cheever looked around to make sure no one was watching, then followed him inside.

I glanced down at Buster, who was glued to my leg. My dog wanted no part of this. I made him go inside anyway.

* * *

The interior of Bash's trailer was like a cave. The walls and ceiling were painted black, the curtains tightly drawn. Natural light was not welcome here. An oversized leather chair with a TV remote on its cushion sat in the room's center. On the floor in front of the chair was a plastic bowl half filled with buttered popcorn.

Bash's throne.

Across from the chair, a wide-screen plasma TV was mounted on the wall. I stared at the TV, slack-jawed. On its screen, a bikini-clad Melinda Peters hung by her wrists inside someone's closet, her manicured toes scraping the floor. A cell phone lay by her feet, and I thought back to last night's call.

Bash staggered around the trailer, clutching his face. Cheever grabbed him by the shoulders and threw him into the leather chair.

"Please don't hit me again," the DJ begged.

"You gonna behave?" Cheever asked.

"I didn't do anything."

"Answer me, asshole."

"Yeah, I'll behave."

Cheever pointed at the screen. "Is that live?"

"Yeah, it's live."

"They're playing voyeur cam with her, aren't they?"

Bash hid the smirk forming on his face. "Something like that."

"When are your buddies going to kill her?"

"Tonight, after Skell gets back to Fort Lauderdale. He wants to see it."

"Were they going to broadcast it to him?"

"No. He was going to Jonny's place to watch."

I could not take my eyes off Melinda. The voyeur cam

turned, and the Cuban who had shot out my windshield on 595 appeared on the big screen. It was Jonny Perez, wearing a bright red bandanna around his head and clutching a can of beer. He smiled and waved at the camera while doing a crazy little dance.

"Why is he dancing?" I asked.

"He's playing 'Midnight Rambler,' " Bash said. "It's what we play when the girls are being tortured."

"We?" I asked.

Bash nodded. Sensing that I wanted a more complete answer, he used the remote to start a CD player sitting on the floor beneath the TV. Out of its speakers came the opening harmonica riff from the live version of "Midnight Rambler." The music was like a demonic chuckle.

I took a deep breath. If I saw any more, I was going to explode.

"Where's your address book?"

"In my bedroom. I'll get it for you."

He started to get out of his chair, and Cheever shoved him back down.

"I told you not to move," Cheever said.

"I was just going to get the address book for him," Bash said.

"Don't you want Jack to go in there?"

Bash shook his head. "No."

"Why not?" Cheever asked.

"He won't like it," Bash said.

Bash's bedroom was in the rear of the trailer and reeked of cigarettes and a decayed conscience. There were no real furnishings, just a water bed and an upturned orange crate that served as a night table.

The address book lay on the crate. I found Jonny Perez

under the J's. He lived in West Sunrise, which was as close as you could get to the Everglades without falling in.

As I slipped the address book into my pocket I realized I wasn't alone. The bedroom's ceiling was papered with photographs of naked women. It looked like pervert heaven, only with a twisted difference. The photographs were not torn from an X-rated magazine or copied off a pornographic website. They were real. They were the victims.

I choked up. The poses were sexual, the women smiling through clenched teeth. All eight were there. I silently recited their names as I pulled them down.

The last photograph was of Lola, a pretty Jamaican prostitute whose story I'd never known. I'd talked her into making her johns wear rubbers and getting doctor's checkups, and she'd lasted twelve years without getting sick. As strange as it sounded, I took a lot of pride in that.

I let Lola's photograph float to the bed. It flipped over as it landed, revealing writing on the back.

#7.

I checked the backs of the other photographs. They were also numbered. I realized this was how Bash and the rest of the gang saw their victims, as nameless objects. In their eyes, they were not worthy of proper names or identities, just numbers.

I gathered up the photographs. They were evidence, but a part of me didn't want anyone to see them. The victims had suffered enough, and having these images passed around a police station or at a trial seemed one more senseless indignity. As I weighed what to do with them, a man's screams shattered my thoughts.

* * *

I ran into the next room, and found Cheever punching Bash. Cheever outweighed me by forty pounds, and it took all of my strength to pull him off the struggling DJ.

"What are you trying to do?" I asked.

"Kill the son of a bitch," Cheever said.

"Why? What did he do?"

"Look at the goddamn TV."

I looked across the room at the giant screen. Jonny Perez and a second Hispanic were dancing naked around Melinda while using pieces of paper to cut her arms and legs. Each time she screamed, they cut her again. They seemed to be feasting on her fear.

"I caught Bash laughing under his breath, getting his rocks off," Cheever said.

"I need to talk to him, Claude."

"Wasn't the address book in the bedroom?"

"I've got the address book," I said. "I need to ask him something."

Cheever walked across the trailer to where my dog was sitting in the corner. He crossed his arms and stared murderously at Bash.

"Go ahead," he said.

I knelt down beside Bash's oversized chair. The DJ was red in the face and was having a hard time breathing. I grasped his arm and pinched it.

"You said something on your show that I want explained," I said. "You said Melinda had more dirt on me. What was she going to say?"

Bash started to reply, then thought better of it. I answered my own question.

"Was she going to say I was the Midnight Rambler?"

The DJ shut his eyes.

"Yes," he whispered.

"That's why you've been attacking me on the radio, isn't it?"

The DJ nodded.

"Was that Skell's idea?"

"Yes. Skell thought it would take the heat off him."

Since Carmella Lopez's body had been discovered in her sister's backyard, I'd been painted to look like the kind of monster that I'd spent my life chasing. Now I knew why.

"He's all yours," I told Cheever.

Bash opened his eyes and looked pleadingly at me. "What about our deal? You guys said you'd help me if I cooperated."

"Fat chance," Cheever told him.

"But you guys said—"

"The only deal you're getting is a one-way ticket to Starke," Cheever said. "Either you'll get the needle shoved in your arm, or someone will shove a broomstick up your ass. Those are your options."

"But we had a *deal.*"

"We lied, buttercup."

Bash's eyes floated to the giant screen. Jonny Perez had ripped away Melinda's bikini top and was cutting perfect circles around her perfect breasts. Bash tore his eyes away long enough to look at me.

"No deal?" he asked.

"No deal," I said.

Bash started to protest, then went rigid in his chair. He slapped his hand over his heart like a dramatic actor in a play. I knew what was happening, and pulled him out of his chair and laid him on the floor. Then I began to pound his chest. But it was too late. He had already stopped breathing.

CHAPTER FORTY-TWO

Heart attacks are strange. Some could last for hours, the way my sister's did. Others were over in the blink of an eye. Bash's was quick, and he was dead in less than thirty seconds. I could do nothing but watch.

Years earlier, I had plowed into a deer on a moonless night, and stood on the side of the road to comfort the poor thing. As the deer died, a smokelike substance escaped from its chest. I told a doctor I knew, and he'd said that he'd seen the same thing with many terminal patients. The substance, he believed, was their soul.

I looked for Bash's soul to escape but saw nothing. Cheever edged up beside me.

"Is he dead?"

"Yes," I said under my breath.

"Shit, Jack, what am I going to do?" Cheever asked.

I looked at him, not understanding.

"I might get pinned with this," he said.

"Because you punched him in the mouth," I said.

"Yeah, and I provoked him. The review board will have a field day. I don't want to go through what you went through."

I didn't blame Cheever for feeling this way. If I'd learned anything from my experience with Simon Skell, the only people society expected to follow the laws were those who enforced them.

The trailer had a small kitchen. I got a rag out of the sink and washed away the blood from Bash's lips. Then I scrubbed down anything Cheever or I had touched.

"How well did you know him?" I asked.

"I came by the station when he had porno stars visiting," Cheever said. "I knew he was a sick puppy, but not this sick."

"Did you ever use your real name at the station?"

"No."

"Good."

I shifted my attention to the wide-screen TV. Jonny Perez and the other Hispanic had stopped torturing Melinda and were no longer in the picture. Melinda was looking directly into the camera, fighting back tears.

"We're coming," I said to the screen.

We went to the door and I whistled for my dog. Then I looked at Bash lying dead on the floor. His face looked as if he'd been dead a long time. As we walked out, "Midnight Rambler" was still playing on the CD player.

We left the station and drove our cars to a deserted strip center. We got out of our vehicles, and I took Bash's address book from my pocket and showed Cheever the listing for Jonny Perez.

Perez lived in a marginal neighborhood in Sunrise. Cheever suggested that we take his car and leave mine behind. He believed his filthy vehicle was less likely to arouse suspicion as we searched for Perez's hideout.

I agreed, and soon we were heading west on 595 in his car. Cheever drove with his body hunched over the wheel and his eyes glued to the highway. I sensed he was trying to shake off Bash's death, and tried to comfort him.

"Don't blame yourself for what happened back there," I said.

He shook his head without taking his eyes off the road.

"Bash got what was coming to him," I said.

Several miles passed before Cheever replied.

"I need to ask you something," he said.

"What's that?"

"Do you love Melinda? I have to know, Jack."

The question stunned me, and I jerked sideways in my seat.

"How many times do I have to tell you, Claude? I didn't sleep with her. Not yesterday, not last week, not last year. We never got it on."

"But do you love her?"

"No!"

The pain showed in Cheever's face.

"I'm sorry, Jack, but you're the reason she and I broke up."

"How is that possible?"

"She said your name one night in bed. She had this thing about me wearing my badge on my T-shirt. She looked at it and said your name."

I hadn't forgotten the cartoon drawings I'd seen on Melinda's kitchen table, and the stick figure with a badge pinned to his chest. That figure had been holding hands with a female stick figure and standing before a house with smoke billowing from its chimney. Now I understood its significance.

"I'm sorry that happened to you," I said.

Cheever nodded regretfully.

"So am I," he said.

* * *

Cheever took the Sawgrass Expressway to the Sunrise exit and soon got lost. Sunrise had been built by developers and was a mishmash of identical-sounding street names. Fifteen excruciating minutes later we found Perez's street and did a quick sweep. The houses were small, their windows covered with security bars. An alley ran behind the properties. It made spying easy, and we crawled down it and braked behind Perez's place. His house was a single-story concrete-block structure with a tar-paper roof and rotted hurricane shutters. A bike with two flats sat on the back porch.

"What a dump," Cheever said.

I looked around the backyard. It was a disaster area, with newspapers floating in the dirty swimming pool and no grass. The place felt unattended to.

"I don't think Perez lives here," I said.

"Then where is he?" Cheever asked.

Perez's trick of cutting the cable in his victims' backyards was fresh in my mind, and I gazed at the telephone poles lining the alley. It didn't take me long to find a thick black wire running from Perez's supposed house to the house next door. This house had some serious landscaping, plus a padlocked prefabricated storage shed in the backyard. Sitting in the carport was Perez's white van.

"They're in the house next door," I said.

Cheever parked on the street, and we walked down the alley to look at the second house. It appeared to be a normal middle-class dwelling, except for the shed. It was way too big for the property.

"Wonder what's inside that thing?" Cheever said.

"Let's have a look," I said.

A five-foot-high chain-link fence ringed the property. I

picked up Buster and dropped him over the fence. Then Cheever and I climbed the fence and crossed the backyard. We took down the shed's door with our shoulders.

The shed's interior was easily a hundred degrees. I hit the light switch, and we cautiously entered. Hanging from the walls were tools and trenching equipment. Something was making me uneasy, and I drew my gun. So did Cheever.

We stood with our backs to each other and looked around. My eyes fell on a metal worktable that ran the length of one wall. Beneath the table sat eight coolers, each large enough to hold a human body. Buster was sniffing them, his tail wagging furiously.

I examined the cooler closest to me. It had a label with writing on it. I had to squint to read what it said.

#1.

The cooler beside it said #2, and the cooler beside that one said #3.

I walked the row and read the label on each cooler. They were numbered just like the photographs that had papered Bash's bedroom. No names, no identities.

Just numbers.

I decided to open cooler #1 first. I put my hand on the lid, and the image of Carmella Lopez lying in her sister's backyard came back to me.

"Want me to do that?" Cheever asked.

I shook my head.

"You sure, Jack? You look pale."

"Positive," I said.

I popped the lid. The cooler was empty. The smell of ammonia nearly knocked me sideways. I caught my breath, then opened the rest. They were all empty.

A glittering object inside the last cooler caught my eye. I held it up to the light. It was a gold earring.

"Perez must have already dumped the bodies," Cheever said.

I put my hands on the worktable and took a moment to compose myself. I had desperately wanted the bodies to be here. Finding the victims was the only way I was going to be able to get on with my life. Cheever put a comforting hand on my shoulder.

"Sorry, buddy," he said.

I nodded without looking at him.

"Let's go rescue Melinda," he said.

I reached for the light switch, then noticed a map taped to the wall. It was of Broward County and had colored thumbtacks stuck in it, just like the map in my office. The thumbtacks were stuck in the same spots as on my map. Perez had chronicled where he'd nabbed his victims, just as I had. Only there was a thumbtack on his map that wasn't on mine. It was on the north end of Dania Beach, where I lived. I wondered what its significance was, and decided I'd have to ask him. I turned out the light.

We entered the backyard. Cheever stood by the end of the shed and cautiously peeked around the corner. I edged up beside him.

"I hear them talking inside the house," he whispered.

"How many are there?"

"I'm not sure. You speak Spanish, don't you?"

"A little," I said.

"Maybe you can understand what they're saying."

We switched places, and I stuck my head around the shed. Jonny Perez's face was visible through a screened window on the back of the house. He was washing his hands in the kitchen sink while carrying on a conversation. He moved away from the window.

"He's talking to his brother Paco, and some guy named Alberto," I whispered. "They're discussing a restaurant they want to visit after they kill Melinda."

"So we're outnumbered," Cheever said.

"Looks that way."

Cheever pulled out his cell phone and powered it up.

"Time for reinforcements," he said.

"You calling the cops?" I asked.

"Yes."

I thought about the ramifications of bringing in the Broward cops, and how Bobby Russo was going to react after hearing what we'd been up to.

"Give me the phone," I said.

"Why?" Cheever asked.

"I've got a better idea."

CHAPTER FORTY-THREE

I called Ken Linderman. Even though I'd abandoned him a few hours ago, I knew he'd help us. He wanted Skell as bad as I did.

"I need your help," I said.

I explained our situation without going into specifics. Cell phone conversations could be picked up by a variety of monitoring devices, and I didn't want to tip our hand to Perez or anyone else who might be electronically eavesdropping. Twenty minutes later, Linderman was standing on the sidewalk with us. Theis was with him.

"That was a shitty thing you did this morning, Jack," Linderman said.

"What happened after I left?" I asked.

"Goddamn police grilled me for an hour like I was a perp," he said. "If Coffen hadn't shot at me through his desk, I'd probably still be talking to them."

"Did everything get resolved?"

"Yes, no thanks to you."

I was past the point of apologizing for my behavior and led the FBI agents down the alley. I pointed over the fence at the back of Perez's house. "Melinda Peters is being held inside that house by Jonny Perez, his brother Paco, and a guy named Alberto," I said. "They're going to kill her once Skell gets here. Skell has told them he wants to watch."

Linderman and Theis acted stunned.

"How do you know this?" Linderman asked.

I had decided not to tell Linderman about our encounter with Neil Bash. It would only get Cheever in trouble.

"A little bird told me," I said.

We walked back to the street, and Linderman unlocked the rear of his 4Runner. The backseat had been replaced with a metal footlocker, and he removed two Kevlar vests and a pair of Mossberg 500 shotguns. He tossed the vests to Cheever and me.

"I remembered this time," he said.

Cheever and I put on the vests. Then the four of us went into a huddle.

"Here's the game plan," Linderman said. "Theis and Cheever will go to the front door of Perez's house posing as deliverymen. At the same time, Jack and I will come through the back door and trap Perez and his buddies. We'll coordinate our steps using our cell phones. Any questions?"

There were none. We wished each other good luck and broke up. I grabbed Buster and followed Linderman down the alley.

"What is it with you and that dog?" Linderman asked.

"We're getting married," I said.

We stopped at Perez's place, and I tossed Buster into the yard, then hopped the fence. Linderman handed me his shotgun and climbed the fence as well. His cell rang, and he took the call standing behind the shed.

"Damn it," he said, hanging up. "Theis just spotted a school bus. He wants to wait until it's left the neighborhood."

Storming a house with children around was never a

good idea, and we went inside the shed. Linderman took out a pack of cigarettes and lit up. As he smoked he propped his foot on one of the coolers lying beneath the workbench.

"Perez put the victims' bodies in those," I said.

Embarrassed, he removed his foot from the cooler.

"They're empty now," I added.

"Any idea where he disposed of them?" Linderman asked.

"No," I said. "But before this is over, I'm going to find out."

Linderman ground his cigarette into the dirt floor.

"What if Perez won't tell you?" he asked.

"Then I'll make him," I said.

Linderman gave me a long, hard stare.

"Are you ever going to let go of this?" he asked.

It was a question I'd asked myself a hundred times. I gathered my thoughts before responding.

"Do you know what Dia de los Muertos is?" I asked.

"It's a holiday down in Mexico. Day of the Dead."

"It's also a religious belief," I said. "In the village where my wife was born, they believe the spirits of the dead watch over us, and that it's our responsibility to treat their memories with respect. If we don't, those spirits will haunt us for the rest of our lives."

"Do you believe that, Jack? Do you believe the victims will haunt you if you don't find out what happened to them?"

I nodded solemnly. It was my only explanation for how far I'd gone over the past six months.

"Then I guess we'll have to make Perez tell us," Linderman said.

We were beginning to sweat and went outside. I peeked

around the corner of the shed at the house. A portable radio sat on the kitchen windowsill, and I heard Neil Bash's abrasive voice. It made me shudder, and I wondered how long it would take Perez to realize Bash's show wasn't being broadcast live.

"We're running out of time," I said.

Linderman didn't ask me to explain. He called Theis.

"Let's get this show on the road," he said.

CHAPTER FORTY-FOUR

Any cop will tell you that there is no more frightening sound than a shell being jacked into a shotgun. I knew the sound still sent chills down my spine, and I watched Linderman pump his Mossberg and march out from behind the shed.

I drew my Colt and followed Linderman across the backyard with sweat pouring down my back. Through the open kitchen window came Neil Bash's voice on the radio. There was something otherworldly about hearing Bash and knowing he was dead. Buster's cold nose pressed against my leg.

"Time to lose your fiancé," Linderman said.

I pointed at a shady spot beside the house.

"Sit," I said.

My dog made me proud and went into a perfect sit in the shade.

Linderman stopped at the back door and raised his leg. The door was dead bolted and took several hard kicks to bring down. We both rushed inside. The kitchen was L-shaped, with fading linoleum floors and stacks of dirty dishes piled high in the sink. On the radio Bash was talking about a heavy-metal concert that had taken place several months ago.

"Damn," I said under my breath.

Linderman was moving fast. I followed him down a short unlit hallway into a living room with mismatched furniture and a weight bench in the corner. Jonny Perez, his brother Paco, and a dark-skinned guy whom I assumed was Alberto stood in the room's center, pointing automatic handguns at Theis and Cheever, who stood inside the front doorway with their arms stretched to the ceiling. A pair of binoculars lay on the couch by the window.

"FBI," Linderman announced. "Drop your weapons."

Jonny Perez glanced suspiciously over his shoulder at us.

"No. You drop *your* weapons," he said in perfect English.

"That's not an option," Linderman said.

Perez whispered in Spanish to his brother. Paco turned and pointed his automatic at the far wall of the living room.

"If you don't drop your weapons," Perez said, "my brother will shoot through the wall and kill the girl in the bedroom."

"Do that, and we'll kill you," Linderman said.

"I ain't afraid of dying," Perez said.

"Me neither," Paco said.

The third guy, Alberto, simply grunted.

Linderman hesitated. He didn't want to lose Theis and his hostage. Sensing weakness, Perez let out a sickening laugh.

"Jack," Cheever called out.

I focused on my friend while continuing to train my Colt on the others. Cheever was sweating as badly as I was. But his face was defiant.

"Don't you dare trade with them, Jack," Cheever said.

"Shut up, Claude," I said.

"Don't do it."

"I said shut up."

"No, you shut up," he said, his voice rising. "You'll only end up dead, and so will both of us. I'm telling you not to do it. Hear me?"

I looked into Cheever's eyes and realized he meant every word of what he'd just said. Then I looked at Theis. The FBI agent dipped his chin, making it unanimous. They were both wearing bulletproof vests, while Perez, Paco, and Alberto were not. It was the last thought to go through my mind as I squeezed the Colt's trigger.

Paco was the closest to me, so I shot him in the chest. The bullet penetrated his heart—what cops call a kill shot. The gun dropped from his hand, and he fell onto the couch as if he'd decided to take a nap.

At the same time Linderman's shotgun let out a deafening roar. The blast hit Alberto in the waist, doubling him over like he'd been sliced in half. Alberto fell backwards and joined Paco on the couch.

Perez was not touched, and he fired several rounds into Cheever and Theis, causing both men to groan and crumple to the floor. Perez glanced over his shoulder at me, then took off running. Within moments he was out the door. I ran after him.

"Take him out," Linderman shouted.

I stopped at the open doorway. The school bus had dropped a slew of happy kids onto the sidewalk. They were playing tag, oblivious to what was going on. I blocked them out as best I could, aimed at Perez, and fired.

The bullet popped Perez in the ass, and he flew through the air like someone doing the triple jump, then landed on the front lawn, holding his buttocks and screaming in pain. Half the kids ran away, while the rest simply ran around him.

I went down the path and frisked Perez. He was clean, and I retrieved his gun off the lawn. Cheever came down the path covered in blood.

"Lie down before you bleed to death," I told him.

"I'm okay," Cheever said.

"You don't look okay."

"They're flesh wounds. Go find Melinda. I'll watch this little shit."

I tossed him Perez's gun and went inside the house. Theis lay on the floor inside the doorway with his eyes shut. He had taken a bullet in the side of the neck. Linderman was pressing a towel to the wound while talking Theis through it.

"Did you call 911?" I asked.

"Yes. Is Perez dead?"

"Shot him in the ass."

Linderman glared at me. I wanted to tell him not to worry; I was never trying out for the FBI. Instead, I went looking for Melinda.

The back of the house felt like a crash pad, not a place anyone had spent much time in. There were two cramped bedrooms, each with a mattress on the floor and a small electric fan beside it. Walking down a hallway, I came to a closed door.

I twisted the knob and entered. The room had no furniture, save for a video camera and tripod in the room's center and a boom box on the floor. The camera was pointed at a closed closet door. I opened it expecting to find Melinda. Instead, I let out a startled cry.

Hanging from a metal pole was a naked young woman I'd never seen before. A purple rag was stuck in her mouth to keep her from screaming. Everything about her looked dead, except for her face. There was a trace of pink in both cheeks, and I pulled the rag free and untied her wrists. She fell limply into my arms, and I gently laid her down on the floor.

"Wake up. Come on, you can do it," I said.

At first she did not respond. Then a cough escaped her throat. It was a tiny sound, like a dead car battery with a spark of life. Her eyelids fluttered, and she started to breath normally. She stared at me without lifting her head off the floor.

"You're not Skell, are you?" she asked.

I shook my head, and she started to cry.

"I was a present for Skell," she said.

"Did they tell you that?"

"Yes. Over and over."

"There's an ambulance coming," I said. "Everything is going to be all right."

She was eighteen if she was a day, and conscious that she was lying naked in front of a stranger. I went to the bathroom, grabbed two bath towels, and used them to cover her. If one thing defined the gang's victims, it was their beauty. Every one of them was a feast for the eyes. Even in her distressed state, she was no exception, and I watched her hand slip out from beneath a towel and encircle my wrist.

"What's your name?" she asked.

"Jack Carpenter."

"One of my kidnappers talked about you," she said. "He showed your picture to the others. He said if you showed up, they should kill you because you'd kill them. It wasn't a very good picture, though."

I did everything I could not to laugh.

"You're a brave young woman," I said. "I need to ask you a question."

"Sure," she said.

"There was another young woman the gang was holding. Her name is Melinda. Do you know where she is?"

"She was in one of the other bedrooms. I heard her cry a couple of times. I think they took her away."

"When?"

"Early this morning, while it was still dark."

"Did they say where they were taking her?"

She thought about it.

"If they did, I didn't hear them."

"Did they take her in a car?"

She shook her head. Her fingers tightened around my wrist.

"Would you do me a favor, Mr. Carpenter?"

"Sure," I said.

"Would you lend me your cell phone, so I can call my mother?"

I took out my cell phone and slipped it into her hand. Then I rose from the floor. I needed to go stick my gun in Jonny Perez's face and find out where he'd taken Melinda. Based upon what the girl had told me, I didn't think it was very far.

"I'll be right back," I said.

CHAPTER FORTY-FIVE

Jack, Jack, get in here! Hurry!"

I ran through the house. Linderman was still tending to Theis, who lay on his back by the open front door. Linderman pointed outside.

"Perez is making a run for it," the FBI agent said.

I drew my Colt and stuck my head through the door. Cheever lay on the grass with a pocketknife stuck in his leg, while Jonny Perez hobbled down the sidewalk clutching the handgun I'd taken from him. Linderman slapped my leg.

"Finish the job, Jack."

"Yes, sir," I said.

I hurried down the front path. Elementary school kids filled the street, riding bikes and skateboards, kicking and throwing balls. The neighborhood had a lot of crime, and I guessed the kids had seen their share of bloodshed. As I passed Cheever he spoke.

"God, am I fucking stupid," he said.

I chased Perez down the sidewalk. The bullet in his ass was making it impossible for him to run, and he glanced fearfully over his shoulder. Seeing me, his eyes went wide. I yelled for him to stop, and Perez grabbed a chubby little kid pushing a scooter and threw him to the pavement.

The little guy started bawling for his mommy, and I ran into the street to avoid stepping on him. As I did, Perez staggered up the path of a run-down house and banged frantically on the front door. The door sprung open, and a skinny Rastafarian with shoulder-length dreadlocks and bloodshot eyes poked his head out.

"What's up, Jonny?" the Rasta asked.

"The police are onto us," Perez said.

"That's bullshit," the Rasta said.

They disappeared inside the house. I ran up the path and stuck my head through the open doorway. The living room was filled with towering marijuana plants and burning fluorescent lights, and reggae music was blaring over a pair of old-fashioned speakers. I stepped inside and was greeted by a screaming motion detector.

Perez appeared on the other side of the living room, cradling a machine pistol. It was the weapon of choice among drug dealers and could fire a hundred rounds a minute. I beat a path out the front door with bullets flying all around me. On the street, kids screamed and ran for cover.

I hid behind a thick hibiscus hedge at the side of the house. Finally the torrent of bullets stopped. I counted to five, then poked my head out. Perez wasn't standing in the doorway, and the house was quiet. Still, I had no intention of going back inside. The walls looked like plasterboard, and Perez could easily kill me from another room.

I heard a door slam, then voices coming from the backyard. Staying low, I sneaked around the side of the house. The backyard was a jungle of tall Bermuda grass and dying citrus trees, with a detached garage facing the alley. I saw Perez carrying Melinda over his shoulder in a fireman's carry. The Rasta walked beside him, cradling the machine pistol. I didn't have a clear shot and watched them disappear into the garage.

Moments later I heard a car being started. Then I heard the Rasta exhorting Perez to take his foot off the gas and stop flooding the engine. I ran into the alley and aimed my Colt at the garage door.

The garage door automatically lifted, and a black Mustang convertible pulled out. The vehicle had been backed into the garage and came straight toward me. Melinda was sandwiched between Perez and the Rasta in the front seat. She wore a man's white T-shirt and baseball cap. She was alive, and our eyes met. Then she screamed.

"Jack! Help me!"

I had a shot at Perez. But I was just as likely to hit Melinda. I didn't take it, and Perez hit the gas and attempted to run me over. I leaped out of the car's path and rolled onto the grass. Before the Mustang had reached the street, I was on my feet and got off several rounds. There was a loud *Bam!* as the right rear tire exploded. The car drove away, sagging to one side like a wounded animal.

I stood with my gun hanging by my side and Melinda's voice ringing in my ears. I reached for my cell to call Linderman, then remembered I'd given it to the girl. I began to tremble. This wasn't how it was supposed to end.

The sound of a car horn brought me back to reality. Linderman was burning down the alley in his 4Runner with Buster occupying the passenger seat. He braked in front of me, and I hopped in, sharing the seat with my dog.

"Perez and his buddy got away with Melinda," I said.

"For the love of Christ, Jack," he said.

He drove to the alley's end and hit the brakes. "Which way did they go?"

"To the right," I said. "How's Theis?"

"The medics arrived a couple of minutes ago. He'll live."

"How about Cheever?"

"He'll live, too."

We drove around the neighborhood in silence. The gunfire had sent everyone inside, and the streets were clear. There was no sign of the Mustang save for several pieces of shredded tire lying in the middle of the road.

"I got one of his tires," I explained.

"Describe the car," Linderman said.

I described the getaway car. Linderman called the Broward County Police Helicopter Unit on his cell phone and passed along the information to a dispatcher. Hanging up, he jabbed me in the arm with his forefinger.

"You need to start going to the firing range."

"I didn't want to hit Melinda," I explained.

He shot me an exasperated look. "Jonny Perez is a cold-blooded killer. Our responsibility is to get him off the streets before he kills again. You had two cracks at him, and he got away."

"You think I could have taken him out, but didn't?"

"You said you wanted to talk to Perez about the victims. I'd like to question him as much as you would, but this isn't a perfect world."

"Question him about what?" I asked.

At the next intersection Linderman hit the brakes. He took a stack of photographs from the backseat and dropped them in my lap. I leafed through a dozen black-and-white glossies of an apartment complex taken from the outside. In one shot, a sign was visible. It read University of Miami, Coral Gables Campus.

"Theis found those photographs on Coffen's computer," he explained.

"Your daughter's dormitory," I said.

"Yes, my daughter's dorm. They were taken five years ago."

"Is that when she disappeared?"

"Yes, Jack, that's when she disappeared."

I leaned back in my seat with my dog pressed to my side. Linderman had found evidence that tied Skell's gang to his daughter's disappearance, and yet he still wanted me to take out Perez. It said a lot about who he was and how he viewed his job.

I looked at the badge pinned to his lapel and thought of the badge resting in the desk in my office. I supposed that was what separated us. He was always going to be a law enforcement officer, and I was never going to be one again.

His cell rang. He took the call, then looked sideways at me.

"A police helicopter just spotted Perez's car abandoned on the shoulder of 595. Want another crack at them?"

The offer surprised me. I'd figured Linderman was finished with me.

"I sure do," I said.

CHAPTER FORTY-SIX

Fort Lauderdale has three categories of drivers. Crazies, blue hairs, and people without licenses. Despite the blue flasher on the dashboard of Linderman's 4Runner, not a single vehicle on 595 got out of our way.

"Screw this," Linderman said.

He drove onto the shoulder and hit the gas. I held on to my dog while looking for the getaway car. Less than a mile up the highway, a black Mustang convertible sat abandoned. Three tattooed guys with crowbars were in the process of dismantling it.

"There's the car Perez was driving," I said.

"Who are those clowns?" Linderman asked.

"Your everyday car thieves."

"Look for the police chopper."

My eyes scanned the sky and found the police chopper hovering over a strip center near where the Mustang had been ditched. Pointing, I said, "Over there."

Linderman pulled into the strip center and parked. It was a slow day, and only a handful of cars were in the lot. We got out, and Linderman waved his arms in the air to signal the chopper. The pilot saw us and dipped down, momentarily eclipsing the sun.

The pilot was a woman with blond hair. She pointed at

the anchor store in the strip. It was called Mattress Giant and was going out of business. Linderman gave the okay sign, and she went back up. Linderman got his shotgun from the 4Runner.

"You still have bullets?" he asked.

I touched the bullets resting in my pocket.

"Yes."

"Good. Go around to the back of the mattress store, and call me on your cell. If things look okay, we'll enter the store at the same time, and trap them."

"I left my phone back at Perez's house," I said.

He shot me a disapproving look. Between my marksmanship and not having my cell, I could tell his opinion of me wasn't very high.

"You're in luck. I've got a spare," he said.

He removed a bright red cell phone from his jacket pocket, and tossed it to me. It was a newer model and reminded me of one my daughter carried.

"I found it on the lawn at Perez's house," he explained. "I'm guessing it fell out of Cheever's pocket. You have my number?"

I had his number memorized, and nodded.

"Good. Call me when you reach the back. Okay?"

He was talking to me like I was a kid. I said okay, and walked around the strip center with the phone in my hand. I flipped it open, and a greeting in Spanish appeared on its face. Cheever didn't speak Spanish, and I realized it didn't belong to him.

It was Jonny Perez's.

As I came around the strip center, Buster let out a menacing growl. The Rasta stood by the service door to Mattress Giant. He had the machine pistol trained on two male employees, both of whom wore dress shirts and neckties and had their hands clasped on their heads like POWs.

My eyes searched for Perez. Behind the building was a small parking lot, with signs indicating the spots were for employees only. Perez was in the rear of the lot, forcing Melinda into a blue Chevy Nova, his gun shoved into her back.

I went into a crouch and aimed my weapon. I had a shot at Perez, only it wasn't a good one, and there was a chance I might hit Melinda. I thought about what Linderman had said in the car. Then I squeezed the trigger.

The bullet winged Perez in the head. He let out a startled yell and grabbed his ear. Then he pulled Melinda in front of him and turned her into a human shield.

"Stay back!" he shouted.

I kept my gun trained on Perez. The Rasta remained by the service door, his machine pistol pointed at the employees.

"Jack, help me!" Melinda yelled.

"I'm trying," I called back.

"I love you, Jack."

"I know you do," I said under my breath.

Some hostages shut down when faced with death. Melinda did the opposite, and started throwing her elbows and stomping her heels on Perez's toes. It was one of the bravest things I'd ever seen. Perez lowered his hand and put her in a choke hold. His ear was gone, and blood was streaming down the side of his neck.

"Let her go, and I won't come after you," I called out.

Perez's eyes said he wasn't buying it.

"Come on," I said.

Perez aimed his weapon at me. I ducked behind the

building and heard a sickening thud. I stole a look around the corner. He had knocked Melinda unconscious and was putting her into the Nova.

"Cover me!" Perez yelled.

I came out from hiding. The Rasta had finally found his nerve. He aimed the machine pistol at me, and we exchanged shots. It was obvious he'd never handled an automatic weapon before, and the bullets sprayed harmlessly into the ground. I kept firing and saw him go down.

I sprinted across the lot with Buster hugging my side. Perez had jumped into the Nova and was backing out. He spun the wheel like a professional driver, hopped the curb, and headed down a connector road toward 595. I could do nothing but watch.

The back door of the mattress store opened, and Linderman hustled over.

"Jack, are you okay?"

I stood helplessly with my Colt dangling by my side.

"He's getting away," I said.

Linderman found the chopper in the sky and waved the pilot down. He pointed at the interstate, and the pilot took off after the Nova. We walked back to the store, and Linderman addressed the two employees.

"Whose car was that?"

One of the employees was short, the other tall. They both lowered their hands.

"Mine," the taller one said.

"What's the tag number?"

"It's in my wallet."

"Where's that?"

"Inside."

"I need to see it."

They started to go inside. I looked down at the Rasta.

Shot in the waist, he was barely alive, his eyes blinking rapidly. If anyone knew where Perez was headed, it was him. Kneeling, I pulled his head into my lap and shielded his eyes from the sun.

"What are you doing?" Linderman asked.

"Maybe he can help us," I said.

"Don't hold your breath," he said.

They went inside. As the back door closed, the Rasta gazed up at me.

"*You the boyfriend?*" he whispered in a Jamaican accent.

"What boyfriend?" I asked.

"*Jonny said his woman was cheating on him, and he wanted to teach her a lesson.*"

"Is that why you kept her in your house?"

The Rasta nodded weakly.

"Jonny is a killer," I said. "He lied to you."

The Rasta shut his eyes and took a deep breath.

"Will you tell me something?" I asked.

The Rasta's eyes opened, but he did not answer me.

"Where's Jonny taking her? You must have some idea."

The Rasta looked through me, his face losing its strength.

"Jonny was going to leave you behind," I said. "He didn't give a rat's ass about you. You don't owe him anything."

The Rasta thought about it, then spoke.

"*Jonny's taking her to the ocean. He said he was going to surprise you.*"

"Surprise me how?"

"*I dunno, man.*"

"Was he taking her to a boat?"

The Rasta blinked in the affirmative. His right hand was hovering over his pants pocket. I stuck my fingers into the pocket and pulled out a plastic key ring from which a single key dangled. I held the key up to the Rasta's face.

"Is this your boat?" I asked.

"Jonny's. He let me use it sometimes."

"Did he keep it in a marina?"

"Yeah."

"Do you know which one?"

"Don't know the name. It's on one of the canals."

There was a roar of sirens, and I lifted my gaze as six police cruisers pulled into the lot. The cruisers surrounded us in a tight circle. Twelve doors opened simultaneously, and more guns than I could count were pointed at my head.

"Don't shoot," I said.

CHAPTER FORTY-SEVEN

A pair of cops threw me against a wall. I told them an FBI agent was inside the store who could explain everything, and the cops told me to keep my mouth shut. While I was being patted down I glanced at Buster. My dog was parked in the building's shade with a concerned look on his face.

Then Linderman came out and set the cops straight. There were times when I wanted to hug the guy, and this was one of them. Linderman convinced the cops to give me my Colt back. As I slipped it into its pocket holster Buster came out from the shadows and pressed up against my leg.

By now the Rasta was unconscious, and two cops were doing their best to keep him breathing. I stood over him for a minute, then realized he probably wouldn't be opening his eyes for a while.

I followed Linderman into the mattress store. Once we were inside, he turned around and put his hand on my shoulder. It wasn't a gesture I expected from him.

"I've got shitty news," Linderman said.

I braced myself.

"The police chopper lost the Nova."

"How is that possible?"

Linderman explained how Perez had driven east on 595, gotten onto I-95 north, and taken the Broward Boulevard exit into downtown Fort Lauderdale. From there, Perez had driven to A1A and headed south, going through an underground tunnel in the heart of downtown. That was where the chopper had lost the car.

"I know where Perez is taking her," I said.

Linderman dropped his hand. "You do?"

I showed him the Rasta's key ring. "Perez is going to dump Melinda in the ocean. You need to call the police and tell them to search Perez's house. There should be a bill from a marina where he keeps his boat."

"Why wouldn't Perez just shoot her and dump the body?" Linderman asked.

I shook my head. "The gang was setting me up. They were going to kill Melinda and make it look like I did it."

"You?"

"They were trying to convince people I was the Midnight Rambler, and take the heat off Skell."

I watched Linderman punch in the Broward cops' phone number on his cell. Raising the phone to his face, he said, "You're always thinking, aren't you, Jack?"

I realized he was complimenting me and smiled grimly.

The mattress store was filled with beds. While Linderman was on his phone, I sat down on the edge of a king-size bed and removed Perez's cell phone from my pocket. It was still powered up, and I went straight into the address book, hoping to find the number for the marina.

The address book had several dozen entries. No full names were listed, just first and last initials. There was NB, who I assumed was Neil Bash, and PC, who I guessed was Paul Coffen. A listing near the end jumped out at me.

LS.

It could have been anybody, but my gut told me it was Leonard Snook. The listing had two numbers: one work, the other a cell. Both had 305 area codes, which was Miami/Dade County. I punched in the work number. It rang through, and a woman picked up.

"Law office," the woman said sternly.

"Is he in?" I asked.

"Is who in?" she asked suspiciously.

"Leonard Snook."

"Mr. Snook is out of the office. If you'd like, you can leave a message."

I said no thanks and hung up. Snook represented Simon Skell and Cecil Cooper, and now I had evidence he was connected to Jonny Perez. There was no law against representing abductors and serial killers, and I found myself hoping that Snook could be persuaded to help us find Perez before he killed Melinda. I pulled up his cell number from the address book and called it. After several rings he answered.

"I can't talk to you right now, Jonny," the lawyer said in a whisper. "We just got into Fort Lauderdale, and Simon's giving a news conference to a bunch of dimwitted reporters. I'll call you back when he's done."

Before I could reply, Snook ended the call. I couldn't believe what I'd just heard, and rose from the bed. On the other side of the store, the two employees stood by a desk drinking coffee. I walked over to them.

"Is there a TV in the store?" I asked.

They pointed at a portable TV sitting on the desk. It was so small, I hadn't even noticed it. I picked up the remote and channel-surfed. Skell's news conference was on the local ABC affiliate. He was staying at a nearby hotel.

Skell stood in front of a podium answering questions, his wife and attorney flanking him. He still wore the Old Navy sweatshirt and blue jeans. I jacked up the volume.

"What will you do, now that you're free?" a reporter asked.

"Go back to my work," Skell said.

"Do you hold a grudge against Jack Carpenter for what he did to you?" the same reporter asked.

Skell leaned into the mikes. "Jack Carpenter will get what's coming to him."

"Are you angry at him?"

"He'll get what's coming to him," Skell repeated.

"Is it true there's a movie deal in the works?" another reporter called out.

Leonard Snook stepped up to the mike and announced that a major motion picture deal was in the works, with a famous Hollywood actor being considered to play his client. There was also a six-figure book contract with a prominent New York publishing house.

"Who's writing it?" a reporter asked.

"I am," Snook said.

Something inside of me snapped. Attorneys made money representing scumbags, but Snook was profiting on his client's victims' misfortune. It was evil, pure and simple.

Without thinking of the ramifications, I called Snook back. On the TV, Snook pulled out his cell and looked at it disapprovingly, then stepped out of the picture. Seconds later, his voice came on the line.

"For Christ's sake, Jonny, I can't talk to you right now. I'll call you back when I'm done."

"This isn't Jonny," I said.

Snook paused. In the background, I could hear Skell talking to the reporters.

"Then who am I speaking to?" he asked.

"Jack Carpenter," I replied.

Snook gasped.

"What do you want?" he finally said.

"Tell Skell I have a message for him," I said.

"A message?"

"That's right. And for you, too."

"What's your message?"

"Tell him that Paul Coffen, Neil Bash, and Paco Perez are waiting for him in hell. Will you do that for me, Leonard?"

"Is this some kind of twisted joke?"

"No joke," I said.

Snook hung up.

I stared at the portable TV. There was a time delay on the transmission, and several seconds passed before Snook reentered the picture. He edged up to Skell and whispered in his client's ear.

Skell was directly facing the camera when he heard the news. His jaw clenched and his nostrils flared. I'd seen this look on the faces of other killers. It was called sociopathic rage. Skell was ready to blow.

Suddenly the news conference was over, and Skell walked away from the podium with his entourage in tow.

CHAPTER FORTY-EIGHT

I turned off the portable TV and walked to the front of the mattress store. Linderman stood by the windows, gazing out on the parking lot while talking on his cell phone. I could tell by his posture and subdued voice that the police had not found the stolen Nova. I coughed, and he turned to stare at me.

"You need to call Special Agent Saunders," I said.

He clamped his hand over the receiver.

"I'm on a call," he said.

"Do as I say, and call him."

"Just . . ."

"Right now," I said. "Skell is going to make a run for it. I tipped him off."

Linderman's shoulder twitched, and for a second I thought he was going to punch me in the mouth. He said good-bye and ended the call.

"Why in God's name did you do that?"

"I popped my cork and called Snook on Perez's cell phone," I said.

"For the love of Christ, Jack."

Linderman called Special Agent Saunders and explained the situation. Putting his hand over the receiver, he said, "Saunders is sitting with his partner in a surveillance van outside the Executive Suites in Fort Lauderdale. They're watching Skell's motel room and listening through the walls to their conversations. Skell's in there with his wife and attorney. Everything is fine. Skell isn't going anywhere."

The Executive Suites was located on Military Trail near a busy shopping center. It was a crummy place to be holding news conferences, especially considering the big money Skell was making from the book and movie deals. I guessed Skell had an ulterior motive for staying there and grabbed the phone out of Linderman's hand.

"Scott, this is Jack Carpenter," I said into the phone. "I did a dumb thing, and I don't want you to have to pay for it. You need to grab Skell."

"On what grounds?" Saunders said.

"Make something up," I said.

"I can't do that."

"Why not? You're the law."

"Two reasons. Skell just got released from prison, and his lawyer is with him," Saunders said. "Arresting him is a one-way ticket to North Dakota."

North Dakota was where FBI agents got sent as punishment. I handed the phone back to Linderman. He ended the call and folded the phone.

"We need to go over to the Executive Suites," I said.

"I just told you Jack, everything's under control."

"No, it's not," I said.

"You're sure about this?"

"Yes."

Linderman's shoulder twitched again. Then he pulled his keys out of his pocket, and I followed him out the door.

Traffic in Broward was as unpredictable as the weather.

Although the Executive Suites was not far, the drive took twenty minutes. We pulled into the parking lot, cursing.

The FBI's surveillance van was parked in a handicap spot and was painted to look like a dry-cleaning service. Linderman tapped three times on the rear door. The door opened, and Saunders hopped out.

"Skell hasn't gone anywhere," Saunders said, lighting a cigarette. "His suite is right in view, and there are no back windows he can escape through."

"Has he had any visitors?" I asked.

"Chase Winters, the movie producer, paid him a visit fifteen minutes ago," Saunders said. "He's also staying at the hotel."

"What did he want?" I asked.

"He was bringing some stuff to Skell."

"What kind of stuff?"

Saunders shook his head.

"Did you film Winters going into Skell's room?"

Saunders nodded while exhaling a large purple plume.

"I need to see it," I said.

We climbed into the back of the van. The interior was filled with sophisticated electronic monitoring equipment. Saunders's partner sat up front wearing a pair of headphones, and he gave us the thumbs-up.

One wall of the van was nothing but digital monitors. Saunders played the tape of Winters going into Skell's suite. Winters wore loose-fitting designer clothes, a baseball cap, and shades. His diamond earring sparkled as he walked. Clutched to his chest was an open cardboard box containing several bottles of champagne. Dangling from his fingers was a plastic bag from CVS.

Winters used his foot to knock on the door to Skell's suite. The door opened, and Skell stuck his head out. He looked around, then put his arm around Winters's shoulder and ushered him inside.

The tape ended. Saunders hit a button, and the monitor switched back to real time.

"I want to know what's inside that bag from CVS," I said.

Saunders looked at Linderman as if seeking confirmation.

"I think that's a good idea," Linderman said.

Saunders called the CVS pharmacy on the corner. A minute later he had an answer.

"Chase Winters made six purchases on his Visa Card," Saunders said. "Razors, shaving cream, a box of cotton balls, rubbing alcohol, a package of sewing needles, and a can of black shoe polish."

Linderman looked at me. "What did he want with that stuff?"

I shook my head. There was no way of knowing what Skell was up to.

"The movie producer is coming out," Saunders's partner announced.

On the monitor we saw Chase Winters emerge from Skell's suite. He was holding the cardboard box up to his chest, and his baseball cap was pulled down low. His diamond earring continued to sparkle. He walked to his own suite, unlocked the door, and went in.

Something didn't feel right. Without thinking I lifted my head, and banged the roof of the van. The pain made me see the discrepancy.

"Play the tape again," I said.

Linderman and Saunders stared at me.

"Come on," I said.

Saunders replayed the tape. I brought my face to the

screen and stared at Winters's feet. He was wearing black tennis sneakers. They didn't match his outfit, and I was reminded of Shannon Dockery's abduction at Disney. Her abductors had painted her shoes instead of switching them because shoe sizes were hard to predict.

Then I knew. The man we'd just seen wasn't Chase Winters. It was Skell, wearing Winters's clothes and earring, his sneakers colored with dark shoe polish. He had staged his escape right beneath our noses.

"That's Skell," I shouted.

The FBI agents beat me out of the van and across the lot. With weapons drawn, they took down the door to Winters's suite. I waited a few seconds before following them inside. This was their show, not mine.

The living room was empty, save for the cardboard box lying on the floor. I walked into the bedroom and found Saunders and his partner climbing through an open window that led to a courtyard behind the motel. They had checked Skell's suite for escape windows, but not Winters's suite. My nightmare had become reality. Skell was free.

As Saunders and his partner ran across the courtyard in pursuit, Linderman frantically punched numbers into his cell phone and called for backup.

"Where's the other teams?" I asked.

Linderman looked at me, not understanding.

"You said there would be three teams of agents assigned to watch Skell. Where are the other two teams?"

Linderman shook his head. He didn't know. I cursed and started to leave.

"Where are you going?" Linderman asked.

"Next door," I said. "I want to see what he did to them."

CHAPTER FORTY-NINE

The door to Skell's suite was unlocked. So as not to taint the crime scene, I twisted the knob using my shirttail, then used my shoe to open the door.

I stuck my head into the darkened space. So did my dog, who'd climbed out of the 4Runner to join me.

The living room had its shades drawn, and it took a moment for my eyes to adjust. The sounds of a man's tortured breathing filled the void and painted pictures in the dark too gruesome to describe. I opened the door all the way and let sunlight flood the room.

A hazy cloud of cigarette smoke hung lifelessly in the air, as did the sweet smell of champagne. I drew my Colt as I stepped inside.

"Ahhh."

The voice was muffled. My eyes scanned the room's interior. Leonard Snook sat in the corner, tied to a chair with a bedsheet. A sock was stuck in his mouth, and his face was turning a violent shade of blue. He had also soiled himself.

"How's the book coming?" I asked.

"Uhhh."

"I should let you die, you know that."

"Ahhh."

I pulled the sock out of his mouth, and Snook sucked down air.

"Tell me what happened," I said.

Snook began to weep. The shock was so great he could not speak. I kicked the leg of the chair with my foot. The jolt made him sit upright.

"Start talking," I said.

"He made me watch," the attorney sobbed.

"Did he kill them in front of you?"

Snook shut his eyes, forcing out tears.

"Yes."

"The FBI was listening to the room," I said. "You had to know that. Why didn't you scream for help?"

"He said if I screamed, he'd kill me."

"You're a coward," I said.

"Untie me, please."

I heard Buster whining. He was standing at the bedroom door with his hackles up. I left Snook and went to the door. It was closed, and I covered my hand with my shirttail before twisting the knob. Then I went in.

The bedroom was dark, and I flicked on the lights as I entered. A man lay on the bed in his underwear. The left side of his head was crushed in, and his throat was slit from ear to ear. His eyes were wide open, as was his mouth. I looked at the recognizable portion of his face and decided it was Chase Winters.

A broken champagne bottle lay beside Winters's body. I guessed that Skell had killed him while celebrating, then stolen his clothes. The wounds Skell had inflicted were so severe that Winters had bled out, and I pulled my dog back so he didn't step in it.

I made Buster sit in the corner, then noticed several loose sheets of paper lying on the floor beside the bed. I picked one up without bothering to cover my hand. It was the cover page to a movie contract with Paramount Pictures for a film based on the life of Simon Skell. The working title was *Midnight Rambler*.

My dog let out a pitiful whine. He could smell the death and despair and pure evil that had inhabited the room. I looked around the room for Lorna Sue Mutter. She wasn't in the closet or stuffed beneath the bed. I noticed a sliver of light streaming out from beneath the bathroom door. I crossed the room and knocked gently on the door.

"Lorna Sue?"

Nothing. I tapped again.

"Are you in there?"

Still nothing. I wanted to believe she might still be alive, even though I felt certain she wasn't. Despite our run-in outside the police station, I did not hate her. She had found it within her heart to love a monster. If more people had done that with Skell, he might not have become the person he was.

"I'm coming in."

My body pressed against the bathroom door, and I heard it click open. I pushed the door open a few inches, and Buster pushed it open a few more.

The bathroom was large and contained a shower stall and a tub. The sink was filled with clippings from Skell's beard. On the floor I spied a bloody cotton ball, which Skell had used to pierce his own ear.

Lorna Sue Mutter lay in the tub, submerged in water. She was faceup, and her big hair floated in the water like a dead animal. Like Winters, her eyes and mouth were wide open. I'd heard it said that death was the ultimate aphrodisiac, but the look on Lorna Sue's face told me otherwise. It was the look of betrayal, and love gone horribly bad.

CHAPTER FIFTY

I walked outside into the blinding sunshine. A police cruiser pulled into the parking lot, and two cops hurried inside. Linderman stood nearby with his phone pressed to his ear and a disgusted look on his face. He said, "All three of them dead?"

"He spared Snook," I said.

"You never know when you'll need a good lawyer."

"You on hold?"

"Waiting for the police," he said.

Although I knew the answer to my next question, I asked it anyway.

"Any trace of Skell?"

"Looks like he stole a car and took off. Tell me what you think of this."

He removed a photograph from his pocket and handed it to me. It showed Melinda lying provocatively on a bed without any clothes on. She was smiling through clenched teeth.

"Saunders found it in the courtyard behind the hotel," Linderman said. "He thinks Skell dropped it running away."

"How would Skell have gotten this?"

"Snook must have given it to him."

I stared at the photo. Melinda looked just like the other victims I'd seen in Bash's trailer. That surprised me, and I flipped the photo over. There was writing on the back.

#9.

The number's significance was slow to register. When it did, I showed the writing to Linderman. He didn't understand, and I grabbed his arm.

"I was wrong," I said.

"About what?"

"Skell isn't obsessed with Melinda."

"I thought you said she had sent him over the edge."

I pointed at the #9 on the back of the photograph.

"This is how the gang identifies the victims, by numbers. Melinda's just another number to him. She isn't what fuels his rages."

The FBI had given Linderman an award for his accomplishments in hunting down serial killers. Understanding a serial killer's motivation was the only possible way of stopping them. He took the photo from my hands and studied it.

"Then why did Skell come to Fort Lauderdale?" he asked.

"To frame me."

"Why not let his gang do that?"

"The gang tried. They killed a prostitute named Joy Chambers and tried to pin it on me. They left enough evidence behind that the police knew it wasn't me."

"So Skell wanted to make sure they didn't blow it this time."

"Yes."

Linderman nodded. Then he took out his car keys.

"Get in the car," he said.

"Why? Where are we going?"

"To the beach. The Rasta told you Jonny Perez was taking Melinda to a marina so he could dump her body in the ocean, right?"

"That's right," I said. "Only the Rasta didn't remember the marina's name."

"Your office is at a marina, isn't it?"

We drove to Tugboat Louie's with the blue light flashing on the dashboard of the 4Runner. This time, traffic got out of our way. I called Bobby Russo and told him what was going on. Then I called Kumar and told him to be on the lookout for the police.

Kumar was standing in the parking lot as we pulled in. His oversized bow tie was undone, and he looked upset. Two police cruisers were parked by the front door with their bubble lights flashing. A Jimmy Buffet song about getting wasted filled the air.

Linderman and I hopped out of the 4Runner and approached Kumar.

"Jack! I'm so glad you are here," Kumar said. "The police arrived five minutes ago, just like you said they would. Can you please tell me what's going on?"

I introduced Linderman. Seeing the badge pinned to Linderman's lapel, Kumar fell silent.

"I need to talk to you about a man named Jonny Perez," Linderman said.

"I know this man," Kumar said.

"You do?"

"Oh, yes. Perez keeps a boat in my dry dock. He's a strange character, that is for sure."

"How recently have you seen him?" Linderman asked.

"Twenty minutes ago," Kumar said. "Is he involved in this?"

I ran around the parking lot looking for the stolen Nova. It was illegally parked in a handicap spot. I searched the interior and popped the trunk. No Melinda.

I went back to where Kumar was standing with Linderman.

"Perez was walking with a limp," Kumar said. "His shirt was pulled out, and it was stained in the back. He had a beautiful woman with him, very tall and very blond, and she looked drunk. They were walking to the dry dock, and several times she nearly fell down. It was obvious she should have been at home, sleeping it off."

"Didn't you find his behavior strange?" Linderman asked.

"I own a bar," Kumar said. "I see a lot of strange behavior."

"What happened then?"

"As they reached the dry dock, the woman fell and couldn't get up," Kumar said. "I went over and offered my assistance. Then a second man appeared and started to help Perez. They appeared to be friends, so I left."

"What did this second man look like?" Linderman asked.

"He had a baseball cap on and sunglasses. I didn't get a good look at his face. I did notice that he was missing a finger on both his hands."

"Did you see them leave in Perez's boat?"

Kumar nodded. "Perez owns a Boston Whaler. It's probably the smallest boat in the marina. I saw the boat leave with the three of them in it."

"Did they go inland, or out to the ocean?" I asked.

"To the ocean," Kumar said.

"Anything else you remember?" Linderman asked.

Kumar scratched his chin. "I did find one thing strange."

"What's that?" we both asked.

"The man who runs the dry dock is not on good terms with Perez. They have had words many times. I was surprised he got Perez's boat out so quickly."

A good ole boy named Clyde ran the dry dock. Clyde had issues with dark skin and foreign accents. I took off running toward the dry dock, knowing what Perez and Skell must have done to persuade Clyde to get Perez's boat.

CHAPTER FIFTY-ONE

The dry dock was a blue-and-gold manufactured aluminum building designed like an airplane hangar. Inside, powerboats rested on steel-framed bunks stacked one atop the other, right up to the vaulted ceiling. A portable hydraulic lift, used to move the boats, sat in the corner as I entered. Normally, Clyde sat in a beach chair beside the lift, listening to country and western music while spitting tobacco juice on the ground.

Clyde's chair was empty, and his radio was turned off. I looked around the building for a sign of where he might have gone. The building did not have air-conditioning, and the air hung hot and still. Buster had disappeared, and I could hear him whining and scratching on wood. I followed the sound to a storage closet in the back.

"Good dog," I said.

I pulled open the heavy sliding door. Sunlight filled the closet's interior, and I saw a sunburned man lying on the floor, holding his stomach with both hands and moaning. A large stain covered the bottom of his denim shirt.

"Clyde?"

"Don't hurt me," he begged.

"It's Jack Carpenter. Where are you hit?"

"That bastard Perez shot me in the stomach," Clyde said.

Linderman entered the building. I called him over, and we pulled Clyde out of the closet by his ankles. Linderman started to tend to Clyde's wound while I dialed 911.

"Jack, he's okay," Linderman said.

"How can he be okay?"

Linderman tossed me a pint metal flask that he'd pulled from Clyde's pants. The flask had a bullet hole in it. Holding it to my nose, I smelled rum. I saw Clyde tenderly rub his stomach.

"Lucky you," I said.

Linderman called the Broward office of the FBI and asked for a cutter to be sent to the mouth of the canal leading out of Tugboat Louie's. The FBI, which was responsible for handling criminal investigations in waters twelve miles off shore, kept a high-speed cutter and crew on twenty-four-hour alert in nearby Port Everglades. It was the best chance we had of finding Perez's boat.

Linderman and I walked outside the hangar and waited for the cutter to arrive. Kumar came down the dock and pulled me into the hangar's cool shade.

"Jack, will you please tell me what's going on?"

Normally, it was best to say nothing during an investigation. But Kumar was my friend, and I couldn't keep him in the dark.

"The man you saw with Perez was Simon Skell, the Midnight Rambler. The woman was kidnapped. They're going to take her out and throw her overboard."

"And I let him get away," Kumar said.

"You did everything you could," I said.

"No, I did not. There is something I did not tell your FBI friend."

"What's that?"

"Over the past six months, Perez took his boat out many times, always when it was late at night. Several employees saw him and thought it was suspicious."

"How many times did Perez do this?"

"Six or seven."

"Did you see him do this?"

"Once. There was a ferocious storm. I watched from my office window. Perez took a sack from his van and carried it down to his boat. It looked heavy."

I thought back to the empty coolers I'd seen in Perez's shed. For the past six months he'd been coming here, taking his boat out, and dumping the bodies.

"Jesus," I said under my breath.

Kumar's shoulders sagged, and he walked back to the bar muttering under his breath. I knew that his inability to stop Perez would weigh on him for a long time.

Fifteen agonizing minutes later, the FBI cutter motored up to Tugboat Louie's, and the captain jumped onto the dock. He was in his fifties and fair-skinned, the sunblock on his face as bright as war paint. He explained that his vessel had just completed a sweep of the waters both north and south of us and had not spotted Perez's boat.

"The ocean's choppy, and there's a small craft advisory in effect until later tonight," the captain said. "My guess is, Perez is hiding in the mangroves. When it's clear, he'll dump his victim. It would help our search if we could get a description of his boat."

Clyde stepped forward. He'd put on a fresh shirt and seemed eager to put the incident with the flask behind him. He described Perez's boat to the captain. When he was finished, the captain made him start over. It was an old interrogator's trick, and Clyde's description became more detailed the second time, right down to the bad paint job and sputtering Honda engine.

"Anything you'd like to add?" the captain asked when Clyde was done.

"The Hispanic in the boat has a death wish," I said.

"That's good to know," the captain said.

He jumped on the cutter and motored away. I stood on the dock and watched, the sound of the cutter's engines reverberating across the marina.

"What do we do now?" I asked Linderman.

"We wait," Linderman said.

"I'm not good at waiting," I said.

Linderman slapped me on the back. He reminded me of a Little League coach I'd had who liked to slap his players on the back when the team was getting trounced.

"Keep the faith, Jack," he said.

We walked down the dock to Tugboat Louie's bar. On the way, I counted the steps. There were exactly 120. It was a number I would never forget: 120 steps from my office was the boat used to dispose of the women I'd spent six months looking for.

God was cruel.

"I need some coffee," Linderman said.

We went inside the bar. The cops' presence had cleared the place out, and Robert Palmer's "Addicted to Love" blasted the empty room. We took a pair of stools and waited to be served. My sense of helplessness would not go away. I needed to do something, or I would start pulling my hair out and make everyone around me crazy.

Buster sat by my feet. He was panting, and I scratched behind his ears. I'd read that this calmed dogs down and wondered if it would have the same effect on me. Right now, I was willing to give just about anything a try.

"Jack, Jack!" a familiar voice rang out.

I lifted my eyes. Kumar stood at the bottom of the stairwell behind the bar, motioning excitedly to me.

"What's up?" I asked.

"I have figured out where they are taking the lady," Kumar said.

CHAPTER FIFTY-TWO

The scrape of my stool was enough to make Buster jump.

"You did? How?"

"I used a nautical chart," Kumar said. "Come upstairs, and I'll show you."

We followed Kumar upstairs to his office. A large nautical chart hung on the wall behind his desk. It was for boaters and showed the shoreline, minimum and maximum water depths, and aids and hazards to navigation for Broward County. Grabbing a pencil, Kumar began drawing lines on the chart.

"Here is what I'm thinking," Kumar said. "The engine on Perez's boat is less than a hundred horsepower and not very strong. Even in calm seas, he can't go far without fear of capsizing. More than likely, he'll stay close to the shoreline to dump the lady. He'll probably pick a deep area that can be found on a fisherman's map, or a chart like this one."

"Do fish like deep areas?" Linderman asked.

"Oh, yes," Kumar said. "They are safe places for them to breed."

Kumar drew three lines across the nautical chart. Each started at his marina and went down the canal to the ocean. Reaching the ocean, the lines veered off in different directions. One went north, one south, and one due east. None went very far.

As I stared at the lines, my heart began to race. The line going south ended at a spot in the ocean that I knew better than any fisherman in the state. North Dania Beach, within spitting distance of the Sunset. Had I not been so damn tired, I would have guessed it before now.

Perez and Skell were going to dump Melinda in the waters where I swam every day.

Linderman burned down Dania Beach Boulevard and practically flew over the bridge. He pulled into the Sunset with a squeal of brakes, and I jumped out with my dog.

"I'll be right back," I said.

I ran to my room and changed into bathing trunks. Then I tossed my Colt and a pair of binoculars into my snorkeling bag and headed for the door. Buster had climbed onto my bed and passed out.

I hurried downstairs. Entering the bar, I caught Sonny and the Seven Dwarfs in a rare moment of sobriety. They were slurping coffee and eating doughnuts, and they stared at me as if I was a ghost.

"Where the hell you been?" Sonny asked.

"Road trip. Why?"

"We were worried about you, man."

This crew didn't worry about anything. Then it dawned on me what Sonny was saying. He and the Dwarfs were worried that I'd done something to myself.

"I'm fine," I said. "Look, I need your help."

Whitey jumped off his stool and saluted me.

"Help's my middle name, captain."

I pulled the binoculars from the bag and tossed them to him.

"Go to the window and look due north for a Boston Whaler hugging the shoreline. There will be two guys in the boat. One is Hispanic and is in a lot of pain. The other is about my size and has surfer-white blond hair. There's also a beautiful blonde with them who's either doped up or unconscious."

Whitey went to the window and lifted the binoculars to his face.

"What are they up to?" he asked.

"They're going to throw the woman over," I added.

"Oh, my Lord," Whitey said.

I found Linderman standing by the shoreline, talking to the captain of the FBI cutter on his cell. I heard him tell the captain to bring his cutter to the northern tip of Dania Beach. Fitting on my mask and flippers, I threw my bag over my shoulder and waded in.

"Where do you think you're going?" Linderman asked, finishing his call.

"Out there," I said.

"Don't do it, Jack. If Perez shows, you'll be a sitting duck."

A wave broke over my legs, and I felt the ocean's unmistakable pull.

"I've got a gun in my bag," I said.

"Ever try shooting while treading water? It doesn't work."

I stared out helplessly at the ocean.

"I can't just stand here."

"Jack, I've had enough of your bullshit," Linderman said. "I'm ordering you to stay here with me. If you disobey me, I'm going to jump in and drag your ass out of the water. Am I making myself clear?"

I have a way of getting on people's nerves that pushes

them to the breaking point. I'd reached that juncture with Linderman, and I reluctantly tossed my bag on the shoreline. Then I plopped down in the sand. Thirty seconds later, Whitey appeared in the bar's open doorway, flailing his arms.

"I saw the boat," Whitey yelled. "I saw the boat!"

I stood up in my spot.

"Are you sure?" I called back.

"Positive, captain. It's coming from due north and has two men in it. There's another boat chasing it."

I said to hell with Linderman and dove into the water.

CHAPTER FIFTY-THREE

I swam with a strength that I didn't know I possessed. Passing the Sunset, I shifted my gaze northward. Several hundred yards away a boat was motoring toward me with Jonny Perez hunched over in the stern. The sun was in his face, and his eyes were slits. Angry black flies swarmed around him, attacking his wounds. He was in pain, yet his posture was defiant.

Skell stood in the bow, bare chested. His skin was as white as milk, his torso lean and sinewy. He'd gotten several tattoos while in prison, all of them in vibrant colors. From a distance they looked like scars.

Skell was yelling at Perez, telling him to make the boat go faster. His voice was high-pitched, almost a scream. His sociopathic rage had taken over.

I swam toward the boat, my flippers propelling me effortlessly through the water. I was directly in their line of vision, but they weren't looking my way. In the distance I could see the FBI cutter, coming fast.

"This is the spot," Perez called out.

"You sure?" Skell shouted back.

"Yeah, man."

"Then let's do it."

Perez stopped the engine, and the boat came to a halt.

Bending down, Skell lifted Melinda out of the boat and stood upright with her in his arms. She looked dead, and for a moment I thought I was too late. Then her fingers fluttered like a butterfly's wings. It did something to my heart, and I hurtled myself toward her.

A loud blast ripped through the air. The cutter was a hundred yards away, and a man wearing an FBI slicker stood on the bow, wielding a bullhorn.

"This is the FBI," the man announced. "Stop what you're doing and put your hands into the air."

"Cover me," Skell said.

Perez pulled a gun from his waistband. He turned and faced the cutter.

"I repeat, stop what you're doing!"

"Fuck you!" Perez screamed.

On the cutter another man wearing an FBI slicker appeared. He had a rifle, which he aimed at Perez. The shot ripped across the ocean.

Perez grabbed his arm. Then he fell, rocking the boat.

"Put the girl down," ordered the man with the bullhorn.

I was fifteen feet from the boat. Looking at Skell, I knew he wasn't going to comply. Killing was what defined his existence and would keep him alive in my memory long after he was gone. With a defiant yell, he tossed Melinda into the water.

Diving beneath the boat, I watched Melinda sink. Her body looked weightless, almost poetic. Reaching the ocean floor, she slipped behind a coral ledge and disappeared from my sight.

I propelled myself toward her. I had never been this deep before and had no idea what I was getting into. The thought was unsettling. Then I remembered Melinda's testimony at Skell's trial, and the courage it had taken to go down that road.

I owed her.

A dark shadow loomed overhead. Thinking it was the FBI cutter, I looked up and saw that I was wrong. It was Skell, chasing me.

Skell had ripped off the rest of his clothes and was naked. The crazed look in his eyes was still there. Clutched in his hand was a knife normally used to fillet fish. He used the knife to slice the water like he was in a street fight.

In seconds he was on top of me. I swam backwards with my flippers until I was safely away from him. He stopped over the spot where Melinda had disappeared and started treading water. Then he motioned to me.

I instantly understood. Skell was going to stay right where he was. Either I engaged him and we fought it out, or I stayed back and let Melinda drown.

Those were my options.

I charged him.

The element of surprise was mine. I grabbed his wrist with one hand and punched him in the face with the other. It had to hurt, because he made a noise that was loud enough for me to hear underwater.

Then Skell cut me.

It wasn't a deep gash, just a run of the blade across my left forearm. But the ribbon of blood was enough to get my attention. It clouded the water and told me I was in trouble. Again I propelled myself backwards.

Skell remained where he was. I got set to charge him again, then felt an enormous thrush of water. It was a feeling that every swimmer dreaded. A big fish was lurking behind me.

I froze as a male lemon shark swam past. It was easily three hundred pounds. The shark was checking us out, just as the school of sharks had checked me out the other day. I placed my hand on its side and guided it toward Skell.

Skell's face darkened. He didn't understand that the shark wouldn't hurt him and was only guarding something on the ocean's floor. He didn't understand that there was no immediate danger. As the shark got within his range he thrust his knife into its side.

There was a violent thrashing, followed by an explosion of blood and bubbles. I ducked to get out of its way and watched the shark go straight down.

I righted myself and stared through my steamy mask. Skell hadn't moved from his spot. A chunk of shark flesh was impaled on the point of his knife. He picked it off and stuck it into his mouth. Then he began to chew.

Again I felt a powerful thrush of water. The wounded lemon shark raced past and grabbed Skell's head in its powerful jaws. The crazed look on Skell's face changed to one of pure terror. He struggled violently, but could not break free.

My lungs were about to burst, and I propelled myself up. Moments before my head broke the surface, I listened hard, and was certain I could hear Skell screaming.

CHAPTER FIFTY-FOUR

Air had never tasted so sweet. The FBI cutter was parked next to Perez's boat. Two men wearing wet suits and scuba equipment were on deck, preparing to take the plunge.

"Over here," I yelled to them.

They jumped into the water and swam over to me.

"Where's the guy who threw the girl into the water?" one of the divers asked.

"Dead," I said.

"How about the girl?"

"Follow me. I'll show you."

I took them down to the coral ledge and pointed at the spot where I'd last seen Melinda. The divers glided effortlessly past me. I stopped at the ledge and waited. The pressure was intense, and my head began to throb. After what seemed like an eternity, the divers swam past, holding Melinda between their arms. With her flowing blond hair she looked just like a mermaid. I said a silent prayer as she passed.

One of the divers spotted me. With his head, he indicated the ocean floor. It was a simple gesture, one I didn't understand.

I started to follow him up. The diver stopped and repeated the gesture. I looked through his mask at his eyes and saw pain.

I swam back to the ledge and looked straight down. The first thing that caught my eye was the school of lemon sharks swimming below, the next the hull of a boat covered in a fine brown silt. As the silt moved with the current, other shapes appeared. Then my throat constricted, and I saw what the diver had seen: the decomposed bodies of Chantel, Maggie, Carmen, Jen, Krista, Brie, and Lola, each with lead weights tied around her ankles and wrists. They were lying so close together they could have formed a circle had they still been alive. Perez had dumped their bodies there in an effort to frame me, and I thought back to all the times I'd swum here in the past six months. Once a day, sometimes more. Perhaps Rose was right. Perhaps their spirits were clinging to me, so strong was their desire for vindication. Perhaps this was why I couldn't let go.

A minute later, I was standing on the cutter's deck with the crew, watching a pair of medics try to revive Melinda with a noisy machine called AutoPulse that mechanically pumped air into her watery lungs. Her face was a ghostly blue, and she looked more a part of the next world than of this one.

Perez's boat drifted nearby. Perez had tumbled out of it, and the crew seemed confident that the sharks had finished him off. I wasn't going to be happy until Perez's body was found, and I talked the divers into going down and searching for him.

"Do you know her?" one of the medics asked.

"Yes," I said.

"Well, start talking to her. She needs all the help she can get."

I got on my knees and put my lips to Melinda's ear. It was hard talking to someone who looked dead, but I tried. I told her that if she didn't start breathing, I wasn't going to speak to her again. I told her to fight. I told her anything that came to mind.

"Keep it up," the medic said encouragingly.

I kept talking and talking. Dime-sized spots of pink appeared on her cheeks.

"Here she comes," the medic said.

We all leaned in. Like a baby chick hatching from an egg, she popped back to life. Her first breath was a violent hacking sound. Then she started breathing normally. She looked all around as if seeing the world for the first time. The crew began to applaud.

I saw motion in the water and glanced over the side. The two divers had reappeared. Seeing me, they both shook their heads.

"Jack, is that you?" Melinda said.

I turned and looked at her.

"Hey," I said.

"Is this real?"

"What do you mean?"

"Did I die, or is this real?"

"You're alive," I said. "This is real."

"Are they gone?"

"Yes."

She lowered her voice. "Am I safe?"

I glanced at Perez's empty boat. I did not have the heart to tell her that his body was unaccounted for. Better for her to be happy, even if it was just for a little while.

"Yes, Melinda, you're safe," I said.

CHAPTER FIFTY-FIVE

The Queen of Heaven Cemetery in north Fort Lauderdale was a special place for me. Both of my parents were buried there, and so was my sister. So it only seemed fitting that I should bury Skell's victims there as well.

Wearing a dark suit I'd purchased at a thrift shop the day before, I watched as the seven bodies I'd found in the ocean were lowered into the freshly dug ground. With the last of my money and an old credit card, I'd purchased seven plots, seven coffins, and seven tombstones. I still didn't know how I was going to pay the bill, but that really didn't matter. It was the only way I knew to properly say good-bye.

Rose and Jessie stood alongside me, holding fresh flowers to put on the graves. A few days ago they'd appeared on my doorstep and offered to help with the funeral. I could not have managed without them.

When the last coffin was lowered into the earth, Rose handed me a Bible, and I read a passage from Psalms about God's eternal love and forgiveness. It was the same passage that I'd read at my parents' funerals, and my sister's. As I spoke, my tears stained the page on which the words were written.

Finished, I closed the Bible and bowed my head. Then an earthmover filled the graves with dirt, and it was over.

My wife and daughter slipped their arms through mine, and in silence we walked back to my car. It was a beautiful morning; the air was crisp and clear, the cloudless sky an aching blue. I found myself taking solace in that.

"Jack, that woman is staring at us," Rose said.

I lifted my eyes from the pebble walkway. Behind a tombstone twenty feet away stood a Hispanic woman holding a bouquet of wilted flowers. She wore a black dress, a black hat, and sunglasses, and she appeared to be in mourning. I wondered if she'd known one of the victims, or perhaps was a relative. She glanced furtively at my wife and daughter, then turned and abruptly walked away, her heels clacking noisily.

"How rude," my wife said.

"Maybe it was one of those pesky reporters in disguise," my daughter said.

"Maybe so," I said.

We continued our walk. I'd been contacted by plenty of reporters in the past week, all of whom wanted to tell my story. I'd also heard from Bobby Russo, who'd hinted that an unnamed job with the police department was waiting for me, should I choose to return. I'd become everyone's favorite guy, not that I particularly cared. These same people had helped Skell walk out of prison, and I wanted nothing to do with them.

Reaching the parking lot, I found Buster asleep on the driver's seat of my car. I let him out, and he jumped on me, his tail wagging furiously.

"Daddy, someone left you something," my daughter said.

Tucked beneath the windshield wipers were a white envelope and a single wilted flower. I pulled them both free and looked for a trash bin.

"Aren't you going to open the envelope?" my daughter asked.

"No," I said.

"But it might be something important."

I tossed the envelope to her.

"Have at it," I said.

Jessie tore open the envelope and removed a cassette tape.

"I thought these things were obsolete," my daughter said.

Tape cassettes were obsolete, except in my car. Once the engine was started, I slipped the cassette into the tape player, and the three of us sat and listened. At first, nothing but crackling static came out of the speakers. Then we heard the blast of a harmonica, followed by Mick Jagger's young, raw voice. Then the music started.

"What the heck is this?" my daughter asked.

An invisible knife twisted in my gut. As I gazed over endless rows of tombstones that graced the landscape, I searched for the Hispanic woman dressed in black, knowing that I hadn't seen a woman at all but an old enemy who was trying to track me down.

It was the opening lyrics to "Midnight Rambler."

The live version.

ACKNOWLEDGMENTS

I would like to gratefully acknowledge several people for their help during the writing of this novel. They include Shane James, Ed Jones, Christine Kling, Shawn Redmond, and the ever-helpful Fred Rea.

A special thanks to the folks at Ballantine Books, who continue to support me in everything I do. Thank you, Gina Centrello, Dana Isaacson, Elizabeth McGuire, and my terrific editor, Linda Marrow.

During the early stages of this manuscript, several people made suggestions that helped shape this book, and to them I owe a huge debt of gratitude. Thanks to my wife, Laura; my agent, Chris Calhoun; and his assistant and editor extraordinaire, Dong Won Song.

Above all, I must thank Andrew Vita, Team Adam Consultant with the National Center for Missing and Exploited Children and former Associate Director/Enforcement for the Bureau of Alcohol, Tobacco, and Firearms. Without his help, this book could not have been written.

Read on for a sneak peek at
James Swain's next novel

THE NIGHT STALKER

Noise was one of the few things that moved freely inside a prison.

The haunting echo of my own footsteps followed me down the long, windowless corridor inside the maximum-security wing of Florida State Prison in Starke. I'd visited many prisons, and the smell was always the same: a choking mixture of piss, shit, fear, and desperation, wiped down by harsh antiseptics.

Walking through an electronically operated steel door, I was patted down by two stone-faced guards. Satisfied that I was not carrying weapons or contraband, they passed me off to a smirking inmate with a hideous purple birthmark on the side of his face. He took off at a brisk pace, and I followed him into the cell block that housed death row inmates.

"What's your name?" I asked.

"Garvin," he replied, not breaking stride.

"What are you in for?"

"I shot up my family during Thanksgiving dinner."

I walked past the cells in death row with my eyes to the floor. I felt their occupants' presence like a fist pounding my back.

When we arrived at an empty cell, Garvin slid back

the door and stepped to the side. "Wait inside here," he said.

"What if no one comes?"

"Make some noise, and I'll come get you."

"Promise?"

"Yessuh."

I entered the cell, a ten-by-ten concrete square with two wood benches anchored to the floor and a small wood table. Garvin slammed the door behind me, making me jump. He chuckled as he walked away.

I took the bench nearest the door and stuck a piece of gum into my mouth. I chewed so hard it made my jaw ache. I'd put scores of bad guys into Starke, and I didn't want to be here any longer than I had to.

I stared at the table. Inmates were not supposed to have anything sharp, but the table said otherwise. Names and dates and ugly epithets were carved into every inch of the wood. One name stood out over the others.

Abb Grimes.

I had been involved in Abb's case, and I knew his story. A Fort Lauderdale native, he'd quit high school at seventeen, done a stint in the navy, gotten married and had a kid, and gone to work driving a newspaper delivery truck—an ordinary guy, except that he liked to kill young woman.

Abb's killings had all followed a pattern. Late at night, he'd leave his house and walk to the neighborhood grocery. There he'd hide behind the Dumpsters. When a young homeless woman would show up looking for food, he'd drag her into the woods, rape and strangle her, then stuff her body in a large garbage bag, tossing it into a Dumpster.

As mass murders went, it was nearly perfect. The victims were women no one cared about, and the bodies were disposed of for him. It might have gone on forever, only one night a surveillance camera caught Abb in the act.

The morning following his last nocturnal killing, a store manager viewed the tape. On it, Abb could be seen standing by the Dumpsters with the body of a young woman draped in his arms. He appeared to be laughing.

The manager called 911, the police came and found the woman's body in the Dumpster. They got a search warrant and went to Abb's home. In his garage they found a cardboard box containing women's underpants. None of the pairs were the same.

Their next stop was the Pompano Beach landfill, where trash in Broward County was taken. Using earthmovers and cadaver dogs, they moved several acres of trash, digging up the bodies of seventeen strangled women.

Eleven of the women were carrying ID. As head of the Broward County Sheriff Department's missing persons unit, it had been my job to contact their families. It had been one of the hardest things I'd ever done.

The remaining seven women were still Jane Does. I'd hoped to identify them one day and put their memories to rest. Only I'd lost my job and never gotten it done.

It still ate at me.

Hearing footsteps, I went to the cell door. Wearing leg irons and handcuffs, flanked by two guards, Abb shuffled down the hall. Tall and powerfully built, he had an angular jaw and eyes too small for his face. During his trial, the prosecution had called him "The Night Stalker," which had been a TV show that had lasted one season. It had scared the hell out of everyone who'd seen it. The name fit.

"Stand back," a guard ordered.

I retreated, and the three men entered. Abb sat on the opposing bench, while the two guards remained standing.

An attractive brunette carrying a briefcase followed them in. Her haircut was masculine, and she was all business. We briskly shook hands.

"I'm Piper Stone, Abb's attorney," she said.

"Jack Carpenter," I said.

"Thank you for coming."

We sat down on the bench and faced Abb. As strange as it sounded, he was my client, so I waited for him to start.

Abb cleared his throat. He had a voice like gravel, and I guessed he didn't use it much. "I'm going to die soon," Abb said. "Did my lawyer tell you that?"

"No, she didn't," I said.

"They're going to execute me in four days," Abb said. "Think you can find my grandson before then?"

Abb's grandson, Sampson Grimes, had disappeared from his bedroom three nights ago. I'd read about it in the Fort Lauderdale newspapers and knew that the police had been stymied in their efforts to locate him.

"I'm going to try," I said. "Now why don't you tell me what happened?"

Abb nodded, then stared at the floor. "I get an hour each day to exercise in the yard. "Two days ago, a photograph of my grandson and a ransom note got slipped into my pocket. I didn't see who did it."

"Do you still have the note and photo?" I asked.

"I gave them to Ms. Stone."

I looked at Stone. "I'd like to see them."

Stone unclasped her briefcase and handed me the items. The photo showed a tow-headed little boy with a face like the Gerber baby lying on a blanket. His clothes looked clean, as did his face and hands, and his eyes showed no sign of fear. I took these as a sign that his captor was not abusing him. Lying on the blanket was a copy of the *Fort Lauderdale Sun-Sentinel* with the date prominently displayed. It was a trick used by kidnappers to show that their victims were still alive.

I shifted my attention to the ransom note. Written in pencil, it said, *"STOP TALKING TO THE FBI OR SAMPSON WILL DIE."* The handwriting surprised me. Most kidnappers used typewriters or glued letters cut from a magazine. This guy was obviously confident he was not going to get caught.

"What are you talking to the FBI about?" I asked.

"I'm in their VICAP program," Abb said. "I was supposed to go under hypnosis to help them identify those Jane Does. I still don't remember the things I did."

VICAP was the FBI's Violent Criminal Apprehension Program. Cops had an expression when criminals entered programs like VICAP and agreed to help the police. They called it "taking a shot at heaven."

"Does the FBI know you were contacted by your grandson's kidnapper?" I asked.

Abb shook his head.

"How about the police?"

Abb shook his head again.

"Why haven't you told them?"

"Because I want you to find him," Abb said.

"Why?" I asked.

"I've met six guys in Starke that are serving life for kidnapping little kids. You put them here. That's why."

I slipped the ransom note into my pocket.

"Good enough," I said.

"You're going to take the job?" he asked.

"Yes."

"Good."

I stood up from the bench and so did Stone. One of the guards slid back the cell door for us. I started to leave and saw something resembling hope in Abb's eyes. I decided to level with him.

"Your grandson's case is three days old," I said. "That's a long time when it comes to a kidnapping. I need to do a lot of groundwork and talk to a lot of people."

Abb looked up at me. "What are you trying to say?"

"I may not find Sampson before they execute you."

"Four days isn't enough?"

"I won't know until I start looking."

"I was hoping you—"

I cut him off. "I don't make promises."

"But—"

"That's the deal," I said.

Abb cast his eyes to the floor. He had asked me here because he did not want to go to his death knowing he'd caused an innocent child to suffer. I had to think it was one of the more decent things he'd done in his life.

He was still looking at the floor when we left.